The Last Black President

By Lamar Anthony Chesterton

Caroline Press
Drawer 1344
Alto, N.M. 88312 - 1344

ISBN: 978-0-6152-4580-5

Available on Lulu.com in book form or download.

This work is dedicated to all those gifted with compassion and the courage to use that gift to make this a better world.

Lamar Anthony Chesterton, May 7, 2008

Chapter I

The country had suffered through 8 months of the Presidential Primary season. The less fortunate segment of the public, those who were not ensconced in watching professional baseball, football and now basketball, or for the other gender - Oprah and Court TV, were treated to one meaningless presidential aspirant's debate after another – nearly one a month. In length, the debates at one hour each were tolerable. The two hours of interpretation that followed on each of the cable shows and that echoed into the network newscasts were more than any patriot could endure - let alone some more casual citizen. Worse yet, the cable commentators kept their two hour ritual going four to five days after each debate – even though not one of the major candidates (anointed by the press using some dubious criteria) had said anything profound, or even important. On the other hand, candidates who might have had something interesting to say were rarely given an opportunity to speak.

But the country learned quite a bit from those hundreds of hours of television. Interviews and talk shows ad nauseum were done with panels of experts on such important topics as candidate body language, the Angel Moroni's revelations, the relationship of Jesus to Satan, the inner workings of the New York City fire department, the Mafia's influence in politics, the role of prayer in children (particularly children who later on become presidential candidates), and what should the next president do about steroid use in baseball. After all, the national pastime had been tarnished. Who in the record books should be asterisked?

One useful discussion that went missing on the public was choreography. All of the so called "front runners" – had become so skillful in reversing position after position – on abortion, gay marriage, Iraq, Iran, taxes, immigration, etc, etc. - that they could not be matched by even the most skilled dancer. Quick change artists paled by comparison. The only things they didn't change were their noses – though it looked like some of them had had sagging eyes propped up. The only positive progress was on the art of the non answer that was to be accomplished in 150 words or less. It had been honed to a new high – even outdoing the Great Gipper (the master of obfuscation and the champion of appealing, in not so subtle a manner, to some of the country's dumber and baser instincts).

It is very probable that the terrorists – where ever they might be - were listening in to the debates with rapt attention. Maybe they even enjoyed them. For certain they were paying closer attention to some of the issues, and where the candidates stood vis-à-vis some of the major lobby forces in the US, than were the majority of the American public – after all they had more at stake. It's also reasonable to speculate that after 8 months of this drivel some of the more astute terrorist leaders had even concluded that there was no need to blow up the United States. If wisdom and political courage were some measure of a country's strength, it wasn't unreasonable to think the country would just implode. Wait them out!

Wading through this drivel month after month would force even the most uninformed American to wonder if the country had lost its sanity. Were this taking place in Africa rather than the US it would be presumed that the gods had gone crazy. Where are the good candidates? Where are the leaders? This used to be a great country! It produced some of the greatest leaders in the history of mankind. What's going on? It was common knowledge that sperm counts in young males had decreased over the last few generations. Some were asking if the DNA content had changed as well.

Whether or not the media set the tone for the debates that had taxed the country these many months, or that there was just such a sorry set of candidates, or that the country was falling just like Rome did, was difficult to determine. But the cable stations followed by Fox News and the networks either set the tone or did their share to set it. The situation left some to ask, "Whatever happened to the League of Women Voters?" They had sponsored debates for nearly 40 years. They seemed to have just disappeared off the face of the earth.

First on the debate road was CNN. They led off with their hottest "anchor man" [can you really be an anchor man when you're on the tube three hrs a day?] Blaze Lupos in the saddle, asking some of the most irrelevant questions imaginable – worse they were mushy softballs! Supposedly Lupos' first set of questions was written by a panel of experts - political scientists from several Ivy League colleges. If that were accurate – enough said for the Ivy League. Who's running those places? And, it got even better – Lupos had the temerity as that first debate moved forward to begin morphing into a commentator/questioner who not only understood the nuances of the questions he was asking, but understood the appropriate answers in all their detail as well. Somehow he must have envisioned himself as an Edward R. Morrow. Where were the Murrows, the Cronkhites or the Severides when you needed them? Second rate candidates, second rate newsmen.

But the questions got even less intelligent after CNN came up with the brilliant idea of asking listeners to submit YouTube questions. Many individuals are not familiar with YouTube - it's a curious business. Individuals or groups of individuals make videos of themselves, of others or of things they think are interesting. Next they post them on the Internet for the world to see. The postings also presume that someone out there cares about some minuscule aspect of some nobody's life. Enough said for the benefits of the 8 hr day and the five day work week.

It's not too unreasonable to think that anyone who might be capable of asking a probing question would probably not know of the mechanics for making YouTube presentations. The two don't seem go together.

But one has to ask: Was the media – in particular CNN - involved in a mild conspiracy? A conspiracy aimed at raising ratings – advertising dollars? Was this the motive for sponsoring the presidential debates? Could you rig the whole deal and make it pay? Why not? News is big business. Billions of dollars are to be made.

For the third Republican debate, sponsored by CNN, 30% of the YouTube questions selected were on immigration issues. Hardly a hot topic - and hardly at the top of most American's priority list, nor one that the country seemed to want to solve. Immigration was on hold for this season - everybody knew it. Granted immigration - if you were an illegal trying to earn an honest living and trying to support your family - is an important topic, but, by and large, only to the kooky liberal fringe and 15 million Illegals – and, the latter don't vote.

So why might a major cable player bias his questions picking? Well if you have a "news and commentary" program on that network where 80% of the air time is dedicated to issues surrounding immigration, making the illegal issue a "hot" debate issue could be profitable. The junior Senator from North Dakota raised the possibility of a profit motivation in the sponsorship of the debates in one of the senate hearings – it did not gain any traction.

*   *   *

Among the 7 or so diminutives that called themselves Republicans, Senator Marjory Hunter, widow of the two-term ex governor of New Jersey had gotten the endorsement of the Iowa caucuses and taken 44% of the vote in the New Hampshire primary which was enough to take first position. Polls in South Carolina and Florida were indicating that she had sufficient strength to be considered the likely nominee of the Grand Old Party. She also was the only Republican who had a considerable and renewable war chest.

Senator Hunter had waged a very straight forward campaign concentrating on all that was good with the country – an expanding economy, a low tax rate, not a single terrorist attach since 9/11 and, of course, the lower abortion rates and diminished numbers of babies born to single mothers since her party had begun their family values campaign some eight years earlier. She played hard on her Senate experience and also her "executive" experience in her role as a key player in running the state of New Jersey when she was the first lady. She claimed to have played a major role in cleaning up the scandal in the New Jersey State Police who were "racial profiling" motorists along the NJ Turnpike and other shenanigans during her husbands tenure.

The other side of the aisle was equally deficient in candidates of any substance. There were eight of them. They had exhausted the country with their endless rhetoric on the dire problems facing the nation – global warming, income inequality, health care, immigration, infrastructure problems, and, of course, Iraq and Iran. Democrats seem to have a skill, even a penchant, for identifying problems in the country and in the world. Unfortunately, they never seem to be able to come up with viable solutions. Or, if they do, there is so much squabbling within the party that they just can't implement. – at least not since LBJ was in office.

How ironic! Republicans can get things done, but they just don't seem to know what to do, or when they do it can border on the ridiculous. Maybe their talent for getting things done comes from the fact that so many Republicans run small to medium sized business. You need to execute to be successful in business, and if you know the formula for putting a business together and have watched someone else do it (like your father or grandfather) – even without an MBA and without being a genius – you can get the job done. Also you make a lot of money which makes you think you really are smart.

Alternatively, many Republicans may just have gotten their training by starting out as paper boys. Paper routes are great training grounds. You learn to organize, to be disciplined, to be patient, to be customer oriented, and you learn the joy of counting money and how it feels to have your own money. You also learn that the girls like young men who can buy them ice cream cones. With testosterone starting to bubble up in these young entrepreneurs that knowledge may well start the imprinting process.

*　　　*　　　*

On the Democrat side, the Iowa caucuses had produced no real favorite; despite millions of campaign dollars spent and with candidates spending so much time in Iowa they were almost eligible for residency. None of the 9 candidates had more than 23% of the vote in New Hampshire. Polls were indicating that South Carolinians were not about to project any of the candidates to the top.

Enter Morris Bloomfield, Mayor of New York City – nearing the end of his second term in office. Bloomfield a self made multi billionaire – Wall Street - was best known for preferring to live in a townhouse on the Upper East Side of the city rather than Gracie Mansion – the NYC mayoral residence – and for taking the subway downtown to City Hall each work day. He was one of the new breed of billionaire politicians who were popping up all over the country, all of whom had made their fortunes in the world of finance. Bloomfield could best be described as a very likeable fellow (not at all combative, but a wee bit abrasive – or maybe it was just his New York accent), Harvard educated, seemingly intelligent and very pleasant looking. He was not that overly handsome where women might have voted for him just for his looks. On the other hand, he didn't have that "pretty boy" look – which some men have even though they might be in their mid 60's as he was. That might turn male voters off.

Bloomfield had not done anything remarkable as Mayor of the City but was well regarded for being a good fiscal conservative who had put the City's finances in good order. He was well traveled and had visited the major capitals of the world – in his capacity as Mayor of New York City – and he had done all of that at his own expense. He even paid all of the expenses of his aides – so no one had any real gripe, except that he was not "minding the store" during those absences. But New Yorkers don't really get excited about such things. As long as the subways are running everyone is happy. Bloomfield had also used his great wealth wisely giving to favorite charities and causes that might further his ambitions. He was a born political animal almost in sheep's clothing – and very expensive clothing at that.

Bloomfield had sized up the Democrat primary contest accurately well before the South Carolina primary. In fact, he had shared his thoughts with his small circle of confidants – two Wall Street buddies who were now dollar a year men for the City, a college roommate from Harvard, and his former wife's brother, a plastic surgeon in Brooklyn whom he had been close to for nearly 40 years. Well before the Iowa contest started Bloomfield concluded that none of the candidates had the depth, charisma or appeal to win the nomination, let alone the presidency. In a very methodical and clandestine fashion, he and his inner circle, had laid out a "Blitzkrieg" campaign to pluck the Democrat nomination from the very hands of the unsuspecting hopefuls.

A major part of Bloomfield's strategy, while the primaries were in progress, was well planned, well timed and well placed speeches that would draw just enough attention in the media. In that way he would be on record with a position on some issue he would make in his campaign, but he would not draw so much attention that he would appear to be running for anything. He gave speeches at the Business School of his alma-mater, Harvard, at an AMA convention in Chicago, at a dedication of a museum he had donated in Tel Aviv - that was done at a Synagogue in Brooklyn via a satellite hookup, at Grambling State University – a black institution in Louisiana, and at the Columbia School of Journalism.

From the content and structure of those speeches, Bloomfield made clear that he was conversant, even knowledgeable, on all of the key issues. In them, he outlined, and carefully defined areas of concern and in each case defined in very broad strokes his strategy for winning the war on Terrorism, for stabilization of the Middle East, for dealing with trade and trade barriers and for dealing with global climate change.

With an incredible TV advertising campaign of a magnitude not witnessed before, the blessing of and anointing by the media as well as party faithful anxious to win back the presidency after what many considered the most incompetent and morally corrupt administration in the history of the country, Bloomfield had the nomination in his pocket 40 days after he launched the Blitzkrieg. The results of Super Tuesday were a given.

The Presidential election was shaping up to be politically one of the more interesting contests in recent history, and, in fact, a history making one at that. The country would have either its first Women President or its first Jewish President.

*　　*　　*

Early May through mid October is not the time to be in Jackson, Mississippi – despite what the natives claim. The superlatives for hot and humid are inadequate to describe the living condition there. Everything moves in slow motion – traffic, people, even the dogs running loose kind of saunter not wanting to generate any excess body heat. Prior to air conditioning most of the inhabitants hid themselves at mid day, only emerging in the early evening, and then searching for even the mildest breeze.

Jackson is the capital city of Mississippi. Most people don't know that. In fact, most people don't know much about Mississippi. The current minority whip of the US Senate is actually from Mississippi. Most people know his name, Senator Kent Mott, but would be hard pressed to tell the state he represents. Even hurricane Katrina that whipped the gulf coast of Mississippi and left its toll of devastation and human misery - yet to be repaired or resolved 3 years post hit - is rarely associated with Mississippi. Nothing belongs to Mississippi – not even Katrina.

What has historically belonged to Mississippi is poverty, a poor educational system and a state whose infrastructure either suffers, or was never built. And, as far as history is concerned most know that Mississippi was involved in the civil war, was in the confederacy and that's about all. It would not be an exaggeration to state that the last news evoking event that occurred in that state was a brief mention when Katrina landed and prior to that a few events during the Civil War – in particular the Battle of Vicksburg.

So it was unusual when the Governor of the state of Mississippi – Maynard Jefferson DeFrie – declared, as loud as you can declare if you live in Mississippi, that he had been moved by his personal Savior, Jesus Christ, to call a press conference and to announce his "candidacy for President of the United States of America". He had stated that he had wanted to wait until July 4th, but that it was imperative to call his press conference at this time – Thursday, May 1st - for reasons he would share at a later date. More than likely, Maynard knew he was throwing his hat in the ring at a very late date and wanted to give the impression that he was not concerned about that.

The numbers of newspapers that responded to the press announcement were impressive, given the location and difficulty associated with getting to Jackson, Mississippi as well as the stated purpose of the press conference. Most of the reporters were in their late 20's to early 30's – probably rookies - and nearly two thirds of them were women. Of the major papers, the *New York*

Times, Washington Post, Miami Herald, St. Louis Post Dispatch and the *Atlanta Journal-Constitution* were present. There were a number of reporters from regional newspapers like the *Natchez Sun, Hattiesburg Clarion,* and, of course, the *Jackson Clarion-Ledger*. On the TV side CNN, MSNBC and ABC had sent camera crews, the latter two being from local affiliates.

None of the press that was in attendance that hot and steamy day as well as their more seasoned colleagues, who had stayed home, knew anything about the current Governor. No one could recall him, or for that matter any one else, from the state of Mississippi in recent memory, calling a national press conference. In fact, with the exception of the local press, no one of the national press knew anything about Maynard J. DeFrie, except for the few brief comments that accompanied the press announcement. One of his titles that were mentioned in the briefing paper was The Reverend MR DeFrie.

*   *   *

On the steps of the majestic State Capital Building – referred to locally as the "new capital" - was arranged a lectern behind which on a landing portion of the steps were thirteen folding chairs. The middle chair was occupied by a large, very large, black man who chatted amiably with individuals seated to his left and right. To his right was a white baldish gentleman, probably in his late 60's, not a picture of health and not wearing his well worn suit well. Further to the right were seated four black men, two with clerical collars, and last, an elderly white woman, who sat with pen in hand holding a note pad on her lap as if she were going to take notes of the event. On the left of the large black man sat a symmetrically arranged group, by color and not by gender. On his immediate left was an attractive white woman who appeared to be in her mid 50's. To her left were seated two black men, both with clerical collars, two well dressed black women in their early 40's, and finally an elderly man who at one time had been blond and whose hair now bore the mottled faded colors of aging.

When it was apparent that all of the press that were present and ready to pay attention – they stood in rows on the steps just below the lectern – the large black man stood up, and very slowly and deliberately walked to the lectern. He moved with a sense of confidence, smiled softly as he approached the lectern, looking over the assembled crowd – he seemed to move in slow motion. When he stood, and as he walked forward, it was apparent he was even larger than he appeared in the seated position. Many in the press presumed he would be introducing the Governor.

In a very slow, melodic and deliberate voice he began. "For those of you who do not know who I am, I am Maynard Jefferson DeFrie. I am the Governor of the state of Mississippi. Today, on the steps of this magnificent capital building, adorned with our blazing golden eagle – the symbol of strength and integrity - I announce my candidacy for President of the United States of America. I will be seeking the nomination of the Green Party. It is my goal to win this election, and to change the course of this country."

He paused momentarily, looking directly at the assembled press to gauge their reaction to his words. "Why me? Why?"

"Why would this black man – and I should add - very large black man (a soft snicker floated through the assembled crowd) - standing before you have the temerity to think that this country needs him? That he could be president of this Union which over these nearly 250 years has become the most powerful, and the most influential country the world has ever known."

"My reasons are as simple as they are complicated. As you will learn in due course I began my career as a pastor of a small racially mixed church in Hattiesburg, Mississippi. That is where I started. And, because my mission in life has always been, and will continue to be pastoral, to be God's servant, I see a country that has lost its way, and I need to do something to help us find the way."

"I see a country that has lost its way on issue after issue. I see a country that was once great, a country that once produced great and generous people in large numbers. I see a country divided by the very rich, the not so rich and the working poor. A country that allows corporate and powerful interests to dictate social policy – be it health care, taxation, foreign policy etc. etc. etc. A country of immense riches that can not maintain its infrastructure, cannot provide first quality education to all of its citizens, cannot provide decent housing, quality health care for all and decent jobs for so many of our brothers and sisters."

"I see a country of troubled citizenry who worry about their futures, who are seeing the toll that free trade has brought, whose jobs are either outsourced or, if I can use the expression, in sourced. And by that I mean the import of low cost labor that threatens the very existence of vast numbers of Americans."

"Those are just some of the issues we will address during my campaign. Moreover, I will campaign and speak on specifics. Americans are not morons. Thomas Jefferson, whose sir-name I carry as my middle name, believed that the basis of democracy is an educated populous and the wisdom of the common man. I believe that with all my heart and soul."

"And so my fellow citizens, I not only announce my candidacy for the Presidency today, I dedicate myself with all of my resolve, all of my energies, all of my intellect and all of my spirit to returning this once great country, these once great peoples back to the days where integrity meant something, where corporations were responsible, where we were our brothers keepers. And, let me quickly add, I do not campaign on a platform of free lunches for anyone. Each of us will do our share, each of us must – we must become patriots again. We must be a United States."

"So when I say we shall become our brothers keeper, I do not ask for welfare for anyone be it individual, corporate or for other nation states. We are all God's children and we all must give an account of ourselves to those we live with and to our Creator– we all must contribute. I want to recreate a country where we look out for our brothers and sisters as we would have them look out for us."

"As my campaign unfolds, and that begins today, I will enumerate the problems that exist in our country - problems most Americans are very well aware of - and I will outline what I believe we need to do."

"We live in a country where more than 80% of the population does not approve of the direction that the country is heading, yet neither the leading Democrat Party or Republican Party Candidates, nor any of their competitors has addressed that concern. I will appeal to that 70% whose sense it is that we need to change course as well as the 30% who approve of where the country is going. I will do my best to appeal to the latter group with facts and reason."

"Americans are good and decent peoples – all of us. We have a history of doing what is right – up until recent history every nation in the world knew that about us and admired us for that quality and for our generosity. We also know how to deal with those who do not share those qualities. As we move forward, I believe I can convince you that my goal is to serve 100% of the people, and not just special interests. That is my promise to you. So it is now time for me to get to work. Let me begin by asking our guests who have taken the trouble of journeying to this obscure part of the country, if I can answer any questions at this time."

When Maynard finished there was polite applause from the press, some loud applause from the assembled crowd, mainly blacks, and two or three "Amen Brother Maynard." "Praise be God." "Thank you Jesus." And, a final "Hallelujah - Hallelujah." – with emphasis on the third syllable – "lu".

Maynard looked to the press but no one immediately came forward with a question. Perhaps, he had intimidated them, possibly they thought he was some kind of nut, or maybe they were trying to digest what he had said. Governor DeFrie could be intimidating just by his sheer size. He had the body and the fluid gate of a man who had been a trained athlete during his youth. In reality, he stood about 6 feet 4 inches. He had the shoulders of an NFL lineman which he might have been had fate been different, or alternatively had he not heard a different calling.

With all his size he was a graceful man. He had a beautiful squarish head – a handsome head with well spaced and large eyes, and well formed features. He wore his jet black hair close cropped as black athletes of his era did. His temples had grayed giving him a distinguished and kindly look. He was, indeed, a handsome and imposing black man. After the press conference, the reporter from the *Atlanta Journal-Constitution*, an older black man, commented that Maynard bore a strong resemblance – even his broad smile - to Roosevelt "Rosey" Greer, a NFL star of yesteryear who also served as one of Bobby Kennedy's bodyguards in that fateful campaign where Kennedy was assassinated.

Following an uneasy moment or two, an attractive young woman raised her hand. Immediately, a young black man holding a portable microphone was before her, handing her the mike and gentling moving other reporters standing near her to the side, so as to create space for her. In an initially inaudible and nervous voice she began: "Governor, I'm Carla Rothman with the *New York Times*. In your announcement you stated the country has lost its way, and on that many might agree. However, your suggestion that it is your pastoral duty to save the country is of concern. Is it your intention, presuming you are elected President to obliterate the line between church and state that our constitution mandates?"

Maynard smiled, first looking directly at Ms Rothman and then over the assembled crowd. He began, "First let me thank you for your efforts in coming all the way down Jackson, Mississippi from New York City to be with us on this important day – I know that is a difficult trip, there are no non-stop flights to Jackson from the North, or for that matter from the East, West or South." – The crowd tittered softly, some rolled their eyes in agreement. "Let me also thank the rest of you for being here, your efforts are appreciated, and I hope you will find this day not only worthwhile but an occasion to be remembered – one of those events you might someday want to share with your grandchildren."

"Let me answer your question Miss Rothman in this fashion. I believe with all of my intellect, my heart and my soul in the Constitution of the United States. Along with the Declaration of Independence and the New Testament it is the most sacred writing I know of. As you know the Constitution forbids the government from establishing, or more accurately Congress shall make no law respecting any religion, and guarantees all of us our Religious freedoms. We even have the right through free speech to question, to argue religion as well as the freedom not to believe. So, no I will not in any way obliterate, blur, or modify the original intentions of our founding fathers."

At the precise moment Maynard finished his last sentence, and still holding onto the microphone, Carla Rothman quickly added a follow up question. "Governor, it has become an accepted practice for politicians seeking office, or for Judges seeking confirmation, to take one position before taking office and quite a different position when they are confirmed. I am not questioning your integrity, Governor, but how do we know you will not do the same?"

"The easiest way, Miss Rothman, to allay your concerns is to remember that Leopards don't change their spots – or at least not this Leopard. I have been the Governor of the State of Mississippi now for 7 years, before that I served two terms in the State Senate and before that I served one term in the US House of Representatives. Parenthetically, I would probably still be in the US congress were it not for the electoral sweeping our Republican friends accomplished in 1984, but that's another story."

"But to continue, my record is not only spotless on this issue, it has been tested. As much as I respect the Ten Commandments, look through the halls of our state buildings in Jackson and around the entire state– you will not find them. And, if you dig further you will see that was an issue in my first term.

My position there is one of record. If you further examine all of my public service you will see that I have without fail always respected the Constitutional separation of Church and State. Christ, himself, stated clearly and explicitly this very same concept – and Jesus Christ is my Savior. So I would be a hypocrite to do or think otherwise."

No sooner had Maynard finished with Ms. Rothman's questions, when a least 5-6 hands shot up, the owners of which were anxious to get the Governor's attention. Maynard gestured permission to speak towards a tall black young man whose head was clearly visible over the others - again the black young man with the microphone was on the spot in a flash.

The questioner stretching himself a bit taller than he actually was, began – "Governor DeFrie, I am Archer McNabb with the *Washington Post*, and I would like to ask you what I think is the most obvious question."

"Sir, why did you not enter the Democrat Party primaries that have been going on these past many months, after all your briefing paper lists you as having run on the Democratic ticket for Congress, for the state Senate and for Governor of the state?"

"Thank you for your question Mr. McNabb", the Governor began. "If you had had a chance to check further – maybe a Google search - you would know that I have been a life long Democrat. I have worked hard for the Party and been a good soldier. However, the party that I swore my allegiance to some 40 plus years ago is not the Democrat Party of today. Today's Democratic politicians in the Congress are in reality Republicans who pretend to adhere to the principles and beliefs laid down by Franklin D. Roosevelt, John F. Kennedy or Lyndon Baines Johnson. Men and women who were my contemporaries in the party now bow to, and take from special interests. The special interests of the Democrat Party used to be the welfare of the people."

"Just take a look at who is running in the Democratic Primary Contest. Or, reflect back on the Candidates the Democrats have run for the Presidency. They represent corporate

America – not the people. Their solutions to America's many problems are corporate benefiting solutions."

"Let me add one more reason regarding my not entering the Democrat Primary. Currently, in the primaries of both parties there are twenty one serious candidates. Among those combatants there are two – one in each party – who have a different message. A message that suggests they have a very different view of America's problems than their opponents."

"I am sure you know whom I am referring to – Congressman Daniel Kaminski from Ohio and Congressman Don Saulzer from Texas. Have you noticed how much time the media has given these candidates?"

"Hardly any! Why? Because they are out of the main stream – and, since our media filters everything with a bias filter that does the American public great harm, two very able candidates have little or no chance of becoming president. That, Mr. McNabb, is how the system operates."

"Let me add, my good man, that I am a realist. I am also a problem solver as my record demonstrates. For me to do God's will and for me to move this country in its rightful direction, I will need to take a different route – I know that route! And, you will see that in due course."

A very youthful reporter who identified himself as being from Mobile, Alabama but who mumbled both his name and his affiliation was able to get Maynard's attention and asked, "Sir, given your Christian disposition can we assume the ban on Stem-Cell research that the current Administration has imposed will remain in effect?"

Maynard took a deep breath. "Son, one of the things you and your colleagues will learn about Maynard DeFrie as we move forward together is not to assume anything about me. One of my first acts, if it be God's will that I be President, is to lift the ban on Stem-Cell Research."

"It pains me greatly that so many Americans are caught in this terrible moral dilemma while thousands upon thousands suffer. And, suffer without hope."

"A significant part of this whole stem cell issue and, therefore, the dilemma, itself, is ignorance!"

"Politicians and lay folk argue whether it is right or wrong to toss embryos that are left over from in-vitro fertilization procedures, when, in fact, they could be used to prepare embryonic stem cells. The first point is what is to know what we are talking about. These are fertilized ova – human egg cells - they are not embryos. They are roughly four/five day old fertilized eggs, and at that stage we are talking about 100 – 150 cells. You can't even see them with the naked eye!"

"So, is that an embryo? It is human? I'm sorry, my friend, I don't think so. It might have the potential to become an embryo, but in my judgment it is not. Humans look and act like humans. Most significantly, humans have well developed brains – the most glorious gift to us from our Creator. Our brains are the part of us that truly differentiate us from animals. And, the greatest sin – the greatest offense to God - is not to use our brains."

"To me it seems clear – to use the vernacular, almost a no brainer (no pun intended) - that it is morally corrupt, morally wrong to toss something down the drain, or something to be kept frozen forever – some mass of cells - that some misinformed and misguided groups of individuals are calling embryos, when they could be used to save lives and alleviate pain. Would not a loving God want the same? I have never heard any of the opponents of Stem-Cell research ask 'what would Jesus want?' Or possibly, through their lack of knowledge they are just asking the wrong question."

"I know what Jesus would want. You bet I know what he would want! He would want us to use the marvelous minds that our Creator blessed us with and not get caught in moral dilemmas that are, in fact, not dilemmas at all."

The assembled press began to realize they were dealing with a different sort of man. Maynard Jefferson DeFrie's responses to thorny questions were almost professorial in their content, but in no way was he talking down to his audience. His answers also contained a small sprinkling of Southern Baptist

preacher who was greatly concerned for his flock. Maynard
Jefferson DeFrie was a man confident in his views, confident in
himself and confident in the knowledge of what he was saying,
and of where he was going.

Not only did he not duck questions, he had the courage to
answer the question head on and to take the questioner well
beyond his expectations. And, he did that in a deep baritone
voice, - a comforting, convincing voice - that he could modulate
at will, and in an almost symphonic fashion. His voice and
manner of speaking were mildly reminiscent of the late Dr.
Martin Luther King, Jr. - not quite as melodic, nor as deep, but in
the same genre.

The sun had not let up. Even though the shade of the
Capitol building was beginning to shade the press event, it had
becoming unbearably hot. The elderly white gentleman with the
ill fitting worn suit who was seated near the Governor when the
press conference started made his way to the podium. Placing his
hand on Maynard's shoulder, he gently took hold of the
microphone and announced – "we need to be bringing this
meeting to a close as the Governor must move on to other very
pressing engagements." He was about to thank the press for
coming when he caught himself in mid sentence. He continued -
"However, since at this very moment the Governor is tugging at
the back of my suit, we will take two more questions." Maynard
looked down at his much smaller frail colleague and smiled.

The black young man who manned the hand held
microphone threaded his way quickly through the press group
and handed the mike to a young black female reporter whom
Maynard had pointed to. "Governor DeFrie, I'm Lisa Westbrook
with the *Natchez Sun*, and you mentioned health care."

"Do you have a plan to solve the current debacle in
healthcare? Do you any have thoughts on how to hold down the
rising cost of medical delivery, and what about those who cannot
afford health insurance?"

While Ms Westbrook was asking her question, Maynard's
eyes were focused upward to the sky. Was this something he did

when he was thinking how he might answer some difficult question? A number of people do that without even realizing that they do. Or was he looking for divine revelation? Slowly lowering his gaze and in a soft almost velvety voice he turned looking in her direction, but not directly at her, he began – "Miss Westbrook, the questions you have asked are ones that have pained me greatly. Mississippi is a poor state, and we do the very best we can in treating of sick, of giving well care to newborns, of keeping our elderly healthy – yes, we do the best we can. We have per capita probably the largest Medicaid program in the country."

"But to return directly to your question – yes we have a health care debacle in this country, and it is getting worse."

"So, before I tell you what we need to do, let me give you some numbers that we need to think about, and, perhaps, you already know them. First, despite the tremendous investment Americans make each and every year in Health Care, we rank in the high 30's in the world in the effective delivery of that care – not first like so many of us think. Now that is on average – clearly many in our country get the best possible care – but as I said that ranking is an average. Secondly, for every health care dollar invested in this country 31 cents goes to health insurance companies for their administrative role."

"Now, you don't have to take my word for that, you ought to check it yourself – that figure comes from a Harvard Medical School study done about 3 years ago. Of course, the insurance industry has their study - they claim their administrative costs are only 15 cents for every health care dollar spent. .....Who are you going to believe? Are we going to believe an industry that pays millions of dollars in annual salaries to each of its Executives? I don't know about you, but I don't!"

"Now we have another issue to deal with regarding health care costs and that is litigation. According to a reliable study done only last year – the name of the accounting firm that did the study escapes me at the moment – as much as 25 cents of every health dollar goes to litigation related issues. So Miss

Westerbrook (sic) we have already lost half of what we spend on healthcare to the insurance industry and to the litigation industry."

"I say we can get a major portion of that money back. How?? First we cap litigation to 10 cents on the dollar, because there are legitimate and real claims that need to be paid – medical mistakes happen. Everyone knows that, physicians and care givers are human – they make mistakes – all mistakes can't be avoided. We are going to be able to cap litigation at 10% because we are going to get rid of the litigators!"

"How do we do that? We establish a board of medical experts, intelligent lay persons and trial lawyers." When the Governor mentioned 'lawyers' a soft snicker moved through the crowd. With missing a beat, he added, "After all trial lawyers do know a lot about these issues. And, if we establish an effective board we will be able administer and pay claims at the 10% level I mentioned and not at the 40 to 50% we are currently giving to the litigators and their clients."

"So that I don't threaten the livelihood of every personal injury lawyers in the country, let me add that I believe trial lawyers serve an important function in our country. Taking away medical malpractice cases still leaves them with plenty important work to do."

"Simultaneously with capping medical claims to 10 cents on the dollar, we will reduce the administrative cost of health care delivery to 5%."

"And, how do we do that? We extend Medicare to everyone. We institute Universal Health Care like the rest of the civilized world! And, by instituting just these two reforms we get rid of two components that have been bleeding the health care system – the malpractice lawyers and the health care insurance industry. Hallelujah!"

"I see you looking at my funny-like, Miss Westerbrook (sic). You probably think I am pipe dreaming – particularly with my 5% administrative cost number – don't you? Or maybe you are wondering if we can really rid ourselves of those monstrous blood suckers?"

Maynard paused for a moment, hoping for some kind of reaction from Ms Westbrook. She didn't flinch. Maynard continued, "Well, Miss Westerbrook (sic) did you know that Medicare is administered at a cost of 2 cents on a dollar?............ Well, it is! Let me refer you to an excellent analysis done by a Professor Milton Burnstein at Washington University in St. Louis. It is an excellent study and very revealing. If Medicare can administer at 2%, I am giving a twofold comfort factor with my 5% costs."

"Before, I go on to our last question; I want to add one additional comment. And that is, Americans have been deceived, and deceived repeatedly these past nearly 30 years by the Republicans, and that has been done with the very willing complicity of the Democrats. This deception was started in 1981 by the President who the Republicans revere and worship to this very day – the man they refer to as the Great Communicator, Mr. Reagan himself. Republicans, for reasons I cannot comprehend place him on the very same pedestal as Abraham Lincoln – I just don't get that."

"In any case, you will also remember some of the very first words that gentlemen –may he rest in peace as he was, without doubt, an amiable and well intentioned fellow – stated, loud and clear. He said that the problem with Government was the Government itself. And, that, my friends, was a policy statement that was repeated daily for 8 years and, very importantly, that was occurring in a confluence of time when corporations and their business interests were expanding exponentially. And so, we deregulate and we privatize everything. We don't have soldiers in Iraq doing guard duty – we have Halliburton. Our soldiers don't peel potatoes – we have brother of Halliburton. And on, and on it goes. Our government has become the tool of corporations. Big businesses are empires, and they are run by non-elected individuals responsible only to investors. And, I add, not little investors like us - and, certainly not we the people."

"To accomplish their aims the opponents of government use, among other means, a very clever tactic. They led us to believe the government can't do anything right. I claim they give the government a bum rap. It is almost a conspiracy. They repeatedly state that the government can't do anything right. And while we, the people, get deceived a bunch of some bodies are making billions off of our backs."

"I know of Federal Agencies that function very, very well. The only glaring exceptions I can think of are the few that were blessed with some mighty incompetent leadership – put in charge by the current administration. The US government as does the State of Mississippi has thousands of dedicated workers, and believe me they are not well paid. Let us not forget that all of our wars have been fought by government employees – I cannot think of any more dedicated individuals. I cannot imagine any warriors performing better than our soldiers."

"And, if we need to remind these anti government folks about other successes, let's not forget about NASA. They put a man on the moon! And, 20 years before that a bunch of government scientists built the atomic bomb. Remarkably, they did it in eighteen months. Those are, no doubt, two of the greatest achievements we have made in this country."

"To be fair I need to add one more point. There are a few Federal and State Agencies that are filled with bureaucracy. The new Republican Governor in Louisiana learned that when his state finally got money from Washington to rebuild after Katrina. But he also learned quickly to take those bureaucracies by the horns and make them function for the benefit of Louisiana. He has done an incredible job getting those agencies to do their jobs. That is what good leadership and good management are all about. That is what politicians who are interested in first serving the people are all about."

Given that this would be the last question, almost all of the assembled press tried to get Maynard's attention. For some reason, - maybe just instinctual or because he was a head taller than the rest – he nodded to Archer McNabb of the *Washington Post* who had already had his chance. None-the-less, McNabb reintroduced himself and asked, "Governor DeFrie, Iraq and the war on terrorism are not getting as much press these days as they were six months to a year ago. However, they are still important issues. Do you have a different solution from that of the Administration, or – if elected – would you continue the same policies?"

Maynard winced, hesitated and wet his lips before beginning. He did really not want to address this issue so early in the campaign. However, he knew he had to respond – it was too important a matter to duck. Looking down to the ground in front of the lectern and then towards McNabb he said, "The Iraq situation is not only a mess, it is a moving target, and so most presidential aspirants don't want to touch it - And, of course, that's why it get so little press these days, other than the weekly car bombings."

"Let me say, however, that had I been President after September 11th I would have taken an entirely different approach. Actually, I would have taken an entirely different approach to the whole terrorism issues well before 9/11 happened. We certainly should have known it was coming – after all we had been hit at home and abroad well before that. But that's hindsight."

"The best policy that I can envision has already been delineated by one of the Republican Presidential candidate, Congressman Don Saulzer – someone who has gotten almost no attention in that campaign. What Congressman Saulzer asserts is that the root cause of terrorism is the very fact that we have such a major military presence in so many Middle Eastern countries. We have been meddling in their affairs for more than 70 years. Further, I can think of no strategic basis for our being there other than to insure a supply of oil that will be vital to our economy. And we only need to do that until we make the transition to alternative energy sources. And, departing from the Congressman's point of view, I would propose that we can insure and safe guard our interests without a physical presence on their land. There are clearly other ways to accomplish appropriate safe guards."

Maynard had hardly finished his last sentence when an unidentified reporter blurted out, "But what about Israel? What about our long standing commitment to Israel, and our strategic interests there?"

Maynard paused. He wanted to be forthright, but he knew he had to answer this question carefully – too much was at stake. The Governor understood well the influence and resources of the Pro Israel Lobby in America. He did not want to offend this powerful group. He knew how emotionally illogical so many of them could be. However, because he as a black man and understood human nature well, he could understand them and empathize with so many of their experiences. He also knew that no matter what he said someone would misinterpret his words.

"I did not get who asked that question. But my first thoughts are that we need to take a more global, and a more realistic view of the Middle East. Firstly, the Israelis have done an incredible job building a country that in its modernity rivals our own, or for that matter all of the major European countries. It is truly miracle brought about by an intelligent and industrious people. Furthermore, as you all know, Israel has one of the most advanced militaries in the world – rivaled by no country in the Middle East – not by any stretch of the imagination. Israel is a nuclear power and they have stockpiled more than 300 nuclear weapons."

"I add - we can take significant credit for that by virtue of the billions of dollars in aid and military assistance we have provided to our loyal ally over these many years. But I also need to give the lion's share of that success to Israel, and add that they personify the saying 'God helps those who help themselves'. I think it is also safe for me to say that Israel has proven it can take care of itself. And, we are all aware of how well Israel looks after its own interests."

"It would be naive of us, and insulting to Israel to classify that modern country as 'adolescent'. If the US disappeared off the face of the earth, Israel would survive. Consequently, I think the time has come for us to play a more evenhanded role in the Middle East. Having played a major role in achieving the objective of Israel's survival when it was necessary to do that, our objective now needs to be peace for Israel and its neighbors. And, I might add, the time has come for America to look out for its strategic interests – our world is changing rapidly."

When Maynard had finished, he mopped his brow, looked over the crowd and thanked all who had endured the heat and humidity of the day. The elderly gentlemen with the ill fitting and worn suit came to the lectern – never introducing himself - added his thanks and invited all present to a small reception in the Capital rotunda.

*   *   *

Maynard's press conference announcing his candidacy for the Presidency got very little media attention – what little it did attract was not well reported, and in fact largely erroneous. Short articles, and few of them, entitled – "Evangelical Minister Green Party Candidate", "Jesus Inspires Presidential Run", "Mississippi Minister for President", "Maynard Who(?) for President – appeared somewhere between page 8 and 15 of about ten newspapers. The *New York Times* ran a two paragraph article on page 3 of the "Arts" section entitled "Mississippi Governor DuPreis (sic) Green Party Candidates". The *Washington Post* got it right: "Mississippi Governor DeFrie Presidential Candidate."

Maynard did not fare as well on network Television. The evening anchors for ABC and NBC gave a one liner about the press conference in Jackson where DeFrie announced his candidacy. Fortunately, cable news – CNN and MSNBC - with their insatiable need to fill air time, showed, respectively, the first half and the entirety of Maynard's opening statement.

Chapter II

Maynard Jefferson DeFrie was born on December 27, 1943 in Metairie, Louisiana, a suburb of New Orleans. Metairie lies south of Lake Pontchartrain, and northwest of the City of New Orleans. Metairie is not a city, it has no government, and, in fact, is governed by a Council from Jefferson Parish of which it is a part. The name of this city - 'Metairie'- is derived roughly from the French word for 'farm'. More accurately, it describes a form of French farming where a landowner would lease land to a tenant in return for 50% of the crop. Indeed, Maynard's ancestors – or at least his grandfather whom he never knew – had been sharecroppers. Maynard often speculated that his sir name - 'DeFrie'- was probably connected to that sharecropper background and, accordingly, the French influence on Metairie.

On more than one occasion it had occurred to Maynard that his name could well be a corruption of similarly sounding French names such as D'Aprix or DuPrey, and that he must have had some French ancestry. That notion was also not inconsistent with old photographs of Maynard's father who had a finely shaped nose and non Negroid lips despite his very dark skin color. Maynard, on the other hand, had a significantly broader nose, yet well formed and not typically Negroid.

Maynard never had the opportunity to know his father. His father, Justin DeFrie, was killed near the end of World War II on French soil near Prudemanche, France - August of 1944. He was twenty years old and had only been in the service for 11 months. In a moderate twist of irony in Prudemanche there is an ancient Inn named LaMetarie, perhaps the only such Inn so named in all of France.

A private in the recently integrated Army, Maynard's father had volunteered to be a driver in a very dangerous ongoing mission called the Red Ball Express. This effort involved a continuous convoy of trucks that would be supplying food, fuel, ammunitions, and other essentials to American troops who were hurtling towards Nazi Germany under the leadership of General George Patton. At that time, American troops were so rapidly advancing towards Germany and as there was no other means of transport of vital supplies - the French rail system had been bombed into oblivion – the Red Ball express was invented and pressed into service. Maynard's father and two black companions on their very first transport run were killed almost instantly when their truck carrying gasoline exploded after being strafed by German fighter planes. No remains were recovered.

In spite of that major misfortune which included that Maynard would never have the positive aspects of male influence in his formative years, Maynard was raised by two strong and rather remarkable women – his mother, Ernestine, who never remarried, and his maternal grandmother, Beulah McDermott, whom he often in his adult years referred to alternatively as his 'Black Saint' or 'The Black Madonna'. He was indeed the apple of their eyes, and deservedly so. Maynard understood instinctively at a very early age the impact of having no adult male in his household and, consequently, from that time he knew that much was expected of him. That was consistent with his ambitions and his personality. A day dreamer from a very early age, Maynard dreamed visions that some day he would be a famous man – famous in so many different venues that he had no idea which he would eventually pursue. They were, indeed, incredible and more than moderately unrealistic visions for a young boy coming from so humble a background with only the most meager of resources available to him.

Maynard's mother, Ernestine McDermott DeFrie, grew up in the lower 9th ward of New Orleans a predominantly Negro area squeezed between Lake Pontchartrain and the Mississippi. After completing 8th grade she left school to do her part in helping her family financially – not uncommon for Negro young women living in the south in the 1940's and during the war. For nearly 5 years Ernestine worked for and lived with the family of a prominent New Orleans Surgeon, Gorges Merieux, and his wife, Isabelle, a nurse.

She had been hired initially to work as a domestic and to assist with the care of the Merieux children. Dr. Merieux was on the staff of Tulane University Hospital and also operated at East Jefferson Hospital in Metairie. He maintained a professional office at their residence - a moderate sized Victorian mansion located in the 16th ward and next door to the residence of the Archbishop of New Orleans – and Isabelle assisted him with patients and with the general running of the office. At that time the 16th ward was an old well established section of New Orleans – a very desirable place to live.

Ernestine had not been an outstanding student, but she did like to read, and was naturally curious. Her 5 years with the Merieux family influenced Ernestine greatly. In time she graduated from her domestic chores to cleaning Dr. Merieux's office and that included cleaning and sterilizing surgical instruments that Dr. Merieux used for minor surgical cases in his office. Eventually that led to her assisting Isabelle who would be assisting Dr. Merieux with a variety of routine and minor office procedures on patients.

It was from the experience of those years that Ernestine became familiar with being in the close company of whites and, most importantly, being comfortable and at ease with them. This was an entirely new and different experience for her - in stark contrast to her early life in the 9th Ward where she had effectively no interactions with Whites. She would in time pass this comfort she had gained in working for and living with the Merieux family and that familiarity onto her son. It would have a profound influence on his life.

Ernestine also benefited from her experience with the Merieux family in two other ways. First, her introduction to the world of medical care would lead her into nursing – initially as a nurse's aide – a vocation she would maintain for the remainder of her life, and a vocation that Dr. Merieux and his wife had helped her greatly to achieve. Additionally, Ernestine met her husband, the man who would become Maynard's father, while in the employ of the Merieux family.

Justin DeFrie whose induction into the Army had been delayed by an emergency appendectomy that Dr. Merieux performed at East Jefferson Hospital had come into Dr. Merieux's office - quite by mistake - to have his stitches removed. He had been instructed to meet Dr. Merieux in the emergency ward at East Jefferson. There was instant chemistry between Ernestine and Justin in that first meeting – clearly visible to Dr. Merieux who understood such things – that flourished in the next four days before Justin was off to boot camp following his induction into the Army.

Ernestine and Justin would be together one other time. That short interval followed Justin's completion of basic training at Fort Hood, in Texas and ended with him going off by train to Chicago and eventually to Fort Dix in New Jersey in preparation for deployment to France. In that short interval Ernestine and Justin married and conceived Maynard – though not necessarily in that order.

*   *   *

St. Catherine of Siena has the distinction of being the first parish church established in the Metairie area. Five years later, in

1926, the Sisters of Charity – originally coming from San Antonio, Texas – opened a grade school in a small building adjacent to the parish church. Maynard's grandmother, Beulah McDermott, worked as a cleaning lady for the Sisters for nearly ten years prior to Maynard's birth. Beulah did that six days a week for 51 weeks of each year, making three bus connections each way to get from the 9th Ward to the Metairie area and finally having to walk the last mile.

She was hard working and dedicated to her work in which she took great pride. She had an engaging personality and was well liked by the Sisters, particularly the school Principal, Sister Maria Catharine. From the time Maynard was three years old, Beulah had made the effort to bring her grandson to two annual events where the Sisters included employees and children of employees – the annual Christmas Mass for Employees and reception that followed, and a May Day celebration. On each of those occasions Maynard was presented to Sister Maria Catharine with a small bouquets of flowers in hand that Beulah had fashioned for him.

Thus it was no surprise that Maynard would be allowed to begin his schooling at St. Catherine's even though neither he, nor his mother or grandmother, were Catholic, or that he would be the only negro child in his class and one of a three other negro children in the entire school. Sister Maria Catharine arranged a small scholarship for Maynard that made his tuition about half of that of children who actually belonged to the St. Catherine Parish.

From St. Catherine's, Maynard – still not Catholic – with the encouragement and support of Sister Maria Catharine went on to St. Augustine High School in the city of New Orleans. St. Augustine's is a Catholic high school established in 1951 for Negro boys of Catholic families in the New Orleans area. It was appropriately named as St. Augustine was, indeed, African coming from Hippo in the northern part of that Dark Continent. A very significant number of very successful American blacks in the professions, performing arts and professional sports count themselves as Alumni of St. Augustine.

Maynard prospered at St. Augustine in academics and athletics. By 10th grade he was standing 6'2" and weighed nearly 200 pounds. Maynard was a gifted athlete in speed and in agility as well as physical size. In his junior and senior years he led the "Purple Knights" to two Catholic league championships as a bruising full back on offense and as an aggressive nose guard on defense. It was these accomplishments as well as his well above average grades that gave him a choice of selecting from several institutions. He had been recruited by Grambling College, University of Texas, University of Georgia, University of Alabama and Tulane University, and had been offered by each 'a full ride' (tuition, room and board, plus a small allowance). Maynard chose Tulane University because it would allow him to meet the responsibly he had assumed for the well being of his mother and grandmother. Ernestine and Beulah had not wanted Maynard to make that sacrifice, but he was adamant. They both knew that when Maynard saw the 'right' path, there was no changing his mind. And so, Tulane it would be, and he would commute on a daily basis.

At Tulane Maynard decided to major in Chemistry – something he really enjoyed at St. Augustine's – and minor in Biology. Ernestine had very much encouraged him to pursue medicine as a career. Thus his choice of major and minor would permit him that avenue, if he were so moved. He also entertained the possibility of a career in professional football. He was not unrealistic in that desire – his high school coach at St Augustine had arranged scholarships for many graduates to attend college and several had gone onto professional football. Maynard's coach believed he had the physical and mental gifts to compete at that level.

On the Tulane football field, Maynard had fewer choices than he had in the colleges he could choose from. He had hoped that he would continue at running back or alternatively at the nose guard position that he truly enjoyed. In his freshman year, by which time he had bulked up to 225 pounds and was now standing 6'4" he was forcibly moved to offensive guard. It was a position that utilized his size, speed and agility, but he still didn't enjoy it. As a team player Maynard made the necessary adjustment.

The 1963 football season for Tulane University, when Maynard played starting right guard as a sophomore, was truly a miserable year. The season started off with six straight losses. Maynard had no real experience with losing, and he was not pleased with the small return he was getting for all of his efforts. His analysis of what 1964 season might be - based on seniors that would be leaving and new sophomores that would be joining the varsity - was not at all optimistic. This trend of thought led Maynard to rethink his immediate and future career choices. From discussions Maynard had with his adviser – one of his chemistry professors -he concluded that by attending summer school and taking one additional chemistry course that it would be possible with a heavy junior schedule to graduate in three years. He was almost right on both accounts. The 1964 football team, of which he would continued to be a part, won 3 games and lost 7. And, he would be able to graduate at the end of his junior year if he took his chemistry course along with one additional science course for which he chose comparative anatomy – thus adding to his credentials should he chose a medical career.

*   *   *

In the summer following his graduation from Tulane, Maynard still had not made a career choice. He knew two careers that he was not wanting to pursue: they were medicine and professional sports (he was also gifted at baseball). Quite by accident early in that summer Maynard ran into one of his high school teachers, a Brother Peter Weiss, a Brooklynite who had joined the Josephite Fathers late in life - the Josephite Fathers ran St. Augustine and were a Catholic order whose mission was not confined just to St. Augustine, but to the education of American Negro boys.

Brother Weiss had taken a liking to Maynard in his first year at St. Augustine, and they remained close throughout his high school years. Indeed, Brother Weiss was instrumental in Maynard's college choice, encouraging him towards Tulane which he believed would offer Maynard the best education of those schools from which he had offers. It was at Brother Weiss' suggestion following that accidental meeting and with Brother Weiss' repeated intersession that Maynard applied for and was offered his first job. He would teach chemistry at a private Catholic school for girls run by Josephite sisters called Villa Joseph-Marie, a part of St. Joseph's Manor in Newtown, Pennsylvania.

Maynard taught for three years at 'Villa', and also had some success coaching the high school soccer team. He had never played soccer, knew little about it and he had little experience with young girls, but they did win a league title in his second year at Villa. For the first time in his life, Maynard was experiencing the world outside of Louisiana. The brief trips he made with the football team to surrounding states had provided him with little contrasting experience. Maynard made the most of this new exposure by making frequent visits to Philadelphia, Washington D.C. and New York City as both a sightseer and as a cultural sponge – he missed very little and absorbed everything.

Maynard also made it a point to visit some of the very prestigious universities in the region – University of Pennsylvania, Princeton University, Rutgers and New York University where he enjoyed a number of social events, attended a variety of seminars and enrolled – at Rutgers -in two education courses in the second and third summers he had spent in the East. His intent with the education courses was to prepare himself for a teaching certificate – a requirement that did not exist at 'Villa' as it was a private school operating within the Philadelphia archdiocese. Maynard was thinking at that time that teaching and coaching at one of the high schools in Philadelphia or in Trenton might be a good career choice for him.

During this time Maynard maintained contact with Brother Weiss by letter on a regular basis and with an occasional phone call. Prompted – or more appropriately – pestered by Brother Peter Weiss, Maynard eventually journeyed to Baltimore and spent a long weekend at the Seminary where Brother Weiss had trained and was ordained – St. Joseph's Manor in Baltimore. Brother Weiss claimed that Maynard would enjoy Baltimore, that it was a good sport city – home of the Baltimore Colts and Baltimore Orioles, two of Maynard's favorites – and that the Seminary would be a convenient place to stay, plus he would have a chance to meet some of Brother Weiss' old friends. It was clear to Maynard what Brother Weiss really had in mind.

That visit was to have a profound effect on Maynard's future. It created a lot of inner turmoil that caused Maynard to reevaluate his life goals as well as causing him much pain. Was he doing what he was meant to be doing? A spiritual person Maynard had long hoped that when had found his calling he would know it immediately. It was from this experience, Maynard's long relationship with Catholic schools, his familiarity, liking, appreciation and admiration for the Sisters and Brothers who had taught him since he was a child - and who had influenced his life immensely - that Maynard decided he would dedicate his life to the most meaningful thing he could conceive of - doing Jesus' work.

Raised by a mother and grandmother whose lives were very much intertwined with their church – the Baptist Church – for their social needs, but whose spiritual needs were satisfied by their personal relationship with Jesus, Maynard could not bring himself to become a part of the mystery of the Catholic faith. For him there was no mystery in his relationship with Jesus – they were brothers and Jesus was his savior. That was what he learned from very early on. He knew that as well as he knew his own name, as well as he knew the love of Ernestine and Beulah. He also knew that the Baptist approach to Christianity that served the spiritual needs of Ernestine and Beulah would not satisfy his intellectual needs.

Based on that analysis and those emotions, however flawed they may be, Maynard applied for admission to the Yale Divinity School and Princeton Theological Seminary. He was accepted to both programs but accepted the Princeton Theological Seminary – a graduate school of the Presbyterian Church (USA) – and would be an ordained minister in three years. One of his reasons for choosing Princeton was proximity to Newtown, Pennsylvania which would make moving relatively easy, inexpensive and still allow him to maintain some friendships he had made in the Philadelphia area.

Another reason was that the admissions office at the Theology Seminary had promised to help him find a position – possibly as a line coaching assistant to the Princeton University football team. That position, he was told, would make him a University employee – a small stretch – and it would provide him with some tuition reduction as well as making him welcome to eat, free of charge, at training table with the players he would be coaching. Maynard was a line coaching Assistant for the three years he was at Princeton. He would now be able to expand his world to include Boston, New Haven, Ithaca, Hanover and Providence – all places where the Princeton football team played.

*   *   *

Upon his ordination, the Reverend Maynard Jefferson DeFrie accepted a pastorate at a small, integrated Presbyterian Church in a racially mixed section of Hattiesburg, Mississippi. He was successful in his work both professionally and personally. After two years of hard work his church had prospered, his flock had grown and he was pleased that he was doing God's work. He was very well liked. One parishioner, a graduate of Mississippi State University who had only recently begun attending services and who happened to be a very attractive young black woman – a grade school teacher as well - liked Maynard even more than most of his parishioners. She liked him enough to join his church, become a Presbyterian, and enough to get him to his own alter in the fourth year of his pastorate.

In spite of Maynard's apparent success, his healthy marriage and with the expectation of his third child, he was not completely fulfilled. He had ministered to his flock for nearly 8 years and he was now 37 years of age. He knew in his heart and his mind that he had made significant progress on his mission, but he was being worn down by the thought he could do more – much more. But what would that be?

Initially Maynard was not sure what his next vocation might be. He had lived through decisions that had caused him similar turmoil before. In time he came to the conclusion that he could best do God's work, and that he could best give love and honor to his Savior by a vocation that affected more aspects of peoples lives than just the spiritual side – as important as that was to him.

Maynard Jefferson DeFrie's analysis led him to the conclusion that he should enter politics. That would be the road that would enable him to do more good works than his ministry afforded him – enable him to be the Sheppard of a much larger flock. An avid follower of politics from the time he had arrived in Mississippi, it was apparent to Maynard that the Democratic Congressman representing his district for the last 24 years would not be running as his health had failed significantly in the last 18 months. He was correct in his thinking about the up coming vacancy and he was prepared. Maynard Jefferson DeFrie secured the Democratic Party nomination, ran for the US congress from his district in 1982 and won. He was on his way.

*   *   *

Maynard had no more achieved this milestone in his life when he set his next goal. Ambitious people do that. That next goal would be the US Senate or Governor of the state of Mississippi, his adopted home – depending on how the winds of fortune might blow. He was also thinking of the goal he would set upon achieving one of those objectives, and that was by the time he was in his early 60's he would be President of the United States of America. He was confident that he would succeed. He would plan diligently and accordingly.

The path on which Maynard had embarked and appeared to be successfully launched lasted only two years. When Ronald Reagan was re-elected in 1984 by a landslide, Maynard along with many other freshman Democrat Congressman were voted out of office. That set back might have caused men of lesser intellect, character and resolve to rethink their mission. That was not Maynard's style; he was an individual who needed to understand why he had not achieved some particular goal. What had he done wrong? Where were the errors in his thinking?

Consequently, Maynard took a very different approach to his dilemma. Rather than rethink the goal of his mission, he would rethink his strategy for achieving those goals. He realized that in politics the vicissitudes that are part of politics operate more intensely at the national level than they do at the state level. He had learned that the mood of the country can swing – almost turn - rapidly and with significant momentum. Accordingly, Maynard would readjust his course, this time using state offices to achieve his goal of becoming Governor – now his first choice – or alternatively that same route to become a US Senator.

After serving two terms in the State of Mississippi House of Representatives and one term in the State Senate, Maynard was elected Governor of the State of Mississippi in 2000. He was the first Black Governor of Mississippi and the first Black Governor of a state in the Deep South. He was 56 years of age.

Maynard DeFrie had climbed this steep ladder almost entirely on his own. He was totally unlike so many politicians who from an early age are voracious political animals that cultivate coteries of friends with a purpose - friends whom they will use to leverage themselves to the next step in their careers. In spite of the fact that Maynard was a gregarious individual who enjoyed and liked people, he was deep down a loner who as he once said spent most of is waking hours within the confines of his own head. There were no 'Friends of Maynard' either helping him or hanging on to his coat tails. From being an only child and having no other males in his home to commiserate with - or even play with - Maynard had become accustomed to being alone and he learned that whatever he would achieve in life, he would have to do on his own.

Because Maynard was such a complex individual, he could easily be misread. There were many individuals who thought Maynard was arrogant, when, in reality he was a very humble person. That humility like all of Maynard's inner workings was not easy for the casual observer to perceive. Apparently he was thought to be arrogant, primarily because Maynard was so confident in his knowledge of issues and of areas he had studied well. Furthermore, the manner in which he delivered his ideas, and the manner in which he presented himself were not typical of a humble individual. In conversation, Maynard would often times tilt his head a slight bit backward – looking through the lower part of his eyes -which gave some the impression that he was arrogant, maybe even imperious. It was merely a personal habit that Maynard had acquired, one that he was not aware of, and one with no conscious meaning on his part.

Those few confidents that Maynard had, all knew well that he could take criticism and would even solicit it. He would often repeat that the only way we can achieve perfection – or, more appropriately he would say, try to achieve perfection – is to hear the views of others and to listen to their criticisms of our ideas. On the other hand, once Maynard had taken a position on some issue – a position honed by thorough and exhaustive examination and rethinking – he was hard to dislodge. He could come on like the bull of a man he was.

However, on many occasions Maynard would take a comment someone might have made, and made even casually, 'home to bed' with him – as he would say. After a few days of rethinking he might modify his position. Maynard J. DeFrie was not a man stuck on fixed ideas. He was a man who realized that each day brings new information and new insights that need to be factored into the mix of information that complex situations require. He was good at doing that, and had no qualms at admitting he had rethought an issue. Unlike most politicians who squirm when they have been caught 'modifying' some particular view, Maynard was forthright. He had factored in new information, rethought the issue and modified his view.

Chapter III

Governor Maynard J. DeFrie had not been inattentive to his long range ambitions during his campaign for Governor and during his years in the Governor's office. Every effort he made in his campaign at the state level - be it strategy, organizational or with the media – he tested, tweaked and reevaluated with the intention that it could be leveraged when he would go onto the national scene. He used the same tactic in governing his state – learn and understand the fundamentals of what works in gaining the support of this generation of Mississippians, of Americans. Maynard had vowed to himself that he would never put himself, his campaigning or his future in the hands of professionals. He would make it a point to learn what they knew and to understand their experience, but all final strategic decisions would be Maynard's.

In his campaign for the governorship, Maynard ran on a very progressive platform – a campaign for radical changes that would call for major investments in education, in infrastructure, in economic development, in health care and in research and development, particularly in the area of bio-agriculture, at the state's institutions of higher learning. The strategy of the campaign and its design had a simple and ambitious goal: rocketing Mississippi forward, and out of the sleepy – almost Rip Van Winklish - Southern state it had been for hundreds of years.

During his campaign, Maynard traveled to every corner of the State of Mississippi. He visited nearly every church in the State – black or white – and every Masonic Hall, American Legion, Elk or Moose Lodge and each an every nursing home.

Maynard had learned well some very important lessons from his short teaching career. He knew, or could sense, when his audience was with him – following each part of an intricate analysis. Alternatively, he knew when he had lost them, or if they were either not paying attention or were skeptical. Good teachers learn to read the facial expressions of their students and to pay attention to their body language. Good teachers also know how to turn an audience on a dime when they have lost them. Maynard used these abilities well throughout his campaigns and in his governing.

In campaigning, Maynard had several stump speeches. He had put great effort into them – each was very well thought through. The strategy of his presentations was to form a connection to his audience – a bond of trust. He did that by first making a few statements that showed how appreciative he was for the opportunity of speaking to them, by understatement about himself and by a demonstration that he was, indeed, not a haughty man – he was one of them.

Most times Maynard would introduce himself, rather than have someone praise him for things he did not want praise for. He would do that by walking deliberately and slowly to the podium, firmly place his hands, then look around the entire assemblage, and begin speaking with a most sincere and kindly smile on his face, "My name is Maynard Jefferson DeFrie and I am here to seek your vote for the Governorship of this great state of Mississippi. I want you all to know – with every ounce of humility in my soul - what a privilege it is for me to be running for the highest office in the State of Mississippi. Whether or not, at this very moment you support my candidacy I want to thank you for allowing me that honor, and I thank you for being here."

"And, I also want to thank for the opportunity to discuss with you vital issues affecting our State of Mississippi, and to share with you my proposals to address those issues. I thank you also for the opportunity to convince you that I might deserve your trust. When I have covered the issues I have come here to discuss with you, I invite your questions, your challenges, or for that matter, concerns that you might have that I have not addressed. I promise you that I will be direct in my answers, and also that I will stay as long as you need me to. "

Maynard would follow those introductory remarks with a short inspirational message designed to transform the bond of trust he had already created into a communal bond. For example, he would in a very genuine way extol the unique virtues of Americans and specifically Mississippians. "We are a hard working people; we are honest, generous, patriotic and proud of what we stand for." He would augment those comments by giving examples of Mississippi history that demonstrated the points he had just made.

He would follow that by saying, "Do you folks realize how unique we Mississippians are?" Pausing for a reaction from his audience, "We are a state that lacks so many resources; we have no ocean we having only our Gulf Coast which unfortunately so often betrays us. We are in so many ways on the crossroads to nowhere."

"Yet, we are rich. Yes, rich in our people. Mississippi produces some of the most extraordinary Americans of any state in the Union. Most Americans don't know that. Most Americans don't even know what the name of our Capital is, let alone that they idolize the accomplishments of so many individuals who are the progeny that this great state. I dare say that on a per capita basis – we are truly the Champions!!

His audiences always met that last comment with great applause, and without missing a beat Maynard would begin dropping the names of famous Mississippians, and quickly follow on with a few words about their accomplishments. His list of names was long, very long and depending on the background of his audience he would use them to make connections on a very personal level. He could do this because Mississippians knew and revered these individuals.

If he wanted to mention civil rights – Maynard would talk glowingly about the character and courage of the Evers brothers, Medgar and Charles. For popular music his list was extraordinary but he would limit it to Tammy Wynette, Elvis Pressley, Bo Diddley, Jimmy Buffet, and BB. King along with a dozen others. For literary contributions, Maynard's favorites were Eudora Welty, William Faulkner and Tennessee Williams.

When he wanted to connect to the celebrity world he called up the accomplishments of Oprah Winfrey, Craig Claiborne, Jim Henson and Leontyne Price, and for Hollywood he had James Earl Jones and Sela Ward. For sports he used the trio of Jerry Rice, Walter Payton and Red Barber, even though there were so many famed Mississippians in that world. And, that was just Maynard's 'A list'. Maynard knew the details – place of birth in Mississippi, high school, manner in which they had achieved their goals and their fame – for each of those Mississippians whom he might mention. He was encyclopedic in his knowledge.

When Maynard had finished this portion of his presen-tation, he would end by saying, "What is the magic of this land – this sacred mud - that has bestowed on so many of us the ability to achieve greatness? What is it about us that has made our Creator so generous? We are truly blessed! Thank you, Lord. Thank you Jesus!" Inevitably, the crowd rose to its feet in rapt applause. Maynard had connected – they were a part of him.

After warming up his audience, demonstrating his human side, the power of his intellect, his devotion to the state of Mississippi and his desire to bring change, he would then address pertinent state issues and the programs he would implement. He would also touch lightly on national issues such as Free Trade, immigration and state vs. federal government responsibilities in their connection to the state of Mississippi.

Maynard knew that you can only hold the attention of a mixed audience for 35 minutes. Accordingly, he completed his introductory and substantive comments in that time frame. When he had completed his presentations at these 'town hall meetings', he would open the meeting for questions. He knew that if he needed to add detail to any of his proposals, he could do it in the question and answer part of the meetings. It was a rare occasion when questions, answers and commentary took less than 50 minutes.

After Maynard's election and inauguration, he continued to make his 'rounds' – journeying around the State of Mississippi to all the places he had visited on his campaign. He did this nearly every weekend during his first two years in office. On those visits, he would report the progress on his agenda and round up support for specific items that were being resisted in the State Legislature.

It was suspected by many that his visits were not entirely chosen at random, but, instead, many were in the very districts of recalcitrant legislators. Whatever Governor DeFrie was doing it was effective as he could be assured that anywhere from 50 to 150 letters would arrive on the desks of individuals who either opposed his initiatives or were looking to bargain for their votes.

Maynard made one other innovation on his campaign trail and continued it with modification when he journeyed around the state conducting his "town meetings' after his inauguration. During the campaign and afterwards he collected thousands upon thousands of e-mail addresses. On a weekly basis each recipient was e-mailed a three paragraph letter entitled "What Mississippians Need to Know". Maynard knew that no one wants to read more than three paragraphs. Consequently, the points he wanted to make were stated concisely, and, if, the reader wanted more detailed information they were referred to specific web sites where they could obtain all the information they needed with merely a double click; or they were directed to Maynard's web site.

After his election, Maynard changed the title of his weekly e-mail to "Mississippi Moving Forward". Recipients were not only informed of the progress that was being made on Maynard's agenda, but of other relevant issues in the state and also in the nation when it was relative to Mississippians. Those recipients who were willing to reveal their birthdays as well as their e-mail addresses also received greetings on those occasions.

*   *   *

Beginning in the third year of Maynard's Governorship, it was his plan to expand his sphere on a more national basis. He also needed to address the race issue, and address that head on. Was the country ready for a Black president? Were Blacks ready for a Black President? Maynard had compelling reasons to believe that within Mississippi he had gained the respect of his white constituents, and that in reality at the political level Mississippians had become color blind. He also had the strong support of Black Mississippians. He was also convinced that he could resonate with Black voters around the country. It was now time to test where the rest of the white population of the country stood.

Maynard was not expecting this to be an easy row to hoe, he instinctively always knew that Southern whites – not Northern ones - would be more accepting of him and other Blacks who had worked hard to achieve, and who knew how to function in civil society. He knew this to be the case in spite of the fact that conventional wisdom might say otherwise. Maynard understood human nature, he understood racism and he always had the courage to think out side of the box. He was an original.

In June of 2003, Governor DeFrie gave commencement speeches at the University of Mississippi and at Mississippi State University. The themes of his talks were similar. He gave a short analysis of where the country had been these last fifty years and presented an analysis to the graduating classes of where the country might be going in the next half century. He spoke about the economics of globalization, about all of the long range consequences that would accompany global climate change, on the Bill of Rights and our personal freedoms, and on the affects of modern technology on the human spirit. He entitled his speech "Twenty fifty-four". The graduates seem to like the Orwellian title.

The speech was long by Maynard's standards – one full hour – and was politely received by the graduating classes considering the heat of the day - even though the commencement services had been moved to the early evening. From Maynard's point of view his efforts were a success, since both Time Magazine and Newsweek carried excerpts in the following week, and both were complimentary of its content.

Maynard was pleased for many important reasons. Focusing on college aged students was a key part of his strategy to answer some of the fundamental questions he had raised for himself – vis-à-vis the possibility of a Black President. He realized that by the year 2008 college aged students would be in the workplace, some might be married and some raising children. Most importantly they would be voters, potentially they could be volunteers, and to some degree they might also reflect their parents thinking. If Maynard's ideas about the issues facing the country resonated with them – they could be disciples. Maynard also reasoned college campuses all over the country were always seeking speakers. The positive commentary made in Time and Newsweek was, in fact, free advertising. That along with contacts Maynard had made over the years would ensure a busy speaking schedule.

Beginning in the fall of 2003, Governor Maynard DeFrie visited, on average, three campuses a month. He accepted no honoraria – the going rate $5000 – 15,000 – and he was not embarrassed to have his hosts pick up his coach air fare, accommodate him for the evening, and he always agreed to sit down to dinner with groups of them. He particularly enjoyed the

Political Science majors and that subset of them that would be going on to law school.

Initially, Maynard focused on colleges and Universities in Southern nearby states – Texas, Florida, Alabama, Louisiana and Tennessee. By November of 2005, Maynard had visited and spoken at over 100 institutions all over the country. By his estimate he had made 20,000 potential disciples. He also had accumulated nearly 18,000 new e-mail addresses to add to his collection as well as cell phone numbers – text messages would be forthcoming.

Maynard had structured his life in a very orderly fashion. He had done this from the time he was a child performing his chores and keeping his small room in order without supervision. He understood not having material items that most of his classmates had – some items most would consider necessities. He also understood waste, and Maynard was not one to waste opportunity and he took pleasure in leveraging his opportunities. Consequently, on almost every occasion when he had a prepaid ticket to visit some institution – typically on a Friday – Maynard coupled that with an additional visit on Saturday. These were to Church groups and Lodges just as he had done in his campaigning in Mississippi and in governing his state. Most mortals could not maintain such a taxing schedule, while, at the same time, governing a state. It was evident that Maynard not only had the body of a bull – he had the energy. He was tireless.

*   *   *

Governor Maynard Jefferson DeFrie's next monumental issue was money. Granted that he was careful in spending his own or the state of Mississippi's money, none-the-less he understood he would get nowhere without financial resources. Maynard further understood that campaign monies come from a politician's base. But he also knew that his base in Mississippi did not have the wealth or resources to be of real value to him.

On December 6th of 2006, Maynard mailed 70 Christmas Cards in envelopes that identified them as coming from the Office of the Governor of the State of Mississippi. Each Card was hand written by the Governor personally and closed with his writing, "May the Joy of Jesus' Love be in your Heart this Christmas Season." And, signed them "Maynard Jefferson DeFrie."

In each card was a handwritten invitation at the top of which was printed in large red letters – CONFIDENTIAL. The invitation said, "I would be honored if you would join me for a Prayer Breakfast, in Honolulu, Hawaii on Friday, February 9th, 2007 at 9 a.m. In addition to breaking bread with you, it would be my pleasure to lead our gathering in thanking our Savior Jesus Christ for all of the bounty he has bestowed on us." The invitation was signed, "Reverend Maynard J. DeFrie."

Of the 70 recipients of this unusual invitation 37 were Professional Black athletes who would be participating in the NFL Pro Bowl that would be held in Honolulu on the Sunday following Maynard's prayer breakfast. The remainder of the invitations was sent to other Professional Black athletes – football, basketball and baseball -who Maynard knew would be attending this event. The invitations contained no request for R.S.V.P. Under Maynard's signature, he had written, "I look forward to the pleasure of making your acquaintance, and I look forward to discussions of common interests."

On Friday morning, February 9, 2007, 72 Black men – the majority at the physical peak of their lives – assembled at the Hawaii-Hilton Village Beach Hotel in Honolulu in a private dining room that had a commanding view of the Pacific Ocean. Maynard greeted them as they entered the room; he introduced himself and welcomed each of them by name, save two elderly men, whom he did not recognize. In preparation for this event, Maynard had studied photos of all of his guests. As was his habit he had committed to memory pertinent personal and professional information on each individual.

When all were seated, Maynard stood, asked each man to take hold of the hand of his neighbor – forming a complete circle - and offered a short prayer. He blessed the food they were about to eat, and prayed for Jesus' protection for all those present who might immanently be facing the danger of bodily injuries that were so much a part of their profession.

From the hand written note on Maynard's Christmas card, the hand written invitation and Maynard's warmth and persona, each man assembled had the sense that they were in the company of a very special person. Yet they did not exactly understand why that was so.

As the assembled guests ate their breakfasts and chatted softly about the past season, the upcoming Sunday event and reminisced over various past interactions they had had with each other, Maynard moved from table to table greeting again his guests. He marveled at them - these most unusual men – so familiar to him from the homework he had done, yet individuals that he had only just met. At every table, Maynard simul-taneously chatted amiably while slowly moving around the table stopping at every other seat and placing one of his large hands firmly on a shoulder of each individual and his nearby neighbor. He thanked them for taking the time to be with him.

At the table where the uninvited additional two guests – elderly gray haired Black men - were seated, Maynard pause to reintroduce himself, not exactly knowing who these individuals were, why they were there, and, most certainly, not recognizing them. To his great surprise they were teammates from his losing years at Tulane. Both had gone on to play professional football with only moderate success, both coached high school football teams in Louisiana, and both had coached and mentored two of Maynard's honored guests when they were in high school.

When the vision of these two gentlemen in their youthful faces slowly formed in Maynard's brain, he was overwhelmed. As he embraced his long lost teammates his eyes became watery as did theirs. That electrifying moment observed by all reverberated through the room at the speed of light. From soft whispers that moved from table to table all soon learned what was behind that which had just transpired. These were Maynard's old teammates from Tulane. Maynard Jefferson DeFrie had, indeed, been an outstanding athlete in his own right. He was regarded as an exceptional talent, and there was every reason to speculate that he had the potential to be a Pro Bowler had he chosen that path. Maynard DeFrie was by every measure a 'man for all seasons.' Maynard's light – bright that it was in the eyes of these new acquaintances – had grown even brighter with this revelation.

When breakfast was completed, Maynard stood up and first thanked his honored guests. Next, he paused for a moment and as only Maynard could do, a large smile flashed over his face and he began, "I am smiling now because a vision of my grandmother, Beulah McDermott – may her soul rest in peace – just came to me."

"If my Grandma were here with us at this very moment she would be tickled beyond any of your imaginations. Not only would she embrace each of you just like each of you belonged to her.........she would cry out "'thank you Jesus – thank you Jesus' for such beautiful Negro men "

"We were called Negroes when I was a boy and that's how my Grandma would have said it. I am sure at this very moment she would be going from table to table, touching you, pinching you in such a kindly fashion on each of your cheeks. And, if you were standing, she would put her arm around your back and pat you on the behind."

"That was my Grandma – she would be proud. Proud of each and every one of you. Proud of these mighty sons of Africa. That's what she would say! And, so do I."

"I am proud of you because you represent dedication, you represent pride and you have risen to the top of your profession. Few men can say that."

"You also represent something else. You bear witness that a Black man is unlimited in what he can achieve. Not just on the playing field, but in every endeavor"

"When I was a boy, most Black athletes – and then we were called 'colored' or Negro and some other names – had little opportunity to be educated. I remember Joe Louis being interviewed after his fight with Jersey Joe Walcott – and, that was on the radio! Louis who was a PhD in pugilistics never had the opportunity of education. I am ashamed of myself now for what I thought at the time, but I was embarrassed. I vowed that someday I would do my part to make that different – to prove that Black men are as capable as any other."

"Fortunately, for me and for you, so many courageous Black men and women from the previous generation made that very same vow. They succeeded in doing the impossible. Can you imagine the courage - the resolve?"

"These most incredible individuals were successful in achieving what they had set out to do. Unfortunately, in so many cases, they made the ultimate sacrifice. And it is we, the living, who have had the benefit of standing on their mighty shoulders."

"And as I speak I can't help thinking about the Reverend Martin Luther King, Jr. At this very moment his handsome Black face blazons its way through my brain, his resonant and incredible voice reverberates in my head. If only he could see us here today, and I believe he can, what a miracle that would be. On every night of my life since 1968, I have prayed to Brother Martin, thanking him and asking him to help me keep my resolve as I try to do God's work."

"Great and courageous men like Brother Martin paved the way for you and me – we must never forget, and our children must never forget that."

Maynard paused for a moment, realizing he had allowed his emotions to divert him from his message, but he was pleased with what he had said about Brother Martin.

"Today so many things are different. I have heard almost all of you being interviewed on the television at one time or another; you speak the words of educated men – you express yourself marvelously. I glow when I hear you on the television."

"I add that two of our honored guests announce the very games you play – this is a different world. This is a better world. No one could have imagined that 60 years ago."

"In every other profession, Blacks – men and women, both - have assumed positions of leadership, of honor. We have had Black governors, Blacks in the House of Representatives, in the Senate, in the Cabinet and in the highest ranks in the Military. And, we owe that to all those who have gone before us – our forbearers. It is also important to remember those who were not Black – they, too, championed the cause of Civil Rights, and there were many of them. They were touched by the love of Jesus and the notion that all men are brothers."

"We must also keep in mind that we, too, have done our part. We have dedicated ourselves to hard work – hard work is the key to achieving any meaningful goal. You, of all people, most certainly know that. We must also take pride in our ancestry and in ourselves. But we must never forget that without opportunity no amount of work will overcome rock solid barriers. Hence, we must not be haughty – that would be an offense to each of us and to Brother Jesus."

"There is one other point I need to make before I go on. And, that is – we must not think that the work of those who came before us is finished. The response that we, we as a country, made to New Orleans after Katrina was a disgrace."

"No doubt much of that was incompetence, but I think we would be fools to think that a white city so devastated would have received such treatment. In Jackson, we have literally hundreds of refugees from New Orleans who still struggle to get their daily bread. And Katrina didn't happen yesterday."

Maynard paused for a few moment, took a sip of water while he was shuffling some notes with his left hand. He continued, "There is one position in this country that we Blacks have not achieved, and, perhaps, until now never considered achieving. That position, my dear brothers, is occupancy of the White House – the Presidency of the United States."

"The real issue on having a Black President is that the only way every Black child in this country can know that he or she can be President of the United States is for there - to be a Black President! It is that simple! And, I add the only way each and every Black child can know that there is no limit to what they can be – that there is no limit on them for using their God given talents for whatever they may choose – is for a Black man to have the opportunity to sit in the highest office of the country – the Presidency."

Maynard stopped speaking for a moment, sensing he had hit a resonant cord with his guests. As he paused a flash of memory came to him from his childhood. He could remember himself proclaiming to his beloved Grandma that someday he would be President of the United States of America. He could also remember the utter shock, sorrow and disappointment when she responded, "Maynard, Negro boys can't become President, but you could become a doctor."

It was the most hopeless response he had ever experienced. He was twelve years old when that happened, and he could still – some 50 or so years later - remember fighting back the tears and biting his lower lip, not wanting his Grandmother to see him cry. He hurt – real physical pain – for weeks after that happened. Maynard did not share this memory with his audience.

When he continued speaking, he said, "If you will look under your place mats you will find an envelope with the Mississippi seal on it, and with your name written below. In that envelope, is a short copy of my Resume. There is also a letter – marked 'Confidential' - that I have written to you. The letter tells you that I, Maynard Jefferson DeFrie, have made the decision to run for the Presidency of the United States as an independent candidate." There was a collective gasp in the audience, but no one stood up and said, "you must be nuts" or stormed out. Instead they all waited to hear what Maynard would say next.

"This is not been a hasty decision. And, I tell you sincerely that I didn't begin working towards this end yesterday -

I have been actively working diligently towards this goal for seven years. And, if there is anything you will learn about Maynard DeFrie – if you decide to stick by me - is that he is diligent, he is thorough and he does his homework. On that I give you my word."

Maynard's two Tulane teammates almost in unison rose to their feet and applauded. With that gesture they confirmed that this was a man whom they - from their own experiences with him - knew would keep his word.

"The decision to seek the Presidency" Maynard continued "is one I made some twenty years ago. In my letter to you I have detailed the basis for that decision, and how I evolved to it. I have, also, outlined the great issues facing our country as I see them– and they are most certainly great ones, and they will be difficult to solve. At your leisure, you will be able read my list of changes that this country must make to avoid the disaster that will surely come our way if we do not alter our course."

"Since I am going to be seeking help from each of you to achieve this goal, let me highlight some of the changes I believe we need to make."

"First tax reform – we need to reestablish the middle class, we cannot have a super-rich class that gobbles up all the resources. We cannot have a system of government that funnels riches upward to those who do not need riches. We need to bring our brothers and sisters up from the lowest classes. That will require money. Money for programs to help those who want to help themselves."

"Second, Health Care – we need universal health care, and we need to do that without the insurance companies. Already we have made too many paper shufflers and bean counters millionaires. The time has come for us to stop doing that."

"Third, we need an entire redo of our foreign policy. We meddle in every part of the world with the exception of the very regions that need our help. If we put 10% of the resources we have poured into Iraq and the Middle East into Africa, we could give millions of our fellow humans hope. Hope for a life worth living – hope that a man can raise his family in safety and without fear of savagery."

"The time for us to disentangle ourselves from the Middle East has come; in fact, we have had no business being there, particularly, in the manner we have involved ourselves, these past 80-90 years. But that is another story."

"Fourth, we need a fair and human solution to the immigration problem in this country. We need a policy that is fair to immigrants and fair to those Americans who are negatively affected by immigrant workers"

"And finally, fifth – I have more but I don't want to overwhelm you, and most of you have a game to play tomorrow – we need to repair the infrastructure of what was once a great country. We will do that by investing right here in the USA. And, when we do that not only do we improve our country, we create opportunity. We create jobs. And, that is a vital issue – believe me when I say that."

"I want to follow up on my last point. I want to speak to the issue that I believe to be the most critical issue facing each in this room. And that is the job and opportunity issue." Pausing momentarily, Maynard continued, "The job creation issue is of absolutely paramount importance to every American Black. I cannot emphasize that point enough!"

"We now have freedoms, we now have opportunity – our children can attend any college or graduate school where they can qualify."

"But something has been happening in the world and in this country which no one seems to talk about. Of course, if you control everything and you are on the top enjoying the benefits of being there, why talk about it?"

"Everything is becoming more competitive. Good jobs, top notch universities, opportunities of all kinds are becoming harder and harder for average Americans. That has been going on for more than 30 years, and it will get worse. For every decent job there are hundreds of applicants."

"Just as an example, when I was flying from Los Angeles to Honolulu yesterday I sat next to a young lady in coach who told me that she was coming here to audition for the Honolulu Symphony. She is a flute player – she has what seemed to me some very excellent credentials."

"I just assumed it would be an easy position to land. Guess how many other flute players she is competing with? Can you believe 400!? That's right 400!"

"I would have thought there were not more than 400 flute players in the entire country. That is what our children and their children will be facing. All of the good jobs will not be available to us for reasons I will cover unless there are some fundamental changes made."

"And, why is that? Why won't jobs and opportunities be available to us, or for that matter any other American kid with no connections?"

"The answer is simple. There is an aristocracy forming in this country at a level never seen before. If you are not connected you will stand out in the cold. You will stand out in the cold just like you were invisible."

"If you don't believe me take a look at Hollywood! If you are not the son or daughter of somebody - somebody who made it in the industry when that was possible on talent alone or a somebody who wields influence in the industry – you don't stand a chance of breaking into the acting world."

"I don't know what movies you might have seen on your flights coming here. In getting from Jackson, Mississippi to here, two movies were played. Guess what? They were starring 'son's of' – if you know what I mean. Nepotism has become the order of the day!"

"There is a great irony to all of this. Each of us has heard year after year commentary upon commentary – most of it veiled in its intent – against affirmative action."

"Parenthetically, I never heard anyone speak about the doors that were held wide open for the present occupant of the

White House. If that character really got to where he is, based on his talents – I'll be a monkey's uncle."

"So what is the take home message? And why, other than to be in your magnificent company, did I call you here? "

"My message is simple! If we allow an aristocracy to be created in this country – and that is what happens in a two class society, and two class societies are fostered by unfair taxing policies and by starving public institutions, public works that foster opportunity for all people – the Black man is finished. And, so is any White kid with no connections."

Maynard stopped for a moment, sipped some water and added in an almost apologetic voice, "I hope I did not offend any of you by what I just said. It occurs to me that maybe some of you might just well be aristocrats!" That created quite a bit of muffled laughter around the room.

Before continuing Maynard dug for some folded papers he had in his jacket pocket, seemed to be having difficulty reading what must have been some hastily scribbled notes, and then turned to look out the window at the Ocean. He looked a little puzzled as if he were wondering what the weather were doing. He was in fact concern that he had worn out his audience and that he hadn't even gotten to the point of telling them what he wanted of them. He raised his left hand, his index finger pointing skyward and said, "Ok, so what do I want from you?"

"First, let me assert that I think we have a common bond. My true belief is that I represent each of you, and that each of us have been brothers in a life long struggle. That is what I believe in my heart."

"I also believe that I can be the instrument to insure that what we, and those who came before us, have all struggled for, and what we have worked so hard for continues . It must go on to insure that there will be opportunity for all of our children and every Black child in this country."

"I also believe that our country – a country that has been good to each of us in spite of what we have had to endure – is in dire trouble. I want you to join with me, to join with me my efforts to change the course."

"For me to do that, I need resources! Resources as in money. So I am asking each of you – the 70 I invited to join me here – to become donors, and, I add, large donors for this effort."

From a table near the back of the room, in a surprisingly high voice, a question was asked, "Mister Reverend, you have already told us that if you become President our taxes are going up. And, from the programs you mentioned I would guess that will be a substantial increase. Now you tell us you want us to support you in your effort to become President. So, if I can be so bold, how much do you want from us?"

Maynard responded, "I need 17 million dollars to begin a credible effort. I am hoping that each of you will either donate from your own pockets or from whomever's pockets you have access to 250 thousand dollars. All I ask you at this moment is to think about doing that and to think about what I have said today, and, if you need to I am available to answer anything you might want to know." The questioner stood up and strode to the door, never turning back. As the door pulled shut, Maynard quipped - "I guess we are down to 16.75 million!" Some nervous laughter followed.

At that moment, one of Maynard's uninvited guests stood up. "Maynard, first I need to tell you that I have never in my 63 years had an experience like I had today. I was not looking forward to making this trip as I have had to deal with a number of ailments this past year, but this has made all my efforts worthwhile. Believe me when I say that. Everything you said today has in one way, or another, been a concern to me."

He continued, "I am not really a rich man – my resources don't compare with anyone in this room. And, I have no experience in political matters, but I will pledge to you that I will do all I can in getting you one of those quarter million dollars you need. What I need to know is – isn't there a limit on how much an individual can contribute to a candidate?"

Maynard responded, "There is a campaign limit – I think it's about $2000 per individual or $4000 per couple. There are, however, a number of creative ways to increase that amount. You can have family members – brothers and their wives, cousins – or even friends make contributions for you. There are many of ways to do that. Or, you can use your own money to run ads. For example, if you run a full page ad in the *New York Times* or the *Washington Post* that's going to cost you around $85,000 a pop. You can also use your own money to sponsor a variety of fund raisers."

"If you will make your commitment, we can help you do that within the law. I need to tell you that I am not going to let myself get hung up with the issues of campaign financing. The entire system is a charade, and that is something we will need to fix. Candidates are buying offices – that is not what our founding fathers envisioned."

"What I am looking for is 'starter money'. And, I am asking you, a very special and privileged group, whom I believe cares about the future of Blacks in America and for America, itself, for that. I am confident that once we get rolling, we will be able to raise whatever we need from small contributions. From the people!"

Maynard brought the meeting to a close with a short prayer asking Jesus to Bless all those present and to give all the wisdom, courage and generosity to do God's work. Maynard spent the next 40 minutes answering questions, clarifying points he had made.

Hotel maintenance employees had filtered into the room and were beginning to break down tables and reset the room for its next schedule event. They were polite in not asking the group to vacate the room, but they banged enough tables and chairs to make it uncomfortable enough to encourage people to begin leaving. By that time Maynard had in hand commitments from 36 of his guests giving him a total for the day of 9 million dollars.

Within the two weeks following the Pro Bowl game, the remaining 23 attendees who had stayed through Maynard's entire presentation made their pledges. There were also pledges from 8 other athletes who were not at the Breakfast. Maynard's war chest would contain 17 million dollars. He had achieved a key milestone. He had managed to hurdle a major barrier in a very creative way. Few would have conceived of so brilliant and logical a plan. Maynard was pleased.

Chapter IV

In the 15 months between February 9, 2007 – the date of the Pro Bowl Prayer Breakfast in Honolulu – and May, 2008 when Maynard announced his candidacy for the Presidency, a technologically linked grassroots organization was being assembled according to a plan laid out Maynard himself. The goal of the organization was to have one campaign office – 400 to 1200 sq ft depending on the cost of local office space - located in every county of the country which amount to about 3100 offices.

In reality only 2153 were eventually established as so many counties are so sparsely populated the return on investment would not be worthwhile. Each office was to be linked to all of the others via telephone or cable carrier through a server that was to be located at a campaign headquarters in Jackson, Mississippi. All telephoning was to be done through free internet services, all cell phones used by staff were to be on single network provider so that calls between any staff wherever they might be would be free of charge. The server would have to be set up so that any or all staff could be reached by cell phone text messaging.

To accomplish this countrywide coverage, Maynard had laid the groundwork for the establishment of civically motivated organizations on 220 campuses all over the country that were called "College Students for Change." These organizations were an outgrowth of the follow-on relationships Maynard had established with some of the highly motivated civic minded students who had met the Governor when he visited their campuses. He had cultivated those relationships with his weekly e-mails on relevant topics that he had written specifically for his new college friends. He would additionally have text messages sent to them to alert them on some important issue – on TV, on the Internet or in a weekly newsmagazine.

Maynard had cemented his relationship with 90 of these students over spring break 2007 by inviting each of them to represent their college at a 3 day forum at the University of Mississippi in Oxford, Mississippi the subject of which was: "Civic Responsibility in a Capitalistic World and in the American Democracy." This event would be the first major investment that Maynard would be making in his campaign for the Presidency. It would be the first use of the 'war chest' he had accumulated with the monies contributed by his consortium of professional athletes.

For the conference, each attendee was mailed a reading list compiled by Maynard – with input from guest speakers that Maynard had invited - a plane ticket, a dormitory room assignment and a brochure on 'Ole Miss.' The structure of the Forum was four 35 minute lectures each day followed by a 70 minute discussion period. At the end of any morning or afternoon session participants were encouraged to raise any issue they wanted.

Lectures were presented by five University of Mississippi professors – three from the history department and two from political science. Prof. Zbigniew Brzezinski of Columbia University and former advisor to President Clinton gave three lectures and led the ensuring discussions. David Gergen, former Advisor to Presidents Nixon, Ford and Clinton - currently a

Professor of Public Service at Harvard - gave two lectures with discussions.

Henry Kissinger, Secretary of State under President Nixon was invited but did not respond. Maynard gave the first lecture and a short summary lecture at the closing dinner of the Forum. It was a resounding success. The Forum at Ole Miss and the closing dinner which was catered at 'Rowan Oak' the home of one of Mississippi's most famous sons, William Faulkner made a lasting impression on the attendees.

The most important consequence of the 2007 Spring break Ole Miss Forum – other than a jump start on Maynard's goal of combating the complacency that had engulfed college campuses in the last 15 – 20 years – was that Governor DeFrie had made 90 disciples. Given what his Savior – Jesus – had done with 12 disciples, he was more than pleased.

It was these disciples who by May 2007 had established on their 90 campuses plus another 140 other campuses, the "College Students for Change" organizations that would become champions of Maynard's Presidential aspirations once he had signaled his intent. In the summer of 2007, 422 newly graduated volunteers on ten campuses around the country - working for only room and board, travel expenses and $35/week spending money were working out the - 'hypothetical' - logistics of finding, managing and manning of 3100 county campaign organizations. This was the number of county organizations that Governor DeFrie had suggested a viable candidate for the Presidency might need.

The summer volunteers had concluded only 2100 county offices would be needed. Their planning included the logistics and steps necessary for having these campaign offices in place and functioning by mid January of 2008. And, that included the recruiting of locals who would dedicate themselves to the ardors of a campaign effort. On their own, they had constructed Internet capabilities for communicating any and all information that might be needed in a campaign, and they had built an elegant interactive web page that only needed substantive material added – such as a

Candidate's name and his positions on key issues - for it to be fully functional.

They had also put together all of the mechanics that would be needed to do Internet fund raising. In that connection, they had organized and compiled all of the e-mail addresses that Maynard had accumulated over the years. They were also able to 'locate' e-mail lists that were categorized in many helpful ways. From voter registration lists for the entire country and Internet searches, they created data bases that could be used for mailings, or for phone calling.

While this grassroots strategy and planning was going on, Maynard had also launched another equally important effort – a legal corps. Maynard knew that there would be significant legal issues as he moved down the campaign trail. Good aggressive lawyers would be vital. He also knew that there would be several issues concerning getting his name on ballots in various states, and he needed a legal analysis of that, and the where with all to fight those battles.

Lastly, he had decided to make a legal challenge regarding public funding of campaigns. As the law stood, matching funds were restricted to candidates whose parties had polled more than 5% in the previous election. If Maynard were to run as an independent, there would be no matching funds.

If he were to run as the Green Party candidate – which he leaned to because getting on the ballots of every state would be easier - there would also be no matching funds. The highest percentage that any Green Party Candidate ever achieved was less than 3% - that was Ralph Nader in 2000. Maynard's position would be that if a candidate had polled more than 5% within 90 days of the election, it would be discriminatory not to give that Candidate matching funds. Maynard saw a link to the equal opportunity laws that had survived numerous court challenges. From his point of view, he was, to some very large extent, applying for a job!

To establish his legal corps, Maynard was successful in recruiting volunteers from the NAACP whom he believed would be interested in helping him with some of the issues he wanted to raise. He was also able to enlist three lawyers who were retired alumni of Ralph Nader's 'raiders'. Governor DeFrie had assembled a very competent team, and a team that really understood and delighted in challenges.

*   *   *

On the Tuesday after Governor DeFrie announced he would be a Candidate for the Green Party nominee for the Presidency, a call was received at the Governor's office from the producer of the Larry King Show on CNN. The call was forwarded to Michael O'Connor, the Governor's Administrative Assistant who learned that Larry King wanted to interview the Governor on an upcoming show. O'Connor learned that King broadcasts his shows from one of three identical studios in Washington, D.C., New York City and Los Angeles, and the first opportunity for an interview would be in Los Angeles on Thursday or Friday – May 8th or 9th – since King would be spending the weekend at his vacation home in Utah. If the Governor was unable to journey to Los Angeles, King's producer suggested that the interview could be done via satellite hookup.

O'Connor knew that the Governor would never make a West coast trip for a single 2-3 hour meeting as the expenditure of time involved amounted to 2 entire days. He also knew that the Governor always felt his physical presence was an asset in any negotiation or meeting. Accordingly, he mentioned that the Governor had reason to be in New York City the following week - which was not exactly true - and indicated that an interview at that location might be possible. It was agreed – subject to confirmation from the Governor – that he would appear on the Larry King Show on Tuesday, May 13th. O'Connor took down the address of King's studio and agreed that the Governor would arrive 90 minutes before air time so that he and King could go over some ground rules and become acquainted.

What O'Connor had not told King's producer was that the Governor was scheduled to be in Dallas on the 13th to have lunch and go over some campaign ad copy that two of his Dallas Cowboy supporters would be paying for. They also had lined up three potential donors they wanted the Governor to meet - professional athletes from the Dallas Mavericks basketball team, one of whom was a 'White boy' as they jokingly called him. O'Connor also knew that it was easier to get to New York from Dallas than it would be from Jackson. In fact, to fly on American Airlines from Jackson to New York City, the connection is through Dallas.

After consultation with Governor DeFrie, O'Connor confirmed the Governor's appearance with King's producer, and he directed that travel arrangements be made for the Governor. Maynard would take an American Airlines flight from Jackson to Dallas at 9:30 am arriving at 11:05, have his meeting with his supporters in a private conference room at the Admiral's Club at the Dallas-Fort Worth Airport, and leave for New York City on a 2:30 pm flight. He would arrive at LaGuardia Airport at 7:00 pm. That would give him adequate time with a short cab ride to be at King's studio by 7:30.

On May 13th Maynard's connecting flight from Dallas to New York City was delayed 40 minutes on takeoff and another 30 minutes on landing. He arrived at his gate at LaGuardia at 8:15 pm. He was in King's office 10 minutes before air time.

With only time to make quick introductions and grab a cup of coffee, King and Governor DeFrie sat before the cameras awaiting the 9 pm start of the program. King seemed very pleased to have the Governor as his guest and welcomed his warmly to his show. After giving a brief background of the Governor, stating that he had read the transcript of the Governor's press conference announcing his candidacy, and mentioning that he – King – had heard that the Governor was getting strong financial backing from professional Black athletes, King began with his first question.

"Governor I have red transcripts of some of your speeches and heard recordings of some of them also. I see that you refer to people of your race as Colored, Negro and Black. How do you like to be referred to, Governor?"

Maynard smiled, "Larry – and I hope I can call you Larry – (to which King nodded approval, graciously), you can call me Governor, if you like you can call me Maynard, or Reverend, or just plain DeFrie. And if you would like to, I give you permission to call me Mr. Jefferson, as my Grandmother would call me if she thought I was too uppity." King laughed, indicating he had in no way meant to offend the Governor and was ready to move on to more substantive issues.

"Governor, when you made your press announcement, you said something like you had been called on by Jesus to become President of this country. Is that accurate?"

Maynard wet his lips. "Larry, first of all I am a Christian and I have a strong relationship with Jesus – he is my Savior. Now Jesus didn't come to me and say 'Mr. Maynard, time for you to be the President' – no, he didn't come at all. But as a Christian, Jesus is always in my heart and in my mind, so that when I make a decision - no matter what that decision is - I would hope that it would be the same decision that Jesus would make."

"Now let me add something else, Larry. If you live in Mississippi and if you are the Governor of Mississippi as I am, how much attention do you think you are going to get when you decide to call a press conference announcing that your are running for President? Well the answer is not that much! So if I can get Jesus to help me get some attention, that's what I am going to do."

King started to chuckle at Maynard's candor and the way he structured his answer. He responded, "So you are a melodramatic Christian. Is that what you are telling me? Maybe you're a little bit Jewish like me!" Both had a good laugh.

King resumed, "Let's talk about some of your views on the Middle East – probably the most important trouble spot in the world. In the transcript of your press conference, you were very complimentary to Israel and the Israeli people. You also indicated that it was time for us to get out of the Middle East which would leave Israel on its own. Don't you think we have a special relationship with Israel – don't you think that we must stay there to guarantee Israel's safety?"

"Larry, let me first say that Israel has one of the most powerful and most modern militaries in the world. You know that, and I know that. Israel has stockpiled over 300 nuclear weapons. Do you really think that if every Middle Eastern country all at the same time decided to attack Israel there would be any contests? To think that there would be is totally unrealistic. So I don't think we need to be Israel's protector. If fact being her protector has caused many of the problems we face. But that is another story."

"Now to answer your question regarding a special relationship with Israel, I can only say that I have a special relationship with Israel because I am a Christian and Christianity has roots in Judaism. There is another reason that I personally feel a special relationship with Israel and that is because I have so many very close Jewish friends. My Jewish friends feel close ties to Israel, so in respect for them and because of my great affection for them, I feel the bond."

"But is that logical? Is that why I am supposed to have close ties with Israel, and to take the side of Israel no matter what she does to her Palestinian neighbors? Am I supposed to feel that way because I really don't know any Palestinians? I don't think so, Larry. Palestinians are humans – they are children of God just as the Israelis are. I have always believed that God does not play favorites – I believe that God loves all of his children equally. So to answer your question, I would think that any basis for a special relationship has to depend on some other reasons. Such as strategic interests, and what is the moral thing to do. Wouldn't that make more sense?"

"Let me add one other point, Larry, which is that in my experience is the thing humans resent above all others is unfairness, or even the perception of unfairness. Our country has taken the side of Israel regardless of what it does, regardless of what means it uses to defend itself, or to expand it territories. Larry, it is immoral for us to do that. Furthermore, it is also not in our best strategic interests to do that."

King adjusted his glasses, scratched his nose and stated, "Governor, you are making statements like some of those that Jimmy Carter made in his book, and for that and that horrible title he chose to give his book, he has been called an anti-Semite. Governor, are you and anti-Semite?"

"Larry, I am no more an anti-Semite than you are. I am anti-nothing. In fact, I am pro human. My goal in life is to bring peace, to bring love – that is what my Jesus requires of me. My goal is to help people live a good life – to keep them healthy, to minimize their sufferings, to make them as content as possible and to help them be in harmony with their God."

"But back to your question. To suggest that Maynard DeFrie, or Jimmy Carter, is an anti-Semite is really silly. I read Carter's book, my conclusion is that Jimmy Carter is a great friend of Israel. Parenthetically and ironically, some American Jews won't read Carter's book. It really is in their best interests to do so."

"In any case, Larry, Carter makes statements in his book about Israel policy which are absolutely true. He makes accusations that prominent American Jews have made. Does he or any of us have to turn a blind eye? Can't we disagree with Israel policy when they have acted inhumanely? When they have used tactics outside the Geneva conference – like using Cluster bombs, isn't that our right – isn't our duty to speak up? After all Israel is a country? What does speaking out have to do with being anti-Semitic which as I understand the term is against individuals who happen to be Semites? Furthermore, Larry, Israel is a country with about a 30% Arabic population."

"One more point, Larry. If you were to condemn some of the atrocities that have gone on in Darfur or some other parts of

Africa, does that mean you are a racist? I sure don't think so. And, I am sure you don't think so, either."

King responded, "Well I understand your points Governor, but don't you think the history of Jews make things a little different. How can you ignore the Holocaust? How do you ignore the fact that Jews have been discriminated for thousands of years?"

Maynard hesitated and then placed his right elbow on the table in front of him, and slowly lowered his head into the crotch formed by the pointer finger of his right hand and his thumb which he had extended backwards. Speaking almost into the table before him, he said "Larry, people of my race have been persecuted, killed, raped and tortured for 400 years on this continent, and for 1000 years before that in Europe."

"It still goes on. Don't you remember the incident in Texas where a Black man was tied to a truck and dragged until he was dead? Don't you think enough Blacks have been murdered to qualify our race for a Holocaust? And if you do, what human sympathy do we get for that? What advantage are we supposed to get?"

"I'll tell you what we got Larry; we got some affirmative action that let a handful of Black kids get into graduate and professional schools. But back to the point, Larry. Are the benefits of affirmative action comparable to our country being complicit in the destruction of a country or to the slaughter of its people? By that logic, I would think that Americans should have a very special relationship with Blacks."

"And, there are some Blacks who think that. In a few cases you might hear Blacks claiming they are being discriminated against because they are Black, and for that they are looking to gain some advantage. But that is a small minority of the Black population. Most Blacks are not looking for anything for the suffering of their forbearers. All they want is opportunity, and the freedom to work hard, raise their families, see their children have successes and maybe enjoy some of the pleasures of life."

King interrupted the dialogue to take a commercial, saying, "And we'll be right back." When he resumed the interview he said, "Governor, let's talk about health care. You are proposing Universal Health Care. Isn't that socialized medicine?"

"I guess it is Larry, but what's wrong with that? Don't we have socialized retirement? We call it Social Security, and it works pretty well? Doesn't it? Why aren't we as a country responsible for the health care of our people? Doesn't it make sense to keep people healthy? How can you expect our workers to produce if they are not healthy? Every European country and Canada has socialized medicine. Why shouldn't we?"

King responded, "Well of course it makes sense to keep people healthy, but we do that now with combination of insurance and a free enterprise medical delivery system. We are a country that thrives on free enterprise. Physicians have fought socialized medicine for years. Why would they give up now?"

"Let me back up a little bit, Larry. First, it's important to remember that the US taxpayer has made a tremendous investment in the development of modern medical care. We subsidized the training of doctors; we paid for the research at Universities and Federal institutes that have brought almost all of the improvements we now enjoy. So one could argue, we have something coming back to us. But let me address the Physician issue. You are correct that they have fought for many years socialized medicine. Ironically, their incomes are going down, while the insurance executives are making a killing. HMO's have not been a good friend to doctors."

King raised his left hand, in his right hand he was holding some notes he had written down while Maynard was speaking. He said, "Let's change the discussion a little bit, Governor. Haven't we heard horror story after horror story about Canadian medicine? Aren't Canadians coming to the US for medical treatment? If socialized medicine is so good why do we keep hearing these stories?"

"That's a good question, Larry. The answer is that for the most part we are being lied to. Let's not be naïve! It is in the best interests of all who profit from health care to keep us misinformed – to keep us frightened."

"I can tell you stories where the reverse occurs. We had a family in Jackson who took their child to Montreal for treatment of an eye cancer. They had brought the child to Sloan Kettering for treatment and for 10 days were getting nowhere. The family finally located a center in Montreal that was offering an advanced treatment. Guess what, Larry? They went to Canada and the child is alive!"

"Before I forget, Larry, have you seen that Michel Moore movie, 'Sicko'? Because if you haven't you should. Now I have to tell you that Moore usually goes off the deep end in the way he portrays his material, but for the most part his central ideas are right on the money. Unfortunately, Moore needs to learn that he's not just preaching to his choir. He has to make converts, and because he seems to want to 'stick it to' so many in his audience, he fails, and that's too bad. But the point is Larry, see the movie. It's the very same conversation we are having here."

"Okay. Okay, Governor, but how are you going to accomplish all of this change? What's going to be the role of the Insurance companies? Are you going to sit down with the Insurance companies get them to change their ways of doing business?"

"Heck no, Larry, we are going get the public behind us, get these bills passed and effectively legislate those guys out of business. Let them go push paper for some other industry!"

King seemed a little surprised by Maynard's answer, realized they have covered enough of the Governor's health care program and moved on to a new topic. "Governor, I understand you want to sock it to the rich with some very high taxes. Is that right?"

"Larry, I wouldn't use the word 'sock'. I would rather say that I want the rich to pay their fair share. And, Larry, their fair share is a progressive income tax, not the 34% top bracket we have. What we have today is immoral."

"Governor, those are pretty strong words. So let me ask you this: you used to be a Pastor, didn't the members of your church tithe? And, isn't that a flat tax? Doesn't the Old Testament proscribe tithing? So shouldn't that be the biblical standard?"

"First of all Larry, the members of my church did tithe. But I need to tell you that the more they had, the more they gave, and I never asked them to do that. I just presumed they were giving in accordance with the teaching of Jesus who said, 'unto whomsoever is given much, much is expected, and to whom men have committed much, of him they will ask the more.' That, Larry, is not a flat tax."

"Jesus tells us that a progressive tax is the moral standard. Moreover, a progressive tax gives the government the resources to reinvest in the country and invest in its people. Don't you think that is what Jesus would want?"

"That's very interesting, Governor, I have never heard that about Jesus or the New Testament. I also never heard anyone ask Jesus that question. But what it prompts me to ask is, 'When the New and the Old Testaments give conflicting instructions – or rather teachings – who are we supposed to obey?'"

"Larry, from my point of view it's not a matter of obedience, it's a matter of a moral teaching. But the question you ask about which moral teaching do we follow when there is a conflict. Without hesitation I can tell you that for me it is the teaching of the New Testament, the teachings of Jesus Christ."

"I don't want to turn this into a bible study session, but there are numerous examples of conflict in these writings, and at seminary I made an in depth study of such issues. My conclusion then, and that has not changed, is that the New Testament is the moral and teaching authority when such conflict exists. Furthermore, Larry, if the Old Testament were a complete document, there would be no need for the New Testament."

"Well, that's another interesting point of view, Governor. I never heard that before either. You're beginning to remind me of one of my old Philosophy professors." King chucked and asked, "Governor, if you are going to increase my taxes shouldn't I know what that is going to be and shouldn't I know what you are going to do with all that money?"

"Yes to both questions, Larry. I think a marginal tax rate of 55% on earnings over 2.5 million would be reasonable, and I would lower the current rate to 12% for earnings under 150,000 dollars, tapering that down to 0% for the lowest wage earner. For any earnings above 150,000 I would slowly graduate the rate up to that 55 % number when the earnings hit two million five figure."

"Now to your question of what will I do with all of that money? That will be the fun part! I propose we start with rebuilding our infrastructure – roads, bridges, public works – this country is falling down and we don't need another bridge collapse like we had in Minneapolis to remind us of that need. Next we need to establish a 'Manhattan' type project to convert sunlight directly to electricity. I am sure that can be done and we can be investing in fuel cell technology while we pursue the larger goal."

"We also need to make major reinvests in our public institutions – that would be at the elementary and high school levels and at the college/university level. We must provide every American child with all the opportunity at our disposal."

"Now when we do all of these things, Larry, we are going to create jobs – and they will be good jobs. Under President Number 40 and the current President whom I consider a mutated clone of Number 40 that mutated for the worst, the only kinds of jobs we have created are minimum wage. Who can support a family on 200 dollars a week? We need jobs that pay 5 or 10 times that."

King had been listening intently - as he does most of the time - and it was becoming apparent that he wanted to make another stab in Maynard's tax proposals. "Governor, I am still a little bothered as to why you want me to pay so much tax. Don't you think high taxes are a disincentive?"

Maynard responded, "Larry, when I was growing up Joe DiMaggio was in the 90% marginal tax bracket and I don't recall him not wanting to make more money."

"We need to add, Larry, that most Americans are confused on marginal tax rates. DiMaggio, as I recall, in 1952 was paid $125,000. His taxes were really about 45% of that. It was on his earnings between $105,000 and $125,000 that he paid the 90% rate. Now, I am not suggesting we ever go to those kinds of marginal rates, but it is important for the public to realize that point." King nodded in agreement.

"But, Larry, there is a better reason for you to want to pay more taxes – and it's this. Tax dollars have put in place advantages upon advantages for Americans, particularly high income Americans, and even more so for self-employed Americans. If you own a company you hire trained workers at all levels – from high school through advanced degrees. You don't pay for their education from your own pocket – we the people pay. Almost everything a business uses – we the people have made the lion's share of the investment that made that available".

"And, that same concept is true, Larry, when you fly a plane. If it were left for airlines to pay for navigational technology and the required infrastructure they could not afford it. There would be chaos in the air. Planes would be bumping into each other in the air every hour on the hour, and it would still take us two days to get from coast to coast."

"It was the tremendous investment that – we the people - made in airplane technology in guidance systems that allows them to run their business. And, don't forget, Larry, you and I paid for the training of every pilot we have in this country. That is a multimillion dollar investment in each and every single pilot and co pilot. We paid for that!"

"And, if you will permit me a little sarcasm, Larry, it was we the people who paid through a government organization known as the military for the training of every American pilot. That's right Larry, one of those government organizations that 'can't do anything right'!"

"Larry, it actually exasperates me to hear many businessmen complain about taxes in this country. America is an entrepreneur's paradise! Earlier, you mentioned that I had gotten some support from professional athletes – and that is true. But do you think that Barry Bonds is supposed to be making 100 times more than Joe DiMaggio? Barry can do that because of the system we live in. Barry didn't invent television. It was invented at Motorola by engineers that the public paid to educate."

King brought the interview to a close saying, "Governor, it has been delightful to talk to you. We did not take any callers because we had so much to cover. So I am going to ask you, Sir, can we have you back again?"

Maynard answered in the affirmative. King continued, "And, Governor I have to give you credit for taking on such major forces – I am actually concerned for you. Maybe we should send you down the back elevator."

King chuckled at his last remark, "But Governor I got to tell you, I don't think you are going to get my vote!"

Without skipping a beat, Maynard responded, "Larry, first of all thanks for having me. But I need to disagree with you. I really do think I will get your vote. And, the reason I am going to get your vote is that you are a compassionate person. I have known that about you as I have listened to you over the years. And, I had that confirmed for me just before I left Jackson."

"I had asked one of my assistants to do a Google search on you. She did that and return with a stack of papers. In that stack I found a piece that told of how you have set up a fund to pay for cardiac care for those who cannot afford such care. That's compassion Larry! And take it from me, Jesus and his humble friend, the Governor of Mississippi, also love you for that. So we will see if I get your vote."

Maynard was pleased with the interview. He had hoped he was clear on all the key points he needed to make. King was equally pleased. He was totally taken by Maynard – his size, his intellect, his passion and his courage. Yet he knew as a reporter with many years of experience that he had to maintain his objectivity.

*   *   *

From mid May to July 10th when Maynard was to be in Chicago for the Green Party convention where he would accept the Party's nomination, Maynard's campaign efforts were accelerating at an unbelievable rate. Of the 2153 county campaign offices, 2034 were fully functional – staffed by Maynard's 'paid' volunteers who were getting their $35 a week plus travel expense allowance. At each county office Maynard's volunteers had recruited full complements of committed local volunteers. Maynard's unpaid volunteers had been very successful in recruiting Green Party members at the local level. Even though these new volunteers would not commit themselves to Maynard DeFrie, prior to his receiving the nomination, they had been instructed by Green Party headquarters to cooperate. In that way the Green Party could at the very least benefit from all of Maynard's organizational efforts over the past 14 months.

In this period Maynard had raised an additional 22 million in two rounds of Internet campaign fund drives, and he had found an 'Angel' – or an Angel had found him. The Angel came in the form a Black celebrity entertainer – apparently worth billions - who would commit up to 50 million dollars to Maynard's campaign efforts in the way of paying for fund raising events around the country, for television advertising and for any other use providing it was within the law. The only condition that Maynard would have to agree to was that the individual's identity had to remain anonymous and that Maynard had to make all possible efforts to ensure that anonymity. That was an easy task for him- Maynard could keep confidences.

There was a second condition - and that was this donor would be invited to Maynard's main inauguration ball in the event that he would be elected President. That condition was in reality no condition at all; she was already on Maynard's list of invitees merely for whom she is as well as for the positive influence she had made on the country and for all she had accomplished.

Before the month of May had ended, Maynard had been a principal guest on George Stephanopoulos' program 'This Week', Tim Russert's 'Meet the Press', Chris Mattthews' 'Hardball' and Mike Wallace's 'Fox News Sunday'. He was never able to appear on Bob Schieffer's program because of unending scheduling issues. That was a great disappointment to Maynard as he had a very high regard for Schieffer and had looked forward to meeting him.

On George Stephanopoulos' program, Maynard summarized most of the positions he had already made publicly, but dropped a few bombs that took his host off guard. Maynard came out strong against the profiteering of the Pharmaceutical industry, how the industry executives indulge themselves with perks even the President of the United States can't afford, how they have constructed palaces for themselves and how executives are treated like Princes.

Maynard added that when he had visited three Pharmaceutical firms in the Research Triangle of North Carolina so that he could negotiate Medicaid drug prices for Mississippi, he was overwhelmed by the numbers of limousines 'in waiting'. He remembered telling his aides back in Jackson that one of the requirements for being an Executive in the Pharmaceutical industry is that you can't know how to drive or take a cab.

Besides Maynard's taxing policies putting 'the lid on these guys' – his words – Maynard had vowed to change the law to prevent drug firms from advertising. He likened them to street drug pushers.

Maynard also lit into Wall Street. Acknowledging that a strong financial and banking system is absolutely essential to support the entrepreneurial growth of the country, DeFrie asserted that the system was out of control and needed regulations that fit the times. He promised that an entirely new regulatory framework would be one of his first acts as President.

He would also close loopholes in the tax structure that allow Wall Streeters to 'game the system' (his words). The Governor had a real issue with Hedge fund managers being able to report their income as Capital gains.

Maynard grouped with these investment miscreants the banking industry. He claimed that George, the second – as he called him – had deregulated banks to the point that they were out of control. Who ever conceived of sub-prime loans should be in jail, he exclaimed. He promised to have his attorney general make this one of his first investigations. Maynard also took a swipe at the last Chairman of the Federal Reserve. He claimed he was either asleep at the switch or complicit.

When Maynard had gone through his list, Stephanopoulos looked exhausted and somewhat bewildered. But he was able to ask Maynard, "You have come out strongly against so many vested interests in this country – rightly or wrongly – but how in God's name do you expect to be elected?"

Maynard was unfazed. He shared with Stephanopoulos his analysis which was: 121 million votes were cast in the 2004 Presidential election. If Maynard had to give up 30% of those votes because he had 'ticked a few people off' that left 98 million votes that Maynard could appeal to. Maynard also cited the fact that of all the registered voters in 2004 only 86% voted. To him that meant there were 20 million votes that he could go after.

Lastly, Maynard cited the fact that only 60% of eligible citizens are registered. That meant that there were 80 million votes out there if you could get those people registered and voting. Maynard shared with Stephanopoulos that he had an army of troops who were working hard to bring some of these voters in his corner.

*   *   *

Maynard's session with Mike Wallace on Fox Sunday Morning was a little more heated. Wallace began by asserting that low taxes drive the economy – wealthy people invest.

Because of high income earner investments, he contended jobs are created. Maynard challenged him on several counts. First, he said that low taxes create a two tiered society – the rich and the poor. Next he claimed that the majority of high income earners don't make the kind of risky investments that drive the country forward – the kinds of investments that really create jobs. Why should they? If you have lots of money why put it at risk?

Maynard went on to say his experience is that most wealthy individuals invest very conservatively – they buy art work, bonds, blue chip stocks, investment real estate – all very safe investments that do the country very little benefit. He also added that were he rich and were the accumulation of wealth his main objective, he would do the same.

Maynard went on to say that he was convinced that the kinds of outrageous salaries being paid on Wall Street and in many corporations were the main cause of the housing bubble. He contended that if you are making millions and that if somebody who is selling a house sticks a 5 million dollar For Sale sign on it – even if it's inflated 50% - you are going to buy it, if the 'Little Lady' likes it.

That Maynard stated is what has driven housing prices up. And he said it is the only trickles down effect he has ever seen in the economy. It trickles down so well it inflates the value of all the houses of lesser value. And, that – according to Maynard – is why housing has become unaffordable for middle income earners.

The Wallace interview ended as contentiously as it had started. Wallace first intimated that Maynard was a socialist. When Maynard didn't bite he was much more direct. Maynard countered that capitalism was by far the best form of economy because a businessman can't make a profit if his product is not doing some good for the general public. On the other hand, Maynard added Capitalists have big teeth and just like Pitt Bulls they need to be kept in check. That was one of the obligations a civilized society had to take seriously, he added.

Not happy with the tone of his interview with Wallace, and Maynard's belief that Wallace had been treating him in an overly aggressive manner and almost talking down to him, Maynard had decided he would get the last word in, even if it meant talking over Wallace – which he did, in fact, have to do. Maynard let Wallace know that in his opinion capitalism had degenerated in the last half century and was on very dangerous ground.

He cited price gouging and, in particular, the practice of value pricing – charging a premium for a technology superior product that is cheaper to manufacture than some more expensive product or service it replaces. Maynard asserted this is particularly true for technology that was either discovered or developed with Federal monies. He could not understand why the public should be paying twice.

Maynard didn't stop there. Wallace was aggressively trying to butt in - but Maynard was not to be stopped. The whole notion of pricing of goods based on what the market will bear was troubling to him. Maynard also had a problem with the US patent system granting monopolies on products that are made abroad utilizing virtually slave labor. Maynard asserted that was not the original intent the founding fathers had in mind when they created our patent system.

He believed, like the founding fathers, that giving an Inventor a 17 year monopoly allowed him to establish a business – but it also incentivized others to 'out-invent' him. But, he added, the founding fathers could not foresee manufacturing in China and Indonesia. Maynard mentioned that he had recently taken apart a water pick unit – he was naturally curious and particularly about mechanical items - that had stopped working to see if he could repair it. He said if the general public knew what was inside – at most 2 dollars worth of parts – they would be a little reluctant to pay 60 dollars for such an item.

*   *   *

Maynard's interview with Chris Matthews was hardly "Hardball' – it was a peach. Matthews – a political junky of the first order – had a lively conversation with Maynard on every important issue. Chris enjoyed that immensely. When it was time to end the interview, Matthews told Maynard that he might be a bit more disposed to voting for Maynard than Larry King was, but he was making no promises.

Just as Matthews was about to close the interview and thank Maynard for being his guest, he interrupted himself by say, "Before we close, Governor, I gotta tell you from what I have read about you and from having you here today – you're almost too good to be true! Is there anything about you that is going to shock the country and make people not want to vote for you? And, I apologize Governor, for asking you that."

Without hesitating Governor DeFrie responded, "Chris I am as mortal and human as any other man. I have made mistakes in my life – some very big mistakes. There are things I have done in my life that I am not terribly proud of. And, just like everybody else in this world there are things I have done and said that I wish I could take back. That is part of living and part of maturing. But, believed me Chris, I am not too good to be true; I have my flaws just like most of us, and more than some of us."

Finishing up the interview, Matthews profusely thanked the Governor and wished him well. After Matthews had taken his commercial break and it was now time for him to carry on a discussion with his panel that makes up the second part of his program – he was still pumped up.

Maynard's last of this series of interviews was on The Meet the Press with Tim Russert. Russert was indeed, typical Russert. For a good part of the show, Russert produced document after document trying to prove that Maynard was just as inconsistent as any other politician. He began by showing and reading clips of statements that the Governor had made which were in apparent contradiction to positions Maynard was making in his Campaign for the Presidency. In every case, the Governor was able to give an explanation – the material was either taken out of context, or was a misquote, or a poor choice of words. That seemed to satisfy an even skeptical Russert.

After the first commercial break, Russert, with his eyes twinkling and one of his typical ear to ear smiles on his face, showed Maynard a picture taken of the Governor when he was in college. The picture showed Maynard and some college classmates each wearing campaign Goldwater buttons and handing out campaign literature for Barry Goldwater in 1964. The picture was taken in front of a Goldwater Campaign office in New Orleans. That took Maynard off guard and before he could regain his composure Russert was literally badgering him about how Maynard could be championing liberal-progressive ideas today when he had supported an ultra conservative like Barry Goldwater.

When Maynard had recovered, he smiled and said to Russert, "I've come a long way, haven't I?" Russert almost smiled.

Maynard went on to explain that at the time, and at his youthful age of about 20, he had had no contact with conservative ideas or conservative politicians. Candidly, he admitted that he was politically naïve then and for a long time after. But he also admitted that in 1964 he was quite impressed – even taken - by the vigor and the devotion with which his campaign colleagues had embraced Goldwater. "The energy many of my classmates put into that campaign still boggles my mind" Maynard said softly.

Maynard went on to share with Russert that he could still remember Goldwater's campaign speech: 'A Time for Choosing.' He shared that he had kept that speech in his head for years examining and reexamining every point that Goldwater made, and every facet of each point.

Maynard stated that in time he matured in experience, in his knowledge and understanding of the issues, and also in his understanding of human nature – and, most importantly, human nature as it relates to politics. From that understanding, he concluded Goldwater had it all wrong. Maynard added that from that time forward he would need to seek out political views that were consistent with his experience and his beliefs.

The Governor finished up that topic by saying, "Frankly, Mr. Russert, the romance or flirtation – if you will – was all over for me when I finally realized Goldwater's ideas could not pass 'The Jesus Test'. And, that's not to say that Mr. Goldwater is not a fine person. I am certain he is sincere – he's just plain wrong."

"There is no way that Jesus Christ, in my judgment, could embrace the ideas of Barry Goldwater or be an ultra conservative – it violates so much of what Jesus stands for or preached. So, that's what I mean when I stated that for me it didn't pass the Jesus Test. We are our brothers keepers whether we like it or not."

Russert had also uncovered evidence that when Maynard first went to Philadelphia he had leant his support to a women's group that was advocating a women's right to choose. Maynard admitted to that but responded no further. Russert then wanted to know Maynard's position on abortion.

This was not a subject that Maynard wanted to dwell on. He stated that he did not like abortion, but he could understand that a woman has the right to be in charge of her own body. He said to do otherwise would – in some ways – be like reinstituting slavery. He then went on to list all the efforts he had made in Mississippi to reduce abortions and to foster adoptions. Maynard added that he believed the Supreme Court had spoken on the abortion issue, that it was the law of the land, and that from his point of view it was a state's issue.

Russert pounced on Maynard! He wanted to know how someone so devoted to Jesus could hold such a view. Maynard didn't even wince – looking directly at Russert he said, "Mr. Russert our country sent more than four thousand of our children to Iraq to be killed. And, we did that while this country entertained it selves every night – watching television, going to sporting events, you name it. We and our allies killed at least 250,000 Iraqis – innocent men, women and children. We kill thousands of our people on our highways each year."

"My Jesus tells me that these are the battles I have to fight – battles for the living. My Jesus tells me that abortion saddens him, but he tells me he is saddened even more, in fact he is grieved, to hold in his arms a youthful dying soldier. He is grieved to have to wipe the blood from the wounds of so beautiful a precious youth – a dying soldier in the prime of his life. A dying soldier whose mother, father and loved ones will bear the pain of their loss until the day they die. Those, Mr. Russert, are the tragedies we must concern ourselves about."

Russert was stunned into silence. Without so much as a word, he moved to a commercial break.

Resuming the interview, Russert stated, "Governor when you were on the Chris Matthews Show, Chris Matthews made the statement that you were almost too good to be true. As I recall you said you were human like everybody else."

"What I'd like to know Governor is what does human like everybody else mean when you grow up in a city like New Orleans? Did you belong to a gang? Did you do drugs? Did you ever get arrested? What kind of friends did you have?"

"That's quite a bunch of questions Mr. Russert. Let me begin by saying it was not easy growing up in New Orleans, particularly without a father and also as a black kid. Having said that, to answer your first question, I did not belong to a gang."

"Yes I was arrested once along with a group of my friends, and for no good reason. We were about 14 years old. We had made a lot of noise that frightened some folks and they called the police. After a hearing in juvenile court, we were not charged. And, yes I did smoke grass for a short period in high school, and again during the summer after my freshmen year of college."

Russert was a bit taken aback by Maynard's' candor. For a moment it appeared that he wished he had not opened up this can of worms. But he had, so he asked, "Did you do hard drugs?" (To which the Governor shook his head, no.) "How heavy into marijuana were you in those times you mentioned?"

The Governor answered that his high school experience was more of a period of experimentation as well as yielding to peer pressure. He added candidly that he did not enjoy most of that experience.

In the summer after his freshman year of college, the Governor stated he worked in one of the warehouses along the river loading trucks. He, along with his co workers smoked a fair amount of 'pot' over the course of the summer. As the summer wound down, the Governor stated that he had concluded that marijuana was 'stealing' his motivation – making him feel lazy. The Governor added that it was also an expensive habit. That, he added, always bothered him, particularly since his mother and grandmother were making sacrifices to help him through his schooling. Those facts along with his concern that he did not like being controlled by chemicals led him to quit.

"When you quit, Governor, did you quit for good, or did you fall back into that habit time and time again?

"Mr. Russert, Labor Day of my sophomore year of college was the last time I touched any illegal drugs. For the rest of my life, I never did much smoking at all. On occasion, I enjoy a good cigar. But to be honest, it's only in the last 10 or 15 years that I could afford a good cigar."

"Governor, how do you think your drug experience is going to resonate with the American public? Do you think it in any way disqualifies you from being President of this country?"

"Mr. Russert, we have already had occupants of the White House who had problems of substance abuse – some recently, some more distant in history. Our current President overcame alcoholism. It's very clear to me he has done that very effectively. If fact, I would add, that of all the problems many of us have with him, alcohol is certainly not one of them. His predecessor claimed he smoked marijuana but never inhaled. I can believe that – it's probably true. For my part, I wish he might have smoked a little more marijuana and worked harder on some of his other bad habits!" With the Governors last comment, Russert actually chuckled.

"But let me finish, Mr. Russert, by saying that I believe the American people will judge me on the substance of my character, my integrity, my life experience and what I have accomplished over that life experience. And, they will support me, if I and my campaign can convince them the changes I want to make in Washington are in their best interests."

The interview concluded on an amiable tone. Russert wished the Governor well and added that he was sure they would be meeting again.

*   *   *

Even though Maynard had not anticipated Russert's line of questioning regarding those parts of his own misspent youth, he was relieved they were out so early in the campaign. The Governor's strategy going forwards was to make no further comment. He had said all there was to say. Anything else – if there was anything else – he would let the press dig.

And, dig they did. And, most certainly they talked, and talked, and talked. Nearly 8 days of continuous cable news coverage. They even repeatedly showed video footage of the now vacant lot where stood the warehouse that Maynard had worked in the summer of his sophomore years in college.

Chapter V

The Green Party nominating convention had never drawn much attention, and the convention to be held in Chicago starting on July 10th would have appeared to promise no more than its predecessors. Prior to 2000 the majority of Americans had never heard of the Green Party. Most of those who did thought it was somehow connected to the Sierra Club - a group that promotes conservation, inspired by John Muir, the famed California naturalist of the early 1900's.

There is some basis to the confusion since the Green Party – founded in the 1980's – promotes environmental concerns along with its mainstays of participatory democracy, social justice, diversity and peace. The party's most visible candidate was Ralph Nader who ran for President on the Green Party ticket in 2000. And, even in that case, Nader who only garnered 2.5 % in the Presidential election had more national name recognition than the party itself.

Maynard DeFrie understood all of the negative prospects of a party with so little name recognition and one so loosely organized, but his decision to run as the Green Party candidate could save him about 7-10 million dollars just in costs associated with gathering names that would be needed to get his name on the ballot in all 50 states. He also knew that the Green Party had a base – albeit small but devoted – that he presumed he could energize and integrate into his own organization. That could be turned into a major plus for his campaign. Maynard understood the value of campaign volunteers and he had every intention of using them to his maximum benefit. Philosophically, Maynard embraced almost all of what the Green Party stood for, so he would not be compromising principle.

In early June when Maynard finally met – face to face - with his Black Angel. He discussed with her ways in which she could help his campaign and solicited her ideas as to how he could turn the occasion of his nomination at the Chicago Green Party Convention into a national event. Or, at the very least, he was hoping for an event that would get some media coverage. Despite her urging that he abandon the Green Party – she thought it would add unnecessary baggage – and her suggestion that he run as a true independent, the Black Angel came up with an interesting idea.

She thought that Bruce Springsteen could be induced to do two things that would give Maynard's campaign a big boost. He could compose a theme song for the campaign that Springsteen could perform at the Convention and he could give a concert with his E-String Band at Soldier's Field on Wednesday evening – July 9th - preceding the Convention. It was her idea that the Soldier's Field event could be made into a very effective rally for Maynard and that it would 'T-Up' Springsteen's appearance at the Convention and consequently bring attention to Maynard's nomination.

She reminded Maynard that Bruce Springsteen had never involved himself in political matters. In 2004 so disturbed by the direction of the country under the George W. Bush administration, he was compelled by his own sense of patriotic duty to step forward and try to use his fame and reputation to help remove these 'incompetent and dangerous morons' from office.

Maynard's Black Angel proposed that she would approach Springsteen, offer to cover his expenses – and she expected him to do that for expenses only - deal with the organization issues regarding the event at Soldier's field, and entertain Springsteen during his visit to Chicago. She also intended to make Springsteen her honored guest at a major fund raiser for Maynard at her estate in the Chicago suburbs. Maynard found this to be an offer he could not refuse.

On Wednesday July 9th at 6:30 pm, 66,500 potential supporters of Maynard Jefferson DeFrie – 5000 of them standing wherever they could find room - showed up at Soldier's field to hear a performance by Bruce Springsteen and his E Street Band. After the first set, Springsteen introduced the Governor and told the crowd that this could be the most important message in their lifetime. They listened attentively to Governor Maynard Jefferson DeFrie outline his plan for a New America which he 'demanded' would be a return to the America of our forbearers – an America of 'we the people!' At the conclusion of the program, when Springsteen and Governor Maynard J. DeFrie met together at center stage to thank those in attendance for their support, the crowd erupted into tremulous applause, foot stomping and yells.

Whatever Springsteen and the Governor said on stage that evening would forever remain a mystery. The entire event could have been easily mistaken for the Chicago Cubs winning the World Series – an event that last occurred in 1908, an even one hundred years ago. Not leaving anything to chance – more precisely with good planning - volunteers manned every exit of the stadium. Each participant had been asked in advance to donate $20 for the privilege of attending this event on their way out of the stadium. They were to put their donation in an envelope on which they were requested to write their name and e-mail address.

Instead of the $1.2 million Maynard had expected from that evening, volunteers – still counting at 3 a.m. – had bundled more than 3 million dollars. They also had managed to fill 13 plastic garbage containers – 50 gallons each – with opened donor envelopes that had legible names and e-mail addresses. When these were compiled there were more than 50,000 of them. Volunteers were staggered by the volume of cash, the numbers of 50 and 100 dollars bills that many individuals had contributed and the numbers of individuals who willingly gave their names and e-mail addresses. They were equally impressed when they were told - later on - that Springsteen and his pals had donated their services and covered all of their own expenses.

The Green Party Nominating Convention was, indeed, a colossal success. Even though it did not receive the media coverage of the two conventions that were to follow, it was close. More importantly, it had appealed to the younger audience it was designed to reach – a population that could be activated. Maynard Jefferson DeFrie had achieved all of his objectives. He was a candidate that would be on the ballot in every state of the Union. He had now been fully introduced to the American public, particularly the young base to whom he would focus his case for change. Change in the way things were done in Washington - and change in the direction of the country.

Maynard made the decision to hold back on the Green Party nomination of a Vice President until the Democrats had completed their nominating process in late August. He had his eye on two 'potential' vice presidential candidates and he wanted to see where they stood vis-à-vis the candidacy of his Democratic rival, Morris Bloomfield. He would put his feelers out.

On July 17th only one week after the Green Party Convention in Chicago, CNN, Zogsby and USA Today released poll numbers of voter presidential preferences. Even though the Democrats and the Republicans had not yet had their Conventions, the polls were based on the forgone conclusion that Maynard would be running against Mayor Morris Bloomfield and Senator Marjory Hunter, the respective nominees of the Democratic and Republican parties. With the announcement of those results, Maynard had become more than a blip – he was indeed now on the radar screen with 9% of eligible voters indicating they would vote for him.

*   *   *

Maynard Jefferson DeFrie was created with many special gifts. He was a Black man who began life with very meager material resources but he managed to achieve more than most would ever dare to imagine. He also understood that his resources as measured in human terms - the terms that really count – like his mother, his grandmother, Brother Weiss and all those who had extended their hand to help him make his way– were immense.

One of the more extraordinary gifts that Maynard possessed was apparent to all who knew him well. Maynard was a prophet! But he was not a prophet in the Bible sense. Maynard's mind was so analytical and his thinking so clear that when combined with his ability to simultaneously keep in his mind extraordinary amounts of information – no matter how complex – he could literally predict the future. Maynard routinely could determine how events would play out with uncanny accuracy. He could as he would say 'see over the hill'.

Often times he would detail for his inner circle not only how events would play out, but exactly how a particular individual would react in the course of unfolding events. He could predict what they would say, and how they might respond to what had been said to them. This gift of prophesy was actually a combination of his unique mental capabilities, his ability to read individuals and his understanding of human nature. More often than not it could be an eerie experience to hear him foretell the future.

When Mike O'Conner, the Governor's Administrative Assistant, first joined Maynard's cabinet, he casually made the comment, "let's cross that bridge when we come to it." Maynard informed 'Mr. O'Connor' - in a very warm but firm way - "that's not quite how we do it here. We need to do our best to determine what the bridge will look like, what it will be made of and what's on the other side. And….how are we going to react to what is over there!?"

Maynard took the very same approach to foreign policy and international events. He had predicted precisely the outcome and entire sequence of events that would take place after the US preemptive strike against Iraq following the destruction of the World Trade Center on September 11th. In fact, prior to that he had predicted within four days following 911, the actions that the President and his Neo Conservative advisors would take so that they could divert the 'war on terrorism' to other goals that they had long wanted to achieve – a remaking of the Middle East. In both cases he was exactly right.

It was this gift. - Maynard's gift of analytical prophecy that would make him President of the United States of America on January 20th of 2009. As he had in the past, he would use that gift in his Presidential campaign to predict the strategy that his opponents would use to attempt to defeat him. Then he would either design offenses that would nullify their strategies or counteroffensives that would win the day. His other talents of being able to solve difficult problems, of usually finding an inexpensive or creative way to get some task done coupled with his extraordinary organizational skills and his ability to inspire others made him a very formidable opponent. And, he didn't like loosing.

On the evening of Wednesday July 16th, the day before the Presidential Preference Poll results were published, Maynard met with his campaign committee in the Governor's Library in the Capitol building in Jackson, Mississippi. Of this group of seven, five of them were individuals who had sat behind Maynard when he announced his candidacy for the Presidency on the Capitol steps in May. The elderly baldish gentleman with the ill fitting suit who had tried unsuccessfully to end that Press Conference was Abraham Gellman. Gellman had been appointed Treasurer of the State of Mississippi in 2000 by Maynard. They had known each other since Maynard's one term in Congress – Gellman had been the administrative assistant to the Congressman who was from Maynard's neighboring district.

The elderly gentleman with the mottled blondish hair was Jonathon Parkhouse – Maynard's campaign manager for his 2000 and 2004 gubernatorial campaigns. The elderly White woman who took notes while Maynard was giving his press conference was Miss Grace Pendleton, Maynard's personal secretary who started working with the Governor when he was in the Mississippi House of Representatives. The well dressed Black woman who appeared to be in her 40's – she was actually in her late 50's – was Dr. Rose Lee Jamison, a Professor of Political Science at the University of Mississippi who had taken leave in 2001 to join the Governor's staff. The attractive White woman who appeared to be in her mid 50's was Greta Faulkner - grand daughter of William Faulkner – who was a Professor of Middle Eastern History at the University of Mississippi. Greta Faulkner was an unpaid advisor to the Governor.

The first of the other two attendees was Michael O'Connor, the Governor's Administrative Assistant and an Attorney who joined the Governor when he was in the State House – O'Connor was lying in the University Hospital passing a kidney stone when the Governor gave his press conference. The other participant was Rodger D'Angelis, a PhD graduate student – political science – at the University of Texas, who the Governor had become acquainted with when Maynard was making his college 'rounds' and when D'Angelis was still an undergraduate student. D'Angelis had been working on various assignments related to the Governor's campaign for eighteen months.

After some brief comments on some particulars of the campaign, Maynard asked Miss Pendleton to pass a folder bound with a clear plastic front cover that she placed face down in front of each participant. Maynard then addressed the group, and in a very solemn and serious tone, told them that within these pages are the strategy for us to win the Presidency. He then said he trusted each individual in this room, but that it was of utmost importance that none of them reveal any of this strategy to anyone – not husband, wife, lover or confessor! Maynard stated that if any of them felt they were incapable of maintaining that level of confidence until he had released them from it, they could be excused. When all in attendance made that commitment, Maynard asked them to turn the folder over.

Under large in red letters - 'CONFIDENTIAL'- the title of the report read: "INTERESTS THAT WILL UNDERMINE OUR CAMPAIGN FOR THE PRESIDENCY – STRATEGIES TO DEFEAT EACH OF THEM". The report was written entirely by Maynard. The only other person who knew of its contents was Miss Pendleton who assisted the Governor.

On seeing the title of Maynard's presentation, Abraham Gellman smiled, slowly turning his head side to side. He knew how Maynard's mind functioned and he was anxious to dig into his booklet and learn what Maynard had been up to. He did, however, restrain himself, because he knew that Maynard was going to orchestrate its contents as only Maynard could – presenting each item thoroughly and clearly, and then soliciting critical comment along with new ideas. This would be a lively session.

On the second page of the report Maynard had listed the forces that would come after them with the heavy artillery, and he had listed them in decreasing order of strength and influence. Number one on the list was the Health Care Industry – that included Pharmaceutical firms, the mature part of the Biotech Industry and the HMO's. Listed second was the Military Industrial Complex – along with every developer of military technology and manufacturer of weaponry, Maynard had listed the Pentagon.

The Pro Israel lobby made position number three. Maynard had listed a loose but powerful coalition that included the American Israel Political Affairs Committee [AIPAC], Zionist Organization of America [ZOA] and the Washington Institute for Near East Policy [WINEP]. He also had included several Neo Conservative think tanks [American Enterprise Institute, the Center for Security Policy, Hudson Institute], and several influential columnists and Neo Conservatives such as Charles Krauthammer, William Kristol, Norman Podhoretz,

David Brooks, Paul Wolfowitz and Michel Rubin. These were powerful forces who were financially well resourced and who know how to use political muscle.

Number four on Maynard's list was a coalition that would fight him tooth and nail on his taxing policies. They would be for low and non-progressive income taxes, against any estate tax – death tax as they called it – and against capital gains tax, or tax on already taxed income as they claimed. The members of this coalition would be Wall Street, the Republican Presidential and Vice Presidential Candidates and their Party and the 'super rich'.

Position number five on Maynard's list consisted of two independent groups that could, because of common interests, work together against his campaign. One was the Petroleum Industry that was certain to have issues with Maynard's environmental programs, particularly his 'Manhattan Project' converting sun light directly to electricity using plant biotechnology. The other was the Automobile Industry. They would fight him just based on their expectation of significantly increased fuel mileage standards. When they would learn of his plans for light rail high speed lines and the reintroduction of electrified trolley systems – that would be using advanced technology – to replace diesel buses they manufactured, there would be open warfare.

Maynard had some concerns about the Christian Right Wing and the Evangelical Movement. He did not give them the 'honor' of a numbered listing, but he believed they would fight him, particularly at the grass roots level, for his 'more enlightened' view on abortion. Or, more appropriately, for not being totally committed to pro life as they saw it. Maynard originally had thought he could win them over, but at this point in his campaign he had his doubts. In one of the rare occasions that Maynard used sarcasm he said, "I am not sure these people can think any better than they can read. [He meant the Bible, of course.] But we won't give up on them."

In his report Maynard had also enumerated the groups that would not be against him at the onset of the Presidential

Campaign. It was a very short list, it read: 'we the people'. There was no reference to color.

Before Maynard continued he went over some ground rules for the campaign. First there would be no negative campaigning under any circumstances. The thrust of their campaign would be to go on the offensive with information on the key issues with the primary goal of informing voters. In the event that any erroneous information was injected into the presidential contest, regardless of its source, they must respond immediately with verifiable facts. Secondly, when his campaign was attacked on a personal level with erroneous information or by innuendo – as it surely would be – they would counter by releasing accurate information about the source. There would be no twisting of information or bending of the facts to gain advantage.

Maynard next informed his colleagues that they would not wait for the traditional Labor Day kickoff to begin their campaign. Nor would they wait until the Democrats and Republicans had their Party Conventions in late August and the beginning of September, respectively. His campaign would take the offensive as soon as possible. Maynard predicted that attacks against their campaign would be in full swing long before the Party Conventions, and probably by Mid August. Maynard was adamant that their offensive begin by the third week of July, 'even if half the country is on vacation'. He said at least his volunteers would know where the voters were.

Next on Maynard's agenda was defining an effective strategy to deal with each 'opponent' starting first with the Health Industry who would be losing billions of dollars under Maynard's programs. He reviewed that Industry's history in their attacks on Bill Clinton's Universal Health plan in the 90's and later on in 2000 regarding the Industry's concern that prescription drugs would come under Medicare.

For the latter, the Industry had reasoned that with forced price bargaining by the Government, they would take a huge revenue hit. Most of the group was surprised when Maynard produced documentation that the Health care industry had spent more money then the Republican and Democratic Presidential candidates combined. That Maynard said, "is a force to be reckoned with. That defines what 'deep pockets' really means."

Maynard also cautioned that they should not overestimate the support they might gain from the public in their battle with the Health Care Industry, even though the Public would be the beneficiaries of their efforts. He warned that the Industry would gain sympathy from the many that depend on their services for maintaining good health. He gave as an example the current Medicare Drug benefit. In spite of the fact that it is a terrible program that provides little to seniors, they are now backing it because it provides many of them with a 'few crumbs' and because they have also been brainwashed by the Pharmaceutical companies.

In passing, he added that he was certain that the Industry had forced the President and Congress to pass the Medicare prescription bill, even though it is of one of the worst bills in the history of the country. He repeated that it was the worst bill ever passed by congress, and added "but one of the best handouts the industry had ever garnered." "Ironically," Maynard mused, "they will use the profits from those handouts to fight what is best for the people. And, that includes using a major portion of that money to fight us."

Maynard detailed some of the tactics the Health Industry had used to great effect in their campaign against the Clinton plan. He reminded them of the "Harry and Louise" commercials of a young couple who were greatly and so sincerely concerned about the merits of the Clinton health bill – and how these commercials in their most insidious way had undermined the thinking of the American public on any positive benefits that bill would have given them. "Harry and Louise" was so convincing that the majority of the public believed that the plan would do them great harm. And, accordingly it was killed.

To the counter attacks that were sure to be coming, Maynard proposed that his campaign get to work on television commercials that would feature a homey couple that who would be their very own creation - "Louis and Harriet". In a series of 'episodes' this sincere couple could cover the entire spectrum of 'real' concerns that American families have had to face with health care in recent times. Maynard threw out some ideas - the overwhelming costly changes that had occurred in Health Care since the Clinton attempt in '92, the health care deductions from salaries that most employers are having to institute at ever increasing amounts and the deductible increase on services provided that most had to deal with.

Maynard thought it would be fun and beneficial to their efforts to make "Louis" a Republican small business owner. Then they could do an episode on the difficulties that 'Louis' was facing in covering the Health care insurance for his employees – how that and the ever snow balling affects of a system out of control threatened to put him out of business. "That should ring a bell," he added.

He also thought it would be worthwhile to have "Louis and Harriet" make mention of "Harry and Louise" who they could have known from their college days. By doing that they could use the characters they had created to state how wrong "Harry and Louise" were about the information they had disseminated, how they had misled the public and what a great disservice they had done to the country.

Maynard realized he had spent more time on this issue than he should have but he was compelled to add one more thought. "Wouldn't it be funny – and possibly productive – to have 'Louis' do 'stand up' charades of some of the side effects that Pharmaceutical ads enumerate? That would be a way of poking fun at the Pharmaceutical industry and letting a little 'air' out of their balloons."

Maynard was convinced that in one full day of creative brainstorming, and with some detailed planning, that in short order they could launch a very effective and well received campaign. "The key", Maynard stated was to "take the offensive as soon as possible. And, let me add these commercials don't have to be professional quality. Let's not waste money just to make them." Looking directly at Rodger D'Angelis, he said "Rodger, we have a lot of Volunteer talent. I've seen some of the U-Tube stuff they did for us after I 'announced' – let's get them going on this!'

Maynard next considered the Military Industrial Complex. He speculated that the attacks from this powerful group of industrial/technology interests would come in the form of a ferocious fear campaign. It would be a campaign designed to convince the voting public that the US is vulnerable against all enemies existing or imagined. The aim, of course, would be to keep the Military and their 'cronies' in the Industry in the business of developing and supplying ever more powerful and more complex weapons. He was certain they would pour monies – in quantities of 'as much as it takes' - into supporting the Republican Party Candidate, Senator Marjory Hunter. He said that was obvious because she, like all recent Republicans had honed playing the 'fear the enemy' game to an art form. And, of course, that would appeal to their base and be beneficial to them.

Maynard understood the need to counter their arguments before they began their assault, because he knew 'once they get revved up they will jam those fears down the public's throats'. They will claim that it has been our Military strength that has been the primary reason for keeping the Terrorists off our shores. Maynard's campaign would need to be ready to counter that argument with well thought out answers.

Maynard's strategy for dealing with these forces would be three pronged. The first prong would be to go on the offensive immediately – within two weeks. Prong two would be the use of Television commercials as well as infomercials that play at odd hour throughout the day and night, and accordingly are cheap to air. Prong three would be the Internet. Maynard proposed the production of 30 minute infomercial clips that demonstrate America's mighty military power. He had made some good friends of high ranking independent thinking individuals in the Military over the years, and he was sure they would participate.

He also wanted to make it clear that he was not looking for their endorsement – only that they share their knowledge and expertise. He suggested that much of the material used in the Armed Forces recruiting ads would be suitable. He also would use e-mails campaigns and flyers to disseminate statistics on America's military capabilities vs. all countries of the world.

Maynard also proposed that they could create some 'news cast' type commercials and infomercials depicting how the British were handling Terrorism. The British point of view is that the best way to fight terrorists is with an extensive and well coordinated police effort. Given the numbers of Terrorist attacks that have occurred in the UK and their ability to thwart them, Maynard asserted there should be 'miles of TV footage' that we can use. He believed that it was critical to convince the American Public that the best way to fight the terrorist 'beast' was to do just as the Brits were doing, and to keep hammering how successful the Brits have been. That approach in combination with Foreign Policy changes that he would be proposing should make a compelling argument.

To complete that discussion, Maynard reviewed how John Kerry had tried to convince the voters in 2004 that we must back off on our military efforts and concentrate on policing efforts. Kerry was 'outgunned' in that effort. "The Republicans in the 2004 election made significant efforts to make Kerry's position, and hence Kerry, look ridiculous", Maynard added. "And they were successful in doing that.

We cannot afford that! We have to learn from every mistake that Kerry, or Gore in 2000, made. They underestimated how clever this entrenched group is. And, they also underestimated how mean these Bastards can be. Look what they did to one of their own in the 2000 South Carolina primary!" The group was a bit taken aback by Maynard's use of the 'B' word – he rarely used foul language.

Maynard addressed the number three concern on his list – the Pro Israel Lobby. It was apparent to him that his foreign policy intentions in the Middle East would enrage every participating interest in that powerful conglomerate. Maynard clearly understood that it would be hard – if not impossible - to convince the Pro Israel Lobby that taking US bases out of the Middle East, and having a more evenhanded approach to solving the Palestinian conflict would be in Israel's best interests.

He knew they would feel that way even if the US were to guarantee the creation of a protective shield that would use satellite and drone technology along with US aircraft carriers stationed nearby. Without doubt they would unanimously be convinced that the US was abandoning Israel. To Maynard it was abundantly clear that to many American Jews, Israel was a highly emotional issue - as a Black man he understood that well.

Maynard good naturedly chuckled when he shared that he could tell his dear friend of many, many years, Abraham Gellman, Jewish jokes, but he never remembered Abe laughing at one of his Israel jokes. Maynard must have been making that up – no one had ever heard him tell an ethnic joke. Gellman, none-the-less laughed giving confirmation to what Maynard had said.

In defining the strategy to counter the efforts of the Pro Israel lobby, Maynard noted that part of the effectiveness of the Lobby was its methodology of keeping a low profile – something they have done so successfully. In fact, most American Jews were totally unaware of the efforts of the Lobby because they had little knowledge of what they were actually doing.

The Lobby was more interested in getting things done that were favorable to Israel than they were in publicizing the results of their efforts. Maynard felt that very tactic played to his campaign's hand. Thus they would not come out and directly attack Maynard – that would expose the magnitude of their powerbase, and also let the American public know how influential they have been in promoting total favorability to Israel.

They would instead, Maynard predicted, use specific spokesman to make their attacks. He read aloud a list of likely spokesman. At the top of the list was the Independent Senator from Connecticut. Maynard had put the Senator on top because this gentleman had so effectively and publicly chastised Howard Dean – a 2004 Democratic Presidential Primary candidate who 'dared' suggest that a policy of 'fairness' in the Middle East would be in America's best interests. The Senator from Connecticut let Dean know in no uncertain terms that the US was married to Israel from its inception. Moreover, he got away with saying that, just as if he was saying 'we Americans like apple pie'.

Maynard wanted to have ready several informative commercials. For one he suggested having an image of the Senator standing in front of a poster board that would depict the amounts of money he had been successful in sending to Israel versus the amount that he made efforts to bring to his state of Connecticut. Maynard had never seen that comparison but he knew that with Israel being gifted at the rate of four billion dollars each year for as long as anyone could remember, Connecticut could not be the winner. These commercials were to be ready for use on a defensive basis. In that way no one could accuse Maynard of provoking Pro Israel interests.

Abraham Gellman wanted to know if Maynard intended to use a photo of the Senator wearing his Yarmulke. Maynard chucked and responded, "Only if they get really nasty."

As the meeting draw to a close – nearly midnight – Maynard asked for any other input on campaign tactics – any other ideas? Roger D'Angelis who was heading up the college student volunteer effort that had spanned the country told the group that his volunteers in Tyler County, Texas which has a population of about 25,000 came up with a novel idea that seems to work exceedingly well. They had been experimenting with it for three weeks.

What the Tyler group did was to go around the county getting fast food chains, pizza parlors and local merchants to offer time dated discount coupons. D'Angelis gave some examples: Buy a Whopper and get fries and a soda free, buy a medium sized pizza and get two toppings free plus a dozen wings for an additional dollar or get a 5 dollar discount on $50 worth of groceries at the local Pigley Wiggly.

What the Texas group did was print the coupons on the back side of Maynard's traditional three paragraph campaign missiles – the kind he had used in Mississippi that referred voters who wanted more information to his web site. But there were two hitches: the coupons were only good for two days and the redeemer needed to write in a piece of information which required them to have read the other side to find the missing bit. For those flyers that had food coupons printed on the back the Tyler volunteers had entitled them "Food for thoughtful Voters". They called those that bore discount coupons for services or goods "Smart Voters are Smart Shoppers."

When they first started the effort, the Tyler group was either handing out flyers or placing them under windshield wipers of parked cars. Then they got the bright idea of placing around town the kinds of boxes that free newspapers, autos for sale and real estate offices use to distribute their information. Their boxes – orange crates - were neatly covered with Maynard DeFrie campaign posters and had on them a sign that read "Free value coupons". When these innovators found that this distribution means worked so well, they took the next step. They placed 'Maynard boxes' at three truck/ rest stops on Route 20 that runs through Tyler County. From feedback they got from their local merchant base, they had created a truly mutually synergistic situation. D'Angelis reported that when the Tyler Texas Volunteers got the locals accustomed to their coupon distribution system, they were distributing 9 thousand flyers every two days. By week three of the experiment, they had also burned out their copy machine.

Jonathan Parkhouse apologized for putting something on the table at so late an hour but since the topic of campaign volunteers had been raised, he thought it was appropriate to add an update on campaign volunteers, and share some thoughts he had been toying with for effectively using them. First, he mentioned that in their 2000 or so county offices around the country, they had just over 145,000 volunteers, and that 70,000 of them were college or graduate students. He projected that for the next 8 weeks they would add 5000 volunteers per week. He added that the county offices were manned by volunteers in proportion to the voting population – that was about one volunteer for each 1000 voters.

Next he reminded the Governor of the 'Mormon tactic' that the Governor had first suggested and used in their 2000 gubernatorial campaign. Parkhouse explained for those present who were not familiar with the 'Mormon tactic' exactly what they did. They took their young volunteers – mostly college students – instructed them to dress as young professionals (coat and tie), and sent them in pairs to knock on doors or stop people on the street.

Key to their program was that students were trained. They were taught a script which included introducing themselves as volunteers for Governor DeFrie, stating succinctly why they supported the Governor, asking politely for their support – not vote – answering any questions (again scripted with prepared answers), offering campaign literature as well as stating something about the contents of what they were about to receive and finally getting an address – preferably an e-mail address.

From their 2000 campaign experience, Parkhouse stated that 'one pair' of volunteers could on average have a meaningful interaction with 75 individuals each day – that average included meetings that were door-to-door, on the street, at factory entrances and outside supermarkets. Parkhouse continued that if on average there were 30 trained volunteers at each campaign office – 15 paired volunteers – at that rate they would be contacting about two and a half million people per day. With more than 90 days left to the election, he assured those assembled that every voter in the country should know "who we are and what we stand for, well before Election Day."

Parkhouse added one last thought. He suggested flooding any area, where the Governor would be making a campaign stop, or holding a Town Hall Meeting with the number of volunteers –

or Maynard's Mormons as they were nicknamed in 2000 - that would be needed to cover the entire adult population in two or three days. That would mean they would have to bus in volunteers and cover their expenses for two or three days. Parkhouse had gone over this plan with Gellman in advance of this meeting, and Abraham said they could bear the costs.

As the group was getting up to leave, Greta Faulkner wanted to know, "are we going to get any help from the Bruce Springsteen's of this world?" Maynard nodded. Parkhouse shared that campaign rally concerts that would take place while the Democrats were meeting in Minneapolis and the Republicans in Denver, for their respective conventions, were in advanced stages of planning. He also mentioned that several well know artists and celebrities from the entertainment world – Willie Nelson, for one – and from the sporting world had already agreed to join the Governor when he would be doing his summer campaigning last week of July through the month of August into the first week of September. Maynard had figured a way for him to get his message to vacationing voters while adding to their vacation pleasures.

*   *   *

Governor Maynard Jefferson DeFrie took his opponents for the Presidency totally off guard by having his campaign in full force by the third week of July. On July 26th with Bruce Springsteen and Willie Nelson in hand, he kicked off his campaign for the Presidency with a concert and rally in Yankee Stadium. More than 500 DeFrie Campaign Volunteers had been working Northern New Jersey - Hudson, Bergen and Essex Counties - the power base of New Jersey, the five boroughs of New York and areas north of New York City up into Connecticut for an entire week.

Yankee Stadium has a capacity of about 52,000. However, with infield seating crowds of up to 100,000 have been accommodated, as was the case when Billy Graham preached in

Yankee Stadium in the 50's. For Governor DeFrie's kickoff concert-rally 103,000 exuberant supporters squeezed into Yankee Stadium, while an estimated 17,000 to 21,000 listened just outside the Stadium.

Arnold Gellman and Jonathon Parkhouse had negotiated an arrangement with WOR Channel 9 in New York City – the television station that broadcasts Yankee baseball games – to carry the event. The number of TV viewers of the event was estimated to be some reasonable fraction of those that normally follow Yankee games. On the other hand, it could have been more, given the interest the Yankees had generated in the past season.

At the Yankee Stadium event, Governor DeFrie introduced his running mate Democratic Senator Rod Christianson of Connecticut. Maynard had been acquainted with Christianson for many years having been introduced to him through one of his Tulane classmates who served in the Peace Corps in the Dominican Republic at the same time the Senator was serving there. The Governor liked Rod for his independence, his bi-partisan approach to legislation as well as for his total familiarly with fiscal matters through his Chairmanship of the Banking, Housing and Urban Affairs Committee. He also admired Rod for his role in the passage of the Sarbanes-Oxley law intended to prevent corporate equity scandals such as Enron and the kinds of 'creative financing schemes of the 'Big Five' accounting firms some years before that.

Maynard thought the Senator's experience with heath care issues through his years of committee work made the Senator the ideal candidate to implement his Universal Health Plan. Lastly, Maynard reasoned having the Senator on his ticket would allay any fears that together he and Christianson could not nudge the country out what was appearing to be an ever growing recession.

For the first three weeks of August while the Republican and Democratic Candidates were organizing their Fall Presidential campaigns and purposefully ignoring the Green Party Candidate, Governor DeFrie and Senator Christianson were entirely in control of the Presidential race. Together and separately they held rallies in every metropolitan area that had an NFL franchise. In many cases, they used scheduled sporting events – professional baseball or preseason NFL games – to attract crowds, and in those instances traveled with a retinue of retired professional ball players, White and Black. At each event, swarms of campaign volunteers were active distributing literature and assisting and instructing individuals who had never voted with voting registration.

It was apparent that the Green Party Presidential ticket was not entirely ignored by opposing forces in this period. On Sunday afternoon August 10^{th,} "Harry and Louise" returned to the air to initiate their series that was to inform the country about the dreaded possibilities of 'Socialized Medicine' and the horrors that our unfortunate neighbors to the North who had 'government health care forced on them' were dealing with.

Their timing could not have been worse. On that very evening, they were 'greeted' by 'Louis and Harriet". In that first episode, Maynard's new friends detail how the country had been led astray – insidiously and maliciously by these two 'con artists'. Louis also played on video a portion of one of the 1992 ad clips of "Harry and Louise" that he had saved. Together he and 'Harriet' laughed in amusement at how naïve the country must have been in the 90's to believe such nonsense.

There were another series of commercials directed against Maynard that fell under the so-called '527 ads category – the kinds of ads that John Kerry was 'Swift Boated' with in 2004, and that effectively destroyed his bid for the Presidency. The rules for '527 ads are such that it is impossible to learn the identity of an ad sponsor until long after the election, and sometimes not even then.

One series of many directed at Maynard's candidacy would have been amusing had it not had the potential to turn many voters away from him. For that series of ads no words were spoken, only softly played background music – 'The Song of the Volga Boatmen'. For one ad there was a photograph of Mt

Rushmore depicting the American Presidents – Lincoln, Washington, Teddy Roosevelt and Jefferson. Below them and in the foreground was a composite showing Caesar Chavez, Fidel Castro, Joseph Stalin and the outline of an individual that was left blank. Running across the ad separating the two groups, top from bottom, was a moving banner that read – 'Keep America – America'.

Subsequent ads were more direct. The outline of an individual that had been left blank in the previous ad had been moved more into the background and without too much imagination one could clearly make out that it was Maynard. The series continued with variations. In one the faces of Chavez, Castro and Stalin replaced the carvings of the Presidents on Mount Rushmore and Maynard was standing in the front foreground. That running banner read – 'It's your country – it's your choice.'

Maynard ignored these '527 ads and those that followed because he believed that with his campaign which was now moving forward in full stride he would be strong enough to ignore what he called 'this desperate nonsense' – he once even used the 'BS' word. It was his conviction that his strategy of discussing issues vital to the voters in an intelligent fashion would eventually bear fruit as long as no one panicked. Maynard also believed that the American voter was just not that stupid that they would repeatedly fall for the kinds of tactics and lies that politicians had been using for the past 50 years. His larger concern was to be certain that he would not be excluded from the three presidential debates that were scheduled for September 30th and October 14th and 28th.

Polls data released from three sources on September 10th – one week after the Republican National Convention in Denver had Maynard at 12% with his Republican and Democrat rivals each at 19% of the vote – and with about 45% of the electorate not declaring a preference. Maynard had good reason to believe that his campaign tactics were dealing effectively with the opposition he had anticipated. Given all the effort he had put into his campaign strategy and in its implementation, he was very pleased.

Governor DeFrie was tickled with those results for two very important other reasons. First, there was a pool of 40% of the voters who were still undecided - the ones who were still looking. He had a chance to win them over. Secondly, by his polling 12% there was no way he could be excluded from the debates by the Commission on Presidential Debates – the lobby controlled Washington based 'bipartisan' group that supervises Presidential debates.

The latter issue regarding being excluded from the debates was not trivial to Maynard's campaign. He understood two issues related to that very well. First, he knew he could get his message to ten times as many voters in a single debate than would be the case if he visited every city in the country. That would be very important to his campaign. He needed the public to get to know him, and to understand and believe in his ideas. Maynard knew instinctively that 'it's hard to get folks to take their medicine' even when it can save their lives. They had to like the 'doctor', have faith and believe that he knew what he was doing.

Secondly, Maynard also knew the history of the debate Commission and understood how that group operates. He often told his inner circle that the Commission will go to any extreme to keep third party candidates out of the debates. Maynard reminded his intimates of how the Commission dealt with Ralph Nader in 2000 in the Presidential debate that was held on the Campus of the University of Massachusetts.

Not only was Nader not allowed to participate in that debate, he was forbidden from even entering a viewing of the debate that was held at a satellite site on the Campus. Despite Nader's valiant efforts the Commission prevailed even though he had a valid ticket. Furthermore, the Commission in concert with state officials at the highest levels misused the Massachusetts State Police to bully Nader with the threat of physical removal from the campus as well as arrest.

Maynard claimed 'these guys – referring to the Commission - were some of the meanest SOB's on the face of this earth – they bring out the worst human traits in every level of public service.' In his judgment they were as close to thugs as one could get. He mused 'is this how Hitler came to power?' He wondered out loud 'what has happened to our democracy?'

Chapter VI

O n Tuesday September 30th, Chris Wallace of Fox News
moderated a 90 minute debate in Mandel Hall at the
University of Chicago before an audience of just over 1000 -
dignitaries, faculty and students from the University and other
Universities in the Chicago area. The debate would be on
Domestic issues. The format of the debate would be opening and
closing statements of 2 minutes each, questions to be asked of
participants preferably in rotation or at the discretion of the
Moderator, each participant could challenge any response with a
20 second follow up question and each participant would have
the opportunity to ask each of their rivals two direct questions in
the last 10 minutes of the debate prior to the closing statements.

The first question was on Immigration and it was directed
to Senator Marjory Hunter. The question – 'what were her plans
for addressing the immigration 'crises? After many words about
immigration, about linking immigration to terrorism and about
the toll illegal immigrants were taking on our public services,
Senator Hunter stated she would aggressively enforce laws that
were already on the 'books'. When she became President she
would commit in her first 100 days to funding the completion of

the border fence between the US and Mexico on which construction had been stalled.

She would also deport any illegal aliens who were not properly credentialed. Senator Hunter stated that she would boost surveillance of illegal worker activity by increasing the budget of the INS – Immigration and Naturalization Services – by 60%. She contended that when the jobs dry up – 'and that would be the best way to do that' – then and only then would Immigrants return to their home countries.

When the same question was put to Bloomfield he answered along similar lines, except that he would vigorously prosecute and fine owners of businesses that hired illegal aliens. It was his feeling that business owners were as much to blame for this problem as were the illegal workers. Bloomfield felt that it was actually easier to go after business owners because we know who they are and where they are. Furthermore, he contended that once 10- 15% of businesses employing Illegals were prosecuted, word would get around, and businesses would begin cleaning up their 'act' on their own in a domino like manner. His policies, he asserted, would cause the jobs that these people are holding to disappear and force them to return to their home countries.

When the same question was asked of Maynard, he first stated that American workers have some very legitimate issues that have nothing to do with the laws the Senator and the Mayor are taking about. No one is addressing those issues and all my opponents do is propose wholesale actions that hurt everybody. "Americans", he said, "resent the fact that children born to Illegals automatically become American citizens. And, then these children born of parents who are illegally in this country are provided with many costly privileges that our taxes pay for such as Medicaid, day care, and schooling."

"That", he said, referring to the caring of the children of illegal parents, "may be the humane thing to do. Americans do act with humanity – that is part of our character. It is also what the law requires, because the 14th amendment of the Constitution makes everyone born in America citizens. But is that fair? I personally think there is something unfair about all of this!"

"The next question we have to ask are: do American businesses need these workers? Secondly, are they good, industrious and honest workers? And thirdly, we need to know if they act as good citizens when they are in our country? I think the answer to my first two questions is an unequivocal yes. In every city I have traveled to these past several years Illegal immigrants seem to be working diligently. American businesses seek them out so they must be necessary. To the question - are they all good citizens? And the answer to that question is – of course not, certainly not all of them. And those individuals who are not capable of becoming good citizen must and can be dealt with. That is a given!"

Following those remarks Maynard outlined his solutions. First he would change the 14th amendment to exclude citizenship to children born of parents who are in this country illegally. Maynard went on to say that the 14th amendment was intended to grant citizenship to the children of American slaves who had unfortunately been brought forcibly to this country. He quipped that he didn't know of any slaves that had sneaked into the country.

Continuing, Maynard added that the other parts of his program on Immigration reform were not too dissimilar to the current President's plan – the plan that failed in the congress. Both plans, he claimed, contained a strong element of humanity. However, Maynard believed that the concern for the human element has to be tempered with fairness to all concerned. Not only concern for Illegal aliens, but also to Americans who could be affected negatively by Immigrant intrusion.

In Maynard's plan US born children of illegal aliens who were less than 3 years of age would be deported along with their parents. Secondly, he would once and for all secure our Southern border. Thirdly, any illegal who was employed by the same employer for 2 years, who can prove he has been in this country for 5 years, and who has no criminal record would be placed on a path to citizenship after they have paid a four thousand dollar fine. He would use those monies so collected to secure our Southern border and for conducting English and citizenship classes for this group.

Maynard added one last point. He said that it was unfair that Mexico has foisted this entire problem on Americans and, in effect, are really asking us to solve their economic and social problems. Impoverished illegal aliens are a product of Mexico, he asserted. They are a consequence of an aristocracy in that country that has no concern for the poor and the uneducated. He added that there was no doubt in his mind that the unequal distribution of income created by class structure and unfair taxing was at the heart of Mexico's problem.

Maynard also had an issue with the fact that Mexico has such extraordinary resources – oil and mineral reserves – that were untapped years after they were discovered. He wondered out loud if the very structure of the Mexican society was at fault. Perhaps, the aristocracy was not being challenged to develop the country – perhaps they had no incentive to do that. Maybe life was too good. Maynard completed his thought by promising to apply appropriate pressures on the Mexican government to do their share in solving this problem, if he were elected. He added we have plenty of leverage to accomplish that.

While Maynard was making his last point, Hunter and Bloomfield could hardly contain themselves from jumping on him for the previous remarks he had made as to how he would solve the immigration issue. Almost in unison they asked – "wouldn't the program you are advocating be amnesty?"

Maynard responded, "Yes, it is. But it's a better form and one fairer to Americans than the amnesty that President Reagan granted to Illegal Aliens in the early 80's. And, as I recall, Senator Hunter you supported that." Without missing a beat, he said, "And Mr. Mayor, I guess you were on Wall Street at the time, so I have no idea where you stood on that issue. On the other hand, maybe Illegal aliens hadn't invaded the Investment banking world when you were there." That comment got a good laugh.

Throughout the entire debate whenever Bloomfield was asked a question regardless of its nature, he managed to work in a few digs directed at Governor DeFrie. To one of his answerers he coupled the statement that the budget of New York City and the complexity of running the city were far greater than the entire state of Mississippi. Senator Hunter whenever possible either piled on got in her own jabs. She claimed his 'Socialized Medicine' program would put the country on the 'slippery slope to socialism'. Bloomfield chimed in that we were a country founded on the principles of capitalism, and we had all the social programs we needed. All we had to do was manage them better.

Maynard never responded verbally to any of those comments – nor would the rules allow that. On occasion he would, looking straight ahead, feign a wince. Whenever that happened it was apparent that the students in the audience understood him very well. They cheered and applauded – and had to be quieted down. Throughout the debate, Maynard also made it a point to call Bloomfield – Mr. Mayor – and Senator Hunter – Mrs. Hunter. He knew how to communicate on many levels and in many different ways.

Wallace indicated that the debate was running behind and, therefore, they would need to eliminate that part of the debate plan where candidates would have had the opportunity of to ask direct questions of each other. He said they would move onto questions dealing with the environment, the issue of global warming – if it was an issue - and then allow each of them to make their closing statements.

In response to Wallace's global warming questions, Senator Hunter quoted a number of sources that disputed the entire notion of Global warming. She could not understand how it was possible to have weather where we were having record breaking cold spells in many locations when the globe is supposed to be warming. Hunter was also concerned that the fear mongers would bring on government regulation after regulation that would have grave economic consequences. She finished with, "It is of utmost importance that we keep our global competitiveness. That must be our first concern!"

Bloomfield's answer was different, but not entirely. He acknowledged that there seems to be a warming trend around the globe. He did not, however, think it was a consequence of human activity. Bloomfield made reference to studies that indicated that the Sun's surface was hotter, and he cautioned that the earth could be in one of its normal warming and cooling cycles. He cautioned that it was imperative that governments not rush to wrong and costly solutions to a problem that may not be a problem. He would, however, commit funds to continue to study the matter.

While Hunter and Bloomfield were answering soft groans of exasperation and muffled talking could be heard throughout the hall. When it was Maynard's turn to answer the question, he began by saying even though his undergraduate degree was in Chemistry and Biology he did not have the expertise to evaluate the science involved that supported or opposed Global Climate change. He added that his graduate degree was in theology, but with a soft laugh he said he didn't think that gave him any special insights either despite the proximity of the problem to heaven. That comment got a good laugh and some scattered applause.

Continuing on Maynard said that we would have to rely on experts and it would be critical to find experts who were completely unbiased. Then he paused for a moment, tilted his head back slightly focusing his eyes on the ceiling of the Mandel Hall and began, "When I was a boy growing up near the Mississippi River if you went skinny dipping in the River – and I wasn't supposed to do that – or if you fell in, chances are you would get sick, or at the very least get a major rash. The water was that filthy. It was that polluted beyond anything you imagine.

By the time I was a teenager most of our Great Lakes had been polluted and that was true for most of the rivers in this country. Thousands upon thousands of acres of land have been polluted with industrial toxins, garbage and chemicals. We don't have to look far to see that. Just take a ride over to Gary, Indiana and take a look at the ravages and the environmental toll on that area the steel mills took when they were in full force."

"As a consequence of my life experience and my thinking, I have a very different view on Global Climate Change; I really think it's a matter of simple logic. And, here's what I mean – if we have been capable of fouling our rivers, our lakes, our oceans and fouling our soil to the point that we make them uninhabitable, I would think we have ability to foul up the atmosphere. Why should the atmosphere be exempt? It's only a layer of air 6 – 8 miles around the whole world. That is a volume not significantly greater than our oceans. It seems to me that polluting the atmosphere should be a relatively easy task. After all humans have from the beginning of time been very creative in defiling so many of the great gifts our Creator gave to us. Why would that be exempt?" He added with emphasis, "We have a sacred duty to change that!"

Maynard asserted that we can't wait until every last piece of data is in. Global Climate Change is a problem and we must address it now. He also acknowledged that industrialized nations have shifted most of the world's dirty and polluting manufacture to China and therefore they must be part of the solution. He added that we would need to find creative ways to do that – and he was sure that could be done. As an afterthought Maynard, looking almost professorially, said that if Scientists had not used the term Global Warming but instead called it Global Climate Change - which is what it really is - the Public would have more readily grasped the concept. "Scientists need to engage Madison Avenue once in a while".

When the debate was drawing to a close each candidate was to give a 2 minute closing statement in the order: Hunter, Bloomfield and DeFrie as determined by lot. Hunter and Bloomfield each gave very well rehearsed closing comments each touting their experience, their record and their vision for the future. Hunter went heavy on her experience in the Senate and her understanding of how Washington functions. Bloomfield compared the running of New York City to that of many prosperous countries. He stressed his experience with foreign leaders and relationships he had made during his tenure in office as well as his good connections to the world finance industry from his Wall Street days.

When it was Maynard's turn, he reminded Chris Wallace that he had only used 30 seconds for his opening statement and asked if he could tack that onto his 2 minutes closing statement. Wallace agreed.

"Mr. Wallace", Maynard began. "You asked Mrs. Hunter a question of what American could do domestically to improve our image in the world following some of the foreign policy disasters – that's my word, Mr. Wallace – that have occurred these past 7 years. I would like to use my 2 minute 30 second closing time to answer that question." Wallace nodded approvingly anxious to hear what Governor DeFrie might have to say.

"We have become a divided country. We are becoming a nation of two economies – rich and poor. Patriotism is only a word to most Americans. To my father it meant joining the service in World War II at age 20, volunteering for a very dangerous mission and giving his life to his country. It meant the very same thing for most of your parents or your grandparents."

"On Friday I was to outline a program which addresses the uniting of a divided nation, makes the world see the goodness in Americans that truly exists, and restores the good character of Americans – the good character we inherited from our forefathers. In the 2 minutes I have remaining I will outline that now."

"I believe in the ideal that we should have Universal Service for all graduating high school students in this country. Rather than take on the battle of making it compulsory - I will have enough battles if we win this election – we will propose significant incentives to encourage all of our young people to volunteer two to three years of service to their country. One possible incentive, that I would recommend, could be the future exclusion of income from taxes. We are considering a carry forward income exclusion of $70,000 for each year of service after the completion of two years of service. We will also propose a $7,000 tuition benefit along the same lines."

"The kind of program I envision would be 6 months of basic military training for all who enroll. Those that want to continue on with the Armed Services can do so. Those who want to continue on in a Peace Corp type role could do that also. Those that want to enroll in programs of public service right here in this country – and God knows we can use them - can do that as well."

"If you think about all the benefits a program of this type would do for the country they are considerable. It democratizes our youth, it gives them purpose, it teaches them sacrifice and it will build character. It also gives a nation pause before it enters or considers entering into conflicts – like the one in Iraq. When all of our children are involved decisions of that kind are made with a good deal more prudence and less emotion."

"We have made some preliminary budget projections required to do what I am proposing, and I can tell you that the country can afford it. I can also tell you that the country can not afford to not do it, or we will go down a road where we will no longer be Americans."

"The budget numbers related to this program will be released shortly. But in the meantime I want to make a few points related to affordability. First, a good part of the infrastructure to create a national program of the type I am proposing is in place. We have first rate bases all over the country, and we have been wasting these valuable resources by closing them. It is time to reopen them and use them to their full capacity of serving this country once again. Can you imagine how much better we could respond to national disasters, like Katrina, with bases fully functioning around the country?"

"One last point, if I may Mr. Wallace" – Wallace was indicating Maynard's time was up – "we are spending – I should say wasting - billions of dollars on contractors performing the very same services that our young people did for generations.

The State Department spends huge amounts of money doing exactly what an expanded Peace Corps could do."

When Maynard had finished his comments, there was polite applause. From the expressions on their faces, it was apparent that the audience was trying to absorb what they had just heard. It was all very new thinking for them. As they left Mandel Hall it was clear from their demeanor that they were munching on Maynard's last words. There was very little conversation as they exited Mandel Hall.

Immediately following the debate, it was evident that Maynard had given the country much to think about. He had raised ideas and made suggestions no one had seemed to have thought of. If anyone had had such ideas they had never been made public – at least not in this generation. It was becoming apparent to all Americans that Maynard was 'the original' he was rumored to be in many circles of the Deep South. He had definitely stimulated the country's thinking. He had a similar affect on the Media to the extent they are capable of some original thinking. At the very least Maynard provided the Media with hundreds hours they could devote to ideas he had put on the table.

In the week that followed the Chicago Debate, it was evident Maynard had made a significant impression on the Voters with his performance. The Media, too, was beginning to take him seriously. At the end of that week when it was learned that he, unlike his opponents, had not spent the traditional day before the debate preparing – in fact, merely two hours on the plane from Chicago the day of the debate - his image grew even larger. That was the good news – and it would keep Maynard's campaign doing what they had been doing so successfully and at full speed since late July. On the other hand, Senator Hunter, Mayor Bloomfield and every member of all the opposing groups that were on Maynard's list were now taking aim directly at his head.

*   *   *

The second of the debates took place in Miller Theater at Columbia University, in New York City on Tuesday October 14th. The debate would be conducted by the League of Women Voters. The subject would be Foreign Affairs. By this advanced stage in the campaign, Governor DeFrie's positions on Middle East policy were well disseminated and had been discussed by him in detail on Bob Schieffer's program 'Face the Nation' which he finally was able to schedule and with Tim Russert on a 'Meet the Press' interview.

Governor DeFrie had flown into LaGuardia Airport from Chicago where he had held a noon time rally. At LaGuardia, he had instructed his cab driver – a recent Nigerian immigrant – that he wanted to get to Columbia University, but wanted to be let off at the 116th and Amsterdam Avenue side of the Campus, not on the Broadway side. That would seem an odd request as Miller Theater is, in fact, on the Broadway side of the Campus. However, Maynard's campaign manager, Jonathon Parkhouse, who would be meeting Maynard at the University, had warned Maynard that student protesters organized by Hillel, a Jewish student organization on Campus, might 'be wanting to' take issue with Maynard's Middle East Policies. Parkhouse said they were well organized and could be very aggressive protesters.

Since Maynard had busied himself during the cab ride in going over some notes he had jotted down for the debate, and as it was a gray and drizzly early evening with limited visibility Maynard was surprised when the cab arrived at 116th Street and Broadway – the West entrance to the Columbia Campus. Initially he attempted to communicate with his cab driver that he wanted the other side of the campus. That proved futile – Maynard realized he was fortunate that the driver even understood the Columbia University part of his request- so Maynard paid the driver and decided he would walk North on Broadway, find an entrance to the campus and then enter Miller Theater from that direction. When Maynard saw how poor the visibility was and realized he would be somewhat disguised by the umbrella he was carrying as well as not seeing any protesters congregating, he decided to walk directly east onto Campus along the 116th street walkway.

Maynard was half fortunate. The Hillel 'Spotter" who stood on the Southwest corner of 116th street and Broadway, cell phone in hand, was expecting Governor DeFrie to arrive in a limousine – just as his debate opponents had. His job was to call to his comrades who were massed on the steps of Low Library. Low Library is midway between Broadway and Amsterdam Avenues about 150 yards north of the 116th street campus walkway, and it is about 75 yards northeast of the Miller Theater. The protesters' plan was to march down the steps in the direction of Miller Theater and form a cordon that would prevent Maynard from entering or at least delay his entrance.

Maynard walked onto Campus along 116th street, the rear of Miller Theater was on his left side. Continuing to the far end of Miller Theater, he turned left and began climbing the steps – in the direction of Low Library - so that he could make his way around the Theater to its front entrance. Half way up the steps he was spotted. The protesters came running forward carrying protest signs and Israeli flags. They carried their flags and those signs that were mounted on wooden sticks just like Knights carrying lances. All were aimed at Maynard's head. Maynard had, indeed, become a victim of his own physical stature. He was too easily recognized - the umbrella, the light rain and the poor visibility were not at all effective in disguising him.

Besides jeering at Maynard, the protesters were shouting in unison – 'Israel is America, Israel is America.' The protesters had also constructed a variety of very provocative signs. One depicted Maynard in an SS Uniform, a Hitler style mustache had been added to his face. He was directing faceless individuals onto box cars. Another protest sign had a giant figure of Maynard clothed in traditional Arabic dress standing on a map of the Middle East urinating on Israel. Nuclear tipped missiles from the ground were trained on his genitals.

Maynard made several attempts to communicate with the protesters. He tried to speak over their shouts and begged their leader to allow him the use of the bullhorn he carried. The student leader moved towards Maynard, signaling that he was handing his bullhorn to Maynard. As Maynard drew close, the student pulled the bullhorn back and spat on Maynard. He shouted, "Mississippi Hitler – Kinky haired Hitler – Brother of Ahmadinejad."

The other protesters cheered their approval when they heard Ahmadinejad linked to Maynard. That wily disgusting character – the secular President of Iran – who has been insisting for years that the Holocaust has been greatly exaggerated had been invited to Columbia in the previous fall. In addition to his being treated rudely by the President of the University who, ironically, had invited him, Ahmadinejad was the subject of intense and prolonged protests by the Zionist leaning students at Columbia and from other institutions in New York.

Maynard turned from the protesters and moved quickly up the steps towards the front of Miller Theater. A large contingent of students – some wearing traditional Muslim headdress – had formed a cordon so that Maynard could pass to the entrance unobstructed. He did that without comment.

The debate itself was delayed 20 minutes as about a dozen Hillel protesters had planted themselves in the audience. Campus security had to call in New York City police to help remove them. That beginning – outside and inside of Miller Theater - set the tone of what was to follow.

The Foreign Policy questions were entirely about the Middle East, in particular about Iraq and about terrorism. When questioned about Iraq and Middle East Policy, Maynard restated his positions - diplomatic relations would be established with Iran in the first quarter of '09, he would convene a Middle East summit that would include all the Arab counties and Israel before the end of the 2nd quarter, all US troops would be pulled from Iraq by July 1, all military bases would be closed by August 31st, and the US would maintain a naval force in the region to keep peace, to assure US access to oil and to prevent any other country from meddling in the Middle East. The last part of a 'Monroe' type doctrine for the Middle East was entirely new and caught Mayor Bloomfield and Senator Hunter entirely off guard.

Maynard added that an important part of the entire Peace process in the Middle East would be dependent on Israel's willingness to give up Arab lands confiscated in 1967. In particular, he said there would need to be a solution as to the settlements that Israel had established on the West Bank of the Jordon River – on Palestinian lands. He asserted that the more moderate forces in Israel had always known that those confiscated lands would have to be given up in return for peace, and they had come to terms with that idea.

Maynard proposed that all settlements built within the last 12 years be vacated, not destroyed - he felt that destroying habitable buildings would be seen as vindictive and not help the peace process. He indicated he was willing to use major incentives – like slashing the four billion dollars the US gives to Israel each year – to accomplish his goals. He also added that altering Israel's borders does not threaten their security. They have stockpiled more than 300 nuclear weapons.

Speaking first Bloomfield categorically stated that he was horrified by what Maynard was proposing. He went on to remind Maynard that the US has always had a special relationship with Israel, and that Israel was of strategic interest to the US – he claimed it was not just a 'one way street'.

Maynard repeated his belief that 'all of God's children were deserving of a special relationship with the world's foremost democracy.' "Why would not a Just God demand fairness?!" Governor DeFrie then added that Israel may have been a strategic interest during the Cold War. That was questionable then and certainly not the case now. He referred 'Mr. Mayor' to the recent work of Professors Mearsheimer and Walt, from Harvard and University of Chicago, respectively, who had done a thorough and fair analysis of that very issue. Their conclusion he told Bloomfield was that the US needs to reevaluate that special relationship – particularly, in view of some the things that Israel had 'pulled' on the US. Maynard also repeated that the analysis he was referring to shows that there is no real basis for a strategic interest.

Bloomfield was visibly upset by Maynard's responses. At that point Senator Hunter chimed in the one direct question she could address to Maynard. She asked, "Aren't the interests of Israel and the United states mutual? After all, we both are engaged in a war on terrorism?"

Maynard responded by saying, "The US and Israel issues with terrorism are separate and very different. Terrorists have attacked us because of the issues they have with Israel and because we have been so one sided in our support of Israel. Our problem is not the same as Israel's. Our problem has been caused by them!" Maynard again referred the Senator to a very thorough and scholarly study - the work of Mearsheimer and Walt. "These very issues have been discussed in great depth. And, I need to add that this is the first time anyone has dared to publish such an analysis. Discussion of this kind has been suppressed in this country and we need open discussion. If we don't do that our grandchildren will still be plagued with terrorism."

Mayor Bloomfield used his 20 seconds rebuttal time to ask Maynard how anyone could deal with these crazed suicide bombers. "These people are barbarians and hate us and Israel because we are democracies."

Most mortals might have been worn down by this barrage from two well spoken and assertive individuals who were repeatedly attacking his positions. Furthermore, they made no effort to disguise their anger and disdain of him. Maynard stayed calm and without giving his opponents any sign that they were getting to him, he asked Mayor Bloomfield if he had read Jimmy Carter's recent book.

From Bloomfield's expression it was clear he had not. Maynard added that Carter's book gives an honest and accurate analysis of the issue between the Israelis and the Palestinians and a plan for resolving the crisis. "And, if you would read that book, you would see that the Palestinians are not as crazy and barbaric as you think!"

Maynard added one final thought on the matter of suicide bombers, he asked "Mr. Mayor, don't you think it is odd and totally against anything we can comprehend that well educated and professional humans have been willing to be suicide bombers? If you think that is strange behavior for individuals of that ilk – and I can't see how you can't think that - doesn't it occur to you to ask yourself why they would do that? I think if you would think exactly about that, it might soften some of your ideas. All humans love life. To be so desperate that you would give up your life for your people must mean something."

Speaking over the debate monitors who were trying to move ahead, Bloomfield, still angry and not at all listening to what Maynard had just said, stated that Carter's book and the other one – he could not remember the names of the authors – had been labeled by other scholars as anti Semitic. Maynard answered, "That a lot of nonsense! And, if we don't stop calling each other names and begin addressing these issues in open dialogue we will make no progress. We will never solve the terrorism issue!"

When the debate ended, Mayor Bloomfield and Senator Hunter shook hands. They made no effort to include, or even acknowledge, Maynard. Governor DeFrie graciously walked towards them, thanked them, wished them well and left the stage. They did not respond.

When Maynard met up with his campaign manager, Jonathon Parkhouse, after the debate, Parkhouse informed him that during the debate the Columbia protesters had managed to mobilize other Pro Israel students from every borough of New York City. There were at least 1000 protesters waiting for them outside Miller Theater.

Fortunately for Maynard, Columbia University has a system of maintenance tunnels that interconnect nearly every building on Campus. One of the Hospitality Hosts for the Women's League, a black woman who had attended Columbia years before, had overheard Parkhouse's concern. She led Maynard and Parkhouse safely out of Miller Theater underground to the north side of the campus, 125th street. She had anticipated that the Hillel group would have thought of that possible escape route, and 'borrowed', from one of the maintenance men they encountered, his smock and his Mets baseball cap. She was right in her assumptions. One of the students on guard duty, a New York Mets fan himself, acknowledge Maynard's choice in baseball teams with a high five.

It was following the Columbia debate that Governor DeFrie acquiesced to a request Jonathon Parkhouse had been making for the last month. Maynard finally agreed that his own approach to security was not adequate – but with a smile he was compelled to add that it really made him efficient. He would assemble his own team of bodyguards and accept Secret Service protection.

In his reluctance to make this concession, Maynard told Jonathon, "It's not the zealot with some protest sign that is going to get you. The most they are going to do is yelling at you and maybe spit on you. The ones you can't screen for are the ones who will get you. So just like Brother Martin, we have no choice but to put ourselves in the Lords hands." Parkhouse winced.

*   *   *

On October 27th Maynard flew into Philadelphia, to hold a 10 a.m. rally at City Hall. From there he would be making campaign stops in Norristown, Allentown and make his way to a 4 pm rally in Harrisburg. He would be spending the evening at nearby Gettysburg at the farm of the late General and Former President Dwight D. Eisenhower. The Eisenhower family had continued to maintain the farm. It still served a focal point for the large Eisenhower extended family. Governor DeFrie had been invited by John Eisenhower - a retired General, himself, and son of the Former President - to dine with some of the family members who would be at the farm.

Maynard would also be spending the night at the farm as their guest. On the following day Governor DeFrie would continue campaigning in central Pennsylvania. He would finish the day at State College in the Eisenhower Auditorium on the campus of Penn State University for the third and final debate of the Presidential race.

Maynard was looking forward to meeting John Eisenhower as he had remembered that Eisenhower, a life long Republican, had done something very unusual some years back. He had endorsed John Kerry in the 2004 Presidential race against the Republican incumbent. Maynard was also very grateful for the invitation to the farm home of the Eisenhowers– a home that would give him the opportunity to sense the spirit of a great man, and an opportunity to step on the very earth where the great man had walked. And, he was also hopeful.

As a great admirer of President Eisenhower, Maynard had read several biographies on him and was well acquainted with all his accomplishments as well as the many achievements of this large family. He was also tickled by the idea that his debate on the following evening would be in the Milton Eisenhower Auditorium at Penn State University where the President's brother had served as University President for many years.

At dinner Maynard had been seated between David Eisenhower, the grandson of the President, and his wife, Julie, the daughter of President Richard Nixon. In response to his host's request to say Grace, Maynard rose from his seat, reached down and firmly took the hand of David and Julie Eisenhower, and asked all to form a continuous chain.

"If my grandmother could see me at this very moment, she would lift her head to the heavens and shout 'thank you Jesus!' 'Thank you Jesus' for bringing my Maynard to the table of this great American family. And, like my grandmother, I say 'thank you Jesus' for all you have bestowed on me, for all of your blessings and for bringing me to this home. To have been born on the banks of the Mississippi and to have made this journey to this point in my life is truly an American dream. To be seated between the grandchildren of two great American Presidents. One of whom led us through some of our darkest history and brought us as President peacefully and prosperously into modern times."

"And that other great man, Julie, your father who had the courage and foresight to bring us together with what at the time was our darkest enemy. He was a courageous man. His is a journey I can well identify with and understand." Maynard asked Jesus for his blessing upon the Eisenhower family, the food they were about to eat, and thanked again John Eisenhower for his kind invitation.

When Maynard sat down, Julie Eisenhower firmly took his hand and thanked him for the kind words he had said about her father. Maynard responded that history would judge her father well, and he added "Jesus especially loves those who know struggle. And, only Jesus knows what is truly in a man's heart."

At dinner the conversation was lively and totally political. Every facet of every current issue was discussed in depth. Maynard was totally in his element. He was in company of very intelligent people who loved their country, understood politics at the national and international level, and who were not bound by party loyalties. Their interests were for the good of the country. As the evening concluded John Eisenhower praised Maynard for his courage in trying to halt, or hopefully curtail, the growth of the Military Industrial complex. He admitted that he had wondered so many times if the country had, indeed, forgotten the prophetic words his father had spoken more than a half century ago.

*   *   *

The Milton Eisenhower Auditorium at Penn State University seats 2500. 2000 of those seats were reserved for University students at main and satellite campuses, and were distributed by a lottery drawing. The remaining 500 seats were distributed to faculty and dignitaries from Pennsylvania. The dignitaries included the Governor of Pennsylvania, Ed Randall, US Senators, Arlen Specter and Bob Casey, jr., former

Republican Senator Rick Santorum and the Mayors of Philadelphia and Pittsburg. The debate was monitored by Chris Matthews and David Gregory of the MSNBC-NBC consortium. The topic of the debate was 'the economy'.

By the evening of October 28th, it was well acknowledge that the economy was in serious trouble. A recession was well in progress, oil was selling at $195 a barrel, unemployment was inching up to 9% - it was 13% in Michigan - and it cost one dollar and seventy four cents to buy one Euro. For nearly all Americans it was impossible to conceive of how a country with a budget surplus in 2000 could have ended up with an eleven trillion dollar debt only eight years later. And, the clock on the debt was running at the rate of 1.5 billion dollars a day.

Both Mayor Bloomfield and Senator Hunter advocated making permanent the current President's tax cuts. Bloomfield proposed that the economy could be jump started by eliminating the Capital Gains Tax. Hunter's plan was to lower Capital Gains to 10% and to eliminate all estate tax – the so called 'death tax.' Each had a different plan to bail out the commercial banking industry that was being devastated by the 'Sub Prime' mortgage lending scandal. More aptly put, by the scandal that took place because banks made home loans to individuals who could not afford them and for encouraging them to buy homes that were overpriced.

Maynard's plan could not have been more different. He restated his tax plan of 0% taxes on incomes below $25,000, graduating, cutting tax rates in half for taxable earnings under $130,000 and further graduating the income tax up to 55% on very high wage earners. That top bracket would be imposed on income in excess of $2.5 million dollars. The Governor also enumerated some preliminary ideas on how he might eliminate many of the charitable tax deductions that do the public and the country little good.

Maynard went on to say that he thought the trickledown theory – the rich invest and the benefits trickle down to all those below – was utter nonsense. He claimed the only thing that trickled down was price inflation, because the rich did not have to be concerned about how much they paid for items. He also asserted that the current administration with his low tax policies had only brought the country economic disaster. He also challenged the notion that private investment was superior to well supervised government spending.

On the matter of getting individuals to invest their money in ways that benefit the country and the economy, Maynard had a different plan. He would reduce Capital Gains tax to 4% on those kinds of investments. They would include investments into the development or production of alternative sources of power – he excluded the corn to ethanol industry which he thought was an absurd program promoted by politicians buying favor from farmers and the corn/ethanol companies. Investments in light commuter rail systems would be eligible for the 4% Capital Gains as would be coal to electricity production which produced zero emissions, and that included trapping of all carbon dioxide produced.

Maynard was, of course, challenged on his contention that government investment could be more efficient than the private sector. Maynard countered that the goal of federal investment is to improve the country, to stimulate the economy and not to make a profit. He asserted that the country needed a huge investment in its infrastructure and that would be of universal benefit. He also asked the question of how many more bridges had to fall down – referring to the Minneapolis tragedy – before we wake up.

Mayor Bloomfield accused Maynard of trying to remake the US into a European economy which he asserted was considerably inferior. This comment actually angered Maynard. He paused for a moment to regain his composure and responded "The American public has been fed a pack of anti-government lies for years. There is an anti-government ideology that has dominated the American political discussion which states that low taxes and a weak social safety net are necessary for prosperity. That, my good man, is utter nonsense. The European economy is doing more than O.K. despite the level of taxing and government spending well beyond the ambitions of our most progressive politicians. And, if you don't believe that, look at what has happened to the relative value of the Euro versus our dollar."

One of the last questions dealt with free trade issues. Bloomfield and Hunter were absolute in their devotion to the absence of any kind of trade barrier. Again, Maynard had a different point of view. He stated "If one examines the economic analyses that were done in the 90's when Mr. Clinton was advocating removing trade barriers, the analyses were based on free trade accounting for 5% of the economy. The conclusion then was that free trade would be a benefit to the country. Now we are dealing with an issue that involves 25% of the economy. That, my friends, is a very different issue. And, it is and will continue to have a very negative effect on the livelihood of a great many Americans."

Maynard used part of his closing statement to add one issue that was of concern to him. That issue dealt with the degree of manufacturing that American companies are doing overseas. Maynard, who loved technology and liked to tinker, was of the opinion that if someone else does your manufacturing you lose control of the product. That manufacturer will learn how to apply new technology to the product; will find easier ways to make it, and in time the original owner will be out of luck. Maynard suggested we need to address those issues before it is too late.

Maynard had scored well again. It was apparent to all those who would not be adversely affected by his programs, that a hulking giant whose intellect matched his size had come onto the scene. In spite of the fact that Senator Hunter and Mayor Bloomfield each knew in their hearts they were dealing with a superior intellect who seemed to be able to outwit them and out think them at every turn, they were counting on efforts other than the debates to defeat the Governor.

Accordingly, in these final weeks of the Presidential campaign, Hunter and Bloomfield turned up the heat on the Governor with a vicious negative effort that was without precedent. These opponents of the Governor and their allies used every dirty trick imaginable, along with many they invented for the occasion. It seemed Senator Hunter and Mayor Bloomfield and their respective Republican and Democrat allies were more intent in keeping Maynard from winning the election, even if one of them was to lose to the other. Maynard was their main target. He quickly realized what they were up to, and often commented, "When I promised I could bring the country together, I didn't have in mind unifying the candidates of Republican and Democrat parties and their allies against me!"

*   *   *

The attacks came in many forms. Telephone banks calling voters of both parties offering via innuendo synthesized juicy tidbits about Maynard's past. One theme mainly dealt with cocaine usage – that the Governor had never really overcome his admitted drug usage and had just switched to a more sophisticated category. Another claimed that Maynard was not any different than most Black men and had a huge sexual appetite. Supposedly, he had fathered dozens of illegitimate children all over the country.

Other attacks came in the form of barrages of TV ads placed over the entire country, and particularly in suburban and rural areas, reminding the voters in subtle, and in not so subtle terms, that Maynard Jefferson DeFrie was a black man. The strategy of Maynard's opponents was simple: Americans are fundamentally racists; they will not vote for, nor will they elect a black man President.

Some ads, shown over and over again, were constructed to make the Governor appear larger and broader than the large black man that he was. In those ads Maynard's facial expressions had been altered to give it not only a mean look but the expression of his eyes was one that would invoke fear in the viewer. This, of course, was, totally in contrast to the kindly look Maynard's eyes actually had. In most instances, the Governor was depicted speaking to almost entirely black wildly enthusiastic voters. Just to keep some semblance of balance an occasional few white blue color workers were mixed into the crowd.

The repeated charges that accompanied these many 'beyond negative' ads was that DeFrie wants to take this country down the road to socialism. He was accused of promoting class warfare not seen in this country since the communist sympathizers of the 20's. Along with that charge, the Governor was charged with turning the middle class against the rich. From these ads the conclusion to be drawn was that DeFrie has only contempt for those successful individuals who have achieved the American dream.

Maynard was fortunate that he had the resources to respond to these campaigns. He did that with positive messages making sure every voter knew the facts of and knew where he stood on the vital issues. He could do this because his campaign was well resourced. It was capable of raising 15 – 20 million dollars in a two day internet appeal and was able to do that week after week. Greater than 98 % of those contributions ranged from 10 to 50 dollars. His campaign workers continued with their internet mailings and their precinct style of campaigning.

One of the Governor's favorite response ads, as he called them, was on the charge that he was initiating 'class warfare'. His response was, "if I am being accused of starting class warfare, then it seems there is a war that has been going on for some time against 'we, the people'. It's a war most of us didn't even know about. Because if the government is bailing out Wall street banks and major fat contracts are going to a variety of American Corporations, while we can not even afford first rate care for our returning Iraq soldiers, while we have an abundance of working poor who are without health care, while we are talking about reducing Medicare and Social Security benefits, then there is a war going on. That war is against Middle America. And, Middle America is losing! So if my opponents are claiming the changes I want to make are 'class warfare' – so be it. I would prefer it to be called doing the moral imperative! Restoring democracy!"

*   *   *

By Saturday November 1ˢᵗ Maynard had conducted more than 140 'town hall meetings'. His volunteers had introduced themselves and Maynard to more than 80% of the voting public. They had accumulated 80 million e-mail addresses of voting Americans and had on a regular basis kept them informed of Maynard's program and his progress. Senator Christianson had visited every state in the Union, conducted rallies in every population center in excess of 20,000 voters. They had done a through job.

On Monday November 3ʳᵈ, Maynard and his entourage returned to Jackson, Mississippi. On that evening – the day before the election - Governor DeFrie hosted them at a dinner party in the Governor's Mansion. After dinner, Governor DeFrie, Jonathon Parkhouse, and Abraham Gellman went onto the veranda of the Mansion to enjoy cigars and sample some of Maynard's collection of single malt whiskeys.

Maynard was visibly tired. He had taxed his strong body to its maximum. No one could have kept the schedule he had been on these past many months, could have endured the attacks – personal ones and on his policies. Maynard have never once faltered on his impossible goal. On his impossible dream. He had given his all and he was exhausted.

Relaxing with his two old and dear friends, Maynard tired that he was, his voice hoarse from all the speaking he had done was compelled to share his thoughts.

"Since I was 14 years of age, I have always wondered why Jesus put himself through the tortures he knew he would have to endure and the crucifixion he knew would await him. I also know in my heart of hearts that Jesus suffered as any mortal man suffers. He was cut no break there."

"And, now after this long battle, this long struggle, I think I know how Jesus felt during his lifetime on this earth. And, I don't mean that in any way to be presumptuous. To have to fight a battle to have to endure when all you know is that is what you must do, is a terrible burden on any man. During this whole campaign as I would lie in bed each night I would keep thinking of Jesus and his words of 'accepting this yoke'. Whatever happens in this election, I can say I have been true to myself and I have accepted my yoke."

Maynard put his whiskey down and reached out for the hands of his companions. He told them that all of his religion and all of his life was embodied in Jesus' Sermon on the Mount which he recited to them from memory. When he came to the portion where Jesus teaches how we are to pray, Maynard kneeled down with his companions and recited the words of Jesus, the Lord's Prayer. He did that in his rich and deep baritone voice – his words resonating softly into the night air.

When they stood up, Abraham Gellman's hands began to tremble. His chest began to rhythmically heave almost as if he would convulse. Covering his face with his palms he burst into tears. Gellman had never been so moved, so overcome with emotion, yet he could not fully comprehend his own feelings.

Chapter VII

In spite of the viciousness of the Presidential campaign, well before Election Day – in fact, by mid October nearly two weeks before the third debate - Maynard Jefferson DeFrie had a good feeling about the election. He actually believed that he might have a chance to win the Presidential Election. For him this was not a spiritual feeling, nor did he feel that it was preordained, it was simply a feeling. The Governor believed that his approach of telling the voters in clear unambiguous terms what he believed, the basis for his beliefs and where he wanted to take the country was resonating with the public. He claimed that he could 'see resonance in their eyes and in the way they shook his hand.'

Accordingly, even though it was premature, he began to move forward on his strategy to unite the country and to bring about as rapidly as possible the changes he had promised and campaigned on – Maynard claimed he must have used the word "change" a million times during his campaign. He started moving forward by having a second round of talks with key individuals with whom he had had at least one substantive discussion regarding a possible role in his administration. These were seasoned highly respected individuals of the highest caliber. They were Republicans and Democrats who were politically diverse – conservatives, moderates and liberals. They had one characteristic in common - they were accustomed to working 'across the aisle.'

That was critically important to Maynard. For him to achieve his goals, America had to begin speaking with one voice. It had to be a soft, strong and thoughtful voice - not the shrill tones the country had been subjected to for nearly 20 years. Maynard had quipped during this period that if his methods of governing were successful in getting the country united, Fox News would lose its audience.

*   *   *

Election Day November 4th, 2009 would be a day that would remain etched in Maynard Jefferson DeFrie's mind forever. He awakened early. He and Mrs. DeFrie cast their ballots first thing in the morning in the presence of news photographers. As it was a beautiful day in Jackson, Mississippi, the Governor and Mrs. DeFrie, followed by their Secret Service entourage, strolled from their polling precinct back towards the Governors mansion. On their way they stopped at a coffee shop, greeted well wishers and continued on to the Governors mansion where the Governor and his two dear friends, Parkhouse and Gellman, would spend the day in contact with their campaign network. Other than one incident in Canton, Ohio where DeFrie supporters got into an altercation with an election official concerning eligibility of some newly registered voters – the Canton police had been called in – the day went smoothly for them.

After a light dinner, at about 7 pm the Governor and his colleagues retired to his library where campaign assistants were manning phone banks, while several hovered over computers examining and compiling any exit poll data. Six large screen TVs were placed against the north wall of the library, each tuned to one of the major networks, cable stations or PBS. Two individuals were assigned to monitor those broadcasts which were all being digitally recorded.

By 7:30 pm those states whose polls had closed at 7:00 had sufficient returns for the networks with their computer models to begin declaring winners. In Indiana, Kentucky and Virginia, Senator Hunter was being declared the winner. She was off to a good start. To Governor DeFrie's great disappointment, Vermont even though it only has 3 electoral votes was declared for Morris Bloomfield. The Governor thought he had enthusiastic support in Vermont. Further, all the polling data his campaign had analyzed indicated he would take more than 52% of the vote.

The Vermont result along with the networks declaring Georgia and South Carolina for Maynard were disconcerting. The Governor wondered out loud, "Is it possible we are only going to do well in states that have large Black populations?" He coupled that with his concern that all the polling they had done might be meaningless – a concern he had throughout the campaign. Were voters reluctant to share their prejudices with pollsters? Would they say they would be voting for a Black candidate when, in fact, they had different motives for saying that? The Governor's comments were barely out his mouth, when the very same conversation could be heard on every network that was reporting the election.

The results for those state whose polls had closed at 7:30 – North Carolina, Ohio and West Virginia – seemed to be confirming Governor DeFrie's concerns. Even though polls taken by his campaign and by some of the national pollsters, predicted a substantial victory for the Governor in Ohio, based on early results that state was clearly going into Senator Hunter's column. Maynard was not consoled by the fact that he had been declared winner in North Carolina and West Virginia. He was further disturbed by early results from that part of Florida where the polls close at 7:00 – the Florida panhandle is in a different time zone. The Governor had done poorly all along the Florida east coast, and particularly the Miami/Fort Lauderdale area. It was becoming clear to the Governor and his staff that they would be in for a long, rough and possibly disappointing night.

The first real encouragement of the night for Governor DeFrie came when CBS and NBC were declaring him the winner of Massachusetts, Pennsylvania, Illinois and New Jersey. The other networks were claiming these races were too close to call. If those results held up, the Governor's team believed that if he could win New York State, California and Florida – if the remainder of Florida and its panhandle came out strongly for him – as well as more southern states, they might be able to win.

That enthusiasm was not to last long. At 9:15 pm, 15 minutes after the polls closed in New York, all the networks were projecting that Bloomfield would win the state. Worse yet, the Governor was doing poorly in New York City an area in which he had campaigned hard. Ironically, upstate New York which is traditionally heavily Republican came out strong for DeFrie.

The early returns from Texas, where polls had closed at 9 pm, were proving it to be a two way race between Senator Hunter and Governor DeFrie. Just after 10:30 pm when 35% of the votes were tallied, CNN and NBC were declaring that Governor DeFrie would win Texas' 34 electoral votes. If that result held, and if the Governor could win Michigan, Minnesota, Florida which was doubtful, along with California Governor DeFrie would have 304 electoral votes.

By 11:45 pm, there were sufficient returns from California to declare its 55 electoral votes in Maynard's column. Michigan and Minnesota were still too close to call with the Governor being in a virtual tie with Senator Hunter. It was beginning to look as if Florida for the second time in a decade would decide who would become President of the United States. That did not bode well for the Governor and his team.

At 12:30 am, Governor DeFrie tapped on a water glass to gain the attention of his campaign staff most of whom were charged up with the excitement of the evening. When he finally got their attention, he thanked each of them for all their efforts. He stated that this had been a most incredible evening – a very appropriate end to a historical event. He added that he was exhausted physically and mentally, and that even if he had any energy left he could do nothing to change what was already done – all the votes had been cast. After that the Governor gave a short prayer of gratitude to his Savior thanking Him for this incredible opportunity and for the many blessings that had been bestowed on him and on each of his supporters. When he had finished his prayer, the Governor stated that the results of the election were in the hands of the Lord. With that, he waved all a good night and announced he was going off to bed.

Ten hours later when a still exhausted Governor was awakened by Mrs. DeFrie, Maynard Jefferson DeFrie learned that that he had won Florida by just over 12,000 votes. That gave the Governor 304 electoral votes. With 280 electoral votes needed to win that made him the 44th President of the United States. Senator Hunter received 144 electoral votes, and Morris Bloomfield 51.

When the final tallies were in 172,674,301 Americans had cast ballots for the presidency – a stunning increase of nearly 50 million voters over the 2004 Presidential election. Governor DeFrie had received just under 39% of the popular vote. In many ways that was an incredible achievement, but the Governor knew he would need to win over a substantial portion of those who voted for his opponents if he wanted to implement any of his programs.

*   *   *

On the day following his election, Maynard spent more than 8 hours on the telephone finalizing the first component of that strategy – assembling that part of his bipartisan Cabinet that would deal with foreign policy. When the day was completed President-Elect DeFrie had in place the pillars on which he would build his Administration. As his secretary of state he had selected an internationally respected four star General – a Republican - who had served in that position from 2000 to 2005. For Secretary of Defense, Maynard had convinced the current Secretary to stay in that position and join his Administration. Maynard admired the Secretary of Defense for his broad knowledge, his experience and his willingness to stand up to the highest ranking military officers - even the Commander in Chief. These individuals embodied characteristics, of the kind, that individuals serving in Maynard's Administration would have to have - intelligence, wisdom, patriotism and integrity.

In the few days following Maynard's '8 plus' hour telephone marathon, he also formed a senior advisory group which would work with him, his Secretary of State and his Secretary of Defense. The common goal of this team was to institute a greatly modified Foreign Policy and to reverse the damage of the previous eight years. This group of Advisers included some of the most capable Americans in recent history. They were James Baker, Secretary of State to the 41st President, Zbigniew Brzezinski who had served Presidents Carter and Clinton, and Lee Hamilton, a former congressman from Indiana who had served as Co-Chair of the 911 Commission, and who directs the Woodrow Wilson International Center for Scholars. All had very willingly agreed to serve without pay.

One week after the election, Maynard phoned and offered Morris Bloomfield the office of the Secretary of the Treasury. Maynard believed that Bloomfield's Wall Street resume would beneficial in getting the Federal Deficit in check. Bloomfield was not honored by the offer and was brusque in his refusal. Maynard's lengthy discussion with Senator Hunter regarding different cabinet positions or other roles she might play in his administration were not fruitful. The Senator was, however, very gracious in refusing Maynard's offer.

The other two areas in Maynard's Administration that would require finding some extraordinarily gifted leaders would be for his Universal Health Care program and for his Universal Service. The skills – political and otherwise – for each task are different, but to some measure they are the same. For the Health Care program Maynard felt he needed someone who truly understands how Congress works and who has significant experience with Federal Programs. For the leadership of that program Maynard chose Vice President-Elect Rod Christianson. Maynard was confident that Christianson had the drive the position required and a sufficient knowledge of how Washington works to get the job done.

It was leadership of the Universal Service program that was a larger concern to him. That program had components of the military, it had components of the Peace Corps and it had a component that really didn't exist – service on the national level. As Maynard's ideas on this continued to evolve he had come to believe that for those who were going onto college, one option is that the program could very well be integrated with a college education. Hence, instead of 'work study' programs that many colleges offer, there could be offered 'service study' programs. Maynard particularly liked that idea because he felt a young individual who was doing some tour of duty might realize what skills would improve their performance and use the next step to acquire those skills.

Maynard believed that anything that the country could do for its youth to help them mature, to help them make intelligent decisions would be of benefit to the country, and, of course, to them. In a lighter moment on possible benefits of his Universal Service Program, the Governor once quipped – "just getting these kids off of their cell phones talking to their mommies will do them and the country a world of good." He was convinced that to rebuild America, you needed to rebuild Americans.

Because of the novelty of Maynard's Universal Service program and the goals and purpose that he had for it, Maynard had no intention of putting that program under the military. He believed the Pentagon was powerful enough, and probably would take the program down the wrong road because they think they know everything there is to know about training. He also did not want his program under the State Department because he was convinced the State Department could not be made to function at the grassroots level he envisioned.

As Maynard was mulling over this issue, he remembered an experience from his days at Tulane. In his junior year at Tulane he had gone to a recruitment rally for the Peace Corps with his classmate who eventually joined the Corps. Maynard remembered that he was very impressed because the rally was conducted by a Sergeant Schriver who was part of the Kennedy family – Maynard had never before seen a 'celebrity'. In fact Schriver was President Kennedy's brother-in-law and Kennedy had put Schriver in charge of the Peace Corps.

Maynard also recalled that his Peace Corps buddy had over ensuing years written him and had been glowing in his admiration of Schriver. He credited him with almost single handedly making the Peace Corps the success it was, in spite of all the obstacles that had to be overcome. Maynard's buddy had also shared that Schriver was a most unusual individual. He was a composite of dedication to the mission, compassion and toughness. Maynard was pleased he had remembered that. He had decided he would keep an eye out for a Schriver or Kennedy like individual to lead his program.

*   *   *

It is not unusual for a President-Elect – once his transition team is moving forward – to find some place in the Caribbean where he can recuperate from the rigors of the campaign, and just rest, relax and lie out in the sun. The first week in December is a good time to do that and a favorite place for winners – and occasionally losers – is Caneel Bay, one of the original Rockefeller resorts, on St. John in the Virgin Islands. In addition to private luxury cabins scattered around the Resort, there are a number of very private homes with very limited access that can be leased. On most occasions they are loaned.

On Monday December 1st, a private jet made available to President-Elect DeFrie by one of his major supporters took off well before dawn from Jackson-Evers International Airport. It would be one of the few flights from Jackson-Evers that did not have to make a connecting stop to get to its final destination. The destination of this flight was Malpenza Airport in Milan, Italy. Four of the individuals on that plane were exempted from passing through Airport Security.

The identities of those four men and the destination of the plane would remain unknown to all but the crew who were sworn to secrecy, and to the four other passengers who were Secret Service agents assigned to protect the most important traveler, President-Elect DeFrie. The three other passengers on that plane were the President-Elect's nominee for Secretary of State and two of Maynard's foreign policy advisers, former Congressman Lee Hamilton and Professor Zbigniew Brzezinski. The purpose of the journey was for secret meetings with European leaders. The initial destination was to a private estate, the country home of Silvio Berlusconi, Prime Minister of Italy. The estate is adjacent to the grounds of the Serbelloni Hotel, in Bellagio, Italy on Lake Como – reputed to have been Winston Churchill's favorite place in the entire world.

On Tuesday afternoon Maynard DeFrie and his two colleagues held, in secret, a three hour discussion on the Foreign Policy directions of the United States of America with Berlusconi and two other Italian Officials, Angela Merkel – Prime Minister of Germany, and Gordon Brown – Prime Minister of Great Britain. After dinner they continued their discussions over cigars and brandy. On the following morning after they had an additional 90 minutes of discussions, Maynard and his colleagues journeyed back to Malpenza for their next flight.

By Friday December 5th, Maynard and his small entourage had flown to Tehran, Damascus, Beirut, Tel Aviv, Riyadh and Cairo where they met with the leaders of Iran, Syria, Lebanon, Israel, Saudi Arabia and Egypt. When they were in Israel they were able to motor to an impromptu meeting in Jerusalem with delegates from both Hamas and Fattah.

Ironically, the latter meeting was facilitated in the late afternoon by the Israeli Government following a morning three hour meeting that President-Elect DeFrie and his colleagues had with newly elected Israeli Prime Minister Ehud Herzog and former Prime Minister Benjamin Netanyahu. It was during the morning meeting that Governor DeFrie learned of the strong opposition Herzog and Netanyahu had to his proposed meeting with Palestinians that would include Hamas representation. President-Elect DeFrie was reminded that it was a long standing policy of Israel and the United States not to negotiate or speak with terrorists.

The Governor informed his hosts that there would be a new policy for the United States going forward. He asserted that the only time one should not talk to or negotiate with their enemies is when there is some agenda other than a peaceful outcome. Taken aback, Herzog and Netanyahu understood the point. DeFrie also informed the Israeli leaders of his expectations of Israel moving back to its 1967 borders to the extent that it was feasible. He indicated that the security of Israel was of utmost importance and would play a large role in those negotiations

The President-Elect was not reticent in stating that any West Bank settlements that had been built in the last 12 years would have to be abandoned. He assured the Israelis that the US would provide and guarantee a protective barrier over all Israeli lands. He also unveiled his pledge to keeping all 'troublemakers' out of the area. At the end of that meeting it was clear that could see the merits of Maynard's plans for the Middle East. Herzog was visibly enthusiastic. Netanyahu, on the other hand, would require considerably more coaxing.

*   *   *

One of the pillars of DeFrie's administration would be not only stop nuclear proliferation but to reverse the process – begin ridding the world of such weapons. In Iran, Governor DeFrie secured a solemn promise from Ayatollah Khamenie, Iran's supreme leader, to either abandon the country's nuclear ambition or convert those ambitions to peaceful uses. Khamenie who had succeeded the Ayatollah Khomeini, leader of the Iranian

Revolution in 1979, agreed to open up Iran oil reserves to development by a consortium of US and British companies.

That agreement would be in return for a fair sharing of oil revenues, a resumption of a full diplomatic relationship, a promise of Maynard's Middle East type Monroe Doctrine, the establishment of a Palestinian state and an evenhanded approach to the Palestine – Israel problem. The President-Elect also wanted to resume the exchange student programs that had existed years back between Iranian and the USA and shared with the Ayatollah his ambitions for his Universal Service programs, particularly the overseas services he envisioned.

Maynard was blunt enough to suggest to the Ayatollah that the Iranian President Ahmadinejad was doing Iranians a great disservice. He even went so far as to say that the way in which Ahmadinejad had exerted control over Iranian recent elections would more than likely breed hostility from Iranians. Maynard suggested that Ahmadinejad's rhetoric and actions were not in the best interests of Iran or of World Peace – even if they were merely bombastic. Maynard asserted that Ahmadinejad did not respect the sensitivities of other humans. He added that on the road to peace that would be essential.

As they parted, Khamenie took hold of both of Maynard's hands, offered first thanks for the courtesy of the visit and of Maynard's good intentions. He then said a prayer of blessing to Maynard and his colleagues as they were preparing to leave. He extended his blessings to all those that Maynard would serve.

Before taking his oath of office, Maynard had one other important piece of work to do so that he could 'kick start' the economy on day one. That task regarded the drain of American dollars to China. There would be no way he could fix the economy with dollars flooding out of the country in the direction of China and loaned back to us by the very same people. He understood that would be the case even with his tax policies and his plan to rebuild the infrastructure of the country. He needed to take action.

Since the Chinese government was artificially fixing the value of the dollar at such a disadvantage to the Chinese 'renminbi' – China's People's Currency – the President knew that the exchange rate in combination with low wages in China would continue to create a great hardship for American workers.

Maynard understood that in time inflation would take place in China. It was predictable since as the Chinese improved their living condition, they would want more. They would not be immune to the forces of capitalism. Inflation would force the Chinese to pay higher wages to their workers. But the President also knew that waiting for inflation in China to take place such that it would make American workers more competitive might take too long.

He also knew that by meddling in the currency issue he would not be popular with American investors and Multinational Corporations who were making a fortune off of this unfortunate imbalance. That would not stop him. He was elected by the people!

On the weekend of December 13th, Maynard and the same group that made the European and the Middle Eastern tour with him met secretly with Chinese Premier Wen Jaibao and his aides in Honolulu. They discussed the needs of Chinese in the modernization of their country and the incredible growth that was occurring. They also addressed the importance of improving the lot the Chinese people. Maynard presented his case of how their needs could become in conflict with those of the American people if the current exchange rate situation did not improve. It was a productive meeting.

*   *   *

On Tuesday January 20th at 12 o'clock noon Maynard Jefferson DeFrie took the Oath of Office of the President of the United States of America on the steps of the US Capitol Building. The Oath was administered by Chief Justice Roberts.

The weather was absolutely miserable – overcast and 17 degrees with wind gusting from the northwest at velocities up to 33 mph. In spite of that when President DeFrie began to speak his inaugural address, the weather did not matter any more. All present and all watching on television felt the warmth of this magnificent human. The country looked forward with longing to the potential of a leader found. In spite of the fact that 60% of the populous was skeptical, they, too, were hopeful.

"Fellow Americans! My dear Brothers and sisters of this most incredible country. Today we dedicate ourselves - with all of our energies, with all of our spirit to the renewal of our democracy, to a renewal of this great country, to the return to the principles of our founding fathers, to the return of our role as the moral leader in the world community. We have accepted the latter obligation, because of the many blessing that have been bestowed upon us by our Creator, and we have honored that obligation. The only land on foreign soil we have taken is land to bury our brave dead soldiers who were on that soil to protect and defend those who owned it. No country in the history of the world can make that claim. Today we rededicate ourselves to the principle that all men are created equal, in this country and throughout the entire world. We dedicate ourselves to the principle that we will reach down to all of our brothers who have the will and character to pull themselves up." Maynard continued on stressing the urgency with which change must be made. It was a short speech with just a few points, and it suited Maynard perfectly.

Because it was short - now Maynard could get on with his work. His speech was exactly 246 words long – the very same number of words in Lincoln's Gettysburg Address. Maynard was amused that in spite of all the commentary on his address in the press and on the airways no one had made the word connection to the Lincoln speech. A month later a school girl in Duluth, Minnesota wrote Maynard of her discovery. She received a copy of the Inaugural address signed by the President.

There were nine Inaugural Balls. Maynard's original supporters from Honolulu were scattered throughout the nine events. His Black Angel was part of President and Mrs. DeFrie's entourage that visited each of them. Maynard had not forgotten Springsteen, Willie Nelson and all the others who had worked so hard for his election. He had also not forgotten those key Senators and Congressmen who would be essential to his programs. It was important that he cultivate and establish a strong personal relationship with them. After all he had been elected on the Green Party ticket, and he was the only member of his party who ran successfully. Non partisanship would be the order of the day and of every day to come.

President DeFrie also made a point of reminding each of his Cabinet and staff members who were reveling in the events of the evening that they would be 'in session' at 7:30 am on the following morning. He added that if they intended to have coffee and breakfast buns they should be there by 7 am. He gave them his assurance that he would see to it that they would not starve. They learned lunch and dinner would be brought in. They also learned that this would be their routine.

*   *   *

The President had been so entirely focused on his climb to the Presidency, his strategy for accomplishing that and on the changes he wanted to implement when he achieved that goal that he had neglected to consider one very important issue. He had not fully thought through the fact that in a three way race it is all but impossible to receive a mandate from the voters. There was no logical way that he could argue that his not quite 39% of the popular vote was a mandate. He would need to gain the support of a substantial portion of the 61% of the populace that did not vote for him. His goals for doing that was to extend the strong lines of communication he had fostered with his supporters to the general public. He would also initiate a legislative program with several pieces of legislation that would benefit the majority of the population.

In the area of communications, Maynard DeFrie had every intention of using those tactics in his Presidency that had worked for him in Mississippi. If some method worked and fit well, he loved to mention Occam's razor – 'what is simplest is best.'

To get his 'communications machine' up and running on a national basis, during the transition period between Election Day and the inauguration, Maynard DeFrie assigned his assistant Rodger D'Angelis and his team an important task. D'Angelis who so successfully managed the Governor's college student volunteers was asked to organize and codify every e-mail address and cell phone number they had in their possession. For their more than 60 million e-mail addresses, Maynard wanted 435 separate lists – one for every congressional district in the country.

President DeFrie would begin his term of office with a major policy speech in the first 10 days of his Presidency. He would continue to give a policy address or an up date week after week at the same time. The President maximized his audience by effective use of the media and by initiating his weekly three paragraph e-mails and text message reminders using the communication system D'Angelis had established.

In time this Presidential means of communication evolved to a 15 minute weekly event – Thursday evenings at 10:45 pm EST - similar to FDR's fireside chats, except Maynard's 'chats' were on TV not radio. That allowed him to use props, video clips and appropriately chosen guests to make his points. All of this would be in addition to his weekly press conferences and an occasional press conference called on the spur of the moment.

To achieve his goal of gaining popular support for his Presidency through legislation that would immediately benefit most Americans, the President would pursue the tax reform he had campaigned on. His goal was a substantial reduction of the tax rate on those with taxable incomes of under $100,000 after all deductions were made. He also believed that he could appeal to the good will of those who would be paying substantially higher taxes. He was certain that most Americans, rich or poor, were interested in doing what was right for the country. Further, he believed that his formation of a diverse and bipartisan cabinet would set the tone for where he wanted the country to move, and that approach would help unify the country.

*   *   *

The President launched his Presidency by holding his first Press conference on Friday January 23rd. He began by stating that he would be addressing the Nation on Thursday evening January 29th to outline his legislative program for the year. Continuing on in a very matter of fact fashion, the President announced that by Presidential proclamation he was lifting the ban on Stem Cell research. He added that the White House would release plans on an initiative that would be administered through the National Institutes of Health to move rapidly into Stem Cell research.

With his second Presidential proclamation, President DeFrie lifted the ban on travel to Cuba. This came as a total surprise to everyone including most of the President's cabinet. Following his announcement, the President explained that our policy to Cuba – 'with all due respect to the Cuban American community' - was actually 'silly'. He added that 50 years of trying to bring Fidel Castro down with this ban hasn't worked. He quipped that even though we now have Fidel's brother, Raul Castro, leading Cuba, one or both of the Castro brothers would probably outlive him. It was time to try something new.

American tourism he asserted would bring the 'incurable viruses of capitalism to Cuba. In time he predicted that Cuba would evolve to a socialist-capitalist state much like many European countries. Those assembled – journalists and White House staffers – experienced a combination of amusement and chagrin. The President was right on the money. They all knew that US policy had failed. It was, indeed, silly. And, why had no one said that before?

The President's third announcement dealt with China. Chinese Premier Wen Jaibao had agreed to adjust the value of the renminbi relative to the dollar. Beginning mid February the renminbi would be valued at six to the dollar. By June it would be valued at five renminbi to the dollar, and by end of summer the Premier had agreed to let the Chinese currency float. The President was not certain Wen Jaibao would truly let Chinese currency float, but he would wait and see.

The first two planned currency adjustment would have two major affects on the American economy. First it would make American workers more competitive. Secondly, it would substantially reduce America's debt to China. In reaching this agreement, President DeFrie created a win-win situation for both parties. The American economy would get a large boost, and American resources and technology would be made more readily available to China to help them modernize and expand their economy. President DeFrie had also promised to send 12,000 of his new Peace Corps volunteers – teachers and recent engineering graduates – to rural parts of China just as soon as that program was up and running.

Following the President's prepared messages, there was a lively question and answer period with the White House Press Corps. From the tone of the questioning it was apparent the Press Corps was favorably impressed by this new comer to the Washington scene.

*   *   *

On Thursday, January 29th at 9:30 pm Eastern Standard Time, President Maynard J. DeFrie addressed the Nation from the Oval Office for the first time. In his message, he would lay out an ambitious legislative program for his first year in office. He was to also employ his strategy of giving immediate relief to a long suffering public and in return looking for their support.

After a few brief comments about the fact that less than 39% of the voters 'pulled the lever' for him and that nearly 80%

of the public believed the country was heading down the wrong path, the President stated, "I believe that the election is far enough behind us that we can put partisan politics behind us and begin pulling together. Tonight I lay out programs that I feel strongly will put the Nation on the right path. I will do all that I can to convince you that this path is the right path; the path that will initially benefit most Americans. And, I believe it is this path that in time will benefit all Americans, because even those who will initially oppose these changes will realize it is the right thing to do for their country and for themselves." Pausing, the President continued, "I cannot do that alone. I need all of your help and involvement to move forward."

"It has become apparent to everyone that we have a broken economy. While that goes on, there are many individuals and entities that are bilking the system for all that it is worth. We are becoming a country of the rich and the poor. We are losing our middle class; the very strength of the country in both economic and creative terms. We need to reverse that. And, we need to begin tonight!"

"There is a bill languishing in congress referred to as 'the close the Enron Loophole bill'. That bill which needs to be reviewed and strengthened, and passed quickly deals with regulating energy futures trading – an issue about which most Americans know little. Simply put, the current laws allow speculators to drive up the price of energy. And, that, my fellow citizens, is what has been happening since 2000 when certain regulatory statues were removed."

"Just by making that one simple change, we can lower the cost of a barrel of oil by 25%. That translates into reducing the average current cost of a gallon of regular gasoline to $3.20 from our national average which today is $4.95. To the average American that amounts to a savings of over $25 per week. To a lot of families that is not a lot of money. To a lot of families $4.95 per gallon is also not a lot of money. Unfortunately, to too many other American families, who are struggling both are a huge sum of money. Sad to say, but many people have to feed a family on $25 a week."

"That represents a small beginning on what is a very large problem in this country – energy and energy costs. Tonight I announce that Dr. James Taliaferro, Secretary of the Department of Energy, has formed a Commission that will design a Manhattan Project the goal of which will be to convert sun light into electrical energy. We will complete the development of that technology in 24 months. We plan to have commercial production up and running within 36 months. That is an ambitious goal, but this is an urgent issue!"

"Dr. Taliaferro whom most of you know has taken leave from the faculty of Massachusetts Institute of Technology to serve this government is trained as a physicist as well as a biochemist. He and his colleagues have for several years been doing seminal experiments in using biochemical systems, such as photosynthesis, to create and capture electrical energy."

"Starting back in mid November, Dr. Taliaferro assembled an elite and diverse group of scientists from MIT, Cal Tech, the Carnegie-Mellon Institute, Pennsylvania State University, Michigan State University and the University of Chicago who have been busily laying out parallel programs for achieving this important goal. Part of their efforts will also be devoted to recommending and laying the groundwork for programs to further develop the use of systems that use fossil fuels – coal, oil – in ways that release no carbon dioxide into our atmosphere."

Pausing for a moment, the President reached over to the right side of his desk and retrieved a framed photograph which he held up for the TV camera. To many viewers the two men in the picture were immediately recognizable. They were Thomas Edison and Henry Ford, two American inventive geniuses. This photograph of Edison and Ford taken sometime in the 1920's showed them standing in front of Edison's workshop in Fort Meyers Beach, Florida where both men had winter estates.

After describing the picture, President DeFrie said, "During my initial meetings with Dr. Taliaferro I learned that his mother was the grand daughter of Thomas Edison. I was struck by what an appropriate choice we had made for the leadership of this project. I also learned from Dr. Taliaferro that Thomas Edison and Henry Ford, who were great friends, had spent a very significant amount of their own monies in an effort to develop the electric car and battery technology. Parenthetically, that effort apparently either failed, or it might have been sabotaged."

"And, to further amaze me, Dr. Taliaferro showed me a copy of a handwritten letter Ford had written to Edison on their commitment to this project, and I quote 'of ridding the streets of the noxious gases of the internal combustion engine'. Before another 80 years passes, we, as a country, need to dedicate ourselves to that concept. And, we will. We will create programs and incentives that result in major investments in hybrid engine technology and electric cars of the future. "

Laying the photograph of Edison and Ford down, the President stated that next to the public's suffering from energy costs and the potential consequences of global climate change by the use of fossil fuels, the country is experiencing severe income inequality. He exclaimed, "We are losing the Middle Class! And, we cannot do that and preserve our democracy!"

The President picked up a chart and placed it on an easel so that it could be viewed. The title on the chart read "Tax Reform for Restoring the Middle Class". Under the title was a subtitle that read "Marginal Tax Rate Schedule". The first column was headed "percent tax owed". The second column was headed "Income Ranges or Income brackets". The President made it clear that this table referred to taxable wages or income – total wages or income from which all deductibles had been subtracted. Pointing to each percent in the "percent tax owed" column, the President stated that for all incomes brackets below $128,000 per year the income tax percent would be half of the amount paid in 2007.

President DeFrie gave an example of a family of five earning total wages of $120,000 which would result in $100,000 of taxable income after all deductions were taken. Using his chart and a white board to make some calculations he showed their taxes would be $9,100. In 2007 it was $17,650.

He did two more examples. For a family of four with a taxable income of $35,000 after taking all possible deductions, they would pay $2,200 in taxes which is one half of the $4,400 they paid in 2007. Similarly, a family with $85,000 in taxable income would pay $7,150 in taxes compared with $14,100 in 2007.

The President went on to explain on incomes between $195,000 and $350,000 the Marginal Tax Rates are very similar to what they are now. He stated what had been added were marginal rates for income above $500,000, above $750,000, above $1,000,000 and finally for all taxable income over $2,000,000. The marginal rates corresponding to these new brackets would be 40, 44, 47 and 55%, respectively.

Related to extending marginal brackets to higher income levels, the President stated that Social Security Taxes would no long be capped on the first $120,000 of income but would be on total income. The tax would, however, above $120,000 be half the rate that employers, employees and self employed individuals currently pay.

The President added that his plan would keep Capital Gains Tax at the current 15%. He added that for investments in 'clean energy' such as coal to electricity with the trapping of all Green house gases, he is proposing a 5% Capital Gains Rate. While President DeFrie was on the subject of Capital Gains, he stated he would push hard to close the loophole on Hedge Fund managers who were being allowed to treat ordinary income as Capital Gains.

The President next took aim at Medicare Part D – the prescription drug plan that had become a boondoggle for the Pharmaceutical Industry and a huge cost to the American taxpayer. Holding up a chart entitled "Something is wrong with these Numbers". In the first column of the chart was a list of 12 commonly prescribed medicines. In the second column was listed the cost to Medicare patients for one months supply of each drug. In the third column was a list of what the Veterans Administration (VA) charges. The fourth column listed the cost to Canadians and the last column the price COSTCO – one of the membership warehouse chains – charges its customers.

Using his pointer and looking very professorial, the President stated that for each drug, the VA charges veterans half of what Medicare Part D recipients pay. Using his chart, he next pointed out that the VA and Canadian costs were comparable. And, expressing some degree of feigned surprise, the President pointing first to the Medicare Column cost and next to the COSTCO column showed that it was actually a few dollars cheaper to buy your drugs at COSTCO! Playing on the later revelation, the President exclaimed, "Isn't it amazing, that the Government would save considerable money by sending our Medicare Part D recipients to COSTCO? And, COSTCO is a 'for profit' company!"

The President stated that he would be proposing some major changes to the Medicare drug program. His first goal was to give the Government the same bargaining power for buying drugs from the Pharmaceutical industry in its Medicare program as the VA system has in their drug program. He further stated that with that savings alone not only would the premiums that senior pay for this insurance be reduced substantially, the so called 'doughnut' –Medicare Part D recipients who have received $2200 in benefits need to pay the next $1400 out of pocket before coverage resumes - could be eliminated.

When the President had covered his energy program and reforms on taxes and the Medicare Drug program, he announced that one week from this night he would be addressing the nation again. He would be joined by Vice President Christianson who had been tasked with developing a Universal Health Care Program. The President briefly stated they were considering two plans. In one plan Medicare would be extended to all Americans.

Alternatively, the Administration might copy the German Universal health care plan where private insurance companies administer the program on a non profit basis. The President stated that in Germany in return for that no profit participation which covers a very large part of the insurance companies' fixed costs, those companies get to offer 'deluxe' health care coverage to individuals who want, and can afford premier coverage. He anticipated that the Universal Health Plan would reduce the amount of monies paid by employers and employees for health care by one half.

The President added that he would report on a plan being developed by his military Joint Chief of Staffs on withdrawal from Iraq. He was candid in stating that he had come to realize that immediate withdrawal from Iraq would leave billions of dollars of equipment and weaponry behind. He had no intention of leaving the tools of war behind so that they could be used by that small part of the Muslim world – the Jihadists – to carry on their war with the more modern and moderate Muslims as well as against the Christians and the Jews. Accordingly, the President ordered his Generals to draw up a plan for exiting Iraq in an orderly fashion, leaving nothing behind and doing that in such a way that no American troops are placed in peril.

Lastly, the President stated that his Secretary of Defense would be presenting in the weeks to come a staged reduction of the defense budget from the current 525 billion per year to just over 400 billion. "This will be accomplished over a two year period. The country can ill afford to be feeding the gigantic military-industrial complex as we have been doing. We have become the tail wagged by our own watch dog! That can not be! And, the Secretary informs me we can make these reductions without placing our country in peril, while treating our own soldiers better than is their current condition."

*   *   *

It is traditional for Congress and the Press to give an incoming President the opportunity of three months or 100 days to implement his initiatives. This so called 'Honey Moon' period in President DeFrie's case would be most unusual. In the first place, Congress was not at all prepared for the President to attempt this 'running start'. Some were even annoyed that he would dare attempt it; "who does this is character think he is?"

It was clear that Congress' planned strategy well before he took office was simply to ignore the President. After all, he was a third party candidate with no base. Furthermore, most of the legislature thought the programs he had announced did not stand a 'snow balls chance in hell' – to quote one Senator – of getting to the floor. There were powerful lobbies waiting to pounce on every single one of his initiatives. Some even joked that he would be the first President to never have signed a piece of legislation.

President DeFrie understood the game Congress was playing against him and ultimately against the people. And he realized that they were playing it in concert with their lobby associates. To the extent that he could without being rude he ignored Congress and continued his communication with the public through his press conferences, his policy speeches, and his electronic communication. He was confident that the earthquake of e-mails and letters he anticipated Congress would receive from his constituents would win the day. He was also confident that the common senses solutions he was making and offering would wake the country up.

President DeFrie was anxious to get through this period of gaining Congress' trust as there was much to be done, and much to be undone.

In the weeks to come, the President began to execute on what he considered a vital foreign policy issue – peace between Israel and Palestine. He had been forthright during his campaign about his belief that terrorism was directly linked to the Palestinian-Israeli conflict, as has been stated in the Hamilton Report. He further believed the US has been pouring 'fuel on the fire' and 'salt on the wounds' in this conflict by its long term one sided allegiance to Israel. He was determined to be even handed. This message had not played well for the President among many American Jews as evidenced by the November election results in areas of the country with large Jewish populations. None-the-less, the President believed it was in Israel's best interests to make peace rather than acquisition of real estate.

To assist his efforts within the Jewish community, the President had lined up nearly a dozen prominent Israelis who believed as he did that the current living condition of the Palestinians as well as current policy only enrages and foments hatred. During the months of April and May, he and three or four of his 'foreign guests' conducted town hall type meetings around the country to gain support for his efforts. They were received politely and fielded many difficult questions. In spite of these efforts, the President was not sure he had made any headway. None-the-less, his openness and his lack of pandering to this community seemed to have gained him respect. This was a dialogue that had never occurred before. Many admired him for that.

Once the President believed he had 'his ducks in order,' he began pressuring the Israeli government to begin abandoning West Bank settlements, to begin establishing reasonable boundaries for the 'state' of Palestine and to negotiate in good faith a peace. He also insisted that there be a Middle East summit that would be organized by Israel, Saudi Arabia an Iran. It was not the President's intention to put himself or the US in the middle of these negotiations. He knew well that the four billion dollar annual carrot that Israel relied on from the US would be sufficient to get compliance.

As summer approached, President DeFrie was pleased with his initiatives. It had become clear that he was gaining the confidence and support of the American public who were now helping him put pressure on the Congress to adopt his progressive agenda. The President was also getting high marks in Europe and the rest of the world. Americans who had been abroad since the

Inauguration could sense the change in attitude 'foreigners' had for them. It was reminiscent of the goodwill the rest of the world had for Americans when Presidents like Truman, Eisenhower, Kennedy, Reagan, Bush I and Clinton were in office. A major change!

President DeFrie also knew that in his first four months in office that he had 'ruffled a few feathers'. He was convinced that even those who were initially opposed to his changes, and who might be economically affected, would in time see the wisdom of going down the road he was taking the country. He believed that patriotism, the realization that a capitalistic system that works for the good of all and a country united in spirit and in purpose would win his opponents over.

Chapter VIII

The first seven months of President DeFrie's first term seemed to fly by. On the Wednesday after Labor Day, with nearly all of the President's initiatives moving forward in high gear – in the President's Universal Service program, as one example, 7 million high school seniors were already enlisted, eight closed bases were fully operational – Vice President Christianson suggested to the President that they play 'hooky' for the afternoon. Christianson's plan was that they 'sneak' out of the White House with two Secret Service men – who would be in casual dress – and journey to a rib place he knew of that was not too far from an exit of the Baltimore-Washington Parkway. The President accepted the invitation, and agreed to don a Baltimore Oriole's cap and a Washington Redskin jersey along with an unpressed pair of old shorts. The object was to look casual – something that eerily reminded the President of his attempt to 'sneak' into the Columbia University, New York City debate.

Fortunately for these two petty miscreants they did not arrive at the rib place – the Owl – until well after the lunch hour rush by which time most of the patrons had gone back to work. Additionally, one had to be an Owl to see in this place – the lighting was awful. Seating themselves at a rear corner table, the two most powerful men in the Universe were well concealed. Well concealed enough to finish off a total of three racks of ribs and six beers without being recognized.

Rod Christianson had developed a great deal of admiration and affection for the President during this very intense one year of their partnership. His feelings for the President were equal to those he had for his own brother which he had always described as a very close relationship – twins, he would say, with different ages. Furthermore, he had come to the realization that even though he had had a very favorable impression of the President, when he agreed to be his running mate, he had still grossly underestimated the man.

The Vice President had accumulated in this year abundant evidence that Maynard DeFrie was a giant among men, and was no doubt the most brilliant, strategic and clear thinker he had ever known. The Vice President never ceased to be amazed at how humble and modest the President could be, yet he could be a charging bull when that was required. At first Christianson thought that was a contradiction; he never realized that humans came from such complex molds. Christianson also understood that by his association with the President he would become an important part of history. He knew well that he was serving along side greatness, and he realized that Americans as well as the rest of the world were coming to the same conclusion.

When Christianson sensed the President was relaxed enough to speak on personal terms, he revealed to the President that he was concerned about the pace the President was keeping. He also stated that the President had kept a horrendous schedule well before their coming together. He reminded the President that to his knowledge he had not taken a single day of rest for more than a year. Christianson, with apologies for being 'preachy' told the President that he needed to be concerned about his health, and that he owed it to the public to take care of himself.

President DeFrie was touched by Christianson's remarks. Even though they had never spoken on a personal level, the

President had always felt a good deal of affection for the Vice President and regarded him as a very close friend. The President was also moved because he never remembered anyone with the exception of his grandmother and mother being concerned about his physical being. He confessed to the Vice President that this was the first occasion in years that he had allowed himself to indulge in relaxation – however short this occasion was, and he was enjoying it. He added that he had on more than one occasion thought of how he was abusing his body, but he regarded himself as a work horse that was up to the task. He said he often thought of St. Francis who was relentless on his own body.

Having said all of that, the President asked Christianson for suggestions. Vice President Christianson was well prepared. He had a list. It consisted of events that would take the President out of Washington, D.C. – where he had made himself a working prisoner – and give the President the opportunity to enjoy interacting with the public. He knew the President would like that idea. He knew that if the President could accomplish something useful such as cementing his bond with his countrymen and being the most forceful advocate for his programs, he would buy into the idea.

On the return trip to the White House, the Vice President enumerated his suggested list which contained one event per month outside of Washington, D.C. for the next 9 months. On the list were visits to each of the service academies where the President would have the opportunity of speaking on any one of his many policies.

Christianson believed the President should pay particular attention to the medical community. He needed them, and he needed their dedication to make his Universal Health plan work. He suggested addresses at the annual meetings of American Medical Association, the American Society of Hematologists, and the American Cancer Society. Christianson thought it would be in the administrations best interests if the President addressed one of the major conferences of the Pharmaceutical Industry.

These were meetings which typically draw 12,000 to 20,000 attendees. The President was receptive to these ideas.

When they returned to the White House which was about 5 pm, the President suggested that he and Christianson have a light dinner brought into the Oval Office so that they could continue their conversation. Over dinner, Christianson said that he had one other suggestion for a Presidential visit, but had been reluctant to share it with the President because the audience he had in mind would not be old enough to vote in the President's reelection. President DeFrie was curious and prompted Christianson to amplify.

The Vice President explained that his older brother had talked about the 'seminal' event of his life on numerous occasions. That event which had taken place more than 50 years ago was an address given by President Dwight D. Eisenhower at the Waldorf Astoria to a group of high school seniors. The Vice President's brother, Michael Christianson, whom the President had met, had attended in 1952 a conference of high school newspaper Editors that was sponsored by Columbia University. Eisenhower had spoken at the Award's luncheon. That event crystallized for Michael Christianson the entire concept of service to country and altered the course of his life. Rather than follow his father's and grandfather's footsteps into Medicine, Michael decided he would teach.

The President had not known why Michael entered the field of education – Michael Christianson who held a PhD in education had recently retired as Superintendent of Schools in West Chester County, north of New York City. He found Rod Christianson's story and his request interesting. However, as he was listening a red flag went up. His Columbia experience was a very unpleasant one. He recalled vividly the Pro Israel Columbia students charging down the steps of Low Library 'intent on skewering him with their flag poles.' The President refreshed Christianson's memory concerning that horrible event, and the fact that it had only occurred less than one year ago.

The Vice President was amused. He mentioned that President Eisenhower would not, on the occasion his brother Michael always referred to, visit the Columbia campus either. That's why the luncheon was held at the Waldorf. Apparently the President had forgotten that Dwight Eisenhower had been President of Columbia University prior to becoming President of the country. He apparently did not know that Eisenhower didn't exactly enjoy the Columbia faculty and was 'happy to get the hell out of that place.'

Christianson shared with the President that for the most part Eisenhower only interacted and enjoyed the company of one faculty member when he was at Columbia. That happened to be the football coach, Lou Little. Little, a brilliant individual in his own right, was regarded as the Dean of American College coaches in the 50's and had become friends with Eisenhower when Little coached at Georgetown.

*   *   *

In the weeks following Vice President Christianson's suggestions the President's schedule of visits began to gel. It had become clear that any appearances at one of the major medical or pharmaceutical meetings needed to be arranged at least six months in advance. Consequently, those events were pushed back in the scheduling. Since the President was the Commander in Chief of the Armed forces scheduling visits at the Service Academies was a matter of informing the respective Commandants when the President was coming.

Accordingly, the President would visit the Military Academy at West Point on Veterans Day on November 11th. On that occasion he would speak on the progress and the implementation of his Middle East Foreign Policy. On the second weekend of December, the President would visit the Air Force Academy in Colorado Springs on the occasion of the Academy's Dean's Weekend. He would be speaking on his Universal Service Program and its integration with the Service Academies.

On Monday January 18th of the New Year, the President would visit the US Naval Academy in Annapolis, Maryland. He would use this occasion – Martin Luther King, Jr. Day – to speak on immigration issues. That would include progress on the border fence between Mexico and the US, progress on the government's program of returning recent illegal immigrants to their home countries, and an update on recently implemented programs for those illegal immigrants who qualified to be placed on the path to citizenship.

In spite of all the efforts of Michael Christianson, the Vice Presidents older brother, and of Michael's close friend Chuck O'Connor, who was the Director of the Columbia Scholastic Press group, the Columbia event was becoming impossible to schedule. In part that was because O'Connor was attempting to 'push' the President to speak in March. That traditionally is when his organization has their spring conference – typically around St. Patrick's Day. The President's scheduling people wanted to keep March, April and May open for some of the major Medical Meetings.

In the final analysis O'Connor reluctantly agreed – even though this would be the biggest day of his life – to move his conference to a date in February. The luncheon address would be on Thursday afternoon February 18th in the Grand Ballroom of the New York Hilton Hotel adjacent to Radio City in the heart of downtown. The President would be addressing 4200 high school 'journalists' – 3000 of them in the main ballroom, the remainder in satellite ballrooms.

As was his style, President DeFrie was already planning productive and pleasurable events he could incorporate into these scheduled visits. The President had accumulated many good friends and admirers during his campaign and in this first year of his term. He would be calling them.

*   *   *

The New Year's Eve ushering in 2010 was a time most of the country was looking forward to. In the first place the Eve occurred on a Thursday. That meant everyone had Friday, New Year's Day as a holiday, and for many of them it would mean they would have two more days to recover. For many others it would be two more days to just relax and enjoy the season.

Relaxation for a good portion of the country became more the order of the day than a matter of choice. About one half hour into the New Year the north east coast, the Midwest and almost the entire west coast got walloped by three different storm systems. One storm which headed north up the east coast from Richmond, Virginia left Washingtonians with 11 inches of snow, gusting winds up to 24 miles per hour and temperature in the high teens. Farther north, in Philadelphia, New York City and Boston 18, 22 and 34 inches of snow was reported, respectively. It was fortunate that there were three days for highway departments around the country to deal with the paralysis that had engulfed most the country. They needed all that time to dig out.

But the country was also looking forward to this long New Year's break for different reasons. The country needed a break! Within the last 15 months there were so many changes that had taken place the country needed time to equilibrate. In reality, a three day weekend might hardly be enough time to accomplish that, but that is all the calendar allowed. The list of changes and their magnitude was huge. The first was becoming accustomed to the first Black President of the United States.

Added to that was a new Foreign Policy in the Middle East that seemed to be bearing fruit, a Universal Health care system that would be completely staged in by the end of the year, a major redo and restructuring of the Medicare Drug plan that would in 10 months be made available to all citizens, the President's Universal Service program, a major restructuring of the tax system that very high wage earners had bought into because they had been convinced it was in the best interests of the country, a significant reduction in the Country's deficit and a closing of the dollar drain to China, new federally mandated mileage standards, major federal invests into energy technology (coal liquefaction, atomic energy) along with the President's Manhattan Project - bio conversion of sun light to electricity- and nearly 200 federally funded major construction projects relating to infrastructure in the planning stages around the country. The projects required states to match 20% of Federal dollars.

In an ABC poll taken in the first week of the New Year, the Presidents approval rating was well above 80%. Having started at 41% from a poll released the day following the President's inauguration, the President and his Cabinet had every reason to believe that most Americans were behind them. At the Monday, the 11th of January, Cabinet meeting that followed the release of the ABC results, the President wanted his colleagues to help him prioritize for the New Year. He wanted to focus on his initiatives that were either lagging or had not been introduced to the Congress.

True to the President's desire to have courageous and independent thinkers in his administration, the President was told very bluntly by the Secretary of State that there is a limit to the amount of change that any country can take. He asserted that the American Public needed time to get used to those changes they had already been made. He also cautioned that if some new program is introduced, and if, for some odd reason, it becomes a bust, it will cause those programs that are working to be questioned. 'That's how humans think' the Secretary asserted. The President had not expected such a response, but wanted to hear more.

He did. His Secretary of Defense echoed the entire sentiment of his State Department colleague. However, he added an entirely different twist. As someone who knew how combatants think, he believed this Administration would be naïve and foolish to think that those they have 'pissed off' – his words – were going to give up. The President he claimed had challenged some huge egos – well resourced huge egos – who do not like to lose as a matter of pride. He added, "These folks are very capable of being very vindictive. They are very powerful people and they love their power. And, their greed and lack of concern for people other than their own ilk far often exceeds their patriotism!"

He asserted that this Administration would be foolish to underestimate the financial and human resources that the 'money guys' on Wall Street, the Automobile Industry, the Military suppliers and their cronies in the Pentagon, the Petroleum Industry, the Pharmaceutical Industry and the Insurance firms could muster against them. He added, "Those guys probably control 90% of the wealth and power of this country."

The Secretary of Defense stated that he was certain that at this very minute at least one of them is plotting a strategy to undermine all that the President had accomplished. "And, most certainly, they are working to see that you are not re-elected," he told the President. His last words were "God forbid that even two or three of them team up on us!"

The President had not anticipated his Secretary of Defense's line of thinking even though he knew in his heart that you have to kill a snake otherwise it will always come back and inject you with its venom. He also understood his Secretary of State's warning on making too many changes. As the Cabinet discussion matured it had became clear that the President's entire cabinet was of the same mind. The general thinking was - slow the pace of change down and keep your eyes on the forces you have offended. In a light hearted moment, the President asked, "Ok, so what do we do now? Do we all take a vacation? Or do we go to the mattresses, like they do in the gangster movies?"

Chuckling, Vice President Christianson's response to that was 'not quite' for each case in question. Christianson stated that everyone present had to be on guard to the forces the Secretary of Defense mentioned. Interrupting, politely, the President stated that the Vice President, the Secretaries of State and Defense needed to huddle with him and attempt to anticipate what might be coming.

To the Presidents' question regarding 'taking a vacation', Christianson stated that the President should continue those of his visits out of DC that were already planned, and that he should be thinking about various Summit meetings out of the country.

Taking the liberty of moving the conversation to a light hearted moment, Christianson quipped that many of our former Presidents like to fish. Christianson spent a lot of time bone fishing down at Isle of Morada, in the Florida Keys. He mentioned that on two occasions when he was in the Keys, he had run into the first President Bush who was an avid sport fisherman.

The Vice President knew that if he tossed in that tidbit he would entice the President even further. He knew that the President liked and admired 'Bush-One', as he would call him. He also knew that the President thought the Republicans had treated him badly. After the Vice President had 'set the trap', he was emphatic about taking the President with him on his next trip.

The Cabinet meeting ended with the consensus that for the next 6 months the area of concentration would be on those programs that had already been instituted. They would monitor those programs carefully and make any adjustments that needed to be made. The President would continue his visits and begin planning for one or more Summit meetings.

The group appointed by the President would sit down with him, ASAP, and try to determine what strategies those groups whose economic interests the President's programs had affected negatively might come up with. They needed to be ready with a defense, and if possible a preemptive offense.

*   *   *

Even though it was not his nature to lie back until a job was thoroughly completed, the President was not unhappy with the Cabinet discussion and with their recommendations. He could see the wisdom in what they were saying about pushing forward too rapidly. In addition, the thought of some fishing, something he had not done since his boyhood on the Mississippi, was an attractive one, for two reasons that jumped into his head almost immediately.

First he had never been to the Florida Keys and the temptation of sport fishing plus visiting Harry Truman's modest retreat in Key West – one of those many facts that the President had filed in his head - was appealing. Secondly, ever since the New Year the weather in Washington had been absolutely dismal – cold, damp and gray overcast skies. A little sunshine along with the fishing would be a welcomed blessing.

There were other factors that were at work in the President's mind which made the thought of more time out of the White House appealing. The President had thoroughly enjoyed his visits to West Point in November and to the Air Force Academy in early December. He was totally impressed by the Cadets at each Academy. To him they represented the very best America could produce. They were intelligent, enthusiastic. And "just plain nice bright kids", the President had said on innumerable occasions.

With these successful visits under his belt and his better understanding of the fact that leadership demands interaction with those who are to be led, the President was now looking forward to his upcoming visit to the Naval Academy on Martin Luther King, Jr. day, and to his visit to New York City where he would address the high school journalists.

He also was looking to the bone fishing trip to Isle of Morada that the Vice President had 'insisted on'. That would take place on the last weekend in January, and it would be a three day weekend. The President was boyishly gleeful about that. The last time he had fished that he could remember was when he was 13 years old.

*   *   *

The month of January flew by rapidly. That was a puzzle to the President because in the beginning of February, he had actually referred to January as one of the least productive period in his entire life. He remembered one exception – the two weeks he spent just before graduating from high school lying in the Metairie Hospital recovering from a burst appendix. But where had all the time gone? And, what did he have to show for it?

In reality, President DeFrie had actually accomplished more than enough. Certainly it would have satisfied any normal individual. In addition to a small bout with a very 'pesky' flu that flattened the President for a good part of the second week of the January, he had spent almost an entire afternoon at the Naval Academy starting with lunch at 1 pm in King Hall in the company of nearly 4000 midshipmen, touring the facility in the afternoon and that evening after dinner with the Commandant and Academy faculty he gave his address in Mahan Hall on the Illegal Immigration issue He had also taken his fishing trip with Vice President Christianson to the Florida Keys, and in between that and the Academy visit the President managed to squeeze in his first State of the Union address.

Considering, in addition to all of his other accomplish in that month, that the President wrote all of his speeches, and was meticulous in his wording and in expressing his thoughts so that they were of the utmost clarity, he had more than earned his keep, and the congress and the public knew that and appreciated him. He had good reason to believe that also.

When the President entered the House Chamber to give his State of the Union, Senators and Congressmen from both sides of the aisle struggled to get close enough just to touch him. The applause upon his introduction by the Speaker of the House was a tumultuous standing ovation that never seemed to end. And there was no response to his address by the opposition – Democrat or Republican – just praise in interviews by Senators and Representatives from both parties.. The nation was finally speaking with one voice.

In the President's State of the Union, he covered his plans to reinforce the McCain Feingold law on campaign financing, particularly the dirty business of '527 ads. The President could not see how giving the public the responsibility to determine which lies to believe served democracy. It absolutely confounded him that in addition to telling lies, the 'liars' could remain anonymous. Given the bipartisan behavior of Congress over the past year, the President was confident that he could get reason to prevail. President DeFrie also announced several other initiatives. Among them he was asking the National Institute of Health to undertake a critical study regarding the foods Americans eat. He wanted to know if 'we were hormoning ourselves to death?'

*   *   *

The President's visit to New York City for the February 18th event where he would address the high school journalists who would be attending the Columbia conference presented a number of major security challenges. Unlike his visits to the Service Academies where security was a matter of course, and, for the most part, a relatively small issue, a visit to the New York metropolitan area where some 10 million or more individuals are moving about each day in a totally unregulated environment is an entirely different matter. By comparison with the Academy visits it could be a nightmare.

After one year in office, the President had become accustomed to the Secret Service and to having at least one pair of agents following him around 'like he was Pied Piper' 24 hrs a day. He could not quite understand how he was not even allowed to walk more than 15 feet within the White House without being 'tailed'. None-the-less, he had taken a liking to the Agents who were protecting him and on more than one occasion teased them about their insistence on precise and exact adherence to Secret Service protocols. His protectors were so well trained and such dedicated professionals that they would never even crack a smile when the President 'acted up', as they called it. Any lapse in their concentration could result in consequences that would reverberate throughout the entire world. They understood that and accepted that responsibility.

The first real security issue that the President had to deal with outside of the White House was on his Florida Keys fishing trip. It was complicated by the fact that both he and his Vice President would be needing security, and they would be in the same place at the same time. The Secret Service was not at all happy with that event, and, indeed, had tried vigorously to persuade the President to consider an alternative plan. The president had no intention of being overruled.

When one of the Agents presented the argument that Isle of Morada was no more than 70 miles from Cuba. The President responded that in that regard they had nothing to worry about. In fact he stated "The Castro boys wouldn't think of shooting me. They have accumulated so many American dollars by my lifting the travel ban that I am a valuable asset to them. They are after all pretty bright fellows. In fact, we should tell them I am coming so that they can send some bodyguards to protect me!"

*   *   *

The expense that the Government incurs to provide security to the President, Vice President and their families along with all the expense for the former ones, was something that troubled President DeFrie. He was confident that you could 'feed all the starving people in the world just with half of the money we spend'. He sincerely believed that a good part of the security effort was unnecessary. He also believed that the Secret Service significantly overplayed the potential of threats as a means of keeping their agents mentally alert.

Despite his feelings the Secret Service was totally intent on doing its job. They knew from experience and from their training that there are just too many 'nuts' – home grown and foreign - walking the streets in this country to be cavalier about Presidential security. Even though the terrorists had quieted down in the past one year, the Secret Service always had to be concerned about the possibility that some terrorist would be willing to become a suicide bomber, might launch a shoulder held missile, or might come up with some other means to take out the President. Agents are trained to play a game called 'you are the assassin.' The object of the game? Acting alone or in concert with others, figure out how to breach the security blanket. Where are the holes? As a group the Secret Service all use the expressions 'beware the calm before the storm - And expect the unexpected.' They would take no chances no matter what the threat level.

Accordingly 10 days before the President and his entourage would be leaving for New York City, two pints of blood were drawn from the President – just in case - and couriered to the emergency services at Lennox Hill Hospital which is located at 77th street and Lexington Ave on the upper East side of the city. That would place the emergency room at Lennox 25 blocks north of the Hilton and a few avenues east.

When the President learned that his blood was to be drawn and sent to Lennox Hill, he was moderately uncomfortable with the idea. But as a way of changing the subject, he mentioned that he seemed to recall vaguely reading in a biography of Winston Churchill, that Churchill had been treated at Lennox Hill Hospital for a fall he had taken. The President gave a little wink to the Secret Service Agents who were briefing him on the details of his itinerary and stated that at the least his blood, or 'worst case' he and his blood would be in good company.

On the occasion of Winston Churchill's visit to Lennox Hill Hospital, he had actually been hit by a car crossing a New York City street.

The plan for getting the President to New York City would be to use 'Marine One' the President's helicopter to take him and the First Lady from the White House to Andrews Air force base in Suitland, Maryland where the Presidential planes are kept. From there they would take Air Force One to John F. Kennedy Airport out on Long Island.

From Kennedy they would motorcade north on the Van Wyck Expressway to the Long Island Expressway heading west through the Queens Midtown Tunnel to 34th Street in Manhattan.

At 6th Avenue, the Avenue of the Americas, the motorcade would head north to 53rd Street and enter the Hilton through the service entrance and make their way to the Grand Ballroom via a service elevator.

The Secret Service would not announce any aspect of the President's route thinking that the more logical route would be to land at La Guardia and motorcade from there. Additionally, New York City police who would be leading the motorcade on motorcycles and in patrol cars would be on alert, but they would not be told where they were meeting the motorcade until Air Force One was making its final approach. That information would be transmitted to them on a secure land based telephone line. The latter measures were believed to add some degree of security no matter how small that might be.

The First Lady who would not be attending the Columbia function, but instead would be having lunch at a private residence on Park Avenue and spending the afternoon shopping with her hostess was to be put in a separate vehicle with security detail at Kennedy. She would be taken to her destination which the Secret Service would have already secured. Mrs. DeFrie would be meeting the President in the evening for a dinner private party that Larry King would be hosting for them. King had tantalized the President with the notion that two of the President's favorite actresses who counted themselves among his admirers might be present. The President was looking forward to that.

On February 16th a contingent of the Secret Service was sent to the New York Hilton. In concert with the Manhattan Bureau of the FBI they would secure every aspect of the Hotel and the surrounding areas. Bomb sniffing dogs were used to sweep the area on the 17th and again on the morning of the 18th. The President's motorcade was expected to arrive 15 minutes before 1 pm.

*   *   *

Air Force One lifted off from Andrews Air Force base at 9:47 a.m. on February 18th. The outside temperature was a crisp 18 degrees. The sky was absolutely clear and blue along the entire eastern seaboard. At the President's insistence Air Force One approached New York City by flying directly over the Verrazano-Narrows Bridge at 12,000 feet and up the Hudson River to the George Washington Bridge. From there the plane headed east and south making its way to Kennedy.

The views of the bridges, the Statue of Liberty, the skyscrapers of New York City and the high rise buildings along the New Jersey side of the Hudson were spectacular. The President seated in the Co-pilot's seat was absolutely delighted. He remembered vividly his first visits to the City where the only views he could afford were those seen on foot. Or those that could be seen from the Staten Island Ferry which at that time cost one nickel – well within his budget.

By whatever means they learned – maybe it was just by looking up into the clear blue sky – thousands of New Yorkers, and particularly those living in the boroughs of Brooklyn and Queens realized that Air Force One would be landing at Kennedy. As the Presidential motorcade made its way into the City, cars lined the shoulders of the Van Wyck Expressway and the Long Island Expressway. Many of the occupants leaned on their horns as the Presidential motorcade sped by at 60 mph, others stood on the hoods of their cars or stood on the sills of their car doors waving furiously. It was a very unusual site for a populous not known for outgoing behavior, a populous that had honed non expressive behavior to its ultimate.

At 1:30 pm in the Grand Ballroom of the Hilton New York, Chuck O'Connor, Director of the Columbia Scholastic Press group climbed the three steps onto the Ballroom stage and made his way to the lectern. O'Connor was a crusty old guy in his late 60's who had spent his entire life at Columbia. He did that first as a student and then as an assistant to the founder and Director of the Scholastic Press, a Colonel Joseph Murphy, a crusty old character in his own right. O'Connor had become

Director when the Colonel was forced to retire at the 75 year old age limit of the University.

Following O'Connor onto the stage were eight individuals who were being honored by his Association, including the President of the University, a Lee Bollinger, whom O'Connor didn't particularly care for. The basis for that was Bollinger's rude and embarrassing treatment – according to O'Connor - of a foreign dignitary at a Columbia event some years back. O'Connor claimed that if you are the one to invite a skunk to your home, you are duty bound to act by the rules of civilized society. O'Connor had such negative feelings for the Columbia President that he once confided to his friend Michael Christianson, the Vice President's older brother, that he dreamed he was having dinner with Bollinger. He told Christianson that the thought of that dream and his sitting next to Bollinger upset him for weeks.

When his honored guests were seated in the chairs that had been placed for them on the stage, O'Connor who was beaming from ear to ear wet his lips and looking directly at his student audience, he began. "In 1952, I sat where you sit - not exactly in the same spot, but in the same City and in an almost identical venue. On that occasion I had to chance to be in the company of the President of the United States, Dwight David Eisenhower, and to hear a great American say words that I have kept with me all of my life. That is an event that I will never forget, just as you will never forget this very day."

"Before I introduce the man whom I believe will become the greatest President of our time, I need to thank my dear friend Michael Christianson for making this possible. Some of you from the Westchester area should know Dr. Christianson. And, if you don't, Dr. Christianson was the driving force in creating in Westchester county one of the finest educational systems in the country." Glancing to his left to be sure his guest speaker was on hand, O'Connor turned back to his audience and in as loud a voice as he could muster he said, "Without any further adieu, I give you a man whom we all know and love – a man who does not need nor want a formal introduction – the President of the United States of America, Maynard Jefferson DeFrie."

At the first glimpse of the President in the main ballroom and on giant screen TV's in the satellite rooms, the audience of 4200 – mainly high school students – in a split second, went from a sitting position to standing position to a jumping up and down, just like they were on pogo sticks. The Ballroom erupted into a cacophony of whistles, applause, screams and banging on tables. The entire wait staff of the Ballroom joined in with the same enthusiasm. It took the President five minutes to quiet his audience down and another few minutes to have them take their seats.

The President was beaming. Throughout this remarkable reception he methodically moved his head across the entire audience so that he could see each individual. That was not an easy task as heads kept randomly popping up as the students continued their jumping. He made eye contact with every student who was in his sights. He could feel their respect and admiration. They could sense his warmth and love.

When the President had finally calmed down his youthful audience, he moved his head up and down turning from left to right across the entire Ballroom a broad smile on his face. His first words were, "Wow!" – followed by a pause – "Thank you, thank you very much!" Before he could finish his last phrase, the students were on their feet again applauding, cheering and whistling. Realizing that the 'wow' comment had only reinvigorated his audience, the President raised his arms so as to signal them to quiet them down. Nodding his approval for their self control, he began to speak.

"The most pleasurable part of being President these past 13 months has been the opportunity to interact with and be in the company of young Americans. Some of you may know that I have visited all of our Service Academies; I have also had at the White House high school and college scholars, the NCAA championship football and basketball teams and other young Americans that deserve honor. Words cannot express how impressed I am with the youth of this country. They are intelligent, they are hard workers, they strive to achieve and they are all beautiful."

Before the President got to the serious part of his talk, he wanted to share some long held secrets which in turn truly amused his audience. Apparently, the President had a strong interest in journalism when he attended St. Augustine High School in New Orleans. He loved reading Art Buchwald, a *Washington Post* humorist, whose columns appeared in the New Orleans newspaper, The *Times-Picayune*. In his youth the President believed he was very good at 'spinning a yarn'. He could easily visualize himself writing humor columns for a living.

In his sophomore year he joined the staff of the school newspaper. It was called *The Knight*. Unfortunately, for him his fingers were so large that it was difficult for him to use a typewriter. As a consequence, he had to write his stories long hand and find someone who would type them up for him. To complicate matters even further, two of the subjects he had not excelled in – 'even with the Nuns beating on him in grade school' – were spelling and penmanship. After one semester 'as a journalist' he could no longer find any one who was willing to do his typing. Consequently, he was relegated to folding copies of *The Knight* and distributing them around the school – two jobs he did not think suited him. The President's audience was particularly amused when he wondered out loud 'what his career might have been had he been born with smaller fingers, and in an age where word processors correct your spelling.'

Continuing on to the message the President had come to deliver, he told his student audience, "You are the strength of this country and you are our future! So today I want to talk to you about a serious topic. That topic is about civic responsibility, it is about what we owe to ourselves, what we owe to our country, and what we owe to our fellow man. And, I need to tell you that many in the generation that preceded you have not well exercised their civic responsibility. That means your job and your dedication will of necessity be greater. But I can tell you from my interactions with your brothers and sisters that you are up to the task."

The President spoke for a total of 45 minutes, not counting the 7 or 8 minutes before his audience would let him say one word. There was not a sound to be heard from the entire Ballroom audience, nor from those in the satellite ballrooms where the President could be seen on giant TV screens, other than the President's thoughtful words delivered in beautiful rich and melodic ones. The audience was absolutely mesmerized.

When the President had finished his prepared words, he thanked his host and he thanked his audience for the opportunity to be with them. He raised his arms – palms forward – and said, "God bless you all. May the Good Lord be with you each day of your life and with each step that you take. And, God Bless America." His audience stood from their chairs and erupted in applause that never seemed to end. There was no whistling, there were no screams. There were broad smiles superimposed on serious thoughtful eyes. Many of the young ladies, and a fair number of the young men, had tears streaming down their faces, in spite of the fact that they were totally joyful. One of the young men seemed to be affected even more than the others. He was overheard to have said that he never been so moved in his life. He felt as if he were in the presence of God.

*   *   *

After completing his talk and waving a 'good bye' to his audience, the President turned to shake the hands of each dignitary that was being honored and thanked O'Connor for the opportunity to speak with his journalism delegates. The time was 2:46 p.m. Before Chuck O'Connor could make his way to the lectern to thank the President, the 7 Secret Service Agents who were standing equidistantly spaced on the sides and back of the Ballroom stage ushered the President to the side exit of the stage nearest the service elevator where other agents were stationed.

As the Grand Ballroom is on the third floor of the Hilton, the President's party would be taking the elevator to the service entrance level which is one level below grade. Exiting the service elevator and turning right, the corridor that leads straight to the old service entrance is precisely 40 yards – a distance the President could have covered with blinding speed as a young man. Along this corridor are only two open doorways – one on the right leading to stairways down to a mechanical room, the other directly opposite that led to a loading dock which was intended, following a recent renovation, to replace the service entrance the President would be using. Both doorways along the corridor had been completely secured by the Secret Service, and were manned by Agents carrying submachine guns – two Agents in each doorway. At the end of the corridor just in front of the old service entrance, stood four Secret Service Agents also armed with submachine guns. They were there to provide cover until the President was safe in his armored limousine.

When the group had proceeded about half way down the corridor, the President reached into his jacket pocket fiddling for his cell phone. He wanted to call Mrs. DeFrie to let her know he had finished his speech, and to see how she had enjoyed her luncheon. The President and his entourage were about 30 feet from the exit when he signaled his bodyguards to pause for a moment so that he could dial his phone. Almost simultaneously, there was a loud explosion, seemingly coming from within the corridor. The blast created a dust cloud that made it very difficult to see anything clearly. In the process, two of the Secret Service agents accompanying the President were knocked to the ground. They quickly righted themselves. The concussion of the blast was later realized to have been strong enough to have caused ear bleeds to the two agents who were knocked down.

Within seconds and before the dust cloud had cleared, two gun shots rang out in quick succession. During a pause of no more than three second when groans mixed with gurgling sounds could be heard, three gun shots were fired – again in rapid succession. Before this second set of shots was fired, the armed

Secret Service agents standing in front of the exit slammed open the double exit doors. There was a pause until their eyes could adjust to the external light which now made discernable the scene within the corridor. Immediately, one of the Agents screamed to the medical emergency team that was waiting in readiness to 'get a stretcher in here!' As loud as he could, he screamed "the President is down!" There was a pause, "And, we have an agent down!"

The original intention for leaving the hotel was to exit the old service entrance through a side door adjacent to a pair of double doors that were only used occasionally for moving very large items. That was exactly how the President and his bodyguards had entered the hotel. For their exit, the plan was that two of the four submachine gun armed agents stationed at the service entrance would step through the side door to the outside, and provide cover to the President. They were to have maintained cover until all were safely in the armored vehicle which was the third car in the President's awaiting motorcade.

The two remaining agents were to provide cover back into the hotel and down the passage corridor. They would do this in concert with the Agents securing the doorways that led to the mechanical room and to the loading dock. In addition to the agents who were to first step through the side exit door to provide cover, there were 12 agents armed with high powered rifles that had been strategically positioned outside of the hotel in readiness to protect the President as he entered and exited the Hilton.

In the resulting pandemonium Agent David Solomon took charge immediately. He directed that they devote all their efforts to the President even though Agent Dean Sutherland who apparently had also suffered gun wounds could be heard groaning and was lying across the lower half of the President's body. Solomon abruptly rolled Sutherland's body to the side and rather than wait for a stretcher to be brought in, he ordered four of his colleagues to kneel down by the President – two on each side. He instructed them to get their arms under the President's body, lock hands with their opposing partner and gently lift the President.

Simultaneously, Solomon, who had torn off his own suit coat, folded the coat and placed it under the President's head. Solomon carefully steadied this huge head as he and the four other agents walked - in step - as quickly as they could to the awaiting ambulance. That was not an easy task considering the fact that the President was weighing in at nearly 270 pounds. The ambulance followed by two Chevy Suburbans each filled with Secret Service Agents left the service entrance of the New York Hilton at precisely 3:09 p.m.

Thanks to the quick thinking of the New York City Police Commissioner, Paul R. Kelley, who was on the scene well before the President arrived and who stayed on duty for the entire visit, all traffic was cleared in minutes from 52nd Street on the Avenue of the Americas north to 77th Street, and from there to the entrance to the Lennox Hill Hospital Emergency Service. The ambulance bearing the President arrived in exactly 12 minutes. On board the ambulance two emergency room physicians worked feverishly in that time period to determine the extent of the President's injuries as best they could. They had some success quelling the President's perfuse bleeding from a bullet wound in his chest, even though they knew internal bleeding continued. They were also able to start intravenous fluids. The latter was a very difficult task because of the lurching of the speeding ambulance, and the fact that the President's blood pressure had fallen to 64 over 40 – his veins were near collapse.

The ambulance for Agent Dean Sutherland that Agent Solomon had called for after the President had been taken from the Hilton arrived at 3:20 p.m. By the time he was placed onto a stretcher and moved into the ambulance, his fair complexion had turned pale blue-white. He did not appear to be breathing. The physician, who attended to him en route to Lennox, pronounced him dead on arrival.

At 3:37 p.m. Brian Williams of NBC interrupted the Rachel Ray Show to make an urgent announcement. Ironically, Ray was talking about how simple it was to prepare black eyed peas and ham hocks, one of the President's favorites. Williams in very solemn tones stated, "We have just received a report from the New York Hilton where President Maynard Jefferson DeFrie had just given a speech to high school journalists that an attempt has been made on the President's life. The President has been taken to Lennox Hill Hospital and we understand at this very moment he is in surgery. We have no further details at this time, but we have reporters at the hospital. We will bring you any further information, as we obtain it. I am sure that all Americans and others around the world will keep the President in their thoughts and in their prayers – just as we at NBC are doing." Within minutes every major television and radio station throughout the entire country and around the world broadcast the very same information.

Anyone who heard those broadcasts stopped whatever they were doing immediately. In New York City, in every other city and town, and on every major road in the country, traffic came to a standstill. Bus drivers, truck drivers and passenger car drivers just pulled off the road where ever they could. Most sat motionless, others searched their radios or made cell phone calls seeking any meaningful information.

By 4 p.m. in New York City's Times Square there were more people crowded into the Square than would be there on New Years Eve. Most stood quietly looking up to the NASDAQ electronic bill board, that normally gives stock quotes, waiting for even the minutest bit of information. Many were weeping. Many were praying, silently or out loud. There was a polyglot of prayers for this magnificent and beloved creature. In Radio City, Rockefeller Plaza and in front of the Hilton, with the exception of the area cordoned off by the police, crowds had gathered similarly. They, too, were silent with the exception of maybe one in twenty who shared any news from text messages that they had received with those standing nearby to them.

At 6:40 p.m. at the Lennox Hill Hospital it was announced to the assembled media multitude milling about the lobby of the hospital that a Medical Press Conference would be held in the hospital's Einhorn Auditorium located at 131 East 76th

Street at 7:00 p.m. The conference would be carried live on every major TV and radio station, and would be shown on the NASDAQ electronic billboard in Times Square. Sound would be piped into the Square as well as into the Radio City Plaza adjacent to the New York Hilton and into Rockefeller Plaza.

At precisely 7:00 p.m. a lanky ashen faced black haired man wearing surgical greens over which he wore a ill fitting white lab coat, which was apparently not his own, stepped up to the bank of microphones that had been hastily placed in front of the lectern on the Auditorium stage. With TV lights blaring on him which gave his ashen complexion an almost cadaverous tint and made his deep set dark ringed eyes seem even deeper, it was apparent this man was drained. He was ill at ease in his role and nervously ran the fingers of his right hand through his hair. In his left hand which seemed to have a slight tremor, he appeared to be holding a c-fold paper towel – the kind of paper towel commonly found in rest rooms for hand drying – that he had written on.

He cleared his throat and began to speak. His voice was absolutely hollow. His words: "My name is Anthony Citarella. I am a Cardio-pulmonary surgeon, here at Lennox Hill. I am the Director of the Trauma Center. At 3:22 this afternoon we admitted President DeFrie to the Trauma Center. Immediately we evaluated the injuries he had sustained both by palpitation of his wounds and by radiology. In short order, we brought the President into surgery. We performed a rapid exploratory surgical exam of the interior of his chest, and found that he had sustained a perforation of the right auricle chamber of his heart and a small tear of his pulmonary artery leading to his lungs. The perforation of the right auricle only grazed the chamber and the blood loss from that injury was surprisingly small. The President also suffered a pneumothorax of the right lung. In other words, the President's right lung collapsed from a bullet wound that entered the right side of his chest. We recovered a bullet from his chest cavity."

"During this exploratory part of our procedure we noted that the President had a significantly enlarged heart, and from coloration on portions of his left ventricle we believe the president had at some time in the past suffered one or more small heart attacks. Because of hemorrhage associated with the perforation of the President's right auricle and the tear to his pulmonary artery, both injuries can be life threatening. We repaired both believing we had saved the President. We were able to reverse the pneumothorax with little difficulty."

"As we were closing the President's chest, we noted a precipitous drop in blood pressure. The President went to cardiac arrest. We attempted resuscitation by every means we know of. We worked on the President for over 40 minutes by which time we realized our efforts were futile."

Dr. Citarella's chest began to heave. He wiped his eyes and bit hard on his lower lip trying to regain his composure. In a halting voice he finished by saying, "At 11 minutes after 6 O'clock this evening, February 18th, we pronounced the President dead."

Immediately hands shot up from the assembled reporters who without hesitation slung questions in Dr. Citarella's direction. Citarella raised his right hand, as if to fend them off. "Gentlemen (even though there were women in the audience), you will have to excuse me, you will have to forgive me. I am in no condition either physically or mentally to answer any of your questions. I have just lost the most significant battle of my entire life. Nothing, nothing in the world, could have meant more to me than saving our President's life. May his soul rest in peace."

With his voice cracking, he added "If you have the need for any further information, I am sure my colleague Dr. Mark Goldman would be happy to address them." Goldman waved Citarella off. He was entirely in sync with his Chief. That was the end of the medical conference.

President Maynard Jefferson DeFrie had just turned 66 years of age in the previous December.

*   *   *

For whatever reason, even though no one on February 18th referred to the shooting of the President as an 'assassination', there were two men present at the Medical Press Conference who when it ended were in intense dialogue about that very issue. They were Robert J. Morgenstein, District Attorney of New York County – the county includes Manhattan where the shooting of the President had taken place – and Archer Reese, Attorney General of the United States. Morgenstein who all referred to as the 'Manhattan District Attorney' had held that position for nearly 35 years. He was in his late 70's and never mentioned the word retirement.

Reese had been Attorney General of the State of Mississippi during the time when the President was Governor of that state. He and the President had become close friends when the President was in the Mississippi State Legislature. The President admired Reese, a white man, for doggedly pursuing the murder case of three young Civil Rights workers who were murdered in Mississippi in 1964 by Klansman Edgar Ray Killen, an ordained Baptist Minister. Reese righted that Historic wrong by successfully prosecuting Killen for murder in 2005. Reese happened to be in New York City on February 18th for meetings with the Director of the Manhattan Division of the FBI regarding a mortgage bank fraud case.

The issue that was of concern to Morgenstein and Reese was jurisdiction of the crime that had just occurred. That would be the key to how the deaths of the President and Agent Sutherland would be investigated and prosecuted. Both men vividly remembered, even though Reese was fifteen years younger than Morgenstein, the fiasco that followed the Kennedy assassination in Dallas, Texas in November 1963. The Dallas Police made every attempt to keep 'the Fed's out of the case, and they were quite successful. Taking charge of the investigation and prosecution, they bungle the transfer of Lee Harvey Oswald, the purported assassin who was in their custody, which resulted in his murder. The Dallas Officials' handling of the Kennedy assassination has made it nearly impossible to resolve that case more than 50 years after it occurred.

It was because of those issues that Congress made it a Federal Crime 'to attempt to kill or kidnap any individual who is the President, the President-Elect, the Vice President, and if there is no Vice President the officer who is next in succession to the Office of the President of the United States.' Accordingly the jurisdiction of the case would be Federal, and Attorney General Reese would be in charge of the investigation and prosecution of any individuals charged with such crimes.

Robert Morgenstein had a reputation for being a tough old bird. And, he was. He was well respected and had over his years as the Manhattan District Attorney built an incredible resume of successful investigations and prosecutions. He also possessed a very large ego, and, because of all his years of service and the connections he had made, he was capable of mustering considerable muscle at the local and federal level. The moment Morgenstein learned of the assault on the President he was on the scene, first at the Hilton and next at Lennox Hill Hospital, within minutes. He was determined not to allow the most important case that had occurred on his turf during his 'watch' to slip out of his hands.

Relentlessly negotiating every issue Morgenstein reached an agreement with Attorney General Reese. In principle, Reese would allow Morgenstein access to all information pertaining to the investigation. They had agreement that the President's body would be flown back to Washington on Air Force One in the custody of the Secret Service and two of Morgenstein's deputies. The body would be taken to Walter Reed Army Hospital where an autopsy would be performed in the presence of a witness representing Morgenstein. That witness would be the Medical Examiner for New York City, a Dr. Charles Hershberger, who had served in that position for nearly 27 years. All results of the autopsy and any subsequent testing results would be shared with Dr. Hershberger and accordingly with Morgenstein's office.

On the matter of the crime scene, Morgenstein had agreement that he could assign two New York City detectives to accompany FBI agents during the investigation. The FBI agents would be in charge. Reese had accepted Morgenstein's assertion that his detectives would be helpful in this part of the investigation as they had had significant experience with murders.

The body of Agent Dean Sutherland, who had been shot along with the President at the Hilton, would be taken in the presence of FBI and Secret Service agents to the New York City Medical Examiners office for autopsy. The autopsy would be performed in the presence of these Federal agents and be done by New York City medical examiners. Again all information would be shared. 'Open kimono' as Morgenstein called it.

The President's body was moved from Lennox Hospital to Kennedy Airport at 9:49 pm, a mere twelve hours and two minutes from when Air Force One took off from Andrews Air Force base in Suitland, Maryland that morning.

Chapter IX

In spite of his constitutional duty to do so, Vice President Rod Christianson had only presided over the Senate on those occasions when major bills of President DeFrie's Administration were being voted upon. In all of those situations, it was never a case of the Vice President presiding because of his 'tie-breaker' vote capability. Every initiative that the Administration had proposed had been vigorously debated by both houses and passed by overwhelming majorities. The presence of the Vice President on those occasions was more a matter of ceremony and of keeping good relations with the Senate. It also created a lot of very good press for the Administration.

As has been the case for generations, the duty of presiding over the Senate on a daily basis is normally performed by the 'president pro tempore' – the temporary president - who is selected by the Senate. Hence, when the Vice President decided to preside over the Senate on February 18th for a vote on a bill that was considered minor compared to its predecessors, it was a surprise to all. The bill, in question, would establish and fund a new center for the National Institutes of Health.

To be added to the list of 27 other Institutes and centers such as heart, lung, infectious diseases, cancer and arthritis, would be a Center for Stem Cell Research. The Vice President wanted very much to have his imprimatur on this particular bill, because he had been heavily involved in the drafting of the bill, and for 8 years following the 2000 election he had fought the stem cell research ban vigorously. And, to no avail. Furthermore, the Vice President in that period had experienced the death of one of his very dear friends from Parkinson's disease. It was painful for him to watch his friend wither up and die. He believed that death could have been prevented, and he bore the pain of guilt for not being able to do anything to prevent that.

At 3:10 p.m. the Vice President had completed the vote on the Senate version of the Stem Cell institute bill, and just as he had pronounced the bill passed, the Sergeant at Arms of the Senate came up behind the Vice President and whispered something into the Vice President's ear. He also placed a note in front of the Vice President. The Vice President blanched, his face contorted as if he had experienced a tremendous pain. Forcing himself to regain composure, the Vice President turned to the full Senate and said, "I have just been informed that President Maynard DeFrie has been shot in New York City, and at this moment is being taken to the Trauma Unit at Lennox Hill Hospital. That is all we know at this time." The Vice President paused as if he were trying to catch his breath and continued, "Will the president pro tempore, Senator John Welzer, please take over this session?"

Without another word the Vice President exited the Senate Chamber, as he did he placed his right hand under his jacket and pressed hard on his chest with the palm of his right hand. He quickly made his way out of the Senate chamber and down steps to an awaiting black SUV. From the Capitol building, the Vice President would be taken by his Secret Service contingent to his office so that he could maintain contact with the unfolding events in New York City.

In spite of his pain and anguish, the Vice President's thinking was crystal clear. He directed the Secret Service not to take him to his office in the Eisenhower Executive Office Building, but instead to his office in the West Wing of the White House. Symbolically, the Vice President realized that he needed to be in the White House during these terrible moments.

When the Vice President arrived at his office in the West Wing he was greeted by a medical contingent led by the White House Physician, a Captain Merrill Madrey. They had been directed by the Secret Service to be present upon his arrival. After a quick but thorough examination, during which time a blood sample was taken to determine if the Vice President's cardiac enzymes were elevated – cardiac enzymes are the best indicator of heart muscle damage, and accordingly of a heart attack – Dr. Madrey ordered the Vice President be taken to Walter Reed Army Hospital at once. At Walter Reed an interventional cardiac team was standing by, if that was deemed necessary.

The Vice President refused to be taken to Walter Reed. He informed Dr. Madrey and those in attendance, "This will pass!" In a forceful voice, he added, "we don't have cardiac problems in my family." The Vice President then explained that nearly four years ago when he was still in the Senate, he was informed that his father, a 78 year old retired physician in excellent health, had been killed in an automobile accident coming south on Route 301 on the Eastern Shore to the approach of the Chesapeake Bay Bridge. Upon hearing that news, the then Senator Christianson experienced very severe chest pain.

At that time, Christianson was given four aspirins to chew on by the Senate Emergency Crew and rushed from his Senate office in the Rayburn building to Walter Reed where blood tests indicated he had had a significant heart attack. Accordingly, Cardiologists at Walter Reed performed a routine cardiac catheterization with the intention of clearing out any clogged coronary arteries that might be causing his heart attack. They found that all of his coronary vessels were perfectly open. The attending Cardiologists could not ascribe these good findings to the aspirins Christianson had been given, particularly as he had told them that he had spit them out.

After two days of observation on Senator Christianson, the conclusion was reached that he had suffered a heart spasm. Apparently the spasm was sufficiently violent to cause his heart muscle to destroy enough tissue to elevate his cardiac enzymes. The Vice President said his doctors referred to his rare condition as Prinzmetal's syndrome – a condition where the heart can go into severe spasms, often associated with severe mental trauma.

Dr. Madrey had, indeed, heard of Prinzmetal's syndrome but had never known of a case first hand, nor did he know any other Physicians who did. Uneasy as he was in accepting this huge responsibility he was taking in not ordering that the Vice President be taken to Walter Reed, Madrey, who had broken out into a sweat over his dilemma, acceded to the Vice President's wishes. Madrey understood that if the Vice President could be so severely affected physically, just on hearing that the President had been shot, what did this portend for the Country, if, indeed, the President were to die.

*   *   *

Dr. Madrey's sense of how the country would react was only an educated guess. He had not been born at the time of President John F. Kennedy's assassination, nor for the two assassinations that followed – Martin Luther King, Jr., and Senator Robert F. Kennedy. Consequently, he had no frame of reference. He only knew how much he hurt, without yet knowing the ultimate fate of President DeFrie.

Moments after learning that the President was dead, the Reverend Peter C. Boyd, the Dean of the Washington National Cathedral– more properly known as the Cathedral of St. Peter and St. Paul – ordered that the Peal Bells be rung. They were to be rung each day from 9:11 a.m. to 9:11 p.m. until the President would be buried. They were to pause each day at 6:11 p.m. – the very time the President had died - and they were to remain silent for 15 minutes. Reverend Boyd believed that in this dark moment of tragedy the Nation needed to know that the Church was there – ever present.

He also had in mind the words of Thomas Merton who wrote that 'Bells are meant to remind us that God alone is good and that we belong to Him'. He remembered the more European tradition of tolling the bells when a King or some great personage had died. The ringing of the Peal bells was the Reverend Boyd's way of giving to all Americans the message that the house of God was open to all who could be consoled by faith, and for those who did not believe, it was his way inviting them to use the Communal spirit that the Church can provide to seek solace.

By midday Friday on February 19th, nearly every house of worship across the Nation had followed the Reverend's lead. And, on that day and the following weekend, the Nation stood absolutely still. Other than President Christianson and his cabinet, who needed to seize the reins of government and give the country the illusion that all would be well, and those involved in essential services as well as those who were investigating the assassination of President DeFrie, the entire population was frozen in place. It was as if a dozen World Trade Centers had been taken down simultaneously. The populous was in deep morning and in deep depression. Many stayed in front of their Televisions – listening to details of President DeFrie's life and his accomplishments, details they already knew, weeping as they watched – waiting patiently for any news about the President's assassination. Many sat silently in churches all across the nation.

In New Orleans, the boyhood home of the President, on Saturday the 20th at 11 minutes past six in the evening, a mock Jazz funeral procession took place on the streets of the City. No one seemed to know who had organized the event; it just seemed to take place spontaneously as if all of the participants knew and understood their respective roles. Those funeral parades would continue each night until the President would be buried in Arlington National Cemetery on Sunday, February 10th.

The funeral parade consisted of a typical New Orleans Jazz band, only it was larger. There were about 35 black musicians and a dozen or so white musicians, each dressed in attire that only would be seen in New Orleans on men of this profession. Unlike other New Orleans Jazz Funeral Parades which sometimes have a hint of celebration for the departed, there were no smiles. These men had a task to perform, and they understood what that was.

Behind the band was a mule drawn rickety old hay wagon. On the left side of mule's bridle someone had tied some sickly looking white flowers. On the withers of the mule was draped a soiled folded American flag. The hay wagon must have been 100 or more years old. It was vintage sharecropper.

Holding onto the mule's bridal and leading the mule was a handsome large framed older black man, who walked, with obvious pain, slightly hunched and with a noticeable limp. If he could stand straight he was probably about 6 feet 3 inches. From the lines in his face and the 'salt and pepper' look of his hair, he was likely in his mid 70's. He was dressed in soiled coveralls. They were no doubt his work clothes. His eyes were red rimmed from weeping and glazed over as he performed his noble task. It was clear he was devastated by the assassination, having so recently been elated by the most improbable event of his entire lifetime – the election of a Black man as President of the United States. He was heart-broken. This very small sacrifice for a President he loved with all his heart and soul was something he needed to do even though he had to ice his swollen and blistered feet after each parade.

At the midline of the hay wagon, running in the direction of its travel, was vertically mounted a clearly hand fashioned two sided framed picture holder, which on each side had a picture of President DeFrie. The frame was draped in purple and black. Behind the framed picture of the President and just at the rear of the flat bed hay wagon was an old galvanized rusted wash tub filled with white rose petals.

On the right and left side of the tub sat, respectively, a young black boy, maybe 10 years of age, and a young black girl, probably about the same age. Both were attired as they might have been had they lived 200 years ago. The young boy's hair was closely cropped. The young girl wore her hair in pigtails tied with tiny yellow ribbons. As the procession moved along, these children reached into the wash tub and dropped white rose petals along the path of the funeral parade. In spite of their young age, they too understood their roles, and the significance and symbolism of this event.

On each occasion that the funeral parade took place the parade route was identical. The participants would assemble at the Louis Armstrong Park. At precisely 6:11 p.m. they would begin moving down North Rampart Street in the direction of Canal Street. At Canal Street the processions turned left, heading towards the Mississippi River. At Bourbon Street the group turned left, proceeded to Conti Street where they turned right and then to Royal Street where they turned right again. When they arrived at Canal Street again, they turned left, proceeded to the River Walk and ended their route at the Riverfront Park. On the Saturday night of their first parade, they were followed by about 1200 very solemn individuals, many of whom had come to New Orleans as tourists.

Unlike the route of the parade which never varied, the music that was played on each night of the funeral procession did change. On each night the band only played two pieces. They were played, and played over and over again as the marchers proceeded. One of the pieces was played on each night – the funeral dirge 'Just a Closer Walk with Thee.' To that was added one selection from the group: 'Lead me Savior', 'What a Friend we have in Jesus', 'As I lay my Burden Down', 'Down by the Riverside', 'In the Sweet Bye and Bye', 'Feel So Good', and finally on the evening of the President's funeral, "The Battle Hymn of the Republic.'

It was the musicians intention to perform 'When the Saints go Marching In' on the evening of President DeFrie's funeral. They could not bring themselves to perform that. And, they had good reason. They were troubled by the refrain 'I want to be in that number' that follows 'oh when the saints go marching in'. Maynard Jefferson DeFrie was their Saint. They had no doubt about that. It would be inappropriate to ask that he be 'in that number.' It would be disrespectful to make that request. They understood their God better than that.

Starting on Sunday, and for the next 7 days, the New Orleans event was nationally televised. By Monday there were estimated to have been more than 250,000 mourners lining the streets of the parade route. Each day the numbers increased. Many had driven without stopping to sleep from places more than 1700 miles away. It was as if Americans had to personally make some sacrifice as a way of letting their President know how much they loved and respected him. And. how much they would miss him.

Millions of Americans, probably more than had watched the Super Bowl just weeks before the President was assassinated, sat in front of their Televisions each night viewing the funeral parade. Most were weeping, others were fighting back tears, all were mournful. It was reminiscent of the public's reaction to the assassination of John F. Kennedy when the country sat transfixed in front of their TV's devastated. Uncertain of what would become of their country.

In the Rotunda of the Capitol building where the President lay in State for three days and three nights, despite some of the worst winter weather in years, more than one million Americans made their way to Washington to say one final good bye to a very special someone who had touched their lives. Waiting in the bitter cold in tremendous lines that took as much as than 4 hours to traverse, they persevered just to catch a 5 second glimpse of the President's body. Just long enough to touch the fingers of one hand to their lips, and wave goodbye with that same hand. They were pleased with themselves for having made the effort.

*   *   *

At 5 p.m. Eastern Standard Time, on the Friday and
Saturday following the murder of the President, Rod
Christianson, who had taken the oath for the Office of the
Presidency just following President DeFrie's death, addressed the
nation. He did this from his office in the West Wing of the White
House. There was some debate amongst the President's advisers
regarding the use of the Oval Office. Some thought that would be
comforting to the citizenry, others thought it be taken as
disrespectful. In the end, President Christianson made clear that it
would be some time before he would even consider using the
Oval Office. To him it had become a shrine.

On each of those two occasions, President Christianson,
whose face was drawn from the wear of the tremendous grief he
was suffering, began by assuring the nation, "we will get through
this terrible tragedy." He said, "Americans are strong of
character, they are fair, they are resilient and they are wise." He
cited the unprecedented election of Maynard DeFrie as evidence
of the country's wisdom. He asked, "what other place in the
world, what other people would have recognized the genius,
goodness and potential of our beloved Maynard DeFrie?" He
mentioned all the changes Americans supported in this past year
that this Administration had spearheaded. That supported his
contention that Americans are strong of character and that they
are fair. Following that, Christianson then assured the public that
'our military is on full alert around the entire world.' "America is
safe!"

In regard to the murder of the President, Christianson
suggested that there was, at this time, no evidence of foreign
involvement in the President's assassination. He mentioned that
the Justice Department under Attorney General Asher Reese in
full cooperation with the Federal Bureau of Investigation and
with the added complete resources of the City of New York was
working feverously 'to get to the bottom of this heinous crime.
On both occasions, President Christianson stopped short of

stating that the President's murder was solved, but indicated progress was being made.

On Sunday February 20th, the President addressed the nation, this time at 2 p.m. Eastern Standard Time. In a rambling fashion, he continued to assure the Public that all was well with the country. The President gave some details on the planning for President DeFrie's funeral which included those days and nights that Maynard Jefferson DeFrie's body would 'lay in State'. He gave a web site where details related to the funeral and information on all events of the week could be accessed. He mentioned the funeral parade that had been held in New Orleans on the previous evening, and shared some of the details which, clearly, had moved President Christianson greatly. He indicated that it was his understanding that this event would be repeated and that it would be televised nationally. When the President announced that, most of the country had already seen clips on their local TV stations of the New Orleans event.

President Christianson followed his remarks with two announcements. First he announced the immediate formation of a Commission that would begin the process of reviewing all data and information related to President DeFrie's assassination. That Commission would be led by one of the President's foreign policy advisers, former Congressman Lee Hamilton. In principle, it would be just like the Warren Commission that had been charged with the thorough investigation and review of the Kennedy assassination.

Hamilton would be given the authority, subject only to the President's approval, to appoint six other members of the Commission. The Commission would have broad authority and all of the powers of the Warren Commission such as subpoena of witnesses, payment for information and funds to undertake independent investigation. Somewhat like the Warren Commission, all meetings and testimony could be conducted in private, but a detailed record of those events would be kept, and be reported to the public every 30 days for as long as the Commission was active.

President Christianson also announced that some considerable progress had been made on the investigation of the assassination of President DeFrie. A press conference would be held by Attorney General Reese and the Director of the Federal Bureau of Investigation Harold Riemann. The Press Conference would be held at 4 p.m. Eastern Standard Time.

*   *   *

The 4 p.m. Press Conference was held in a small auditorium two floors below the office of United States Attorney General Archer Reese. At the last moment, Lee Hamilton who had just been appointed to head the commission that would review all aspects of the assassination investigation would join the Attorney General and the Director of the FBI, Harold Riemann who would be giving the Conference along with the Attorney General. Hamilton would not participate in the Conference. He would only be an observer.

Archer Reese was a long time friend and confidant of President DeFrie. Reese was a southern gentleman whose chivalrous nature somehow masked his determination and his extraordinary intellect and insights. The Attorney General was a Mississippi native, born and raised in Vicksburg. He had graduated from the United States Military Academy at West Point, and after his service obligation he had gone to law school at the University of South Carolina. Other than spending 7 years as a criminal defense attorney in Columbia, South Carolina, he had spent his entire career in public service in the state of Mississippi. On his mother's side the Attorney General could trace his ancestry directly back to William Alexander Stuart, brother of famed Confederate Civil War General J.E.B. Stuart. That was a fact he was proud of, but never mentioned. He was a Civil War history buff, and could describe each battle in detail.

Archer Reese besides being a modest man who kept his ego well in check could also be blunt with those he trusted and respected. He only recently had shared with his good friend

'Maynard' that Harold Riemann was a 'dumb ass.' President DeFrie never permitted his close friends to call him Mr. President, he thought that was pompous and could lead a man to thinking he was more than he was. He preferred to be reminded that he was only human – something he learned from translating 'Julius Caesar' from the Latin when he was at St. Augustine High School.

According to Reese the FBI Director's intellect was not close to matching his level of responsibility and power. Reese was also bothered by Riemann's ego. He claimed Riemann was hiding 'a barrel of insecurities' by repeatedly referring to his 'career accomplishments.' And, he postured, particularly with his facial expressions, as a tough guy – an image the Director seemed to think went with his job. In spite of the Attorney General's feelings Riemann actually thought Reese admired him. That was a measure of how well mannered Reese was and of his ability not to reveal his true feelings.

At precisely 4:01 p.m. the Attorney General seated behind and at the middle of a conference table, and flanked by Riemann and Hamilton, began reading from a statement he had prepared. He apologized for reading his statement, but he believed the information had to be transmitted accurately and unambiguously.

"On February 18th of this year, President Maynard Jefferson DeFrie was murdered as he exited the New York Hilton where he had given a speech to high school newspaper editors. The President exited the Ballroom where the speech was given at precisely 2:46 p.m. From the Ballroom he took a service elevator to a service corridor that would lead him to a double door service exit. The distance from the elevator to the exit door is precisely 122 feet. The corridor was well lighted and had been secured by Secret Service Agents. Bomb sniffing dogs had been used to check this area, the day before the President's visit, the morning of his visit, and one hour before he arrived."

"From eye witness accounts provided by Secret Service Agents David Solomon and Ronald Stutz who were both part of the contingent assigned to protect the President, we have determined that the President was assassinated by one of his own Secret Service Agents. That Agent was Dean Southerland, whose body, as you know, was removed from the crime scene and subsequently pronounced 'dead on arrival' when he was taken by ambulance to Lennox Hill Hospital." With that revelation the Press in attendance as well as Lee Hamilton seated to the right of Reese gasped.

"In spite of the fact that an explosion which occurred nearly simultaneously with the sound of gunshots had made visibility difficult, Agents Solomon and Stutz witnessed Agent Southerland draw his service revolver and fire two shots into the President's body. In a futile attempt to protect the President, Agent Solomon brought Agent Southerland down by firing his service revolver at Southerland three times."

"The FBI has been able to corroborate the accounts given by Agents Solomon and Stutz using video recording from two surveillance cameras which, fortunately, are positioned to give a good view of the area where the shootings took place. The video recordings required minimal enhancement by the Bureau in order to be viewed and interpreted accurately."

"In addition to the surveillance video conformation, the FBI laboratory has performed ballistic fingerprinting on the bullets retrieved from the President's body and from those retrieved from Agent Sutherland's body. For the two bullets retrieved from the President, only one could be fingerprinted for all three characteristics normally used to match the bullet to the gun that fired it. For those of you who are unfamiliar with the most modern techniques for bullet fingerprinting they are done by the matching of three characteristics of the bullet.

The most common method which most of you know is called bullet matching. That is done by examining and comparing the marks left on the sides of bullets when they were fired. Fired bullets have unique markings that result from differences in the machined rifling grooves of each gun. Another method is called breach face matching which matches marks left on the base of the cartridge caused by the fact that when a bullet is fired it is forced against the breach which imprints unique marking from the machine markings on the breach. The last fingerprinting method that is used is called Fire Pin Indentation markings, clearly caused by the unique markings left by individual firing pins."

"For one bullet retrieved from the President's body, each of the three fingerprinting characteristics matched identically those of bullets fired from Agent Southerland's service revolver. Because the second bullet that was retrieved was severely distorted, probably from smashing into bone, we were able to only get an identity match for the breach face and for the firing pin indentation. Based on that data, we have concluded that Agent Southerland's service revolver was used to kill the President."

"From an identical analysis of two of the bullets retrieved from Agent Southerland's body, we have unequivocal matches to bullets fired from Agent Solomon's service revolver. Accordingly, the ballistic tests that were done corroborate the accounts given to us by Agents Solomon and Stutz. I need to add that even though by Agent Solomon's account he fired three bullets into Southerland, only two were retrieved. There are a variety of scenarios that we could speculate. Suffice it to say, we are certain that bullets fired from Agent Solomon's revolver killed Agent Southerland."

Pausing to sip some water, Reese continued, "Dean Southerland was 29 years old, unmarried and lived alone in a two bedroom apartment in Alexandria, Virginia. He has been with the Secret Service for eight years, serving two Presidents. His service and employment record to this date has been exemplary. We have some preliminary evidence suggesting that Agent Southerland's actions may have been a 'hate crime'. The FBI has recovered Southerland's laptop computer and have determined that he has accessed several web sites of Neo-Nazi organizations in the United States and in the Netherlands. So far no evidence of communications with any such group has been found. That will be probed further."

"The FBI did find on Agent Southerland's computer several attempts he had made at writing racially related poetry. In particular, we found three documents on which he was working. All are variations, or more appropriately various attempts to write epic poems – if they can be called that. The poem's central figure is 'a filthy Black Knight' who rapes a 'White Virgin' dressed in a red, white and blue gown. Each of the documents was either modified, or worked on in the last three months. We also recovered letters that seem to be written to no one. In those letters there are repeated and repetitious racial epithets. Further examination of the hard drive is in progress."

"The Bureau also recovered from Southerland's apartment three different psychedelic drugs, a small quantity of crack cocaine and six ounces of marijuana. Trace analysis for crack cocaine and marijuana are in process on blood taken from Agent Southerland at autopsy."

"At this point, we have no evidence to suggest that Agent Southerland acted in concert with any other individual or individuals. We expect to be able to answer that question conclusively within the next week." Reese paused, and then said "Thank you for your attention. We will take only five questions at this time. We will make every effort to keep the American public informed as this investigation proceeds."

Three of the questions that followed were particularly interesting. The first dealt with the explosion that had occurred at the very time the President was shot. The question was, "wouldn't the explosion that occurred simultaneously with the shooting of the President indicate that Agent Southerland was acting in concert with other individuals? Could that have been a means in which he had hoped to make his escape?" Attorney General Reese passed that question onto Director Riemann to answer.

Riemann responded that the FBI had done laboratory analysis – he mentioned gas chromatography – on air samples taken in the corridor where the President was shot. Analysis was also done on washings from random places on the walls, ceiling and floor of the area. There were no traces of any compounds known to be explosives or those that might be the chemical products of explosive formulations found in any of the analysis.

To be certain that some unknown explosive had not been used, Director Riemann stated that the FBI had taken air samples and washings from other parts of the service floor as much as 300 feet away from the explosion, and from other areas of the Hotel. Some of the 'blips' - as he called them – that were unidentifiable from the samples taken in the immediate vicinity of the crime, were identical to those found in samples taken in other parts of the Hotel.

Those analyses and the fact that bomb sniffing dogs had scoured the area thoroughly just before the President entered the area, led Riemann to conclude the explosion had to be 'home grown', as he put it. He speculated that a gas leak within the hotel service area could have been ignited when the President used his cell phone. He added that the FBI had monitored the area for gas leaks, but to no avail. He added that the area would continue to be monitored in the event the 'leak' was of a transient nature.

The second interesting question dealt with Agent Solomon. "Is the investigation looking into the possibility that Agent Solomon is somehow involved in the assassination? There are ample historical instances of the assassin being assassinated as a means of making sure there are no witnesses who could incriminate the perpetrators." Reese did not respond to that question immediately. He was actually taken aback by it. That gave Director Riemann the opportunity to demonstrate that he was a seasoned Washington insider whose knowledge of all events 'on the hill' was encyclopedic. Riemann responded that Agent Solomon had been serving in the Secret Service since 1985 and had been assigned to protect President Regan in 1987 and every President since that time. He added that Solomon had been commended for his service many times and his loyalty was unquestionable.

The very last question that was taken at the Press Conference at first seemed silly, but in reality had merit. A reporter from the *Washington Post* wanted to know if there were any possibility that Agent Southerland whose body was still in the morgue in New York City was not the Agent Southerland who served in the Secret Service. Attorney General Reese responded to that question by saying that Southerland's body had been identified positively first by co workers from the Secret Service and secondly by Agent Southerland's father who had been flown to New York from Atlanta, Georgia by the FBI. He added that Southerland's father is a physician and a Professor of Internal Medicine at Emory Medical School in Atlanta. It would be hard to imagine that Dr. Southerland could not positively identify his own son.

Furthermore, Reese stated, "it is a routine operation to fingerprint bodies during autopsy." Addressing the reporter who had asked this question, Reese said, "As interesting as your question is, I am sure that procedure produced a positive identification."

On the last question, Attorney General Reese was entirely correct on the substance of his answer, but there was one, likely trivial, detail he was not aware of. When Dr. Southerland had traveled to New York City to identify his son's body, he first met with the Manhattan Medical Examiner, Dr. Charles Hershberger. Dr. Hershberger, in an attempt to relieve a medical colleague of the anguish of identifying the body of one of his two sons, brought Dr. Southerland into his office to chat about mutual colleagues as well as mutual interests. Both had trained at Bellevue Hospital in New York City, and they actually overlapped in one of those years. Hence, Hershberger could lead his guest gently into identifying the body of his son.

After many pleasantries and some remembrances of events that had taken place when they were at Bellevue, Dr. Hershberger casually handed Dr. Southerland a copy of the autopsy report that had generated by the Medical Examiner. As he did that he began going over some of the details of the report.

Upon carefully reading the first page of the report which, customarily, gives a detailed description of the body, Dr.

Southerland exclaimed, "this can't be my son. My son was never circumcised!" Dr. Hershberger responded, "Isn't it possible that your son had that procedure done recently?" To that, Southerland's answer was that he had golfed with his son at Ocean Reef in Key Largo over the Thanksgiving weekend, and they had showered together. Surely, he would have noticed.

Hershberger persuaded Dr. Southerland to at least to take the next step and view the body so that they could complete the process, and, in effect, put Dr. Southerland out of his misery. Southerland followed Hershberger into the morgue where awaiting them on a gurney was a body covered with a smock.

When the smock covering the body was pulled down revealing the head and upper body, Dr. Southerland without hesitation moved to the body and ran the fingers of both of his hands over the face. Immediately, he was overcome with uncontrollable grief. His face contorted in anguish. Turning in the direction of Dr. Hershberger, shaking his head in disbelief, he muttered, "Oh my God, that's my son!" Dr. Hershberger tried to console Dr. Southerland as best he could. He was not successful.

*   *   *

In the succeeding weeks, the FBI released additional information on events related to the crime scene at the New York Hilton on February 18th. By monitoring the area with a continuous sampling gas chromatograph, the FBI had determined that there was, indeed, an intermittent release of natural gas into the corridor. They found that the gas leak was being caused by a malfunction of a gas fired boiler in the mechanical room just off the corridor where the President was assassinated.

In order to prove that the gas leak was close enough to the area where the explosion had occurred, the FBI conducted tests to show that the concentration of natural gas at the site of the explosion was sufficient to cause ignition. They used a sparking device to trigger their controlled explosions. They were not successful in getting a cell phone to set off the explosion, but they theorized the concentration of natural gas could have been significantly greater on the day the President was assassinated. They also cited the fact that the humidity in the air could affect 'sparking'. February 18th was a particularly cold and dry day in New York City. Hence, there were a number of ways to explain this anomaly.

When these results were presented by Director Riemann to the Attorney General and the members of the Hamilton Commission, Riemann was questioned as to why no one had smelled gas – after all natural gas which has no smell has a 'stink' additive that makes its present very apparent. Riemann theorized that cooking odors could have masked the odor of the natural gas. That seemed a satisfactory explanation.

Director Riemann also presented the results of a massive investigation on the activities of Agent Southerland for the entire year prior to the assassination. There was no evidence that Southerland had substantial contact with any individuals other than his Secret Service colleagues and with his parents and his only brother. He apparently was a bit of a loner. In every case for every individual interviewed by the FBI, not one who had spent any substantial time with Southerland could recall any remark, or any suspicious activity that might indicate in any way what Southerland was capable of such a heinous act.

Furthermore, none of those interviewed, and many had spent considerable time with Southerland, had any indications that Agent Southerland was a racist. One black Secret Service agent claimed that he was convinced Southerland was very fond of him. They were regular teammates on pickup basketball games they played at the White House gym. He could not fathom that Southerland was capable of killing the President, but he knew the details of the investigation and he knew the case against Southerland was compelling.

In any case, Director Riemann had concluded that Southerland had acted alone. There was nothing to tie him to anyone in the outside world. Riemann speculated that Southerland must have either had a dual personality, or that his drug abuse had taken over some of the 'secret recesses of his mind.'

*   *   *

On Wednesday March 31st, in accordance with their charge the Hamilton Commission made their first 30 day report. The essence of the report was that the assassination of President DeFrie was a simple issue. He had been murdered by one of his trusted bodyguards. That bodyguard had been in the Secret Service for a sufficiently long number of years to conclude he was not a plant. Furthermore, it was concluded that Agent Southerland had committed a hate crime based on his personal issue with a black president. The report speculated that Southerland's behavior might have been affected by drugs of abuse. It was concluded that Southerland acted entirely on his own.

The report stated that Agent Solomon had killed Agent Southerland in a heroic but futile attempt to save the President. The report recommended that Solomon be commended for his actions and for his quick thinking in attempting to get the President to the Lennox Hill Trauma center as rapidly as possible.

One odd piece of information that the Commission had uncovered was the fact that Agent Solomon held dual citizenship. Probing further and using unprecedented investigatory powers the Commission was able to learn that following the assassination attempt on President Ronald Regan's life by John Hinckley, Jr. in March 1981, the President made a secret arrangement with the Israeli government. The Commission speculated that this arrangement was apparently prompted by grave concerns of the President's wife, who was openly critical of the Secret Service following the assassination attempt. And, who believed that Israel was doing a significantly better job at training their agents than was the case in this country.

The secret Presidential arrangement provided for the Secret Service Agency to have on its staff, and particularly in the contingent that was to guard the President, Agents of Mossad – the Israeli Intelligence Agency. As part of the aid package to Israel, Mossad would provide two fully trained, experienced agents that were fluent in English. The United States government was to confer citizenship on these individuals. This arrangement was to last for as long as the US and Israel 'remained allied by common interests'. Agent Solomon was one of those agents. The Commission found no evidence of a second Agent.

Chapter X

E ven though the Hamilton Commission had the authority to terminate itself whenever it deemed its work done, the March 31st Report had a tone that indicated the Commission's work was complete. In spite of the fact that those on the Committee had devoted 12 – 14 hours of nearly every day to their task, there was not one shred of evidence that the President's assassination was anything but the work of one man, a closet racist Agent Dean Southerland. There was not even a sniff indicating that Southerland acted in concert with anyone. Hence, the Commission reduced its efforts to one afternoon per week discussing any aspect of the case they deemed worth discussing. They were also hopeful that some new evidence might turn up.

Manhattan District Attorney Robert J. Morgenstein was not happy with the results of the 'murder case', as he called it, of President DeFrie for two very different reasons. The first dealt with the immediate sequence of events that resulted in President DeFrie being shot. To Morgenstein the sequence did not make sense. He claimed it made so little sense that 'it was corny.'

Morgenstein's problem was as follows: If it is assumed that Agent Southerland intended to assassinate the President, why didn't Southerland have an escape strategy? Secondly, if the FBI is correct in that the blast that occurred during the assassination was caused by a gas leak and was triggered by the President's cell phone, would Southerland suddenly have decided to shoot the President, and then use the explosion as a route to escape? To Morgenstein that would be suicide. There were Secret Service Agents armed with submachine guns at every exit. Southerland knew that! No matter which way Southerland might have chosen to escape, he was a dead man.

Morgenstein's conclusion on 'the not making sense issue' was that something had gone wrong with the assassination plot. He believed that there were other events that were intended to have taken place that, for some reason, did not. His gut told him that there had to be some part, or parts, of the plot that were missing, and those parts were supposed to allow Southerland, or Southerland and anyone else involved, to escape. That logic led Morgenstein to convince himself that this was not the work of one man.

It also led him to wonder about Agent Solomon. Was Solomon the hero he was being perceived as for attempting to bring down Agent Southerland in order save the President's life? Or did he quickly realize the assassination plot had gone wrong and that he needed to protect the perpetrators, and also himself? To Morgenstein it was evident that Solomon was a quick thinker. Solomon took charge immediately at the assassination scene and by his rapid actions and directives; valuable minutes were saved in getting President DeFrie to Lennox Hill Hospital.

The second reason that Morgenstein had a problem with the Hamilton Commission's findings was not exactly something he could put his finger on. It was more of an uncomfortable feeling. Something was rattling around inside Morgenstein's head that he could neither connect, nor find an appropriate place for it in his mental file. From his experience with that feeling he knew he could not put this case to bed. The issue that seemed to be bothering Morgenstein was learning that there were Mossad

Agents in the Secret Service. Alone in his office and thinking out loud, he muttered, "What the hell's that all about?"

In the first place, given his intimacy with prominent Israeli Government officials, that information came as a complete shock to him. Secondly, in spite of the fact that Morgenstein was publicly a strong and vigorous supporter of Israel, he had for many years had a real issue with some of the activities of Mossad. Morgenstein, unlike many other supporters of Israel, was not opposed to criticizing that country which he loved and felt such a strong attachment to. After all, Morgenstein was an American, and he believed it was his right to be publicly critical of things he did not agree with. He extended that right to honest criticism of Israeli policies that he believed were not in the long range interests of Israel and its citizens. There were a number of American and Israeli Jews who took issue with his approach. That never seemed to stop him.

In one moment of anger, Morgenstein actually referred to some members of Mossad as thugs and murderers. The secret action where the Israeli government used Mossad against the 'Black September' terrorists, who slaughtered 11 Israeli athletes in the 1972 Munich Olympics, was painful to him years after it happened. In that operation – referred to as 'Wrath of God' - 5 Mossad Agents were given a list of 'presumed guilty' Black September participants by the Israeli government. They were given secret instructions to assassinate everyone on that list.

If caught the Israeli government would deny any knowledge of the matter or deny any connection to these individuals. They would no longer be Agents of Mossad. In the planning of the mission it was made clear that there were to be no extraditions, there would be no trials. All on the list were assumed to be guilty.

Morgenstein called that "Old Testament retribution.' As much as Morgenstein wanted these killers dead, the actions of Mossad on that occasion were not his concept of justice no matter how heinous the crime. In his judgment those on the list were to be captured, extradited – even if the extradition was illegal, brought to trial and punished accordingly. Israelis must not become barbarians, he asserted. He often would add, "We Jews love our culture and our heritage. We are proud of all the contributions we have made to the civilized world for thousands of years, we must never be tempted to fall to subhuman levels. That, really, is our Covenant with God."

Morgenstein had one other issue that troubled him. In November of 1999 his dear friend of many years, the Premier of Israel, Yitzhak Rabin, was assassinated by a right wing ultra Orthodox Israeli law student named, Yigmal Amir. Amir claimed Rabin wanted 'to give our country to the Arabs'. He added that Jews needed 'to be cold-hearted' about such matters. As a reformed Jew, Morgenstein could not fathom how anyone could think in that manner. It concerned him that the Israeli government tolerated such radical groups, and, in fact, had to reach out to them to form coalition governments. That he claimed could bring down a country with so many virtues, and so many virtuous people. It also made him leery of the capabilities of many within the Israeli government.

As a consequence of Morgenstein's issues with the 'DeFrie Case', he made the decision to assign one of his Assistant District Attorneys to keep current on the 'DeFrie Case'. Morgenstein's style, when he was doing something against the grain, was to do it 'sotto voce' – in a soft voice. In that way, if it was a waste of time, by keeping it low key it would not be a big issue. Nor would it be an embarrassment to him.

The Assistant DA that he made this assignment was a 34 year old ambitious attorney named Ralph Campanella. Campanella who grew up in Queens, attended Fordham University for both his undergraduate and law degrees was distantly related to Roy Campanella. Roy Campanella was an All Star Catcher of the Brooklyn Dodgers in the 50's. He had led the Dodgers to the five World Series and was one of the first Blacks to play major league baseball. Ralph Campanella who had a swarthy complexion looked to be of 'Italian' background which for the most part he was.

Assistant DA Campanella, in spite of his young age, had been successful in investigating and prosecuting several important organized crime and racketeering cases. Morgenstein apparently chose Campanella to follow the 'DeFrie Case', because a case that Campanella was bringing to trial involving the Russian, or Brighton Beach, Mafia had fallen apart. On the eve of the trial Campanella's main witness had gone missing. Campanella was disappointed but not surprised. He assumed his witness would turn up sooner or later in the East River.

Campanella knew the Russian Mafia well. In the words of his father, a retired New York City Policeman, he was well aware that unlike the Italian mafia who refrain from harming journalists, prosecutors, judges or even innocent family members, these 'bastards' will kill you just to see if their guns work. Campanella also appreciated the irony of the existence of this criminal group who were mainly non-believing Soviet Jews who had immigrated to the US in the 1970's. That immigration was a result of President Jimmy Carter and others, who in their championing of human rights vigorously supported of the Jackson-Vanik Amendment. These 'do-gooders' were to learn years later that the Jackson-Vanik law, which withheld 'most-favored-nation-status' to countries that restricted Jewish emigration, resulted in welcoming to the US hardened criminals that the Soviet Union was only too happy to get rid of. Since US immigration officials had no access to criminal records, the US had indeed been duped.

Morgenstein wanted Campanella to spend at least two days of each week on the 'DeFrie Case'. In spite of considerable whispered teasing that Campanella was getting from his colleagues - about "how's 'The Case' going?" – Campanella dug into his assignment with a certain level of gusto. It was a case unlike any he had dealt with previously and a case that was of world wide interest. When he had told his wife about his assignment which he made clear she was to keep confidential, she was actually thrilled. Even if that was naïve of her, it also served to spur him on. Accordingly, he spent the two days of the first two weeks of his efforts reading and researching aspects of the Hamilton Commission report.

By week three after Campanella had thoroughly reviewed and researched every scrap of information he could lay his hands on, he had come to the conclusion that Morgenstein 'must be seeing ghosts.' Campanella knew his boss fairly well, and he was beginning to think that Morgenstein was grandstanding. He understood that Morgenstein was not happy with the role he had carved out for himself in the assassination investigation – even though it was a substantial role considering the circumstances.

Campanella also knew that Morgenstein tracked the number of times his name appeared in the *New York Times* on issues related to the assassination of the President. He did not have many inclusions. Campanella's analysis of Morgenstein's personality as well as an exhaustive review of all aspects of the assassination case led him to conclude the Hamilton Commission was correct in their conclusions. Campanella determined he would devote his activities to other cases which needed attention.

*   *   *

Late on Friday afternoon the 23rd of April, Ralph Campanella had cleared his desk for the weekend and was trying to leave a bit early as he was taking his wife for dinner and a show for her 30th birthday. As he was leaving his office the telephone rang. Wanting to ignore the call and let it ring onto his answering machine, he continued to make his way from his office, when the ringing suddenly stopped. Momentarily the phone began to ring again. Thinking it was his wife, who often used telephone rings to signal she was calling; Campanella picked up the phone and said, "This is Ralph Campanella speaking."

A gruff and somewhat difficult to understand voice on the other end of the line stated, "This is Dr. Hollis. I am the Medical Examiner of Dutchess County. I am calling from Poughkeepsie, New York." Campanella interrupted, asking the caller to repeat his name – he, politely, said we must have a bad connection which was not accurate. Hollis reintroduced himself again, and continued. "The reason I am calling you is that the Poughkeepsie Fire Department recovered a body from the Hudson River just south of the Mid-Hudson Bridge. We were actually dragging the river for the body of a 20 year old woman who had committed suicide in late February. We were hopeful that the temperature of the river water had finally warmed enough to cause bloating and bring her body to the surface of the river."

Campanella, trying to get on his way and annoyed that Hollis' chewing of his words made him difficult to understand, interrupted Hollis by stating, "Dr. Hollis. Thanks for your call, but can you tell me what the Poughkeepsie Fire Department's recovery of a body has to do with me?" Immediately, Hollis shot back, "Didn't you recently have a case of a missing witness in some Russian Mafia case you were prosecuting?"

When Campanella acknowledged that, Hollis continued, "Well this is the body of a male, and it has all the earmarks of a Russian mob killing. Besides being weighted down, the hands of the victim have been severed at the wrists; the face is mutilated beyond recognition." In response to that Campanella ask Hollis how he intended to identify the body.

Hollis responded that whoever killed this guy wanted to be sure he couldn't be identified. Not only had they severed his hands and mutilated his face, his teeth had been ripped out. Hollis stated that the only hope they had of identifying the body would be through DNA analysis. Getting to the point of his call, Dr. Hollis inquired if Campanella knew of any one who might be a related to Campanella's witness. Through a comparative analysis of the DNA of a relative with that of the victim, it would be possible to show a familial relationship.

Campanella, who by now had forgiven Hollis for his muffled speech – the silly thought that led to his new found tolerance which kept running through Campanella's head was 'after all this guy has to only communicate with corpses' – by now had his interest peaked. To Hollis, he responded, "Well today is your lucky day!" He informed Hollis, in confidence, that his witness was a Vinnie Mordorella, and that Vinnie was a classic example of the 'good brother – bad brother'.

Vinnie Mordorella was a petty criminal who had been an informant to the New York Police for years. Campanella also thought he was a paid informant for the FBI. In any case, Vinnie – the bad brother – had a brother, Tony Mordorella, who was a New York City Detective. Campanella, wise-cracking that there was no hurry as his case was as dead as the victim, promised to have Tony Mordorella go the Manhattan Medical Examiners office so that they could retrieve cells for analysis.

Tony Mordorella was not anxious to determine if the body in Dr. Hollis's morgue was that of his brother. They had gone their separate routes years ago, and they did not like each other. As a consequence of that it would take Tony Mordorella, with prodding from Campanella who was being prodded by Hollis, two weeks to visit the Medical Examiners office where they would use a 'cheek brush' – very much like a small tooth brush – to scrape some cells from the inside of his mouth. That brush in a sealed container would eventually be sent to Poughkeepsie for DNA analysis. Detective Tony Mordorella had told the lab tech who took his cell sample, "Don't' rush." The sample arrived in Poughkeepsie on Thursday May 13th.

*   *   *

Even though Campanella was not in a hurry to get the DNA analysis from Dr. Hollis, it had occurred to him that he might be able to build a murder case against 'those Russian SOB's'. He began putting out 'the word' to his informants for any information that might be helpful.

On Tuesday May 18th a call came into the receptionist at the Manhattan Office of the District Attorney. The caller, who would not give his name, wanted to know if anyone in the DA's office was working on the assassination case of President DeFrie. Even though the receptionist was not supposed to be privy to that information, she had overheard enough muffled ribbing of Campanella's activities to know he was the one to refer the call to.

Forwarding the call to Campanella, the receptionist said she had someone – who would not give his name - on the phone who wanted to talk to anyone who might be working on the assassination of the President. She 'thought' Campanella might know who that might be.

Campanella picked up his phone, identified himself and waited. The caller was entirely upfront. He identified himself as Ronald Swick, an attorney who had worked as one of Ralph Nader's raiders from the day he finished law school. He had been with Nader starting with Nader's battle with the Detroit Auto Industry regarding their complete disregard for safety in their products and for the lives of their customers. Swick had spent over forty years with Nader.

The thought that Swick 'needed' to share was how relentless and how unscrupulous the Auto Industry had collectively been in their attempts to get Nader. Swick revealed that he had evidence that there was a plot to kill Nader in the 60's. He claimed that it was a serious plot, well financed and well planned. Even though he could not prove his case Swick was convinced the 'auto guys' were involved. He added that it was only the celebrity brought by Nader's publishing of his book – 'Unsafe at any Speed' – that saved Nader's life.

Swick added numerous details to his account of the plot that seemed to add creditability. Swick wanted Campanella to know that many American Corporate guys were a vile bunch and that President DeFrie's policies had cost a very significant number of them millions of dollars in bonuses. DeFrie, he claimed, had also cost their companies and their shareholders billions. Swick asserted it would be naïve not to consider them as possible suspects, rather than 'this ridiculous nonsense' – his words – that the Justice Department, FBI and Hamilton Commission wanted the country to believe.

Swick finished by saying, "At the risk of making a generality, you have no idea how greedy these bastards can be. They love money and power – it's their Gods!" Swick paused, and then added, "You have to understand corporate executives. Many of them really think they are strategists. And, lots of that bunch thinks they are brilliant because they have reached the top of the heap. But they are really game players who have plenty of time on their hands. Believe me it's not hard to be a corporate CEO; they have armies of 'man servants' doing everything for them. That's why they have so much time. That and their penchant for thinking they are strategists is what makes them dangerous! Everything's a game for them. And, they have all the time in the world to play."

During the time that Campanella was listening to Swick on the telephone, Campanella felt there was something odd in the cadence of Swick's voice. For whatever reason, that prompted in Campanella the thought that Swick must be some kind of nut. Continuing to listen, Campanella could not keep that thought from running through his mind. He wondered to himself if that was the kind of individual you needed to be in order to qualify as a Nader Raider. However, when Swick hung up Campanella realized that maybe it was he that was naïve. Maybe it was his own thoughts that were silly, almost childish.

Replaying the telephone call in his head, Campanella began to realize that Swick was sincere in what he was saying, and maybe there was something to it. Campanella considered the possibility that Swick just expressed his ideas forcefully and with a great deal of emotion. Maybe that it what was throwing Campanella off. Furthermore, Swick was only trying to give Campanella the benefit of his experiences. Reflecting on the fact that Nader guys were courageous, fearless and motivated, Campanella realized he was reading Swick wrong. It occurred to him that the Nader people were so much like some little group of Lilliputians who were willing to attack even the most vicious and vile of dragons.

Leaning back motionless in his office chair, Campanella suddenly lurched forward and reached for his telephone. He made seven phone calls, reaching four of the parties he was seeking successfully. For the other three, he left a private number where he could be reached, and a simple message to call back. He never mentioned who was calling. To those four that he reached, Campanella had a simple request. He wanted to know if there was 'any buzz on the street' regarding a contract on the life of the President or anything that might relate to the assassination. In time the other three 'call backs' were asked the same question. Campanella was confident that he could leverage off of the 'tentacles' of his informants, informants he had cultivated in his 9 years in the District Attorney's office. He would wait patiently. There was no need to rush.

After he had made some notes that he neatly placed in the files he was keeping on the 'DeFrie Case', Campanella dialed up his boss. It was time to get together and tap into the 'old man's' insights. Robert J. Morgenstein had too much experience and too much wisdom for Campanella to pass up. Furthermore, Campanella knew that you don't stay in a high profile and demanding job like that of his boss for so many years – more years than Campanella had lived – without having the right stuff. Taking with him a legal pad on which he had written down several notes along with a series of questions, he headed for Morgenstein's office.

*   *   *

Morgenstein was delighted that Campanella had finally come to him with 'something' on the 'DeFrie Case'. He had difficulty hiding his glee at the fact that he had detected from his telephone conversation with Campanella, the voice of a 'convert'. He was anxious to hear exactly what Campanella had on his mind. He had never revealed any of his own thought on the case to Campanella. He did not want to direct his thinking.

Campanella, in a very thorough manner, informed Morgenstein of all of his efforts to date. He shared that in reviewing all of the information and data that he was able to obtain – and, he believed he had been thorough in that connection – in his judgment, there was no point in retracing the avenues that the Justice Department Investigators, the FBI or the Hamilton Commission had taken. Campanella stated, "They were thorough, but they may have had a blind spot." Campanella suggested that since all the members of the Commission had backgrounds in the government and the judicial worlds, maybe they did not understand the corporate world, or the corporate mentality. Morgenstein smiled when he heard these statements.

In that connection, Campanella told Morgenstein of the conversation he had just had with Swick. He explained Swick's background and some of the detail Swick had shared with him concerning the lengths to which the Auto Industry was willing to go to get Nader. Campanella then confessed that Swick made him realize the magnitude of the resources those, who would want to get rid of the President, had, individually, and collectively.

Before Campanella could say another word, Morgenstein literally jumped out of his seat and bounded to the wall of his office where a dry erase porcelain writing board was mounted. Morgenstein exclaimed, "We need to make a listing of the members of billionaire assassination club." The District Attorney was referring to every institution domestic or foreign that had lost one billion dollars or more just in the last 6 months because the President DeFrie's programs.

Without hesitating Morgenstein began to make his list. He began with the Pharmaceutical firms, listing each by name. Next he added the HMO's and other insurance firms that were financially affected by the President's Universal Health Plan. To that list he added the Auto Industry, individually naming those companies that specialize in large luxury vehicles, and the Petroleum Industry that would take a real beating with the President's programs on alternative energies. Companies that profit in weapons of war, or service contracts related to war made the list as well.

When the list had grown to more than a dozen domestic and multinational corporations, Morgenstein stopped. He turned to Campanella and said, "On that Board with a 99% certainly are companies whose executives – either directly or indirectly - are responsible for the President's murder. The remaining 1%, I reserve for political entities that would want the President dead, either for economic reasons, for territory reasons or for ideology. And, on that list, I place the North Koreans, possibly the Russians, and unfortunately Israel."

Morgenstein paused. He was saddened by the comment he had just made about Israel, but he was honor bound to be objective. He knew there were radical groups in Israel who would want President DeFrie dead, if he were to take just one acre from them. And, President DeFrie was already responsible for much more than that in his first six months of office. He also knew the hatred and determination that all radical groups can muster. He understood well that as illogical as radical groups can be when it comes to their ideology, they can be brilliant, rational and precise in their execution of any plan they put their minds to.

Continuing on, Morgenstein added, "My instincts tell me to take the Russians off of that list. They had everything to benefit from DeFrie's continuing to live. The last real issue we had with the Russians dealt with their objections to the Eastern Europe missile base we were building under the last Administration. Now that that is not an issue, I take them off of my list."

Stopping to compose a thought, Morgenstein added, "When you think of it, for the North Koreans to plot to kill the President of the United States, there are significant barriers. Language and physical appearances become major issues. They would have to use Westerners to do the job. That could present some real problems for them. But let's not forget nothing is insurmountable."

Ralph Campanella was moderately overwhelmed by Morgenstein's performance. "The Old Man' sure could get worked up", he thought to himself. But going back to the list of potential perpetrators Morgenstein had come up with, that would be an impossible task to crack. All Campanella could think was: Where does one start?

Given the resources that those members of Morgenstein's 'billionaire club' had available to them individually, and God forbid collectively, there would be no limit on the extremes they would be able to go to in order to assassinate the President. Keeping his thought to himself, he realized that if just a few of this group teamed up, they could purchase not only the Secret Service, but half of the US government. Campanella could feel depression setting in.

The fact that Morgenstein, who was fully animated by this time, was now revealing to Campanella, for the first time and in detail, his analysis of 'the absurdity' of the plot that everyone had bought in to, did not make Campanella feel any better.

In regard to Campanella's concern about the difficulty of 'cracking' the list, Morgenstein had a very different point of view. He explained to Campanella that he understood it would be impossible to narrow his list down, but he shared that he also understood something else – human nature. Morgenstein claimed that he knew the limits of the human mind. It was 'crystal clear' to him what secrets can be kept and which cannot. Morgenstein explained this to Campanella, and told him why assassins are assassinated. An assassin he asserted can not deal with the thought of killing some great personage. In time he will either be moved to boast about his achievement or he will be overwhelmed by the pangs of guilt. Consequently, the name of the game is to kill the assassin. Most any killer can deal with that.

Campanella was not sure he even understood, let along bought into, all of Morgenstein's ideas, or theories as he more appropriately thought of them. None-the-less, he was anxious to hear where Morgenstein was taking him. Without skipping a beat, Morgenstein stated that one key to solving the murder of the

President lay in getting to the right informants. People like to talk, people like to brag, he asserted, adding that was particularly so for this egotistical and self centered generation. He also knew that people like money, "And we are going to dangle that in front of their eyes."

"The second key to solving this murder is that we need to get inside the head of the assassin. And for now we will assume that Southerland's assignment was to kill the President. We are going to figure out how he was going to escape. Our jobs are to find the missing part, or parts, of the plot. And, who else was involved? And, who planned this?"

Ralph Campanella felt good about what the District Attorney had outlined for him. Even if it was nonsense, at least it was a plan. Campanella then revealed that he had already put out the word to his informer network. Morgenstein, whose network of informants and just 'folks' who like to talk was international, would do the same.

Campanella, who by this time was pleased that he had some direction, and who wanted to get on his way so that he could get up to the Bronx for a Yankee – Red Sox game, started to leaved Morgenstein's office. Morgenstein raised his left hand to about eye level and nodding his head at the same time said, "Not so fast, young fella, we've got a lot of work to do." Campanella had been through this before with his Boss. He knew this could be an all nighter, or at least in the wee hours of the night – sometime between midnight and dawn.

*   *   *

District Attorney Morgenstein's secretary made the fateful mistake of checking in with him before she would leave for the day to see if there was anything that she needed to have ready for the morning. Morgenstein, who, by this time, was wiping the porcelain board clean, without turning from his task responded, "We need a fresh pot of coffee and can you get us some corned beef and Swiss cheese sandwiches." Campanella had seen this drill before, he looked at Morgenstein's secretary out of the corner of his eye, and sort of smirked.

Before the coffee arrived, Morgenstein said, "Tonight we are going to play a little game. I am going to give you 70 million dollars. And, you are going to tell me how you are going to assassinate the President of the United States." Campanella had an issue with the 70 million, he said he understood these guys were flush, but he wanted to know 'where did we get this 70 million dollar figure?' Without hesitating Morgenstein shot back, "That, my friend, is probably not more than 30% of the Pharmaceutical Industry paid in their campaign to keep DeFrie out of the White House!" He paused, "That's right they spent at least 200 million. And that was just their industry. What do you think the rest of those bastards shelled out to keep this guy out of office?" Campanella slouched in his chair. It was hard for him to fathom that kind of money, but 'the Old Man' made perfect sense.

The pause to fix their coffees gave the 'two plotters' time to think of where they would go next. But it became clear that Morgenstein had been thinking of this all along, because he asked Campanella, "If you were going to assassinate the President. What is the biggest obstacle?" Without hesitating, Campanella responded, "Getting through some of the toughest and most rigidly controlled security that exists." Morgenstein nodded approval. That he thought was the obvious answer.

"So if you could corrupt the security that would make it easy. Wouldn't it?" Campanella nodded agreement again. Morgenstein continued, "So I just gave you 70 million dollars how are you going to spend it?" Without waiting for Campanella's response, Morgenstein said, "We are going to buy up the Secret Service. And, since we know that's hard to do – after all these guys are all boy scouts – we need to find the ones who have either fallen out of the mold, or who never belonged there in the first place. There may not be many of them, but we will find the ones we can buy."

Ralph Campanella was uncomfortable with the road they were heading down. His Dad had been a New York City policeman and prided himself as never taking so much as a nickel. To the Campanella's integrity was more important than owning the world. None- the- less, Ralph Campanella had enough work and life experience to know that he and his family were probably in the minority.

Sensing Campanella's uneasiness, Morgenstein took a softer track. He asked Campanella how much money he would need to live well and to never have to work again. Campanella couldn't answer that question. He earned 88 thousand dollars a year and he was one of the highest paid Assistant District Attorneys. He was enjoying his life.

Impatient that no answer was forthcoming, Morgenstein said, "I am going to give you 5 million dollars in cash. And, I am going to see that you don't pay tax on that money! If you hide that under you mattress you can take 250 thousand out each year, that will last you 20 years. If I can show you how to invest it and give you a 5% return, you will always have the original 5 million I gave you." Campanella had never thought of this, and he had no reason to, but he was still surprised even though the numbers made sense.

Accepting the notion that you could 'buy' someone for 5 million dollars, Campanella wanted to first know 'how do you find the right candidates?' And, when you find them, 'how do you approach them?'

Morgenstein responded, "That is not that hard to do. We put a 24 hour tail on every agent and we find out who the straight arrows are and who are not. If we tail 20 selected agents for 20 days at 500 bucks a day that costs us 200,000. And, we are starting with 70 million. That's not a big deal. And, if we double the number we tail, we can afford that too."

Morgenstein could see that Campanella was wondering how you could pull this off. The words 'How do you tail Secret Service Agents and get away with it?' were pasted on Campanella's forehead. Morgenstein said, "If you want to know how to do this, it's simple. You walk into a Detective Agency, and you tell them that you think some guy might be banging your wife, but you are not sure who it is. So you give him a list of names. You also tell them your wife is a secretary for the Director of the Secret Service. And, bingo, you've got them tailing 5 Agents. All I need is four agencies to cover my first 20 Agents." Morgenstein paused, "Once we got them tailed, we will know everything about them."

Campanella could see that this was a viable approach. It would not be easy, but it should be possible to track down if this is how Agent Southerland might have been recruited. He was anxious to see who they might catch in this net, although he was skeptical.

*   *   *

Before the week was out Morgenstein had three New York City Detectives working on the DeFrie assassination case. Two, Detectives Andrew Schiavo and Kenneth Silvers, were assigned to 'work' the DC area. That would include surveying the areas' nearly 20 major detective agencies, checking the Washington area local hangouts that governments workers frequented and checking every bookmaker or corner kiosk where someone could place a bet. Morgenstein was convinced they would turn up more than a few 'naughty boy scouts', as he referred to his prey. The third Detective, Daniel Healey, was assigned to dig into Secret Service David Solomon's background, his associates, his non work hour activities, and according to Morgenstein's directive, "Get to know Solomon a well as his mother knows him." The Detective assigned the 'Solomon task' quickly learned that Solomon's mother was indeed dead, but he understood the Boss' request.

The following week was an extraordinarily busy time for Morgenstein and his sleuths. On Tuesday the 25th, Morgenstein's informant network bore the first fruit. From a reliable source they learned that the Russian Mafia in mid January had 'imported' three former Russian Army Snipers. They had come in to the country through Canada and had been hidden somewhere in Brooklyn. Morgenstein's source told him that it was not known if the Russians still were in the country.

The trio, the Russian Mob had imported, had been trained by the Russian Army and had served in Afghanistan. They had also been involved in an exchange training program with Germany. There they were supposed to have become proficient with the Accuracy International AS50 sniper rifle. According to one of New York City's Police firearms experts, the graduation test for a Sniper team – at least in Great Britain – is to be able to 'take out' a human target at 4500 feet, nearly one mile.

When Morgenstein met with Campanella to discuss this new information, Morgenstein was convinced the Brighton Beach mob was not politically motivated. Their interests lay in only acquiring money, the easier the method the better. Furthermore, neither Morgenstein nor Campanella could come up with a viable reason for how the Mob would benefit by the President's death. That led Morgenstein to go down the mental route of 'who were these people working for? - Who are they providing service to?'

In that connection, Campanella reminded his boss of the 'home heating oil for diesel fuel' switch scandal that the Russian Mafia had been involved in just around the time Campanella came to work in the DA's office. The scandal that broke in 1999 cost the federal government nearly 16 billion dollars in lost diesel tax revenue via the switching scam. And, if that were not bad enough the Mob used major New York, New Jersey and Delaware banks to launder their money – likely with complicity on the banks' part.

Campanella continued, "These guys certainly know their way into the oil industry. They must have some good contacts there. And, it's not a big jump from the oil guys to the auto guys." Morgenstein listening intently, nodded in agreement.

*   *   *

Three days later, on Friday afternoon May 28th, at what was apparently his usual time to make calls – 4:30 pm – Dr. Hollis was on the phone to Campanella to share that his DNA data was in. After some small talk most of which Campanella could not hear clearly because of Hollis' muffled telephone speaking manner, Hollis stated, "Well our guy is not your guy. You can tell Tony Mordorella this isn't his brother."

Campanella, not in a rush because he had to meet with Morgenstein at 5:30 anyway, asked Hollis if they were able to get an ID from the National DNA Data Bank. Hollis responded that they had gotten a match. It was to a young fellow doing a surgical residency at St. Mary's Hospital in San Francisco, which is part of the University of California system. Campanella was curious and asked, "How did somebody like that ever get into the National DNA Bank?" Hollis shared that three years ago when he was doing an internship at Cedars Sinai Hospital in Los Angeles this 'guy' was accused of raping a nurse which 'turned out to be all bullshit, he must have jilted her' – Hollis' words. In any case, Campanella learned that in California it is standard practice to take DNA samples on individuals accused of rape.

Before Hollis hung up, for whatever reason he wanted Campanella to know the name of his victim. It was a 'Gene Sudderlin'. Hollis added that since it was still early in California when he finished this call, he was going to try to track down next of kin. For reasons that were not obvious to Campanella, Hollis insisted on giving him his cell phone number and his home phone. Campanella figured that maybe Hollis expected him to solve Sudderlin's murder case. As if he didn't have enough to do.

During Campanella's 5:30 meeting with 'the Boss', he suddenly remembered that it was the Memorial Day Weekend, something he was looking forward to, but had forgotten about entirely. Campanella's wife had booked a room at Trump Plaza in Atlantic City for Saturday and Sunday nights, and they would be leaving very early in the morning for the two and a half hour drive from Queens to Atlantic City.

District Attorney Robert J. Morgenstein had other ideas. He, Campanella, Police Commissioner Kelly, and two investigators from the DA's office would spend Saturday morning at the 'crime scene'. They would walk every step from the service elevator in the corridor of the New York Hilton where the President was murdered to the service exit. They would also traverse the service elevator to and from the Ballroom. And, they would repeat that at least 10 times. It was as if Morgenstein was trying to get the floors, the walls or the ceiling of the Hilton to speak to him. The only speaking they might have done was said 'they were dirty' – the area had been cordoned off since the President's assassination. With each trip they took, Morgenstein would ask, "How would you kill someone in here, under tight surveillance and hope to escape?"

This Saturday morning exercise which bore little, if any, fruit, only served to delay the Campanellas trip to Atlantic City. It also gave Ralph Campanella a splitting headache. Now instead of a two and a half hour trip, because of traffic that had built up while Morgenstein's entourage traipsed to and fro through the murder scene would result in a possible 4 to 5 hour trip.

*   *   *

Roseanne Campanella liked to take drives with her husband. Under those circumstances, he was her captive, and as they had agreed after 6 months of marriage to 'a cell phones off – no radio policy', it was her chance to have his undivided attention. Roseanne was a biologist and taught the advanced placement biology courses at Stella Maris High School in Rockaway Park – a private catholic girls' school. As the school year was coming to an end, she had much to share including plans to take one or two graduate courses over the summer. Hence, the thought of a 5 hour trip even if it was to be stop and go, was not at all a problem to her.

From the moment they crossed the Verrazano Narrows Bridge, then down the New Jersey Turnpike to the Garden State

Parkway and to exit 38, where they would pick up the Atlantic City Expressway, Roseanne gave a detailed progress report on each one of 'her girls'. Ralph would learn the Regents scores for each, where they would be going to college, and even Roseanne's prediction on which ones would have significant careers after college. He would also learn which ones would just be producing more Catholics.

As they entered onto the Atlantic City Expressway, Roseanne apologized for having monopolized all of their 'conversation time'. She honestly wanted to hear what, if anything, was happening on the Assassination investigation. At her request, Ralph brought her up to date with the information they had concerning the Brighton Beach Mob and the Russian Sniper business. Roseanne was fascinated by that information. She made the statement to her husband, "Are you telling me that someone nearly a mile away from us, could kill us?" To that Ralph replied in the affirmative. Roseanne went on to say that if that were so, 'how could you protect anyone?' Ralph's response, "You can't".

When they were off the Expressway and paying that one last pesky toll just as Atlantic City could be seen in the distance, Ralph mentioned to Roseanne some details of his telephone call with Dr. Hollis on Friday afternoon. Roseanne, speaking as a biologist, said she would love to see the DNA analysis and the related report that Hollis had. When Ralph had not mentioned anything about the identification by the DNA, Roseanne wanted to know, "Was that your witness, 'that Mordorella fella?" Ralph responded that it was not. He added that it was the body of a surgical resident from California. When Roseanne was curious how a surgical resident ends up being on a national DNA registry, Ralph shared that he had apparently been accused of rape and had been acquitted.

The thought that innocent individuals could have their DNA on a national registry troubled Roseanne. She wondered out loud if there were legally some ways to have that information expunged. Ralph didn't answer. He was trying to follow the colored casino signs on the side of the road looking for the turn for Trump Plaza, and the traffic was heavy. He had also in a previous trip missed the turnoff and had to make three trips around a 'mini Greek Temple' placed right in the middle of the street – to him it seemed to be where the pigeons of Atlantic City meet - before he could reorient himself.

As the Campanellas pulled up to Valet parking at Trump Plaza, Roseanne wanted to close out the conversation on Dr. Hollis' case. While Ralph was telling the Valet parker that they would be checking in for Saturday and Sunday nights, Roseanne had one last question, the kind of question that women seem to so often need to know the answer to, even it the answer has no real consequence for them. "Did Dr. Hollis tell you the name that came back on the report?" Ralph said, "Yes he did. It was a Gene Sudderlin."

Chapter XI

O n Monday morning, Memorial Day, Roseanne Campanella needed to stop at the player's desk at the Trump Plaza Casino to check a discrepancy on their Trump One Player card. It seems the Campanellas had to pay for a dinner on Sunday evening that was supposed to be 'complimentary. While in line Roseanne noted that there were about twenty apparently retired men and women who were in line ahead of her. For the most part they were black. There were a few older white women. All were neatly dressed, and each wore a black arm band on their left arm. The group was redeeming coupons for $25 slot machine vouchers and for buffet tickets. It was apparent they were one of the multitudes of senior groups that the Casinos import to Atlantic City on each and every day.

Being a 'nosy New Yorker', as Roseanne often referred to herself, she struck up a conversation with the women just in front of her in line – a very pleasant black woman with a very round face. Roseanne was curious as to who these people were, why they wore black arm bands, and why they wore them on their left arms. She learned that they were from a Baptist Church group located on North Broad Street in Philadelphia, just south of the Temple University main campus.

The Church group was wearing the black arm bands in the memory of their fallen President, Maynard Jefferson DeFrie. They would continue to do this until the anniversary of the President's death in 2011. As the woman related this to Roseanne referring to the President as 'Mr. DeFrie', her lower lip quivered, her eyes welled up with tears, and she could barely speak. Roseanne could see how much this woman hurt. She, too, was beginning to choke up. Roseanne also learned that they wore their arm bands on their left arms because it was closer to their hearts. As a biologist Roseanne was not sure this anatomical fact was correct, but she knew they were sincere. So it didn't really matter.

After they had retrieved their car from the Valet Service – about 1:40 pm - Ralph and Roseanne Campanella began their return trip to Queens, reversing the route they had taken on Saturday. As they proceeded on their way, Roseanne shared the encounter she had had with the Baptist Church group who were wearing the black arm bands. She described the emotion of the woman she was talking with. She had to wipe her own eyes as she shared this with her husband. Continuing to drive west, Roseanne and Ralph Campanella continued to talk about President DeFrie and the assassination. They remembered the thrill of being at his rally in Yankee Stadium. They also remembered their despair with his death.

The exit from the Atlantic City Expressway, north to the Garden State Parkway is often missed. The exit seems to come up quickly, is not that prominent and, oftentimes, visitors who have just left Atlantic City are preoccupied with licking their gambling wounds. That was not the case for the Campanellas; Ralph had won 120 dollars and Roseanne had come out 28 dollars ahead. Ralph, apparently deep in thought, made the turn onto the exit heading south, in the direction of Cape May.

Roseanne, who was counting her 28 dollars in winnings for the second time, quickly realized they were going south and exclaimed, "South, south – we are going south!" She paused for a moment, giving a little laugh that they could have made such a silly mistake, and continued, "Grandma Wetzel would be yelling – wir gehen sud! Sud!" That was the extent of the German that Roseanne had learned from her maternal grandmother, and she wasn't even sure if it were correct. Ralph Campanella who had taken one year of German in his 9th grade Public School before enrolling in Fordham Prep was amused because he thought her pronunciation was off. Being gentle, he asked, "Is it 'sood' as in wood? Or is it 'sudd' as in Sudderlin?" Roseanne laughed. She suggested they stick to English.

Proceeding south to the next exit where they could turn under the Parkway and back on to it heading north, Roseanne sat quietly. She had a slight frown on her face which slowly mutated into a very quizzical look. Turning towards her husband, she asked, "Didn't you say the name of the body in Hollis' morgue is Sudderlin?" Ralph Campanella responded, "That's correct."

"Didn't you also say you can never understand Hollis because he mutters?" she continued. To that Ralph Campanella responded that was so. Roseanne then asked, "Well maybe Hollis was saying 'Southerland' and you didn't understand him right!" By this time Ralph Campanella was becoming annoyed. He really didn't know where his wife was going. She didn't make any sense.

Because the Campanellas were still enjoying the last parts of a very romantic weekend – a mini honeymoon as Roseanne called it – Ralph decided to remain solicitous, rather than show any annoyance. Accordingly, he asked Roseanne to explain what she was thinking. Roseanne proceeding on intuition said, "Suppose Hollis was really saying 'Southerland'. Southerland is not that common a name. Doesn't it seem odd that Agent Southerland was just killed after he assassinated the President, and somebody fetches a body out of the Hudson River – which belongs to someone 3000 miles away in San Francisco – with the same name?"

Ralph Campanella realized there was an easy way to allay his wife's suspicions and get her off this absurd track, he would just call Hollis. After all Ralph had Hollis' cell phone number which was in his glove compartment along with a host of other information Campanella normally traveled with. Ralph told Roseanne that he would call Hollis and asked her to retrieve the number out of his stuff in the glove compartment. He asked her to dial the number on his cell phone.

In handing the cell phone to her husband when Hollis' number began to ring, Roseanne had inadvertently pressed the button on her husband's phone which turned on the speaker. After several rings, she heard a garbled, "Dr. Hollis here!" which made her think Hollis was either being awakened from a nap, or that he was just plain hard to understand.

Responding to Hollis, Ralph Campanella said, "Dr. Hollis this is Ralph Campanella from the DA's office. I was wondering if you have any more information on your case. And, in particular I want to be sure I got the name of the victim correct." To that Hollis responded 'Sudderlin'. At that point Roseanne whispered to her husband asking him to have Hollis spell the name.

Dutifully Ralph made that request. To which, Hollis responded, "It's spelled – 'S'- 'O'-'U'-'T'-'H'-'E'-'R'-'L'-'A'- 'N'-'D'! Did you get that?" Ralph Campanella was stunned. He turned to Roseanne; lips pursed nodding that she might be on to something.

Ralph Campanella then asked if Hollis was successful in contacting the family of the victim. Hollis, who did not seem to have a sense of humor, responded, "Well how about this? I contacted 'Gene Sudderlin' himself! The guy is alive!"

Puzzled Ralph Campanella asked Hollis, "Who could the dead guy be? He must be a close relative!" At this point, Roseanne Campanella who knew a lot about DNA testing asked her husband to find out the extent of the match there was of the victim's DNA to that in the data base. Hollis responded that the relationship must be close, it was an exact match.

Roseanne grabbed the cell phone from her husband, introduced herself, shared her Biology background and said she was overhearing the telephone conversation. That was something that Hollis already knew as Ralph Campanella had mentioned near the beginning of his conversation that his phone was on speaker, that his wife was in the car with him, and that he could not find the button to turn the speaker off in the dark.

Continuing Roseanne stated, "Dr. Hollis if there is an exact DNA match to Dr. Southerland in San Francisco, the body your people took from the Hudson is either Gene Southerland, or it has to be an identical twin." Dr. Hollis reluctantly agreed. He added that he did not know if Gene Southerland had a twin. However, he offered that if the Campanellas would be driving for awhile, he would go down to his office, fetch Dr. Southerland's phone number and call them back so that they could contact Southerland, themselves. Without waiting for her husband, Roseanne said, "That would be great!"

Just as the Campanellas were on their last leg home – they had just paid the toll on the Verrazano Narrows Bridge – Ralph's cell phone rang. Since it was against the law to use a hand held cell phone while driving, Roseanne Campanella took the call. It was Dr. Hollis who had Dr. Southerland's cell phone number, his pager number and the St. Mary's Hospital surgical floor number.

Pulling off the highway at his first opportunity, Ralph Campanella dialed Gene Southerland's phone number. His call was forwarded to a voice mail system. Campanella identified himself as being with the New York City District Attorney's office, left his cell and home phone numbers and said that it was 'of utmost importance' for Southerland to call back ASAP, regardless of what time it was. He placed calls to Dr. Southerland's pager service, leaving a call back number there. He also reached the surgical unit at St. Mary's. Dr. Southerland, he learned, was off for the holiday weekend, but would return on Tuesday.

*   *   *

Ralph and Roseanne Campanella were worn out from their weekend of 'relaxation'. The fresh brisk air on the Atlantic City Boardwalk which they walked on every chance they got, the excitement of the Casino games, the late hours and the long drive home through heavy traffic prompted them to have a light dinner and get to bed early. Both also had early mornings. Both had heavy schedules; Roseanne with end of school year matters, and Ralph with 'The Case'.

At precisely 3:30 a.m., their phone began ringing. After about 5 rings, Ralph, groping in the dark, managed to find the phone and mutter into the receiver that the caller had reached 'the Campanellas'. The caller identified himself as Dr. Gene Southerland, and he immediately apologized for the lateness of his call. He added that it was 12:30 a.m. in California so it had to be 'really late' in New York. Campanella thanked Dr. Southerland for returning his call. He added that on this matter he appreciated being awakened. It was too important.

Composing his thoughts Ralph Campanella asked Dr. Southerland if he had spoken to Dr. Hollis from the Medical Examiner's office in Dutchess County. Campanella, of course, knew the answer he was just trying to find out what they talked about. Dr. Southerland answered in the affirmative. He added that Hollis was actually looking for next of kin because they had recovered a body whose DNA was a close match to his DNA. When Campanella asked what Hollis said next, Dr. Southerland responded, "He said, well if I am speaking with Gene Southerland, and if I am looking for a dead man – and you sound very much alive – there must be some mistake. He apologized, gave me some phone numbers – which I really couldn't understand, and hung up." Southerland paused, "That was the extent of the conversation."

By now Campanella was fully awake. He was a little surprised that Hollis was so cavalier in his approach to investigation, but Campanella had more important issues to deal with. "Dr. Southerland", he began, "there is a lot more to this matter than Dr. Hollis shared, and perhaps he was not certain what he was able to tell you."

"The issue is pretty straight forward. The DNA taken from the body that was recovered near Poughkeepsie, New York is an exact match to your own. The chances of that happening at random are in the billions to one. So my question to you is very simple; do you have brother or better yet an identical twin living in the New York area?"

There was a long pause on the telephone. In a soft voice, Dr. Gene Southerland said, "I have a twin brother. He was shot dead during the assassination of President DeFrie. I am sure you know who he is. He 'is' Dean Southerland. Dean was the Secret Service agent who killed the President."

Before Dr. Southerland could continue, Campanella stated, "Dr. Southerland. To be honest with you, I have not had time to think this through, but if you are telling me that you have a twin brother, and I assume you mean an identical twin, than the person who killed the President may not be your brother at all. Unless something very strange is going on here, the body that your family buried in Atlanta was not your brother. And, we need to prove that."

Dr. Southerland seemed to be getting annoyed. His response to Campanella was, "Look my father identified my brother's body in the Manhattan morgue. My father is a physician. He could not make a mistake like that." Pausing, he added, "As much as I would pray that my brother did not kill the President – you have no idea what that would mean to my parents. The thought to our family that my brother killed the President and that he was a racist is devastating. It goes against everything we stand for. However, I have to tell you that what you are saying is not compelling."

Campanella could feel the hurt, the surprise, the reopening of wounds not yet healed in every word Gene Southerland had said. In a conciliatory tone, he stated, "Dr. Southerland, I apologize for springing this on you. I should have waited until we had proof that the body that was identified as your brother was not your brother. I should have also made the effort to tell you this in person."

Pausing for a moment Campanella continued, "Can I ask you to do me a very large favor? Can I ask you to keep this confidential? And, I mean even from your parents. I don't want to cause any more hurt than they have already been through. And for that I sincerely apologize to you." Dr. Southerland, who by now had some opportunity to reflect on what he had just learned, and who realized that Campanella was just doing his job as best he could, agreed to keep the matter confidential. He also got Campanella to agree to share any information that might be uncovered.

*   *   *

By the time that Ralph Campanella finished his telephone conversation with Gene Southerland it was 3:56 a.m. He felt he had already done a days work, but he knew his day was only starting. He also knew that if he waited until he got to the office to inform Robert Morgenstein of these new developments, and of what he had just learned, he would be skewered. Painful as it was, he called the DA's private number at home. Roseanne, well awake by now, was holding on to his hand, giving him whatever comfort she could.

Even though Campanella had awakened Morgenstein from a sound sleep, he knew that as soon as Morgenstein learned of this bombshell, it would be like firing off a Titan rocket. Morgenstein needed to know and understand every detail. On at least three occasions, he muttered, "How in hell could we screw this up? We are going to look like the biggest jackasses since the Dallas police let Jack Ruby kill Oswald!"

Robert Morgenstein showed none of the hesitation of disturbing someone in the middle of the night as Campanella had just done. This was too important. At 4:23 a.m. Dr. Charles Hershberger, Chief Medical Examiner of the City of New York was awakened by the not so 'gentle' voice of the District

Attorney. After Morgenstein had filled in Dr. Hershberger, he asked, "Charlie, how the hell could we screw up the identification of the assailant in the most important case we have ever had in New York City? In the most important case in the country over the last 60 years?"

Morgenstein paused, and then added "Not only did we get the ID of the assassin wrong, we all got suckered into that bull with Southerland's computer and the drugs in his apartment. We should have known that was a plant. It's the oldest trick in the book. The world is going to think we are as dumb as those jackasses in Dallas! And, God were they dumb!"

Hershberger was stunned by the news. In all his years as the City's Medical Examiner, he had never been known to have made a mistake. He was considered 'the Dean' of American Medical Examiners, and was repeatedly the keynote speaker for any important meeting in his field for the last 12 years. He had been invited to give lectures all over the country, and in London and Edinburgh.

He was also baffled. He was able to recall in detail Southerland's father making a positive ID of the body, even though Dr. Southerland initially had doubts that the body was that of his son. He also recalled personally doing the finger print impressions on the body just prior to Dr. Southerland's visit to the morgue. Getting the prints right, he remembered was made difficult because the thumb, index and middle finger of Agent Southerland's right hand were severely scraped. He used the word 'abraded'. For some reason, Hershberger could not recall either handing off those prints for matching, or any subsequent results that might have come in from the New York City Police or from the FBI. In any case, Hershberger, who was dressing as he spoke with Morgenstein, was heading down to the office to look through his files, and he would immediately begin the process of ordering DNA analysis on specimens they had taken from 'body X' – as he called it - during autopsy.

As much as he wanted to move forward swiftly, Robert Morgenstein's next call had to wait until at least 7:30 or 8:00 a.m.

It was important for him to communicate with United States Attorney General Asher Reese. Reese needed to know what Morgenstein's office was finding out, and it was possible that Reese had information that would be useful to Morgenstein. For a few fleeting moments Morgenstein thought he should also call FBI Director Harold Riemann. Upon reflection, the very thought of waking up FBI Director Harold Riemann – the 'Ass' as Morgenstein often referred to him – in the middle of the night although tempting, was not something he wanted to do. He did not call.

Unlike the Mayor of New York City, Morris Bloomfield who took great pride in the fact that he took the subway to and from his Mayoral office, Robert J. Morgenstein enjoyed the perquisites that came with his office. On of those perks was having a New York City Policeman pick the District Attorney up from his home each morning, in an unmarked police car, and deliver him home each evening. Morgenstein could easily justify using this perk. He knew there were a significant number of individuals who had more than one issue with him. Hence, having a trusted New York City policeman as his driver provided him with some level of protection.

Morgenstein also used the time he was in route to his down town office on Hogan Place in lower Manhattan to make calls from his cell phone. On the Tuesday following Memorial Day, Robert Morgenstein did exactly that. He dialed Attorney General Reese's cell phone at 7: 35 a.m. on the assumption that Reese would be en route to his Washington office. His efforts were only partly successful – 'not quite a cigar'. Reese took the call and informed Morgenstein that he would be meeting with President Christianson momentarily. He promised Morgenstein he would call back before noon.

When Reese did call back, Robert Morgenstein filled him in on the fact that the body had been autopsied in New York City, and that same body which had been buried in Atlanta, Georgia, was almost certainly not the body of Agent Dean Southerland. Archer Reese seemed surprised to learn this information, but in reality he was not surprised. He shared with Morgenstein that from the time of President DeFrie's assassination until now, the FBI had received more than 5000 calls offering information related to the killing of the President. Of those calls fewer than 800 callers wanted to remain anonymous.

Furthermore, when the FBI did an analysis of the origination of all of the tips they had received, a disproportionate number came into FBI Offices in Houston, Detroit, Philadelphia, Newark, New Jersey, Wilmington, Delaware and Indianapolis. Reese did not say as much, but all of these areas were home to some of the greatest industrial might, not just in the US, but in the entire world. He also left unsaid that these areas were the homes of the world's major Pharmaceutical companies. Reese also said that many of the tips received by the FBI were coming from women in very important positions such as Executive Secretaries and Executive Administrative Assistants.

As far as the 'hottest' lead they were tracking, Attorney General Reese shared with Morgenstein that the FBI had four Houston executives – two from the oil industry - under heavy surveillance. The tip leading to that surveillance came from a pilot of a Lear 23 – one of the smaller corporate jets. The pilot, a former Navy pilot and a black man, told the FBI of an incident that occurred while he was flying four executives back to Houston on Sunday night January 24th from Naples, Florida, where they had participated in a Senior Pro Amateur golf tournament at the Twin Eagles Country Club.

These 'characters', as he put it, who were drinking heavily made some very incriminating comments. He told the FBI that he was certain they were talking about the President, and he overheard them say that 'Mr. Uppity Nigger was in for a big surprise'. One of them went on to say 'he may be able to kick one wolf's ass, but when a pack of them come at that S.O.B., his fat black ass is gonna be in for a surprise.' When the Pilot went to the back of the jet to get some coffee, his passengers who seemed to realize that 'their whiskey' was 'talking' too much, in a blatant attempt, to confuse the Pilot quickly pretended they were talking about Tiger Woods. Reese said that the FBI had informed him that the co-pilot had corroborated this account.

*   *   *

Dr. Charles Hershberger was at his office well before 6 a.m. Shortly, thereafter, he was joined by two of his senior technicians and his administrative assistant. While he and his technicians were locating and then preparing a tissue sample for DNA analysis from 'Body X', Hershberger directed his administrative assistant to pull together the autopsy report they had made on the body they had thought was Agent Southerland. He ordered his staff to locate every scrap of information related to the case.

Charles Hershberger was meticulous in his record keeping. When he was performing an autopsy he diligently recorded every detail, even the most minute. After that information had been transcribed by an assistant, he would read the entire transcript to be sure it was accurate. Any additional thoughts he had while reading the report were neatly penned in the margins. In addition to that, on all important cases, he literally kept and organized the file. Those files were kept locked in his desk drawer until the case was closed.

Hershberger could recite the contents of each and every file he had worked on from his first case as the City's Medical Examiner. Consequently, he was stunned when he was unable to locate the finger prints that he, himself, had taken from 'Body X". He, his administrative assistant and one of the technicians spent that entire day, and the following two days, going through the files and computer records of each and every case they had in the past year. Someone, and Hershberger was very troubled by who that someone might be, had removed the finger print information from the Southerland file. Hershberger wanted to believe the prints were misfiled.

During a break he took mid afternoon, Dr. Hershberger placed a call to FBI Director Harold Riemann at his Washington,

DC office. Riemann took the call directly. When Riemann was told by Hershberger of these new developments concerning the identity of the assassin, just from the tone of Riemann's telephone voice, it was clear he was visibly upset. In fact, he was angry. He could not understand why the Director of the 'Federal Bureau of Investigation' would have to wait 7 or more hours before he was 'made privy to this vital information.' He gave Hershberger a short lecture on the fact that the FBI under the Justice Department had jurisdiction over this case. He added that if he wanted to be 'a mean prick' – his words – he could pull this entire case from the Manhattan District Attorney whom he referred to sarcastically as 'Mr. Elite of New York's finest.'

The purpose of Hershberger's call was just to get a complete copy of all duplicate records that the FBI had obtained from the New York City Medical Examiners Office regarding 'Agent Southerland's autopsy and any other related information they may have gathered. Of course, there was no way of doing that without sharing information with Riemann. Hershberger who would in the coming days have difficulty admitting that he had neglected to follow up on the finger print identification of 'Agent Southerland' would tell Riemann only what he needed to know in order for him to get Riemann to cooperate. He was not about to share his 'miscue' on the fingerprints with Riemann at this moment. Riemann did agree to courier copies of all of their records to New York.

*   *   *

Morgenstein selected 5:30 p.m. as the 'mutually' convenient time for his meeting with Hershberger, Campanella and one of the New York City Detectives who had been working on the case. It was important that they communicate directly and in person. That was, undoubtedly, a consequence of Morgenstein's dictum that 'e-mail' was the worst form of communication. He also claimed that you were supposed to 'sit in front of your customer' when you wanted to fully understand, rather than use the telephone. He claimed you missed half the information, and that 30% of that was just in the eyes.

At that meeting Hershberger reported that he and his assistants had prepared a DNA sample from 'Body X' and that aliquots of that sample along with those recovered from the Hudson River body, now known with almost certainly to be Agent Southerland, had been curried to the crime lab for analysis as well as to an independent testing laboratory. He stated that the analyses would be completed by late Friday afternoon.

Hershberger also detailed the issue with the 'missing' fingerprints. He shared that he had checked any records that would indicate that he had sent them off for analysis – in the event that he was 'losing it', as he candidly stated. There were no such records.

The next issue that was discussed dealt with the need to exhume 'Body X'. Campanella had already determined it had been entombed in the Southerland Family Mausoleum at Oakland Cemetery, in Atlanta, Georgia. Morgenstein stated that they absolutely needed to wait for the DNA results on the test that were in progress, no matter how small the odds were that the DNA evidence from the body retrieved from the Hudson River was a fluke. He added there was no real rush anyway.

Morgenstein was more concerned with how they would approach Agent Southerland's father, Dr. Southerland. Morgenstein suggested that once they had their DNA proof that 'Body X' was not Dean Southerland, 'Charlie Hershberger' should fly to Atlanta and inform the Southerland family in person. Morgenstein stated that he would be in touch with Attorney General Reese whose help he would solicit regarding handling of the Governor of Georgia. Morgenstein wanted to cut through all the red tape that might be associated with taking the body from the state of Georgia. Getting the Governor involved should expedite that. He also believed that when his office had definitive proof that 'Body X' was not Agent Southerland, the body in fact belonged to the Medical Examiner of New York City.

*   *   *

The results of the DNA testing from the crime lab and the commercial testing lab had to be repeated because somehow the samples taken from the real Agent Southerland's body had become contaminated with 'foreign' DNA. As a consequence, the samples had to be isolated again. The DNA proof necessary to request the exhumation of 'Body X' from Atlanta would be delayed until Tuesday, June 15th.

That wait was not intolerable, because in one of the intervening days – Thursday, June 10th – at 3:20 p.m. Robert Morgenstein received a call from New York City Police Commissioner Paul Kelley. Kelley told the District Attorney that he was at the New York Hilton, and, in fact, in the corridor where President DeFrie was assassinated. Kelley told Morgenstein that he needed to get down to the Hilton. He added that the New York City Bomb squad at this very moment was inspecting a device which they believed was indeed a bomb that may be live and may have malfunctioned.

With Ralph Campanella in hand, Morgenstein arrived at the service entrance to the Hilton 32 minutes after he had received Commissioner Kelley's call. As they approached Kelley, a large framed man, Kelley was attempting to hold back an elderly man of Puerto Rican background. The man dressed in custodial clothes – his name was Peter - needed to tell Morgenstein, whom he recognized immediately, his story. His story about the great discovery he had made.

Apparently, Peter had been sent to the corridor to begin the process of cleaning it up, readying it for painting. The corridor had been cordoned off since the President's assassination. As he was doing that he noticed that something, like a shiny liquid, had dripped down the wall from a 'fire bell'. The bell was affixed to the exterior wall, about 7 feet above the double service doors. The liquid that had dripped reached the top sill of the doors. Being curious because in addition to whatever had oozed from the 'fire bell', the bell itself was considerably larger than any others he had seen in the building, Peter retrieved a ladder that he brought to the area in order to make an inspection. The fire bell in question was nearly 9.5 inches in diameter compared with the typical 6 inch diameter bells normally used in commercial buildings. It was red in color with the usual white center on which was printed 'FIRE'.

Peter shared that after he had climbed up his ladder, he reached up and took the eraser end of a pencil – the eraser had been broken off – and retrieved some of the liquid which he could now see was oily. Bringing the end of the pencil to his nose, he was startled by the sweet and acrid smell. Realizing that something was very wrong, Peter came down the ladder and walked quickly to the maintenance room down the hall where he knew his supervisor was inspecting some boiler overflow. By the time he found his supervisor, who immediately called the New York City Police, Peter had a splitting headache.

When the New York City Police arrived they heard Peter's account of his 'discovery' of the unusually large fire bell that had oozed an oily liquid. He handed them the pencil on which he had retrieved some of the material. After smelling the material, which they could not identify, the Police immediately called the New York City Bomb squad.

Meanwhile, independent of the account that Peter was giving to Morgenstein and Campanella, two members of the Bomb Squad 'dressed for the occasion' in protective gear were on ladders inspecting the 'fire bell' and the oily liquid that had trailed down the wall from the bell. One of them, a Joe Turner, had removed his protective head gear so that he could get a closer look. He also waved his hand over the liquid trail in the direction of his face, so that he could get a whiff of this material. Without a moment's hesitation, Joe yelled down to those below, other members of the squad plus Kelley, Morgenstein and Campanella, "I think we have a nitro glycerin bomb here!"

Turner added, "That's why the fellow who discovered it got such a splitting headache. Nitro does that." As he inspected further, using a high intensity pen light, he was able to get his head close enough to the wall to see through the opening between the bell itself and the housing that was mounted to the wall. Yelling down, he said, "It looks like we've got a doozy here. There is a clear glass vessel inside the lower two thirds of the bell. The vessel has what appears to be a small stress crack and that's what caused the leak. It looks like all the nitro has leaked out."

Morgenstein wanted to know how long it would take them to verify that it was a nitro bomb. Turner responded that they would have to take a sample back to their lab; do an analysis and that would take 7 – 8 hrs. That was not good enough for Morgenstein, he yelled up to Turner, "Isn't there some simple test you can do right here to prove the point?" Turner thought for a moment and responded that there was. He could use a trick he had seen done in an explosives course he had taken at a course he was sent to at the University of Missouri. It was part of the mining program. Morgenstein was emphatic in urging Turner to get going on the test.

Turner instructed his team to bring him a small piece of clay, about a half inch in diameter and a short length of fuse – about 12 inches. He also asked them to get 'Little John' out of their truck. 'Little John' is a device the squad had fabricated themselves for containing small explosions. It resembled a 'diver's helmet' only larger. It had been fabricated by cutting off the bottom third of a 16 inch hollow sphere that had a wall thickness of about ¾ inch. The top portion of the sphere had been welded onto a heavy steel ring. The steel ring which was circular in shape looked like the brim of a very large hat as its' inside diameter was about 12 inches. The underside of the steel ring was fluted such that when 'Little John' was placed over some material to be detonated, the explosive gases would escape to the outside under the steel ring and through the flutes contained in it.

Turner, using rubber gloves, took the small clay ball and 'smooshed' it through the oily liquid that had oozed from the fire bell. When he felt it was well mixed and that he had captured a sufficient quantity of the material, he came down from his ladder, inserted the fuse into the clay ball and laid it on the concrete platform just outside the service doors. He next had two of his team help him place 'Little John' over the clay ball such that the fuse could be ignited.

Turner lighted the fuse, instructed everyone to stand back and Bam! 'Little John' jumped about 2 inches off the ground. Joe Turner was pleased, his little experiment had worked. He had made dynamite. He informed his surprised audience that the ingredients of dynamite are nitroglycerin and clay – an invention that made Alfred Nobel billions.

Morgenstein was also pleased. But he needed to understand three issues. First, did it appear to Turner that there was a triggering device on this 'Bell Bomb'? Turner stated that he suspected so. He could see some kind of circuitry in the upper portion of the bell. It looked like a disassembled cell phone. He also said that on top of the bell there was a small antenna. Next Morgenstein needed to know would there have been enough nitro glycerin in the 'Bell Bomb' to take the exterior wall down. To that Turner responded, that although he was not an expert on nitro, he was certain that the amount would have been sufficient.

Morgenstein's final question was, "Assuming that there was just enough nitro glycerin to take the exterior wall down, what would happen to anyone who might be standing 20 to 30 feet down the corridor?"

Turner pointed out to the District Attorney that the corridor was an odd structure. Within the interior of the building and going back to the service elevator, the corridor was about 10 feet wide and about 8 and a half feet high. However, he pointed out that in moving down the corridor away from the service elevator to the service exit, at about 8 feet from the service doors the ceiling rises to at least 16 feet.

Turner also noted that the exterior wall of the service entrance did not appear to be part of the original structure. He said it looked as if the outside wall had been cut out to make the entrance. That area had been bricked in around the service doors. Based on those observations, Turner said he had a 'strong belief' that given the high placement of the 'Bell Bomb' and the fact that its' placement was just opposite the interior wall above the corridor – he referred to this area as 'the loft space' above the entrance – that interior 'half wall' would have absorbed most of the blast recoil.

He added that in his mind it was conceivable that the exterior wall could have been blown out, and that anyone standing 20 to 30 feet down the corridor would be unharmed. He added that if those individuals knew that a blast was coming they could have quickly dropped to the floor to protect themselves.

Morgenstein had started to leave the Hilton when he thought of one other question he needed to ask Turner. Quickly reversing himself he yelled to Turner, "What about the bomb sniffing dogs? They had those dogs all over this place. How could they miss this nitro bomb?"

Turner responded, "We don't train our dogs to nitroglycerin!" He went on to explain that nitroglycerin is so dangerous to handle most bombers wouldn't touch it. Turner continued, "Whoever put that bell bomb on the wall had to have 'brass ones'. Just transporting it here without it going off is a challenge. Can you imagine them nailing it onto the wall?" Turner paused momentarily. "Actually, it looked like they used some kinda epoxy to hang it. But if they dropped it when they were hanging it they're goners!"

In response to what Turner had told him, Morgenstein needed two other questions answered. First he wanted to know if bomb makers generally knew that bomb sniffing dogs had to be trained specifically to nitroglycerin. Was that common knowledge? Turner said it was possible they knew that, but that was really just a guess on his part.

With his final question, Morgenstein wanted to know if it were possible to detect a nitroglycerin explosion by sampling the air. He was referring to the extensive analysis that the FBI had done with air sampling to determine the nature of the explosion that had occurred when the President was assassinated. Turner thought that would be very difficult. He went to explain that when nitroglycerin explodes the chemical products are nitrogen and carbon monoxide, two gases. Since there is already 80% nitrogen in the air anyway, it would be hard to detect a slight bit more. He added that anyway that excess would level out real quick; they'd never pick it up.

As far as the carbon monoxide goes, Turner thought that by the time the FBI started their analysis, it probably would have been oxidized to carbon dioxide. The ventilation system would have mixed it in with the normal air of the hotel. He also added that there is always plenty of carbon dioxide in the air. "That's what we exhale, and in the City we have a lot of carbon dioxide producers."

By the time District Attorney Morgenstein was satisfied with all the issues surrounding the 'Bell Bomb' and had drained every last bit of information out of the bomb crew and the head of hotel maintenance who had joined the group, it was nearly 8 o'clock. As they were being driven back to the District Attorney's office, Morgenstein told Ralph Campanella to 'pop' up to his office after Campanella had cleared his desk.

Before he released Campanella to perform those chores he had just been assigned, Morgenstein said, "If what Turner says about our dogs not being trained to nitroglycerin and about their not being able to detect nitro after an explosion, it would be pretty brilliant to use it for making a bomb. Wouldn't it?"

Chapter XII

Even though District Attorney Robert J. Morgenstein had a small liquor cabinet in his office, he was not much of a drinker. When he did indulge it would never be during work hours, and he considered his work day to end at 7 p.m. He might pour a drink if he had been working during the day with some special guest – mostly professionals whom he had known for years - and they were getting ready to wind down the day, and go off to dinner. Or he might have a drink alone if he wanted to fully absorb something important that had happened in his life on some particular day. On other rare occasions when he needed to ponder something that was truly important to him, he would pour himself a small amount of Jack Daniels, close the lights in his office and stare at the skyline of lower Manhattan. It was a sight that he truly loved and never tired of. He often claimed he was just admiring his 'Sweetheart' – that lady whom he could see in the distance on any clear night – the Statue of Liberty.

When Ralph Campanella dutifully entered, his 'Boss' was holding a small amount of Jack Daniels he had poured for himself. It was neat, no ice. Nodding to Campanella to join him, he turned his swivel chair just enough so that he could look over lower Manhattan. When Campanella had fixed his Jack Daniels, something he relished, Morgenstein instructed Campanella to position his chair so that he, too, could view the skyline.

As usual Campanella was not exactly sure why Morgenstein had invited him to join him. He was particularly confused as this was only the second time he had been asked to share a drink with his Boss – the first occasion was when Campanella had won his first big case. Leaning back in his chair, Morgenstein held his glass up, peering through the shiny amber liquid and on to the outside view from his corner office; Morgenstein began to speak as if he were delivering a soliloquy not just to Campanella but to anyone who might be in his view even if they were hundreds of yards away. He began, "I am not really sure I like Jack Daniels." He paused, "My father and my grandfather always drank Jack Daniels, and I never knew why." Turning to Campanella, he asked, "Did you know that Kentucky Whiskey is the only whiskey that is native to this country?" Campanella did not seem to know that fact.

"I think my father and my grandfather drank Jack Daniels because it made them feel like Americans. Both of them dearly loved this country. My grandfather, who immigrated to this country at age 12 from Wiesbaden, Germany, never had a desire to go back to his boyhood home. And, it was a good home for him. He came here long before there were any problems for Jews in Germany. But this was his country, he loved the United States."

"Did I ever tell you that my father served in World War II?" Campanella shook his head indicating he did not know that fact. Continuing, Morgenstein said, "My father was 33 years old when he signed up for the Army. And, he did not have to do that. He was a Pharmacist and because that was an essential service here at home, he never would have been drafted. But he wanted to serve his country." Chuckling softly, Morgenstein added, "My father was in the second wave in the Normandy invasion. He never told me he did anything heroic. He only told me that the most difficult thing he did was to carry a machine gun on his back across all of France."

"These were the men who shaped my life. They gave me 'purpose and direction'. Just like your father taught you principles, they did that for me." Sipping his drink, Morgenstein paused and with a bit of a twinkle in his eyes said, "When I was in 9th grade, I came home almost in tears because the kids in my class were teasing me about having a big nose. When I told this to my grandfather, and said maybe I should have plastic surgery, do you know what he said to me?" Without waiting for an answer, he continued, "My grandfather said, 'Jake – he always called me by my middle name – a man's nose is his rudder. He told me you needed a strong rudder to get through life and that the stronger your rudder the less you will be deterred from your goals and from doing what is right."

"I will never forget him telling me that for as long as I live. When my grandfather finished his rudder story, he made me laugh by asking me how some of my Irish school mates would get through life with those little buttons they call noses. He also pointed out to me that George Washington, Julius Caesar, Napoleon and many other great men had big strong rudders. So, I have always from that day forward been proud of my rudder. It has served me well."

Campanella, who was savoring his Jack Daniels, was also enjoying his Boss' stories. Campanella, who was raised in a tight extended family, had also been brought up with his share of stories. Even at his relatively young age, and not yet being a father, Campanella knew that stories of this kind are essential in the rearing of children. They build family pride, self confidence and character. None-the-less, Campanella knew these tales were not why Morgenstein had invited him to his office.

After Morgenstein had refreshed his own glass and Campanella's as well, he turned away from his office window and told his assistant that the events of the past days had caused him tremendous pain. Morgenstein shared that he had hoped against hope that the assassination of the President was the work of some single deranged individual. And, for a brief period that seemed to be the case. But the events of the past week had proven to him that the President's death was the result of a conspiracy. A conspiracy that they may never be able to unravel, because of its' complexity.

Pausing after a small sip of his Jack Daniels, Morgenstein returned to the soliloquy style he had spoken earlier. He said, "For my entire life I have been an optimist. All of my life I have believed in the goodness of man. And, I know that individually most men are good. But when banded together, many men are capable of the most barbarous acts. For the life of me, I can not understand that. It must be something buried in our genes. Something that helped the species to survive, or maybe we are just plain evil."

"For all of my life I have believed in the principles of Thomas Jefferson who believed that there is wisdom in the masses. And, for Jefferson and for me that has been the basis of our democracy. The masses, the voters, are capable of picking their leaders. That's the Jeffersonian ideal. And, those leaders who will be elected by the people will keep the country on an even keel. That is how democracy is supposed to work!"

"But I don't believe that anymore. I stopped believing that during the 2000 Presidential Election and it was confirmed for me indelibly in the 2004 election. In 2000, our Supreme Count decided 'screw the masses', we will decide who becomes President. Can you imagine that 9 old crows who don't have a clue of what it is to live in the real world, who probably can't make the most simple decisions in their own personal lives, decided who would be President in the year 2000? That boggles my mind. It insults my sense of what is Justice. It insults my sense of what it means to be an American."

"And, in 2004 with the ultimate evolution of mass communication – digital TV with sound that rattles the walls – along with the skills of the advertising prostitutes on Madison Avenue who presented the lies of that incompetent in the White House in the cleverest and most skillful ways imaginable, it all ended. If you combine the inherent ability of TV to communicate convincing lies to the public, along with a country where more people believe in the Virgin Birth than believe in evolution, we are doomed.

In the hands of these evil liars, how will they ever be able to discern the truth? It is impossible. And so, Democracy as we have known it in this country is finished. And, we can't just blame it all on the dunce who occupied the White House before DeFrie. He was the first of many that will have their way with this country."

"If the political side is not dismal enough, look at the power of our multinational corporations. They can stop anything they choose to stop because they control the game board – they own the world. They killed Universal Health care in the 90's, a fair Prescription drug plan for the elderly in 2000, and they fought DeFrie, tooth and nail, on every program he pushed through that benefits the people. And, that's only the beginning of what they will do to the world."

"I used to wonder what these nuts who were protesting globalization at the G7 meetings were all about. I must have had my head up my tuckus. What the hell was I thinking? We have surrendered the world to the rule of unelected corporate executives." Morgenstein paused, "Actually we could not stop them. We were the victims of corporate evolution. What is, had to come. Nothing gets smaller, no entity gives up power. And, the corporate world will tell us what we eat, how it is grown, what we are paid, how we are taxed, who gets educated, and on and on it goes. Those guys will totally govern every aspect of our lives. And, their only motive is the bottom line – profits. So don't expect much."

"What really hurts the most is that when Maynard DeFrie became President there was reason to be hopeful. I was overjoyed. There were nights I would be thinking of his speeches or profound comments he had made, and I would be so excited I could not sleep. In this brilliant mind within this huge black man there was hope. His brilliance had allowed him to figure out how to beat these evil bastards. He outwitted them at every turn. It was like watching the most masterful boxer imaginable. But in the end they got him!"

"Maynard Jefferson DeFrie was our last chance to save our democracy. He came from nothing. He came out of nowhere. It was like the coming of the Messiah. And, just like your Messiah, they killed him. DeFrie's murder was the most heinous crime of all time. I would give anything to bring justice to his murder, but I am losing hope. Whether it was one entity that killed the President or a group of them, we could never stop them. And, if one is guilty, they are all guilty. They all had the same intent, the same goal."

It was late and Morgenstein had exhausted himself. He had also worn Campanella out. But Morgenstein was compelled to say these things. They had to be said because Campanella, and multitudes like him, needed to know these realities. If the country could ever be saved and if the country could ever be delivered from evil - brilliance, goodness and the will of the people would not alone accomplish those tasks.

*   *   *

The results of the DNA testing on 'Body X' were delivered to Dr. Hershberger on Thursday, June 10th as promised. Upon comparison with the DNA patterns obtained from the Dean Southerland's body that was recovered from the Hudson River and those of his twin brother Gene, which were on record in the National DNA bank, there was absolutely no relationship of 'Body X' to the Southerlands. Hershberger would proceed to Atlanta to speak with the senior Dr. Southerland. Morgenstein had already greased the wheels of disinterment through Attorney General Reese and the Governor of Georgia. Raymond Morris.

Since 'Body X' was interred in the Southerland Family Mausoleum there would be little delay in moving forward. It would merely be a matter of opening the Mausoleum and removing the body. Hershberger believed that the body could be transported to his facility by the 22nd of June if all went smoothly.

Dr. Hershberger made arrangements to meet Dr. Southerland for a late lunch on the coming Saturday at Bone's Restaurant on Piedmont Rd, one of Hershberger's favorite restaurants in Atlanta. Hershberger used the pretext that he would be meeting with the Atlanta Medical Examiner on a murder case involving a 20 year old coed from Manhasset, Long Island. He had covered himself well having told the Atlanta Medical Examiner that he knew the family, and as a courtesy to them he would come to Atlanta. That was not a total fabrication.

On late Thursday afternoon June 24th, the remains of 'Body X' arrived in New York City. A viscera bag containing organs that had been removed on autopsy, remained with the Medical Examiner in Atlanta, as they would likely be of little value to Dr. Hershberger. On Friday morning, June 25th, Hershberger and his assistants examined the body. The body was in excellent condition except for expected dehydration. Hershberger would have no problem obtaining fingerprints from the corpse. Sticking rigorously to a protocol that Hershberger had outlined for this occasion, photographs were taken, and before the body was touched the photos were compared with those that were taken when the original autopsy was done in February.

The technician who took the digital photographs of the body was relatively new to the Medical Examiners Office. As she was printing out the close up photographs of the body's head, she exclaimed, "Mystery Man has a root problem. Look at this, his hair grew since he's been dead, and you can see little black roots! He must have been dying his hair."

Dr. Hershberger patiently informed his technician that hair follicles die when the body dies, and that it is a myth that hair continues to grow after death. He did, however, add the fact that when the scalp dehydrates, it can appear that hair has grown because more of the hair root is showing. In spite of this seemingly ditzy comment, Hershberger was pleased with his technician's observation. It was not easy to see. When he examine hairs on the scalp with a powerful magnifier, it was clear that each hair had a root end of about 1 to 2 millimeters that was black in contrast to the clearly 'dirty blond' coloring of the hair. Hershberger plucked a few hairs from the corpse's scalp, placed them in a small plastic bag and asked that they be analyzed for hair dyes.

A young pathologist who was assisting Dr. Hershberger, a Dr. Arthur Tischler asked Hershberger if it was known if the 'real' Agent Southerland dyed his hair. Hershberger was about to say that it was not known, but suddenly realized he had visited with Southerland's father in Atlanta just this past Saturday. What little hair that Dean Southerland's father had was clearly 'dirty blond'. Hershberger remembered that vividly. And, more importantly, Dr. Southerland had brought along for their lunch meeting college graduation pictures of his sons. The pictures were in full color. Both boys had the exact shade of hair as the corpse lying in front of Hershberger.

Carefully and quickly obtaining fingerprints from the corpse, Hershberger was anxious to get on with his examination which would be done at a level of scrutiny that had never been required of him before. The dyed hair discrepancy along with the extraordinary facial resemblance of this individual to Dean Southerland indicated to Hershberger that someone or some ones had gone to incredible lengths to create an exact double for Agent Southerland. The combination of the creation of that double along with its substitution for Agent Southerland, after Southerland had been brutally killed in order to enact that substitution, and the mutilation of Southerland's body in order to prevent detection of the substitution, was mind boggling.

Fully cognizant of the task at hand, Dr. Hershberger placed a small sand bag under the neck of the corpse. Even though there was considerable rigor in the body the placement of the sand bag would cause the head to tilt back slightly. Using a powerful light and a strong magnifier, Hershberger observed a scar from a surgical incision under the chin. He palpated the chin of the corpse manually but was unable to detect anything unusual. Dissecting the chin along the scar line and folding back the tissue, Hershberger discovered that plastic surgery had been performed on this individual. There was a chin implant. He removed it. Although he was no expert on plastic surgery, he dictated that he thought from the appearance of the implant that it had been molded specifically for this individual.

Next Dr. Hershberger made a precise midline incision down the length of the nose of the corpse. He started the incision from the eyebrow line down through the columella of the nose – the skin and tissue that separates the nostrils – to its base where it meets the upper lip. Next he made an incision along the eyebrow line. This allowed him to peal away the skin and attached tissue, exposing the nasal bones. It was evident that these bones had been cracked and reset, a standard procedure used in reducing the size and reshaping the nose. From a dissection of the tip of the nose, even though there was no implant – cartilage or otherwise – it was apparent that it, too, had been reshaped.

While Dr. Hershberger was performing these procedures, a fleeting thought popped into his head. For a moment he remembered the experience when Dr. Southerland had come to the morgue to identify his son. In particular, he remembered that when Dr. Southerland first looked over the autopsy report, he had claimed this could not be the body of his son because the penis had been circumcised. Although he was hardly an authority on circumcision, Hershberger knew there were several procedures for performing that surgery. On the basis, that someone with greater expertise in that area might be able to shed some light, Hershberger surgically removed the corpse's penis and placed in a preservative solution.

When Hershberger had finished the autopsy procedure, he sat down on a stool and dictated some final thoughts. After that he cleaned himself up and called Robert Morgenstein to share his findings. Morgenstein was non-plused on learning that the individual who had killed the President was a double who had been created by using extensive plastic surgery and by cosmetic changes. This imposter undoubtedly also had extensive training in mimicking the mannerisms of Agent Southerland, although no one could tell when that switch took place.

What was very clear was that the creation of a double for Agent Southerland and the complex plot – still not fully understood - to kill the President had to have been well planned and well resourced. Somewhere, some entity or entities had to have exercised extraordinary ingenuity and patience to have come up with this plan. And, besides having unlimited resources, they had to have the connections to get the job done.

Robert Morgenstein had listened to Hershberger's report attentively. Unlike himself, Morgenstein never once interrupted to ask a question. He just listened. Morgenstein ended the call by telling Hershberger that 'we all need a break'. He suggested it would be wise to relax and enjoy the weekend. They would convene on Tuesday morning June 29th to see what they could 'sort out.' Morgenstein added that by that time, hopefully, they would have back fingerprint analysis on the prints Dr. Hershberger had made. Morgenstein made it clear that everyone who had been involved in 'the case' would be expected to be in attendance. That would include the three Detectives who were given assignments in the Washington, DC area – Schiavo, Silvers and Healey.

After Hershberger had finished his conversation with the District Attorney, he personally handed copies of the prints he had made on 'Body X' to Detective Andrew Schiavo. For Schiavo, who had just completed his Washington assignment of looking for 'strayed' Secret Service Agents, this was his first day back in the New York office. Schiavo was assigned the task of identifying the prints. Morgenstein had made it clear that they needed to quickly have any information on the owner of those prints in the event a positive identity was made. Still paranoid about the 'misplacement' of the original fingerprints he had taken and filed, Hershberger had Schiavo sign a statement that he had received them.

*   *   *

The intervening days before the Tuesday June 29 meeting were uneventful with one noticeable exception. On Monday, the *New York Times* broke a story concerning what they termed 'the apparent cover up' of the murder of a Secret Service Agent on the Tuesday following the assassination of President DeFrie. The *Times*, acting on an anonymous tip received in mid March, reported that their investigation revealed that the body of Secret Service Agent Michael Roberts was found near the northern edge of the Western Ridge Trail in Rock Creek Park. Roberts an avid jogger was believed to have been running in Rock Creek Park at the time of his death. He was 48 years old.

A couple hiking along the trail used their cell phone to called Washington, DC police when they discovered Roberts' body. The *Times* article suggested the couple, whom they were able to identify from their investigation, called the *Times* anonymously after they had seen no mention of the event either on TV or in the news media for nearly 10 days after they had called in the crime to the police. In the news article, it was also reported that a 50 caliber round had been recovered from the body. From examination of entrance and exit wounds, it had also been determined that a second round had passed completely through Roberts' body. The article stated that 50 caliber rounds are used in many high powered machine guns and in sniper rifles. Mention was made of their use in the Barrett M107 sniper rifle and in most versions of the British made Accuracy International sniper rifles.

For the article, the *Times* had attempted to confirm information they had obtained in their investigation of Agent Roberts' murder by contacting the FBI. A reporter spoke directly with Director Harold Riemann. Without comment, Riemann referred her to the Justice Department. The *Times* learned from an aide to United States Attorney General Archer Reese that the Justice Department was in complete agreement with the Hamilton Commission's findings that Agent Southerland was the lone assassin of the President. It was also learned, that during their assassination investigations of the President murder, Roberts' killing was considered to possibly be related to the on going investigation. Accordingly, that information was not revealed to the press. None-the-less the Attorney General Reese's aide shared that Director Riemann himself had taken personal charge of this investigation. Riemann had concluded that there was absolutely no information linking Roberts killing to the assassination. The aide also confirmed for the *Times* that their information was correct – Roberts had been killed at long range by a high caliber rifle.

*   *   *

At 9:30 am on Tuesday June 29th, Robert J. Morgenstein gathered with his troops in a small conference adjoining his office. Present were Campanella, Hershberger, Detectives Schiavo, Healey and Silvers, and two other Assistant District Attorneys who had been in the DA's office for a total of 38 years. As a courtesy Police Commissioner Paul Kelley had also been invited. He did that because he liked Kelley and because Kelley, in Morgenstein's words 'had a good head'.

Morgenstein, whose face looked particularly somber, presided over the meeting. He told his assembled group that their objective on this morning was to review all of the available evidence, and see if they could construct a short list of possible people who could have been responsible for the President's murder. The conditions required to make that list would be motive and some evidence of culpability as well as the resources to commit what was clearly a very complicated crime. Before they would do that, Morgenstein called on Detective Schiavo to report on what he knew, if anything, about true identity of the assassin. Morgenstein was the only person, besides Schiavo, who knew anything that had been discovered. He had spent an hour starting at 7:30 a.m. with Schiavo that very morning.

Detective Schiavo, in an attempt to relieve the tension that was apparent in his audience, began with the comment, "Well, we finally got a return on all the billions the Home Land Security

Department has cost us!" He went on to say that the airport fingerprinting of all non US citizens had enabled them to identify 'Body X'. "Body X", he said, "is an individual named Ehud Amir. Amir traveled on an Israeli Passport. And, he has been in and out of the US four times in the past 18 months."

Schiavo continued, "Amir cleared immigration at Newark Airport on January 15, 2009. That's a few days before President DeFrie was inaugurated. He traveled on a US Airways flight from Frankfurt, Germany. We determined he rented a car from Budget at the airport and put 784 miles on the car before returning it on the 24th of January. He flew back to Frankfurt that night on US Airways. We should be able to get a lot more information on his whereabouts as we have shared this and everything else we've learned with the FBI."

"On August 10th, Amir came through immigration at Dulles International arriving on a Lufthansa flight, again from Frankfurt. He returned to Frankfurt on the 24th. There was no evidence that he rented a car. On November 10, Amir entered the country through Houston International airport. He flew on a Continental flight, also from Frankfurt, Germany. Home Land Security has records that he left Houston 10 days later. He flew on Continental and his destination was Frankfurt."

"The last entry of Amir into the country was through John F. Kennedy Airport. That was on February 8th of this year. His flight was on American Airlines and it had come from Frankfurt, Germany. We could find no evidence that he rented a car at the Airport", laughing Schiavo continued, "and I don't blame him. Who in their right mind wants to drive around New York City?" Morgenstein was not amused.

"Lastly, there is the possibility that Amir was traveling with companions on this last flight. There were four other men on that flight holding Israeli passports. According to Home Land Security, it is rare to have a single Israeli citizen on that flight, let alone five. We have the names of the other four individuals on the flight holding Israeli Passports.

We know that two of them left the US very recently - On June 26th to be exact. They entered Canada by auto and passed through the immigration check point on Interstate Route 87 North at Champlain, New York. They gave as their reason for visiting Canada - they were going on a guided black bear hunt. Apparently, black bear season closed on the 30th. They showed receipts to confirm their reservations at a lodge near Mount Tremblant. As far as we know the other two individuals are still in the United States."

When Schiavo had completed his report, Detective Dan Healey who had been gathering information of Secret Service Agent David Solomon, reported that if there is such a thing as an Israeli Eagle Scout it would be Solomon. Solomon was a family man, two teenage children, who belonged to an Orthodox Synagogue in Bethesda, Maryland. He coached the congregation's traveling soccer team and did substitute teaching in their Hebrew school. He was an avid hunter. He was well liked.

Detectives Silvers and Schiavo who were assigned the task of looking for Secret Service Agents, who might have strayed from the cultural values of the Service, investigated nearly every Agent through the Detective Agency hoax suggested by the District Attorney. They came up empty handed, except for one Agent. That agent who they learned had retired within weeks of the President's assassination was a heavy gambler. In addition to his gambling addiction the Agent was addicted to working out. His friends considered him 'a running nut.' In the final analysis this Secret Service agent was not considered to be a person of interest because the Detectives were unable to physically locate him. They assumed he had moved out of the area following his retirement.

Silvers and Schiavo whose newspaper interests did not go beyond the *New York Daily News* had not seen the *New York Times* article on the shooting death of Agent Michael Roberts that appeared in the previous day. It was the same Michael Roberts whom they had identified as a heavy gambler, deep in debt.

Ralph Campanella reported on the analysis on the 'Bell Bomb' done by the 'Guru' of the City bomb squad. It turned out that the bomb could easily be dismantled because hair line cracks at the bottom of the container holding the nitroglycerin had allowed all of the nitro to leak out. That rendered the bomb harmless. The structure and assembly of the bomb was ingeniously simple – or 'elegant' to quote the report. Every piece of the bomb had been made by a machinist, including the oversized ringer.

In the lower two thirds of the bell, there was a glass container that clearly had been hand fashioned by a skilled glassblower. It fit neatly into the lower two thirds of the bell. At the bottom of the glass container and through its wall, two electrodes 1/8 inch apart were imbedded. From the outside these electrodes were wired to a small capacitor which was connected to the ringer device on a cell phone. The bomb would function merely by calling the cell phone number. The cell phone ringer would charge the capacitor, the released charge would cause the electrodes to arc and the nitroglycerin would efficiently and violently explode.

In spite of its ingenuity, the report stated that there was one small flaw in the 'Bomb Bell'. The glass blower had used copper wire for the electrodes that he had embedded in the nitroglycerin container. It was hairline cracks around these electrodes that allowed the nitroglycerin to leak out and effectively disarm the bomb. The Bomb Squad Guru noted that had the maker used platinum electrodes whose thermal properties are more compatible with being embedded in glass than the copper he used, the bomb would have functioned exactly as planned.

Campanella also reported that they had obtained the phone number of the cell used in the 'Bell Bomb'. It was a working number. The cell phone functioned perfectly well even though its ringer circuit had been altered. The phone was purchased at a Wal-Mart Connection Center in Saddle Brook, N.J. A prepaid wireless package had been paid for in cash, there was a 100 hundred dollar credit on the account and the phone had not been used.

The individual, who purchased the cell phone at Wal-Mart, gave her name and address as Rita Karpinski, of 326 Greenwood Avenue, Brooklyn, N.Y. That address belonged to a delicatessen. No one by that name lived or worked there. Campanella reported that the FBI had check out 119 Karpinskis in New York State and around the entire country. None of them raised any suspicion. It was concluded that Rita Karpinski had used false identification.

The most important piece of new information regarded the Texas quartet that the FBI had under surveillance following their tip from the corporate jet pilot who was flying this heavily drinking group from Naples, Florida to Houston. That group was returning from a golf tournament. Two of the men were, indeed, oil men; one was the CEO and the other Chairman of the Board of one of the countries largest petroleum firms. Both men, brothers-in-law, were born again Christians. Both were ardent Christian Zionists who made frequent trips to Israel. Curiously, they had branch offices in London and in Frankfurt. In Frankfurt, they maintained a penthouse apartment overlooking the Main River, for the use of corporate executives.

The other two men on board that flight turned out to be the CEO and Executive VP of one of the largest HMO's in the country. That organization had moved from Chicago to Houston two years back.

Given the absence of any other new information, Morgenstein suggested they review what they knew as of this date. They covered: the Russian Mafia and their potential implication in the assassination plot – citing the 'Russian mob style' killing of Agent Southerland, the importation of Russian Snipers and the possibility that the tentacles of the mob could have gotten them into the New York Hilton.

From employees at the Hilton, the mob could have learned that the President would likely use the same entrance/exit route as had other important dignitaries. They could have also surveyed the corridor and determined where a nitroglycerin bomb or bombs might have been placed to create an escape route. They might have also planned the positioning for well placed snipers who could take out those Secret Service Snipers who were guarding the service exit of the Hilton from some distances off. Morgenstein added that much of what he had just said was speculation, but within the realm of possibility.

Morgenstein also suggested there could be some connection between Ahud Amir – along with the group that might have entered the country with him - and the Brighton Beach Russian Mafia in Brooklyn. If the Brighton Beach Mafia were connected to the 'oil guys' through the fuel oil scandal, he asserted that would make a perfect criminal triangle. And, he speculated, one corner of that triangle – the Texas businessmen along with their HMO buddies – would connect with the part of corporate America that had real issues with the President.

Morgenstein added, "Given the religious convictions of the Texas oil guys, and the extreme ideas of the groups they are part of and fund, I can see motives here. According to their beliefs, anything that endangers the continued existence of Israel, they claim, threatens the coming of Armageddon. That would doom their salvation! And they would, I am convinced, deal with that 'Texas style' or 'West Texas style' as they call it. The Texans would be in lock step with Amir and his ilk, if, indeed, Amir was part of a radical Israeli group. Both would be defending Israel, but with different motives. In any case, I am certain it would not be difficult for them to find each other."

Morgenstein was struck by what he had just said. The Texans with their fanatical Christian beliefs, their belief that God spoke directly to them, their incredible wealth and their ties to corporate America could not only be the lynch pin to the Israeli fanatics, they could have been the initiators of this monstrous plot to kill the President. Morgenstein was only trouble by one issue – did they have the brains to conceive of so complicated a plot? He understood well that in many industries, one doesn't have to be brilliant to amass wealth.

When it became clear that there was no more meaningful information to be added, Morgenstein ended their meeting by saying that they would just keep digging, the FBI will keep on digging, and maybe some information on the money trail would come out in time.

Chapter XIII

With the 4th of July coming up, District Attorney Morgenstein decided he would follow his wife's advice and take some time off. It wouldn't be to some far away exotic place. That would take some planning. Instead he would make the 3 hour drive north from New York City to Berkshires in southwestern Massachusetts with his wife. They would stay at an Inn they had gone to for years. He knew the owners well and knew they would make room for him, even at this late date.

One of the few pleasures that Robert Morgenstein would allow himself was to spend a summer afternoon with his wife sitting on lawn chairs on the grass at Tangelwood listening to the Boston Pops Orchestra. They could do that while sipping a fine wine and sharing some good French bread along with his favorite cheese - imported Parmigiano-Reggiano. Fortunately for him, this year the 4th would occur on a Sunday, which meant that Morgenstein would have his Sunday *New York Times* to take with him. For him that was a combination of the most sublime pleasures imaginable. So enjoyable was that Sunday afternoon that the District Attorney informed his office that he could be reached in an emergency on his cell phone as he was staying through the following Sunday. He would be in the office in the afternoon of the 11th.

The Morgensteins had enjoyed their little respite, as the DA referred to it, in the Berkshires. It was a good interlude to moving onto a new case that occurred in his absence. Apparently, one of the wealthier residents of 5th Avenue had been charged with having arranged to have his wife killed in Central Park. It was supposed to look like a mugging that would occur when she ritually took her poodle for a walk in the early evenings. Ironically, her husband did not like her to walk the dog herself. He preferred she hire 'a walker', since it might diminish his appearance of wealth.

When Morgenstein returned from Tangelwood, he reviewed the available evidence against the husband of this 'dog walking lady' and assigned the case to one of his assistant DA's. He had hoped the case might distract him from his true interests of getting closer to the solution of President DeFrie's assassination. It did not.

Towards the end of the third week of July, District Attorney Robert Morgenstein learned that he would be one of the honored guests at a reception given by Mayor Morris Bloomfield for four of those who had made significant contributions to the City over the past 18 months. The dinner would be on Friday August 13th at the Waldorf Astoria. Morgenstein thought it was odd to be holding 'an honoring' – as he called it – in the middle of the summer, when half the City employees were on vacation. But Morgenstein thought many of the things the Mayor did was odd, so he wouldn't spend any time trying to understand why he had picked that date.

As his wife's bridge group would be meeting at their home on the fourth Thursday of the month, July 29th, Morgenstein decided he would not rush home for dinner. Instead he would order in a deli sandwich and work on the short speech he was expected to give at the Mayor's event. Not relishing the thought of preparing his speech, Morgenstein resorted to a trick he had used in college when he felt the need to procrastinate. On those occasions, he would stand in front of a mirror and brush his hair. Between that activity and an intermittent cigarette he could easily put off his task for at least 30 minutes.

Having grown out of his narcissistic age and also having very little hair to brush, the District Attorney resorted to his latest – more mature – trick of procrastination. He would check his e-mail. And, since most of his e-mails were boring, Morgenstein would focus on the "e-mail alerts" that the FBI had initiated some three years back. They could be very interesting.

One e-mail caught his eye. It was dated July 28th. Its subject: "Royal Canadian Police recover body of US government employee". The substance of the message was that a badly decomposed body of a hunter had been recovered near Lake Chaud just north of Mount Tremblant. The body was identified as that of an American Secret Service Agent named David Solomon. Solomon who was hunting black bear in the area had been reported missing on July 1, one day after the bear season had closed. He had driven to Canada on Wednesday the 23rd with a hunting companion, a co-worker. An autopsy would be performed to determine cause of death. The e-mail alert added that at this point it appeared that Agent Solomon was the victim of a hunting accident.

This last piece of news was not just troublesome to Robert Morgenstein. He felt like an explosion had gone off in his head. He wondered if his brain would go on fire. He previously had only one case that did this to him, but it was nothing in comparison to what he was feeling. He kept repeating to himself, "How the hell can this be? How the hell can this be? Is it possible that Solomon needed to be silenced?" Morgenstein wondered out loud if his statement to Ralph Campanella at the beginning of this investigation had come to pass. He had told Campanella that the assassin has to be killed to complete an assassination plot. Otherwise, he will not be able to maintain silence.

Was it possible that Solomon was not trying to save the President's life by shooting Southerland? Was he just completing his assignment? And, what about Agent Roberts whose body had been found in Rock Creek Park? Roberts had been slain with a high power rifle, presumably fired at some distance. The bullet that was recovered from Roberts' body was a 50 caliber. Morgenstein needed to know how and if Roberts fit in to this scheme. Had Roberts allowed himself to be compromised by his gambling addiction? Morgenstein concluded that if Riemann had stated that Roberts was not connected to the assassination after the FBI investigation, the opposite had to be true. Morgenstein was convinced Riemann never got it right.

Other thoughts that were adding to the fire in Morgenstein's brain dealt with some issues that were very personal. He had hoped that if there was to be an Israeli connection in the President's assassination, it would involve the far right 'crazies' – as he called them. Solomon did not fit that profile. Morgenstein also recalled several articles that appeared in the *Jerusalem Post* – the Israeli newspaper published in English – opposing the election of President DeFrie. Even though the *Post* was considered to be a moderate newspaper, there was too much vitriol in those articles to suit Morgenstein. They upset his notion of what was right, and his belief that no foreign country should, in any way, influence the outcome of elections. To him, that was a violation of a fundamental principle of democracy.

Robert Morgenstein felt that if he could not get these ugly thoughts out of his own head, he would go mad. He could not deal with all that he had learned entirely by himself, nor could he deal with all the pain it was causing him. He needed to talk to someone he knew and trusted. He needed to reach out for help. That individual had to be someone who could analyze and make sense of the most troublesome issues that life can bring. Morgenstein was fortunate to know just that person. It was his boyhood friend Saul Freedman who had lived in Jerusalem for the past 50 years.

Saul Freedman, formerly Paul Freedman, who used this Hebrew version of his given name upon immigrating to Israel, had started school with Morgenstein at PS 5, the Port Morris School in the Bronx. They went to high school and college together. They were best friends. Although Saul had no particular attachment to Judaism – he was an agnostic – he decided, after completing his Ph.D. in Philosophy at Yale University that he wanted to live in Israel.

He had never offered his good friend Morgenstein any good rational for doing that. He would only say that he wanted to live as a Jew, and he needed to do that in Israel. Saul would often quip to his good friend, whom he called by his middle name, Jake, because it was Hebrew that he always wanted to live in a country where every delicatessen was 'a Jewish delicatessen.' Morgenstein never failed to laugh at that comment; no matter how many times Saul made it.

As it was 7:23 pm in New York City and only eight hours later – 3:23 a.m. - in Jerusalem where Saul Freedman lived, Morgenstein decided he would wait two hours before placing his call. He knew Saul was an early riser – not that early – so he was not terribly disposed to waking him up. Morgenstein also realized that now that Saul had retired from the University he probably had gotten in to the habit of going to sleep earlier and rising earlier. Saul who held the title of 'Professor Emeritus', having been on the faculty of the Hebrew University of Jerusalem for nearly 50 years, had indeed changed his sleeping pattern.

At 9:15 p.m. Robert Morgenstein dialed the phone number of his good friend Saul Freedman. Freedman answered the telephone after one ring. Upon hearing his friend's apology about waking him so early, Freedman interrupted. He had been awake. He was just heading back to bed having come from the bathroom.

Morgenstein apologized again. But this time he told his friend, it was because he needed someone to talk to about the work he was doing on the assassination of President DeFrie. Morgenstein shared that he and his staff believed they understood the key parts of the case. He told Saul, that if he would just listen, and just maybe ask just one or two of the insightful questions, only Freedman could ask, it might be helpful to him. With an 'OK' signaling agreement from Freedman, Morgenstein began sharing in confidence with his friend all that his office and the Justice Department had learned in their investigation of President DeFrie's assassination.

Freedman, who wanted to understand in depth what Morgenstein was relating, politely interrupted several times to get clarification of some of these very complicated details. When Morgenstein shared the part of his story about his office having compelling evidence that DeFrie's assassin was an Ehud Amir, an Israeli citizen from Herzliya, Israel, Freedman interrupted. Saul asked, "Did you know that son of a bitch, Yigal Amir who killed our friend, Rabin, is from the same town?" Morgenstein did not know that. He was dumbfounded. Saul wondered, "Could your son of a bitch be related to ours? Or be from the same far right extremist group that has done so much harm to Israel?"

For whatever reason, Morgenstein did not respond to Saul's question. He continued to add additional information and related details. When Morgenstein had completed his tale, there was a pause on the line. Finally, Saul Freedman, attempting to lighten the conversation a bit, said, "So what do you want from me, now that you've kept me on the telephone for more than an hour - and, it's still not 6:30 here? Do you want me to solve your case, or do you want me to tell you that it really doesn't make any difference if you do solve the case?

Morgenstein responded in the negative with respect to Saul's two offers. No he wasn't calling for Freedman to solve his case, and no he didn't want Saul to tell him it would not make any difference if he did solve the case. He did say, "I actually needed someone to talk to, someone I could trust. I have been suffering with the burden of this information. I needed to share it. And, frankly, who else could I do that with, but you? When I called I thought you might come up with something to make me feel better. I was looking for one of your insightful thoughts. That's all."

Before Saul Freedman could respond, Morgenstein continued, "But Saul you did say something about Amir which does trigger a thought. Actually, a question. So let me ask it, before I forget it." Morgenstein paused momentarily, "I just shared with you the evidence, however preliminary that powerful corporate forces wanted DeFrie dead and had the financial resources to put together a complicated scheme to kill him. Those investigations are still in progress and the evidence is skimpy, but it will come out in time. I also told you about some evidence we have that our Russian Mafia – those lousy creeps who moved into Brighton beach – might have played a major role to expedite this scheme. And, I have also told you about Amir. I don't have enough evidence to connect the dots, but maybe there is a linkage."

"There is one other thing I need to tell you. And, that concerns David Solomon. Do you remember who David Solomon is?" Freedman responded that he did remember, and continued by saying that 'yes, that's your hero who tried to save the President's life.' To that Morgenstein said, "Well we might be wrong on that. Solomon was killed in a hunting accident in Canada while he was black bear hunting." Pausing to let his friend absorb that information, Morgenstein added, "We also know that two Israelis who entered the country at the same time as Amir, drove to Canada a few days after Solomon did. They were hunting black bear also!"

Morgenstein was waiting for a response from his friend Saul, and when Saul did not, he added, "I just remembered something I forgot and that concerns the Texas oilmen I mentioned. The FBI learned that two of them belong to a fundamentalist far right Christian church in Houston. They are 'born agains' and they are big time Christian Zionists. They are heavy supporters of Israeli Zionist charities, they visit Israel often and they lead pilgrimages to Israel every summer." Morgenstein paused, "those are some of the kinds of screwballs we have to deal with. Plus they have big big bucks which makes them even more dangerous!"

"Look Jake, I don't know how closely you keep up with news in Israel, but let me tell you a few things that might help you. As you know, Yigal Amir was sentenced to life imprisonment for killing Rabin. But in Israel the only ones who understand vengeance and who are capable of taking retribution are 'the Amirs' in this country that we have to deal with. Isn't that ironic?"

"I sometimes wonder how genes were distributed among the Jews. We got 85% bleeding hearts, and 15% of the meanest, most self righteous and vindictive bastards you can imagine. And, that 15% knows they are right! I have always suspected that the 15% were over represented in the group of guys who wrote the Old Testament. No one else could have created a God who could be such a mean 'so and so'. In any case, that Amir-bastard is treated so well, you would not believe it. And, to this day that son of a bitch says 'he is satisfied with what he did.'"

"Before I get too worked up, let me make my point. Amir married a Russian Jew by proxy in 2004. Then about 2 years ago he was allowed conjugal visits, and last year he was allowed out of prison to attend the Briss (circumcision) of his newborn son. Can you imagine that? Conjugal visits?"

"If it were up to me, I would cut his wiener off, freeze it and you know where I'd stick it. That's the kind of conjugal visit I would give him. And, when it comes to a Briss, I'd like to circumcise that Amir bastard, myself. Right behind the ears!"

Morgenstein could see he had gotten his good friend worked up and apologized for that by saying, "Look, I am sorry I got you all worked up. But where are you going with all of this?"

Freedman responded, "Didn't you get it? The connection is: Ahud Amir to the Israeli Russian Jews to the Russian Jews in Russia and from there to Brighton Beach group. I just made your Russian connection for you! Even though we Israelis got the good Russian Jews, if there is such a thing, I am sure some of our Russian Jews connect directly, or by one link, to your Brighton Beach Russian Jews."

"Secondly, I want you to realize how bold and powerful these bastards on the far right are in Israel. You know we have to tolerate them, because that's how our constitution is set up. We are forced to make deals with the devil himself. In any case, the support that the far right gives Amir is unbelievable. And, they do it publicly. There are petitions circulating in Israel today to free him. There are those who worship him for what he did. And, there are a substantial number of them."

Saul continued, "So if you are asking me if there is a connection? I think there is. And, if you are asking me if these crackpots are capable of participating in a plot to kill your President, I am sure of that also. These guys have a lot of talent. They are engineers, doctors, lawyers, you name it. And, I am convinced they are wired wrong. Something is screwy in their heads."

"There is one other thing you ought to know, and that is something that is not common knowledge, except to those who had access to the inner circles of Israeli politics," Saul added. "When the conservatives were coming into power in the early 90's they recruited some right wing religious radicals into Mossad. Those guys make perfect assassins! First you tell them whom to kill. Then tell them those targets are proponents of a Palestinian State, or that they are giving away one square meter of Israeli land. That's all they need to know, for that they would kill their mothers." Saul paused, and added in the strictest confidence that there was an investigation going on in Israel right now concerning possible far right wing religious extremists who had made their way into Mossad by lying about their backgrounds.

Morgenstein needed to address one more issue that was troublesome for him. He said that he could understand the possible connection of Israel's extremists and the religious extremists in the US. All of that made sense to him. What troubled him was where Solomon fit in. From all they knew Solomon was moderate in his beliefs. How could he be connected?

To that Saul responded, "You know there are moderates, or individuals just right of center in Israel who were troubled by DeFrie's policies. And, they were troubled even though they knew his policies were fair, and the right thing to do. They also believed that DeFrie might lead us to a permanent peace, but, candidly, many were concerned that the odds of success might be too low."

"But many of these same people, even though they know Israel is a sophisticated modern country that is perfectly capable of defending itself, suffer from a bit of paranoia. Given our history that's a pretty normal reaction. It will take us another three generations to get over that. And, don't forget we have the Palestinian crazy element lobbing rockets at us all the time. That doesn't give a lot of comfort."

"I need to also tell you that if you could have seen some of the stuff that appeared in Israeli papers when DeFrie was running for the Presidency, you would have been surprised." Pausing for a moment, "In fact you must have been aware of the pressure that was put on American Jews from Israel, and from pro Israel forces in the US not to support DeFrie."

Morgenstein indicated he was aware of that. "Even though a lot of American Jews did not vote for DeFrie, and perhaps for that reason, there were many that did. I certainly did."

"So, if you ask me if there was involvement of some of the more moderate elements in Israel in this plot, I would have to say it is possible. However, I don't think it's probable. I still think you need to focus on the Amirs of this country and their ilk. They are the truly dangerous ones!"

"And, as far as Solomon is concerned, it is very possible that whoever killed him might have thought that Solomon was to close to all of this. Solomon was, apparently, a bright guy; he had a quick mind. Maybe they thought he might in time remember something that would crack this thing wide open."

Saul paused for a moment and then asked, "I want to go back to what I was saying about how weird these religious extremists can be. Do you remember that nut Alan Ziegler who went to high school with us?" Morgenstein did not remember. Freedman continued, "Alan was the ultra ultra orthodox creepy character who went off to Yeshiva in his junior year. You remember the guy who always wore those silly multicolored

Yarmulkes that his grandmother knitted. The guy that had the side locks? He never shaved, not that he had much of a beard."

When Morgenstein indicated that he remembered Alan Ziegler, Freedman continued, "Alan was a good example of these wrongly wired nuts. I won't ask you if you remember, but I was the chess champion of our 8th, 9th and 10th grades. Anyway Alan was a fiercely competitive prick, and he was always challenging me to a game. I always beat him easily. But I can tell you, he worked on his game endlessly. So, Alan challenges me to a match at the end of our sophomore year, and I play him. I am not paying close attention. I make a few moves that put me in a hole. The long and short of it is - Alan beats me."

"And, when he does beat me he jumps up out of his seat and he howls like a roaring lion. I am looking at him, and it looks like he had 'peed' his pants a little. What do you think Alan tells me? He tells me that when he beat me he had a climax! Can you imagine that? Here we are playing chess, which is not a very sexy game, and this nut is having a climax. I am convinced that Alan and a lot of the nuts like him are wired wrong. Something in their heads is short circuited or left out. What does your dick have to do with playing chess?"

After Freedman related the Zeigler story, he felt the need to offer his friend some kind of solace. But all he could think of in the way of being helpful was, "Well at least DeFrie is your last Black President." Morgenstein, taken aback, responded that if that was supposed to console him; he must have not gotten the point. Saul Freedman explained, "Considering the ugly history of race in the United States, don't you think it's a miracle that the American voter would elect a Black President.?"

After Morgenstein agreed, Freedman continued, "That tells me that Americans are finally become color blind. There can be no other reason. And, what that tells me is that there are no more blacks, there are no more whites in the US – there are just Americans. Maynard Jefferson DeFrie will be remembered as the last black President. I think that is remarkable! After him everyone Black or White will be simply American."

Freedman went on to say that President DeFrie would no doubt be the last 'Mensch' to occupy the Presidency as well. He would be the last true man who knows what is right, not just because he thinks it is right, but because it is right. He would be the last man to have the courage and the conviction to act on the fundamental principles of honor, good will and truthfulness that all humans treasure.

"In this world we live in, not only is the 'Mensch' an endangered species, but there is a concerted effort to destroy each of them. A Mensch, no matter what walk of life – business, politics, academics, etcetera, etcetera - cannot turn his back for one moment; the jackals will drag him down and tear him apart. And, that is just what they did to DeFrie."

In his last attempt to console his friend, Freedman made a light hearted remark. He said, "Jake, you take life too seriously. If you think about it we have, at most, 200 years left on this planet, so relax – you can't change anything. Why don't you come to Israel with your wife and spend some time with us. Travel to everyplace in the world you have not been. You've earned your keep. Your parents and grandparents would be proud of you. It's time for you to enjoy yourself."

Morgenstein thanked Freedman for the compliments and the invitation, but he was puzzled about the 200 year thing. He wanted to know what Freedman was talking about. Saul responded, "It has probably taken man seven or eight thousand years to get himself from sitting in front of a fire in some cave to where we sit today. The question is what is it in us humans, what is in our character that drove that process. Why do we progress?"

Pausing to give his friend a moment to think about the question he had proposed, Freedman continued, "I am convinced that the drivers in us come from the very worst characteristics of human nature. Those traits are ego, pride, greed, selfishness, vanity, and on it goes. If man did not have those characteristics, he would never want to be any different than he already is. He would be content with himself and his surroundings."

"It is those very characteristics that drive us to work hard, to achieve, to invent, to do things better than others so that we can impress. They make the gifted and the industrious, among us, more able to spread their seed, and we do all of that because it is the dance written in our genes. And, so, I believe the very worst in us has brought us to where we are today."

"I also believe that those characteristics I just mentioned will also create a planet where humans as we know them, will not be able to survive. Look what is happening around the world. We have ruined the Earth. We have poisoned the ground, the waters and the atmosphere. They are the places where we throw our garbage. And, those garbage pits are reaching their limits."

"We have reached the exalted status where every body in the entire world needs and owns a hair dryer. Everybody in world, and particularly in the US, needs to drive a car which is of the size and inefficiency of a truck. And, worse, no one is concerned. Those who have lived off the fat of the land, and are too stupid to know they are in danger, deny it is all happening. They deny that even when they are shown pictures of the polar caps that are melting. There is violent weather all over the world. And this is only the beginning."

"Every time I fly to New York, I can not get over the color of the sky, and I am talking about clear days. The blueness of the sky we saw growing up in New York is not there anymore. The sky has a gray cast. And, so, I say the very parts of our character that got us to where we are now, will make this planet uninhabitable. So, my guess is we have at best 200 years left."

"What amuses me is that those screwballs who wrote the Last Testament got it right. The world will end. But they got the reasons wrong! That shows you how much they knew. And, with that I say Shalom, my brother. Go enjoy yourself, before it's too late!"

Robert Morgenstein glanced at his watch. It was one minutes past 12. For another 15 -20 minutes he sat motionless, elbows on his desk, his thumbs and index fingers cradling the sides of his forehead. He was deep in thought of what would become of his beloved country. This very land that was his, that he was a part of him. This land which had been so good to him, to his parents and his grandparents. Had it been betrayed by those who worshiped the Trinity of greed, power and money?

Morgenstein was also deeply troubled by what he had learned from Saul Freedman about some of the inner workings of extreme Zionists elements in Israel. Had his second love betrayed him also? Or was it just those individuals who worshiped a Trinity that required blind faith to a vengeful God created by their ancestors, violent hatred for all who did not see the light they saw so clearly and the obligation to eliminate all who threatened their tiny universe? Had they created an incurable virus that had infected this incredible country? Were they the ones who may have infected moderates like David Solomon? Or was Solomon just an innocent bystander who in time might have starting putting pieces of this conspiracy together? That would make him a very dangerous man.

Robert Morgenstein shuddered at the thought that these Trinities – Trinities composed of the very worst elements of extreme capitalism and extreme religion - had overlapped. He was convinced that the entire plot to kill the President would never be fully understood. It was too complicated. It involved too many parts. But he was convinced that he had uncovered the essentials. And, he was convinced that he knew the ingredients that were the motivating factors: extremes of wealth, of greed, of belief and the self appointed obligation to do God's work.

To regain his equilibrium, Robert Morgenstein needed to know if humanity was capable of sustaining at any level an ideal. He was not looking for a utopia, just an ideal. Or was this all a fraud? Had we been kidding ourselves? Were we just incapable? Had his entire career, its endless hours, the battles to enforce the law, the fights for justice all been a waste of effort? All those principles that Morgenstein had based his life on, that he had been taught by his forebears, and all those things which he loved so dearly were crumbling before his very eyes. Slowly he rose and walked over to his liquor cabinet and poured himself 'one finger' of Jack Daniels, glancing out onto the New York skyline as he did.

Returning to his desk, he sat in his office chair, leaned back, lifting his feet on to his desk top and stared at lower Manhattan. After a few sips of his friend 'Jack' who immediately connected Morgenstein in a good way with his past, he looked into the distance so that he could see his beloved 'Sweetheart' of so many years, the Statue of Liberty.

He hoped she would comfort him as she had done so often in the past. In the distance, just above and to the left of the Lady's torch, a cloud formation was passing whose form resembled the upper body of a large man with his left hand extended upward, as if waving goodbye. A vision of his beloved President, Maynard Jefferson DeFrie flashed through his head, and he winced.

Leaning forward so that he could place his glass of Jack Daniels onto to his desk, Morgenstein reached for a small powerful telescope he kept on his desk. He used that to get a better view of all the sites he could see from his office. He claimed at sunset he could often see a smile on his Lady's face. Or at least, on the left side of her face of which he had a perfect view.

Focusing on Lady Liberty's head, for a moment he was startled. Suddenly Morgenstein lurched forward, pulling his feet from his desk and quickly standing. Refocusing on Lady Liberty, he could see that 'his Lady' had tears falling from her left eye. That was on the side of her face that he could see.

Quickly grabbing a tissue to wipe his own eyes so that he could see better, Robert Morgenstein realized he could not distinguish if the tears he was seeing had been in his own eyes, or in the eye of his beloved Sweetheart.

Robert Jacob Morgenstein dropped the telescope he was holding and crumpled into his chair. He put his head onto his folded arms which lay atop his desk, just as he had learned to do at naptime in Kindergarten at PS 5 in the Bronx so many many years ago. He wept uncontrollably.